A Bible And A Fly Swatter
1977

ZaneDoe

This book is a work of fiction. Names, characters, places and incidents either are the product of the author's imagination or are used fictitiously. Any resemblance to actual events or locales or persons, living or dead, is entirely coincidental.

Copyright © 2010 ZaneDoe
All rights reserved.

ISBN: 1-4392-3845-6
ISBN-13: 9781439238455

This Book Is Dedicated To Joseph With Love And Gratitude. And, To Morgan Who Hung In While I Hung On.

Chapter I
Teacup Newfoundland

"I'm not kidding!" he exclaimed, wide-eyed and donning a half-smile. "It's a prosthesis; he got it at a garage sale."

"He bought a leg, a prosthesis, at a garage sale?" she asked almost certain that Clark was kidding.

"Yeah, seriously—it's a fake leg."

"And he made a shifter for his car out of a *fake* leg?" Morgan questioned with a degree of amusement but a deeper degree of disgust.

"Yeah, it's cool. I can show ya——-"

"That's okay," she interrupted, "but Clark, come on, a leg? Isn't that pretty big to use as a shifter? A fake human leg?"

"He adapted it. It's cool. I'll take you over and show it to you."

"Is it a child's leg?"

"I don't know. It's just a fake leg. I don't know whose leg it was." Clark was a bit annoyed at Morgan's apparent lack of appreciation for the mechanic's ingenuity but then, reminding himself that she was a girl, he quickly forgave her.

"Maybe it's a mannequin leg," Morgan suggested then quickly added, "Can you go a little faster, Clark? I really need to get home in a hurry."

Morgan chanced—to get her foot in the door—telling the prospective landlord that her dog was a teacup Newfoundland. Much to Morgan's relief, he didn't question her claim but welcomed Morgan, along with her canine companion, as a renter. She moved in and the landlord was expected to arrive that afternoon with an updated rental agreement. The "teacup" Newfoundland, OP, was in the apartment and Morgan wanted to get her walked and out of sight before the landlord arrived and discovered that the canine in residence was not of the teacup variety.

"*There*, Clark, on the right." She pointed to the two-story apartment building. "Stop. Pull over here," she said in a hurry, trying to emphasize the urgency to the ultra mellow cruiser.

He complied and Morgan hurried out of the car. "Thanks, Clark. I owe you."

"You want me to check on your car?"

"That would be great," she responded in a rush. "I really can't lock that car up tight, so yes; if you could keep an eye on it I'd appreciate it."

"No problembo."

Clark often added letters to the end of words: "righto," "okaydokee," "yessuree." Or sometimes changed words: "anywhoo." Or, used phrases that Morgan really wasn't sure what they meant: "That's the cat's pajamas"; "Well, bee's knees"; "Whodawhoda." They sounded more like the verbal idiosyncrasies of the elderly instead of slang from a nineteen-year-old.

When Morgan reached over to give Clark's shoulder a quick and affectionate squeeze to say thanks, she noticed a change in his expression—a quizzical stare that was focused not on her but on something past her. Morgan turned to see what caught Clark's attention: it was Lorraine, the so-called apartment manager. She *was* hard to ignore and a queer sight to the unfamiliar. It was difficult to tell whether Lorraine was attempting to be discreet, and greatly mistaken, or if it was her intention to let you know that her ghoulish eyes were upon you. Since Lorraine, literally, applied her make-up with a paintbrush (*"No different than those fancy brushes,"* though she blatantly disproved her own theory) she made a frightful picture as she peered through the wide gap in her curtains. Wrapped on her head was something more like a bathrobe than a towel which only added to her bizarre appearance. Lorraine was an angry, and rather unstable, woman who carried a firearm in her closely guarded purse. Morgan had quit stopping to say hello, or even waving a hello, to the keeper of the keys; she decided that she would rather be a swiftly moving target if Lorraine happened to tip the scales into full-blown crazy.

Lorraine had a past *and ideas* that were always fuzzy in translation and she became pathetically scary. At first, Morgan was welcoming and friendly to Lorraine, who spent a great deal of uninvited time in and in front of Morgan's apartment—much to the amusement of George, the next-door neighbor. Morgan could often hear George through his screen door laughing as Lorraine talked, or rambled: George had the several years of experience with Lorraine that Morgan lacked and wasn't fooled by her moments of lucidity.

Then Morgan experienced the first flaming-red flag:

A Bible And A Fly Swatter 1977

"Are you going on vacation?" Lorraine asked Morgan through the screen door, oozing with the hint to come inside. There was nothing out of the ordinary about that question, nothing alarming.

Morgan politely extended an invitation, "Hi Lorraine. Come on in."

"You packing to go on vacation?" Lorraine stood in the center of the living room, eyes fixed on Morgan's folded clothing spread across the couch.

"Sort of——" but before Morgan could explain further, Lorraine stepped over to the window, stared up into the sky with a dreamy look in her eyes and declared, "You should go where I have always wanted to go." She continued to stare up into the sky.

"Where's that?" Morgan looked out the window to see what Lorraine was staring at. There was nothing but blue skies and billowy clouds.

"Mars," she said transfixed on the midday sky.

"Mars?" Naturally thinking that Lorraine was kidding, Morgan responded with an audible laugh. "Well, I'll have to talk to my travel agent," she said in jest wherein Lorraine turned and gave Morgan a glassy-eyed glare that halted Morgan's playful response.

George, who was enjoying a smoke at the front walkway railing, overheard Lorraine's travel suggestion and the sounds of his snickering drifted through the screen door, seemingly noticed only by Morgan. Lorraine's seething death-grip of a stare remained on Morgan until she spoke up. "Well, Mars does sound exotic," Morgan backpedaled in a cheery voice. "But Lorraine, I really need to finish up so maybe we can visit or talk another time, okay?" Lorraine turned and gave a final glance up to the skies then at an unusually slow pace exited through the front screen door.

Lorraine said nothing to George as she passed him on the walkway, as though he wasn't there, and drifted her way back to her own apartment. George, a drink in one hand, a cigarette in the other, opened Morgan's screen door and with a knowing smirk commented, "Ahhh, and she carries a loaded gun." Then George let loose a hearty unrestrained laugh.

"Come in here," Morgan demanded and George obliged. "She carries a loaded gun? Are you kidding? Where?"

"In that purse she clings to. Ask her to see it."

"Why does she carry it?" Morgan was concerned—though George found it absurdly humorous. "Is that legal?"

"You think she cares if it's legal? Give it a few more months, or weeks, you'll quit answering the door when she knocks." George finished his drink, looking at the bottom of the glass to make sure every drop was indeed gone.

He was right. Morgan quit answering the door and did her best to avoid Lorraine when outside of her apartment also. No longer did she leave the solid door open with the screen door closed. It was too easy to get surprised by Lorraine and her indeterminable stare—not a gentle Mona Lisa-like gaze but more the look of a predator.

Morgan assumed that Lorraine would accompany the landlord when he brought over the new rental agreement. Though Lorraine hadn't said a word about OP, Morgan was sure that she had seen her. After a quick trip to the long ivy patch so OP could relieve herself, Morgan rushed back up the stairs to George's apartment.

"Please?" Morgan asked with urgency through George's screen door. "Dan should be here any minute. He wants me to sign a new rental agreement."

"Ah, my big-black-furry child," he joked. "Bring her in." Morgan opened the screen door and guided OP inside. "Come to Uncle George," he said with a silly grin. "Come see your Uncle George."

Inebriated Uncle George.

"As soon as Dan leaves I'll come get her. And please, George, do *not* make her bark, or let her bark." Morgan was worried; George looked like he was in a playful mood and one loud resonating bark would have the landlord knocking on his door.

"He's going to find out she's a big dog at some point. Why don't you just introduce her? She's a good dog, well-behaved." George leaned toward OP, "Aren't you a good dog, aren't you. . ." and began to rough up her coat to which OP responded with a playful, and loud, *bark*.

"See! Don't *do that*." She was concerned that George may have had too much bourbon for this covert task.

"They're gunna know," he insisted while still playing with OP.

"Not if I can help it, George."

"You do know that I lived in an apartment, the one before here, for six months, and they didn't even allow pets."

"No, I didn't know that. And, that's a bit hard to believe."

"Honest." Morgan crossed her heart with her finger. "She came and went with me and they never said a word."

"Were you a Girl Scout, Morgan?" George smiled.

"Brownie, actually," she answered.

"Anyways, I didn't have any choice but to hide OP. I couldn't find a place that would accept a large dog. This place didn't even accept pets but I saw that it had a back alley right outside the bedroom window and they were so willing to rent to me right away that I took it. I figured I'd sneak her around until I could find something else: the risk I had to take, George."

"I'm sort of doing the same thing." She smiled. "But I've got Uncle George to help us now."

"Come on now." George shook his head, "How'd you pull that off?"

Morgan looked outside to check for Dan then gave George a quick answer, "I did what I had to do, George." Morgan gave a slight grin, proud of such an achievement. She had pulled it off without even raising suspicion the entire six months. "I'll tell you later...Dan is going to be here any minute now.

"Please, George, please don't play with her, okay? She gets excited and *she will bark.* One bark and Dan will come flying over here."

"I gotcha covered. Don't worry, don't worry, don't worry." He put his face up to OP's and continued, "You're mom's a worrywart, isn't she. We'll be quiet, won't we, won't we girl…." OP wagged her tail and Morgan gave another warning of quiet before leaving. She wasn't all the way through her apartment door when she heard OP bark. The walls were rather thin and she could hear the playful commotion. Morgan banged another warning of quiet on the kitchen wall to which George banged back and all was quiet.

Lorraine did indeed follow the landlord to Morgan's apartment, like a pet at his heels, but Dan left her standing on the walkway when he entered. Morgan was not inclined to invite her in for various reasons, but mostly on this occasion for fear that she might bring up OP.

Dan was very chatty, very casual. He sat on the couch too close for comfort for Morgan. She read over the contract while Dan rattled on about himself. She could hear Lorraine in the background knocking on George's door (even while intoxicated, George had the good sense not to answer). Morgan tried to focus mainly on the contract while still acknowledging Dan's one-way conversation.

The changes made in the contract were subtle. Morgan took the opportunity to pen in *Newfoundland*, cleverly leaving out the word *Teacup*, on the blank line for pets then signed the contract. Dan didn't notice what she wrote and didn't seem to care; he was on an ecstatic roll about his newly acquired connections to various local bands on their way up in the music scene. To keep Dan's attention off the contract, she feigned enthusiasm for the topic, mentioning that her ex-boyfriend was a guitarist in one of the bands he had been raving about. Dan's eyes lit up and he became even more animated regarding the subject. Unfortunately, this bit of information interested Dan more than Morgan had anticipated. He asked questions about the guitarist, the band and her current affiliations—causing him to stay even longer. He talked on about the various guitarists he knew personally which led to exhausting details about his own attempt at playing the guitar.

Morgan was clueless how to tactfully terminate the conversation, along with his visit. As the time ticked on, her anxiety about OP sounds being heard through the wall had her on edge. It was becoming near impossible to sit calmly on the couch listening to Dan ramble on. She had already heard several thumps and knocks as OP jumped on and off George's couch, sounds she knew well that often included several playful barks. George liked tossing a toy onto the couch for OP to fetch and was amused at how her big body plopped onto the couch and leaped off with verve.

Finally, Dan stood up to stretch. Morgan quickly declared that she had to make an important phone call by "two o'clock" while politely escorting him to the door.

"Well, I guess I should stop by and say 'Hey' to George while I'm here," Dan mentioned as he stepped onto the walkway.

"See you later." Morgan closed the door and ran to the phone to call George.

He picked up in a normal voice but whispered once he heard that it was Morgan.

"Dan's coming to visit you." Morgan panicked.

"If she were a teacup, I could pass her through the back window."

"If she were a teacup, I wouldn't be hiding her at your place—just don't open the door; put her in your room, okay? so she doesn't jump up at the window or bark."

A Bible And A Fly Swatter 1977

"Hold on." George led OP to the bedroom, tossed in a chew bone and closed the door.

Morgan could hear Dan talking to Lorraine on the walkway.

"If we weren't on the second floor I could just put her out the back window," George said once back on the phone.

"That's what I did at the last apartment. The back window was her doggie door."

"Aaaaaah, *so that's how you did it!*" George chuckled.

"Yeah, that and I would drive the car up to the front door, put a hat and sweater on her. She'd jump onto the front seat and then I would race out the front driveway. She looked like a person sitting there if you weren't paying attention." To this George burst out laughing loud enough for Dan and his pet Lorraine to hear him.

"Hey George, it's Dan," shouted the landlord.

"Oh shit, George."

"No problem, don't worry," George said, still in a whisper. He set the phone down and answered the door. Typically he would invite Dan in for a drink, though he would never offer Lorraine a drink since he viewed her as a loose cannon and didn't want to chance igniting her fuse and have a lead projectile heading his way. He told Dan that he was on the phone and would have to visit with him another time. Dan liked to visit and talk about himself. Dan liked to brag. George liked to listen, not because he was impressed or interested but it was a way to gather information; it gave George one-up over the other tenants—George knew Dan's plans ahead of everyone else, except maybe the pet. Dan and Lorraine continued on to Lorraine's apartment and George got back on the phone with Morgan.

"*I got it!*" George was excited. Morgan could feel the joy and enthusiasm in his voice, which typically turned into a laugh. "Uncle George has solved the problem," he continued then let out the raspy smoker's laugh she had anticipated. "I'm gunna cut a hole in the wall of our adjoining closets and we can move OP back and forth through the closet." George was proud of his clever idea. "OP will have her own doggie door."

"Seriously?"

"Of course." George was serious, very serious.

- 7 -

It was a solution that would not meet the approval of the landlord, that was for certain, but one Morgan agreed would make moving and hiding OP a lot easier.

"Should I put a lock on the closet door so you can't come in and raid my fridge?"

With the help of his friend Rusty, George accomplished their secret passageway. It worked well and George savored the delinquent pleasure he got from the whole process; he was also pleased that he could borrow Morgan's vacuum cleaner at will. They frequently left the closet doors open and OP came and went at her choosing. Her toys were evenly spread between the two apartments, though a stockpile of George's socks ended up in Morgan's apartment and sometimes other items of clothing. "Just wash 'em with your stuff and toss 'em back." Morgan felt obligated and did just that, though she was beginning to suspect that George was giving OP his dirty laundry.

Chapter 2
Stealing Grandpa

The phone rang, or quacked. Morgan picked up the duck's head and placed it tightly to her ear. The telephone may have been a humorous gift at the time but it was awkward to use. It was Simon, the giver of the mallard novelty.

"Hey Simon, how are you?" Her brother didn't call often and when he did it wasn't just to say hello; he always had a specific reason. "What's up?"

"I'm fine," he answered as if bothered by the effort. "Just thought I'd call you and let you know that they put Grandpa Aka in a home."

"What do you mean *a home* and who's they?"

"In *a home*, an *old people's home*—*rest* home, *retirement* home. I don't know, whatever you want to call them, that's where they put him."

"*Who* put him and why?"

"I think he was running out of money and couldn't keep paying for that hotel room he was living in or whatever it is he's been living in." Simon sounded impatient. He wasn't all that fond of Grandpa Aka, and didn't care much where he was *or was put* but he knew that Morgan cared. He also knew that the family wasn't going to voluntarily inform her of what they had done and when Morgan discovered Aka gone, Simon knew that she would raise hell until she found him.

"So was it Mom or Grandma or someone else who put him in a home?"

"Yeah, Mom and Grandma put him in some home, someplace in the Bay Area, somewhere. I think it's called The Willows, something like that. The Elms or—-"

"You don't know the name?" Morgan interrupted.

"I don't know: The Coconuts, The Pine Trees. Who knows? Ask Mom."

"I thought that she was in Europe with Grandma. Is she back?"

"Just ask her when she gets back," he responded in a hurry and Morgan knew he was about to tell her that he needed to go. "I need to get going."

"Don't you want to ask me how I'm doing?" she asked with levity.

"Gooooooodbye, Morgan," and Simon hung up.

With the phone still in hand Morgan dialed Jackie's number.

"Hello?" Jackie answered the phone as if hello were a question, which always amused Morgan.

"Hi, Jackie, this is Morgan." Morgan always said who she was which Jackie found amusing.

"I know *your voice*, Morgan. You always say who you are like I wouldn't know," she said, lightheartedly chastising Morgan then finished with a laugh. "So, what's up? How are you? And, how funny you called; I was going to call you." Jackie was chatty, per usual, but Morgan was agitated about the fate of Grandpa Aka and cut right to the point of her call.

"You used to work at a rest home right?"

"Yeah. Why? You thinking of moving?" Again Jackie laughed.

"Seriously, Jackie; Simon called and told me that Grandpa Aka was put in a rest home but he doesn't know which one other than it's named after some trees or something. The Willows or The Pines or some name like that. Does that sound familiar to you?" she queried. "He said it was in the Bay Area."

"There's The Willows in Los Altos, could that be it?" she answered, now sounding earnest and concerned.

"I bet that's it. Do you know where it's located, the street?" Morgan asked as though an emergency.

"I can find out. Why, what's going on? You really sound worried."

"I want to go see the place, make sure it's decent and I want see him too—to make sure he's okay?"

"Why don't you call and see if that's the place first?"

"I'm sure it is. That's the first name that Simon gave, The Willows. I just want to get there. Can you tell me where it is and how to get there?"

"Do you want me to go with you?"

"That'd be nice." Morgan was grateful for the offer. "I can pick you up."

"No, *I'll pick you up*," Jackie's voice snapped enthusiasm. "I have a surprise to show you."

"Okay, but can you pick me up right away, Jackie?"

"Wait till you see it." Jackie was excited even though Morgan wasn't responding in kind.

"Well, come as soon as you can okay?"

"Okay," she answered then continued, "I'm so psyched, Morgan—"

Morgan interrupted Jackie to move things along, "Well, just come get me and show me then. I really want to get to this rest home place as soon as I can."

"Okay. I'll see you in about twenty minutes."

Morgan knew it would never be "about twenty minutes."

Morgan stuck her head through the secret passageway and called out to George, requesting his services as OP's sitter. George was willing. She then waited, impatiently, for Jackie to arrive. She figured that Jackie's excitement stemmed from another gift from her lover, the doctor. Morgan had yet to meet the doctor and she didn't ask much about this man or their relationship; she didn't approve but it was Jackie's choice, Jackie's life. The doctor had Jackie and his wife and Jackie had the doctor and her devoted and naïve boyfriend, Buddy.

Forty-five minutes had passed when Morgan heard several honks from an unfamiliar car that just pulled up the driveway.

"Another gift from Dr. Special?" Morgan shouted down from the balcony. Jackie was sitting in a shiny little sports car. A delighted Jackie smiled and honked the horn several times in response. Morgan pointed to the manager's apartment with an exaggerated frightened expression on her face and called down, "I wouldn't honk too many times if I were you." Jackie cringed with the sudden remembrance of the tales about the fragile and tentative mental state of the apartment manager—gun and all—then lifted her hands from the steering wheel as George stepped out onto the balcony alongside Morgan, cigarette and drink in hand. He nodded to Jackie while checking out her little white car with the red leather interior.

"New car?" he yelled down.

"It's not new. It's a sixty-eight," Jackie shouted back. "It's a nineteen sixty-eight Fiat Dino; it's a convertible."

George turned to Morgan. "Not the brightest light on the Christmas tree is she?"

"Don't be mean, George," Morgan mumbled, though she did find it slightly humorous that Jackie felt she needed to inform George that the car was a convertible when the top was down. George shook his head and headed back into his apartment.

"You ready?" Jackie shouted from her new toy.

"Yes, just give me a minute and I'll be right down."

"Come on, OP," Morgan coaxed her off the bed. OP headed straight for the closet door, the gateway to George. Bent forward toward the gigantic hole in the closet wall Morgan shouted, "George, I'm letting OP through," though

OP was already through the opening to George's apartment. "I'm going to close the closet door, George, so she'll stay in here."

"Okay," George shouted back from the bathroom.

"I'm not sure how long I'll be, is that okay? Do you have plans?" she asked in a hurry.

"No problem," George answered then firmly instructed, "Get going; I'll see ya later."

"Thank you." Morgan backed out of the closet and shut the door behind her. She locked the apartment door, rushed down the side stairs and quickly hopped into Jackie's shiny new car.

"This is a beauty, Jackie," she immediately commented.

Jackie pointed toward the apartment building and asked, "What's with the towels on the windows?" She caught site of the apartment below Lorraine's as she cautiously watched for the loony manager to make an appearance. The windows were adorned with kitchen towels taped to the glass instead of regular curtains. Not decorative kitchen towels but used towels that looked like old, dirty restaurant or worn-out hotel towels. Morgan rarely saw a light on in that apartment or any activity for that matter. She only knew that two men in their thirties lived there; she would see them come and go, always looking down at the ground as they walked across the driveway. Morgan wondered if their odd demeanor was a result of living under Lorraine.

"Decorating on a dime?" Morgan suggested then quickly added, "Let's go."

Jackie backed out of the driveway, turning the wheel too sharp, and went over and off the sidewalk with a clunk.

"Should we take a look?" Morgan asked, worried about possible damage.

"Naaah, it's fine," and Jackie merged with traffic at an impressive speed. "So, how do you like it? *Bitchen car huh?*" Jackie beamed.

"This is a gift from the doctor, right?"

"Yes…he's so good to me," she proclaimed with dreamy eyes.

Morgan wondered if he was "so good" to his wife.

"I don't want to put a damper on anything, but how do you explain this car to Buddy?" Morgan asked in all sincerity.

Jackie didn't answer the guilt-ridden question. Instead, she let Morgan know that she had located the rest home called The Willows and that she knew how to get there. Morgan was uncomfortable about Jackie's affair with

A Bible And A Fly Swatter 1977

the doctor, not just because he was married with children but because she truly liked Buddy, Jackie's boyfriend—other boyfriend. Buddy was one of the kindest and most trusting persons that Morgan had ever met. Jackie referred to him as naïve and sweet. George described him as "dumb as a rock." But Jackie needed her men: they were her drama, her support—in more ways than one—and whatever Morgan said wasn't going to change a thing, except maybe their friendship. Morgan turned the topic to her concerns about the welfare of her grandfather, Aka.

"Is he sick?" Jackie asked, glad to be off the topic of Buddy or any other guilt-producing topic.

"I hope not."

"Is this your grandfather from Hawaii?"

"Yeah, he's my Hawaiian grandfather. He wasn't living in Hawaii. He hasn't been in Hawaii for a long time, at least as far as I know."

"You don't look Hawaiian," Jackie commented as she took a steady stare at Morgan.

"I'm a combo. Everyone thinks that I'm Italian but that's about the only thing I think I don't have in me."

"But *you do* talk with your hands," Jackie pointed out in all seriousness. Morgan could only smile in response.

"I'm not that close to Aka," Morgan said, "but I'm closer to him than anyone else in my family. It wasn't like he was part of the family. I actually met him by accident; I didn't grow up around him."

"Met him by accident?" Jackie looked over at Morgan again—which made Morgan nervous; she preferred that Jackie keep her eyes on the road—particularly when she was doing well over the speed limit and weaving in and out of traffic.

"I was eight years old when I met him or seven years old, something like that; it was the first time I had ever met him and it was only for a short time, maybe fifteen minutes, something like that."

"You never saw him again?" Jackie asked. "I don't get it."

"I went looking for him when I got older; it's a long story. Too long," Morgan answered. "I'll tell you some other time. You need to pay attention to the road, Jackie." She preferred not to engage Jackie in conversation for safety sake. As they drove in silence, trusting Jackie knew the way, Morgan reflected to herself on how she came to meet and know Grandpa Aka:

"When the movie is over," Morgan's mother instructed through the car window, "just wait out front on the bench for me, okay honey. Don't go anywhere. You stay there and wait for me to pick you up when my game's over." Morgan agreed and hurried off to the Stanford Theater. In reflection, dropping a seven or eight-year-old little girl off to attend the movies by herself seemed incautious and irresponsible, but those were different times.

The movie let out and Morgan walked straight down to the wood bench next to the newspaper stand as instructed and there she sat obediently, soaking up the sun and watching cars and people, waiting for her mother's Saturday tennis match to be over. She was most interested in watching the pigeons, which seemed like a flock of pets to little Morgan. She watched as the pigeons surrounded two women who were eating sandwiches across the street at the plaza. The women tore off pieces of bread and tossed them as far as they could to distance the pigeons from them, which awarded only brief resolve; the pigeons scurried right back and paced up and down as they waited for more. Morgan wished that she had something that would attract the pigeons and envied the attention they were giving the women with the sandwiches.

With her focus on the flying pets, Morgan didn't notice that she had acquired company, a bench-mate: an old man in raggedy clothes was occupying the other side of the wooden bench. Morgan turned slightly to have a look at her new bench companion but he didn't look back nor say anything. That was fine with Morgan since she wasn't supposed to talk to strangers anyway. She did wonder if he were hungry though. Morgan had candy in her pocket from the theater; she wasn't supposed to take candy from a stranger but no one said that she couldn't *give* candy to a stranger. Morgan pulled the half-eaten Baby Ruth bar from her pocket, leaned forward, twisted her head around to face the old man and lifted up her candy bar as an offering. He didn't respond. She figured he must like pigeons as much as she did and was focused on the women across the street stealing all the pigeons' attention. Morgan shuffled her feet to gently draw attention to her offering. He still didn't acknowledge her, so she began to rock from thigh to thigh; he would have to notice that, her mother always did and told her to "*stop it.*" He leaned forward resting his forearms atop his knees, his hands dangling and his head was now facing down. With her little girl perspective, Morgan thought he was going to cry and, of course, he was going to cry because he was poor, maybe hungry. And, she could help. She would pray for him later but for now she had half a candy bar and a dime.

"Would you like a dime?" Morgan asked. She was even going to advise him of how he could use the dime effectively at church. He could put the dime in the slot and light a small candle and he could talk to one of God's angels and tell the angel what he wanted and the angel would talk to God for him. If he had a dollar, he could light the big candle and God himself would listen to what he wanted. Morgan was a little Catholic girl and she wholeheartedly believed in the candle plan.

Still leaning forward, he turned his head and shook it to say no, he didn't want her dime.

"I like pigeons, do you?" She had already broken the rule by speaking to the stranger so she may as well continue.

He sat up, leaned back against the bench, gave a slight grin and nodded. "Yes," he said, then looked at Morgan, "I do."

Just then, her mother's car pulled up in front of the bench. Her mother leaned over to reach the passenger side window, rolled it halfway down and said in a raised voice, "You ready, honey?" The old man looked directly at Morgan's mother and sat upright. As Morgan open the car door to climb onto the front seat, the old man said, "Hello Leilani" in a shaky voice. That was her mother's name. *How did he know my mother's name?* she wondered. Her mother responded with a hello, and may have said a few words more but Morgan didn't catch them.

"Put your seatbelt on," her mother demanded as she pulled out into traffic. Morgan snapped the seatbelt together and pulled the strap until it cinched tight against her body as her mother made her way through traffic for home.

"Do you know who that man was?" Morgan's mother asked referring to the old man on the bench.

Morgan thought that she must have seen her talking to him, *a stranger*, and now she was in trouble.

"A hobo?" Morgan answered with a question, hoping that her mother wouldn't be mad if she was just trying to be nice to a poor hobo. She was about to tell her that she offered him her dime when her mother continued.

"That was your real grandfather, Aka," she said, very matter of fact. "My father." And, she said nothing more about it the rest of the way home, or in the years that followed. Morgan said nothing. Asked nothing. She was relieved that she wasn't in trouble but her little mind was perked for days, months: *My "real" grandfather is a hobo?* She never mentioned meeting her "real" grandfather to anyone, not even to her brother. Morgan believed that her mother didn't want anyone to know that her father was a hobo. Questions popped up privately for Morgan regarding this "real" grandfather that never completely faded.

As an adult looking back, such a declaration with no further explanation was a punch even to a child's sensibility. Yet, in looking back, there were various family related topics of interest not broached upon and clearly an unspoken rule that it was to be kept that way. Though Morgan never knew why this insinuated rule was in place, she always abided by it.

Morgan never forgot the old man on the bench, the "real" grandfather, and when she was in her teens she made it her mission to find him. With the knowledge of his name, and the only place she had seen him, Morgan went back to Palo Alto to begin her search.

There was a corner coffee shop called The Creamery, one of the oldest establishments in town. She started her search there and lucked out—first place, first person: the waitress behind the counter not only knew Grandpa Aka, but informed Morgan that he had coffee there almost every day. She even knew where he lived; it was in the old Barker Hotel around the corner. *That was just too easy.* It was obvious to Morgan that no one in her family had wanted to find Aka.

Morgan walked to the Barker Hotel: it literally *was* right around the corner. The hotel was antiquated and looked like no other building in town. The Barker Hotel had large beveled-glass windows with late nineteenth century style gold lettering. The front still had the original dark carved-wood doors that opened to a dank and musty lobby. The staircase with its dark twisted oak banister was the star of the lobby. It turned upward luring one to follow its lead. At the base of the stairs, lined up against the wall, was a row of flat brass mailbox slots. Morgan stepped up to the mailboxes to check for Aka's name. She heard people talking at the top of the stairs and decided to approach them instead. Maybe their reaction to her inquiry about Aka would give her some insight: Was he a pleasant man and they would smile and point the way or would they hesitate at the inquiry and point to his door as if it were a place they would rather avoid.

The faded floral carpet muffled her steps as she ascended the old wood staircase and the musty smell intensified. Once at the top, Morgan discovered that the voices she heard were not in the hallway but were coming through an open door to one of the rooms, and one voice was that of an old man. She

A Bible And A Fly Swatter 1977

slowly approached the side of the open door and discreetly peered into the room. Two men appeared to be negotiating a deal. Aka looked the same, disheveled and old—just like the "hobo" on the bench. He was trying to sell a watch, or maybe it was a bracelet, it was hard to see. Morgan went unnoticed as she watched and listened.

After several more minutes, Morgan felt uncomfortable, even a bit afraid. She wasn't sure why but it didn't matter; she wanted to get out of there as fast and as quietly as possible. Morgan tiptoed away from the open door and scurried down the stairs. Maybe her mother had good reason to shun this man. She left the hotel and went back to The Creamery.

"Did you find Aka?" the helpful waitress asked.

Morgan told about her initial meeting with Aka, the hobo who was her real grandfather, and how she had always wondered about him. But now that she had found him, she was uncomfortable about approaching him. She asked the waitress if Aka was a friendly man and what, if anything, she knew about him.

"So you're Aka's granddaughter?" she asked, looking pleased.

"Yeah, I'm his real granddaughter," Morgan answered while taking a seat at the counter.

"Huh, he never mentioned that he had grandchildren," she said to Morgan then yelled to a coworker that she was taking a break.

"He may not know, actually."

The waitress introduced herself, "My name is Rita."

"I'm Morgan."

"Interesting name." Rita smiled.

Morgan figured since the waitress took a break to talk about Aka, that they must have established a friendship or some kind of special relationship. Over Cokes, Rita told Morgan what she knew about Aka from personal experience and from what she had heard. She said that he was friendly but reserved, that he stayed to himself. He had been coming into the restaurant nearly every day for coffee since she worked there and he always tipped: "Not everyone does, particularly when they're just having coffee." She said she hated to say it but "he might drink a bit, if you know what I mean." She didn't know what he did with his days but that he often stood out against the brick front. Rita had heard that he was very wealthy, at least at one time, and that "he had been somebody but I don't know who." Then she asked Morgan, "Do you?"

- 17 -

"No," she answered. " Well, I know that we are related to Hawaiian royalty. Maybe that's it; maybe that's what made him a "somebody.""

"He surfed, did you know that?" Rita informed with a smile.

Morgan shook her head no. "I don't know much of anything. I feel bad about it. I feel bad that he doesn't know us—me and my brother."

Rita encouraged Morgan to go back to the Barker Hotel, to say hello to Aka and tell him who she was. "You have to, young lady. I don't think he has anyone in this world. Now there's you," she kindly pleaded.

Once again Morgan stood at the top of the stairs, breathing in the moldy smell of the hoary hallway. Aka's door was still open. She nervously stepped up to the door and called out in a near whisper, "Hello?" A question, sounding a lot like Jackie. She leaned in to get a better look. Aka was sitting on a chair next to the bed. On the bed was a clear plastic bag filled with jewelry. Various other pieces of jewelry were sprawled across the bedspread. The presence of a stranger in his doorway didn't seem to alarm him.

"Are you Aka?" Morgan asked. He looked up as if he were waiting for Morgan to continue. "I'm Leilani's daughter."

His jaw loosened, he adjusted his glasses and stood up. Aka's clothes were old and hung on him like they had been purchased in another time or for another man. He looked a man ashamed.

"Is Leilani here?" was the first thing out of his mouth.

Morgan couldn't tell if he was confused or nervous or what as Aka looked down at the floor, then at her, then at the wall and then back down at the floor.

"No, just me." She hated to disappoint him. "I'm Morgan. I met you once. It was a long time ago, on a bench in front of the Stanford Theater." She waited for a response but there was none. "You probably don't remember; it was a long time ago." He shook his head; he didn't remember. Morgan continued talking, more out of nerves than anything else. "It was a long time ago. I was just a little girl. I was sitting on a bench in front of the theater next to you. My mother drove up and picked me up. You said hello to her."

Aka sat back down and shifted around in the chair, looking uncomfortable and self-conscious. Morgan felt as though she was trespassing on more than physical territory by being there without an invitation.

"Did you know you had a granddaughter and a grandson?" Morgan asked.

He responded by patting a request to sit beside him on the bed. She accepted. He looked at the bag of jewelry, not Morgan, picked it up, opened it and offered it to her, still not making eye contact.

"No. No thank you." The offering made Morgan uneasy. "I just wanted to come to see you, to meet you. I never forgot meeting you that one time on the bench. My mother told me that you were my real grandfather." His eyes were faded and foggy. He seemed to be listening but far away at the same time. It all felt confusing to Morgan, emotionally and otherwise. She didn't know what else to say in this one-sided conversation.

After a short bit of silence, she said that she had to go but that she would come back to visit him, if he didn't mind. He said nothing. He was sitting, leaning forward, looking down just the way he sat on the bench so many years ago. So much had changed in her life yet he seemed no different from the first encounter. Morgan left, not knowing if Grandpa Aka was pleased to have met her or had any desire for her to return. However, Morgan did return. She managed to establish a warm relationship with her mysterious grandfather and found him to be intelligent with a rather whimsical sense of humor, and mostly, he was enjoyable to be around.

Jackie and Morgan pulled on to a residential street lined with trees, landscaped yards and well-groomed houses. It was an unusually hot day, so with the top down on Jackie's new car, it felt invigorating cruising down the shaded street and Morgan felt relieved that The Willows was located in such a nice neighborhood—a safe and attractive environment in what looked like an upscale neighborhood. At the end of the street Jackie turned onto a long circular driveway of typical ranch-style house from the 1950's. They found The Willows. Through the bay window they could see a couple, too young to be residents, sitting with elderly people in what appeared to be a large living room. They were enjoying ice cream on this hot day. Again, Morgan felt encouraged by the scene. Jackie carefully maneuvered to avoid the spray from the sprinklers. They noticed a row of very small cottages at the far end of the property.

"Look at all those little tiny cabins," Jackie commented while pulling into a parking space.

Morgan stuck her head over the door to get a better look. "I think that's my grandfather's cane." Aka's cane looked like a narrow knotty tree branch. The handle was the common u-shape but the engraved silver trim made the cane unique and it stood out. It had belonged to Aka's father, a sea captain. "Yep, that's his cane," Morgan confirmed. "He must live in that little cabin." She opened the door to get out and Jackie did the same. With Morgan in the lead, they made their way up the garden path to the little cabin with the cane leaning against the porch wall.

"Grandpa?" Morgan called out through the closed door. "Grandpa Aka, you there?" There was no answer.

"Just open it," Jackie insisted. "Just open the door."

Morgan tried the door; it was unlocked. She opened the door slowly and was halted. She stepped into what could have passed for a sauna. It was sweltering and she hoped not to find Aka inside. Jackie stepped inside behind her.

"Oh God," Jackie exclaimed.

Grandpa Aka was lying on the floor with his pants partially down. He looked to be unconscious, or dead. He was alarmingly still. They rushed to his side. His undershirt was drenched in sweat.

"Grandpa, Grandpa," Morgan repeated.

He opened his eyes, looked directly at her and said in a soft voice as though relieved, "Mokana."

The couple in charge noticed the unfamiliar car parked in the driveway and left the comfort of their air-conditioned living room to investigate. They found Morgan and Jackie leaning over Aka.

"*Who are you?*" the woman asked with a tone of righteous indignation.

This was the couple Morgan had seen in the living room, in the air conditioned room eating ice cream. She roared a response, "*And who the hell are you to keep someone in a sweatbox like this!*" She took a second to make direct eye contact and added, "Eating ice cream while he lies sweating to death on the floor of this sauna."

The woman looked back at the man beside her then asked in a more submissive tone, "Is he *okay?*"

"Isn't that *your* job, to make sure he's *okay?*" Morgan sharply responded while keeping her attention on Aka. Though Aka seemed to be reviving, Morgan and Jackie were quickly becoming overwhelmed by the suffocating heat. Jackie pushed past the woman and opened the door as far as it would go to let in some cooler air while Morgan tried to get Aka's pants up, until she realized that he had urinated on them. Aka had been attempting to reach the bathroom when he was overcome by the heat and passed out. As Morgan looked around the room for a dresser she noticed that there was no air-conditioning system of any kind in the little cabin, not even a fan.

"Where do you keep your clothes, Grandpa?"

He looked in the direction of the bathroom. Three drawers pulled-out from the wall next to the bathroom door. Morgan retrieved some clean clothing and returned to help Jackie prop him upright. The woman from the main house turned and scurried out the door. The man had already left.

"I can get him up myself," Jackie proclaimed with valor. "I've had practice picking up old people that are dead weight." And, Jackie did gather Herculean strength; she lifted Aka up and flopped him onto the bed.

"Jackie, I just want to get him out of here," Morgan said in a desperate tone. She figured the woman racing off was not going to result in sympathetic help or immediate changes to Aka's living conditions. Jackie agreed. They would change his clothes later. "Grandpa," she said with urgency, "I want to take you out of here, is that okay with you?" Grandpa Aka smiled, which both took as grateful permission.

As if in the midst of a combat mission, Morgan grabbed Aka's clothing then together they lifted and carried Aka out of the little cabin and down the path. They moved as quickly as their burdened feet could take them to the new car where, once there, they stopped short, grasping the reality of the car's available space. Both looked bewildered—and at each other—once confronted with the new dilemma. But when they heard the door to the main house, they worked in unison to get grandpa Aka onto the passenger's seat where he immediately fell forward. The couple from the house, with a few others following behind them, yelled out which caused Morgan to immediately squeeze herself into what could hardly be considered a back seat while Jackie supported Aka. Morgan managed to get her arms around Aka to steady him upright and they were off. Jackie made her speedy and dramatic exit down the gravel driveway shooting rocks like bullets as they made their escape. The car had pep, more than Jackie had yet to test out. They spun out onto the paved street, Morgan struggling to hold Aka upright, and raced off as though they had just robbed a bank. As soon as Jackie turned onto the highway, Grandpa Aka informed in a mellow calm voice that his teeth were still back at the cabin. Jackie looked over her shoulder at Morgan for instructions.

"Okay, Grandpa, we'll go get them." Morgan hardly finished her response when Jackie did a gravity-display U-turn, horns blaring from other cars, and headed back to the home. She made an impressive sideways stop in the gravel driveway. Morgan pulled herself from the constraints of the makeshift backseat and ran across the yard to the cabin, found the teeth and shoved them into her pocket. She grabbed Aka's cane as she left the door and raced back to the car—passing and ignoring the flustered couple on her way. Jackie got the opportunity to toss up gravel again with glee as she sped down the drive once more. They were off. *But to where?* was the silent question. Jackie got back onto the highway and just drove. She moved the rearview mirror so she could see Morgan and Morgan could see her eyes, and with her eyes asked where she should go. Morgan raised her eyebrows, shrugged and smiled.

"Where would you like to go, Grandpa?" Morgan asked the reviving Aka.

"Ice cream," he responded.

"You want to go get some ice cream?" she questioned, and Aka nodded a yes.

Jackie headed to the nearest Baskin-Robbins. She took Aka's order for a peach ice-cream cone then got out of the car by herself to fill the order while Morgan continued to help support Aka upright on the seat. As she sat there waiting for Jackie, Morgan became acutely aware that Grandpa Aka was sitting on the seat of Jackie's new Dino with urine and sweat soaked clothing and now he, in his weakened state, was going to attempt to eat an ice-cream cone in her new Fiat. She began waving her head back and forth trying to get Jackie's attention. When Jackie finally noticed, she thought that Morgan was just joking around so she waved her head in the same manner in return, laughed and turned away.

"Grandpa," Morgan asked, "can you hold yourself up now?"

"I can hold myself up, Mokana," Aka answered in a sprier yet calm voice.

"I'll be right back." Morgan squeezed out of the back compartment and went into the ice-cream store to talk to Jackie.

"Did you want an ice-cream cone too?" Jackie asked.

"Jackie, you are such a good friend."

"And you're saying this because?"

"Because you are; here you get a new Dino, come over to show it off—happy and proud—and I go stick my urine-soaked grandpa in it." Morgan lifted her eyebrows. "And you're okay with it."

- 22 -

A Bible And A Fly Swatter 1977

Jackie's expression was like a light bulb flickering. In all the chaos, she had forgotten about Aka's soiled pants. She looked a bit stunned for a moment then she broke into a smile that elevated to a laugh and spurted out, "Oh my God."

"Yeah, oh my God. And, I think we better have that cone in a cup with a spoon unless you want sticky peach added to the mix," Morgan whispered. They glanced out the window at Grandpa Aka who looked quite happy slouched in the front seat of the Dino. Morgan went back to the car and Jackie quickly joined them with a scoop of peach ice cream in a cup with a spoon and an overload of napkins.

"Grandpa, I think we should get you into some clean clothes before we do anything else." Morgan didn't want to wait any longer.

"Okay, Mokana," he said, compliant and ready for whatever was next.

Jackie drove to a gas station and Aka was able to get out of the car on his own and walk to the restroom without assistance. They walked close behind him, handed him his clean clothes as he entered the men's room then waited outside the door. Morgan asked several times, through the closed door, if he were okay and if he needed any help to which Aka responded, "I'm fine, Mokana. I'm fine."

"What does Mokana mean?" Jackie asked.

"My Hawaiian name. Morgan in Hawaiian, at least I think that's what it is; he's always called me that. I never questioned it."

They waited; both wondered what to do next but neither brought up the subject.

The door to the men's room opened and Grandpa Aka held out his stained clothing. Jackie snickered out of view and Morgan told him to throw them away, that she would buy him new pants and tee shirt. Eventually, Aka emerged from the men's room washed, in clean clothing and donning a happy and relieved expression. They all climbed back into the car and Jackie made her way to Interstate 280, also known as the most beautiful freeway in the country. It was a magnificent drive and Grandpa Aka was enjoying himself so much that Jackie didn't want his ride to end soon. She turned off, destined to Half Moon Bay. They stopped to buy sandwiches, drinks and a jacket for Aka then headed to the beach.

The three walked arm-in-arm down to the water where Grandpa Aka insisted on walking off alone.

"Do you think this reminds him of Hawaii?" Jackie asked as they watched Aka slowly maneuver his way through the sand.

"It probably does. The Hawaii of old, I'm sure," Morgan answered. "Resilient guy, huh?"

"He's not using his cane," Jackie pointed out.

"I think he just uses it like a pointer, you know like 'get me that.'"

"Where did he live before he was put at The Willows?" Jackie asked, still watching Aka slowly make his way along the shore. She knew very little about Morgan's grandfather, other than he was from Hawaii where Jackie herself lived for several years.

"The Barker Hotel in Palo Alto. I went looking for him when I was around fifteen years old and found him at the Barker. I'll always remember it. The door to his room was open and he was standing by his bed selling jewelry or something to some man. I stood there watching."

"Did he know who you were?"

"Well, I said who I was." Morgan remembered. "I left, but I continued to go back to visit him but never told my family that I was visiting with him."

"Why?"

"Well, for one, I was hitching hiking down to see him and I didn't want to get grounded."

"Is that what he did for a living, sell jewelry?"

"No. I don't think he was doing anything for a living at that age. I think he was selling off his own jewelry. I don't think Grandpa Aka ever had to work. From what I'm told, he spent his life surfing but I don't know. He was 'The Playboy' according to my grandmother."

Jackie broke into a huge smile and repeated the title "The Playboy" with a giggle.

"Evidently, the family had land in Hawaii somewhere way back when. It was sold off and he had some kind of life-trust arrangement or something. I don't know. I guess he received money every month and supposedly for the remainder of his life. Maybe they didn't anticipate him living this long and the funds ran out. I really don't know. Getting accurate info from family is more trouble than it's worth, actually."

"That's a big deal. Land in Hawaii? Why aren't *you* rich?"

"Endless questions and I guess I have a lifetime to find the answers, or some answers."

A Bible And A Fly Swatter 1977

"Well, do you have an answer to this question?" Jackie looked worried but laughed. "What are we going to do with him?"

Morgan grinned and both began finding comic relief to the new dilemma.

Jackie told of a rest home that was like a resort. Very expensive, and very nice, and she knew Morgan would approve.

"But, will whoever is paying for his care approve?" Morgan pondered aloud.

"Who's paying?"

Morgan shrugged; she really didn't know.

Both reclined onto the sand and forgot about the quandary at hand, enjoying the warmth of the sun and the soothing sounds of the pacific while Grandpa Aka sat alone staring out at the ocean. He had removed his shoes and coat. The wind was blowing against his face, and he too was savoring his time at the beach.

Chapter 3
Sunny Acres

OP's eyes were riveted on the closet door, and quickly her tail began to wag: she heard the clambering of George returning the vacuum cleaner.

"Hey George," Morgan hollered, "would you like some quiche?"

"What kind?" came a muffled response behind the closed door and OP's tail wagged even harder.

"Broccoli, onion and cheese," she answered. "I made it myself."

The closet door opened and George appeared, greeted by an over zealous OP. She had come to love George as had Morgan. He felt as much family as friend.

"I didn't know that you liked to cook?" he commented, adjusting his glasses and perusing the counter. Morgan had cookies and a pie cooling on the counter next to the open window. "You're vacuum cleaner sucks!" he added.

Morgan just looked at him, feeling no need to give the obvious response.

"Well, doesn't suck," George corrected.

"It likes to look at the dust and debris a couple times before it picks it up," she defended. "Work with it."

Morgan held up the quiche. "It's quiche, not really cooking. Well, not the way I make it but you'll like; OP likes it."

George grimaced, "Yeah, OP's real particular. Should I ask how *you* make it before I accept the offer?" George took a seat at the kitchen table.

"And if you eat all of your quiche, like a good boy, you can have a chocolate-chip walnut cookie." Morgan tilted her head and grinned as though conversing with a small child.

"So, what happened with the grandpa? Or should I even ask?"

"Sunny Acres," she answered.

"Sunny Acres what?"

"He's now at a place called Sunny Acres."

George snickered, "Are you serious? *Sunny Acres?*"

"*I know,* I had the same reaction when we drove up—*it sounds like a rest home out of a cartoon.*"

George watched Morgan set the quiche down in front of him; he was pleasantly surprised—the quiche looked normal and very edible.

"I'll get you a fork." Morgan then asked, "Do you want something to drink?"

"Yeah, I do want something to drink. I'll be right back," and George tucked back into the closet to retrieve a drink from his apartment. He returned quickly and Morgan explained the fate of Grandpa Aka.

Jackie and Morgan made their grand attempt at getting Aka into the luxury "residential home" that Jackie had mentioned but they lacked certain credentials and their story also lacked credibility. They borrowed a phone-book from a telephone booth and continued their quest. Dusting the sand off grandpa, making him put his shoes back on, combing his hair and straightening his clothing before entering the new facility seemed to help. The new story about his caretakers being in Europe, the carefully selected names and places added to the story for subtle influence and credibility seemed to work this time. Morgan believed that Jackie's oversized breasts, seductive smile and the shiny Dino glowing through the window also held great influence since the man in the office appeared to believe that Jackie was also Aka's granddaughter. Whatever it was, they managed to place Grandpa Aka in a "retirement home" named Sunny Acres that met with Aka's approval.

"So what happens to Grandpa when the folks come home?" George asked the inevitable question.

"I don't think about it, at least for now." Morgan shrugged. "But, in a week my mother and grandmother will be home from Europe or China or wherever they are, and the next chapter begins." She smiled at George. "You like the quiche?"

Sounds of Lorraine stomping down the walkway sent out an alert. Abruptly, both George and Morgan lifted their heads, their eyes fixed on each other, momentarily frozen in place. They quickly grabbed their quiche, got down on the kitchen floor and snuggled against the sink cabinet out of view of the kitchen window. Lorraine stopped, as anticipated, and peered into the kitchen. They sat like two children playing hide n' seek with their dog joining in, quietly nibbling their food and sharing pieces with OP.

Lorraine lingered by the window for a torturously long time. It seemed forever before they heard her step away from the window. They thought that she would be on her way down the stairs, however, she stopped at Morgan's front door. They heard the screen door open and waited for the knock, which of course they were not going to respond to. Lorraine didn't knock but jiggled the doorknob then pulling it back and forth rattling the door against the door frame. Morgan's mouth shot open in disbelief but George had come to expect such brazen and odd behavior from Lorraine so he only donned a broad smile while reaching for a cookie. Within a few minutes the screen door slammed shut and Lorraine continued on her way down the stairs.

"Oh my God!" Morgan exclaimed, openly horrified. "She was going to open my door. Was she planning on coming inside?" She looked at George who was still grinning. "She thought I wasn't home...*and she was trying to come inside!*"

Morgan stood up slowly and peeked out the window. She watched as Lorraine crossed the street, her hair in an exceptionally high up-do as though she was on her way to some special event.

George smirked a comment, "And I'm betting that wasn't the first time nor will it be the last our non compos mentis has tried that door." He shook his head then laughed. "I wonder if she was packin'?"

"Non compos what?" Morgan asked, still watching Lorraine saunter down the sidewalk toward the bus stop like an old hooker.

"Nuts, our certifiable apartment manager," George answered.

"Well, old lady Non Compos is clutching her purse." Morgan turned to George, "Euuuh, this is just too weird for my taste."

To which George responded, "You know you have eggshells in this quiche?"

The Willows succeeded in making contact with Simon who promptly made contact with his mother and grandmother to inform them that Morgan and an accomplice had "kidnapped" Grandpa Aka from The Willows. Unable to reach Morgan at home, though she left a clearly unfavorable message on her answering machine regarding Aka's removal from The Willows, her mother contacted Jackie who spilled her guts like a first time criminal on the hot seat. No good cop, bad cop routine necessary—Jackie sang like a canary. Morgan's mother had all the details she needed and then some. She called Sunny Acres and approved the temporary relocation. She would deal with everything when she got back to the states. Their trip had been extended so they could visit New Zealand and wouldn't be home for another month, that's if she didn't find another location just too inviting to pass up.

- 29 -

ZaneDoe

Morgan entered Sunny Acres just in time to meet head on with Alice, Mussolini incarnate, the dictator of the Adult Care Residence. Sunny Acres was a decent place in Morgan's opinion, aside from Alice. Alice possessed the grace of a wounded buffalo and the sound of her thundering gate gave warning of impending unpleasantness of one form or another. Morgan couldn't help but wonder *what sadist referred this demon in white shoes to the home of the wrinkled dependent?*

"Good afternoon," Morgan greeted Alice with a forced welcoming smile.

"Oh," she quipped, "is it?" and walked on her way.

Morgan was getting to know a Sunny Acres resident named Janie. She was drawn to this wisp of a woman sitting alone, stroking the dust off the leaf of a large artificial plant. Janie was a resident but there was an air about her that was undeniably different from the others Morgan had encountered. She seemed so much younger than the other residents, in age and spirit. She stood apart. Janie was terribly thin and had a difficult time walking. Morgan had the feeling that Janie would, and did, refuse the assistance of a wheelchair.

At first sight Janie nodded and smiled at Morgan. Morgan felt compelled to stop for a visit. Thus began a friendship.

Alice was heading toward Janie's room so Morgan quickly gave Aka his newspaper. As she rushed toward the door to get to Janie's room—Alice typically tempered herself or excused herself when Janie had company—Aka stopped her.

"Where's my teeth, Mokana?" Aka asked in his calm voice.

"Oh God, Grandpa," she said with sudden surprise. "I forgot about your teeth. I think they're still in Jackie's car, the glove compartment." Aka responded with a tooth-free smile and Morgan promised to bring them to him as soon as possible then hastily asked, "How are you eating without them?"

"I don't need them to eat. They just make me look good," and he put his head down and disappeared into his newspaper.

"I'll be back, Grandpa. I'm going to visit a neighbor of yours."

Aka didn't look up from his paper; he just waved her on her way.

Janie lie in her designated bed enjoying the sunshine through her window, intentionally focused on what was taking place outside the window while Alice rummaged through her roommate's belongings.

"Good afternoon, Mz Janie," Morgan said rather loudly to jolt the rooting and wrangling Alice. It worked. She jumped back from the dresser and looked at Morgan with unmistakable annoyance. Janie rearranged her life-earned wrinkles with a smile, pleased to see that her new friend had startled Alice. Morgan immediately sat down on Janie's bed and asked with her eyes what Alice was doing. Janie tilted her head as if to say, *who knows*. Only a minute or two had passed before Alice was hoofing it out the door. Morgan's presence made her less comfortable, impeding her sense of absolute freedom to rule—- and root. Once her obtrusive presence was out the door, Janie's mood instantaneous lifted. She picked up the fly swatter and with record speed flattened a fly on the window then gave Morgan a look of satisfaction.

"She complains about my fly-spots," Janie said with a smile. "Alice would rather I tolerate the pest than for there to be a spot on the window from its remains."

"Now that the grizzly's out of the room," Morgan commented, "how are you today?"

"At a grizzly's worst, it deserves a better comparison."

Morgan sensed that something was different with Janie. "So, how are you today?"

Janie maneuvered herself to face Morgan. She had a far-away look and Morgan asked directly, "Are you okay, Janie?"

"I had that dream again last night."

"I'm sorry, but what dream?" Morgan asked, she was certain that Janie had not mentioned a dream previously. She waited for Janie to answer but Janie just looked back out the window. Morgan climbed all the way onto the bed and looked out the window beside her. Both sat quietly, staring at what life there was outside the window.

Janie had the long-lived recurring dream, the one that has visited her since she was in her twenties—steadfast and haunting. No precursory event seemed to be the catalyst for this dream; it just came and went through the years like an old bedtime story and as time evolved, so did the emotions evoked by the dream. In the dream Janie is young, or at least that's how she feels. The dream begins with Janie walking alone on a mountain path at a somewhat hurried pace. The skies, overcast and brooding, announce that a storm is on its way. As she hurries along the path, Janie encounters a man and a woman lying in the grass alongside the path—naked and involved, surrounded by soft white light. Beads of iridescent sweat spatter over their bodies. They lie within an opalescent halo unaware of Janie's presence. Moments pass then they suddenly notice Janie, her company doesn't just startle them but terrifies them. All three are temporarily motionless. Janie wants to ease their fear and leave quickly, but she can't move, no matter how hard she tries. The opalescent aura of light cradling the couple begins to fade. As the light fades, the couple begins to fade as well until all are gone. Janie is responsible for the lovers' evanescent fate. And, the dream never goes beyond that point, or hasn't as of yet.

The aftermath of this dream hangs on a bit longer in Janie's latter years and often has her thinking, and feeling, about those loves of her own from her past. She believes that she will never see them again at this point. She wonders if they are still alive, how they might look. Janie doesn't feel much different inside as she did in her youth just her casing has so drastically changed. Would an encounter tug at their hearts or would the sight of their weathered faces ruin the memories. Janie is very aware of how her blue eyes have faded, how her mouth has turned down in an unintentional frown. Her skin now draped her bones instead of her muscles. She wondered if there was a recognizable feature left to prove that she was truly Janie if she were to meet those from her past. It seemed silly to be concerned about it, to even think about it, but she did. A once notably desirable woman, Janie was painfully aware that the only one looking at her body with any kind of desire was the undertaker. But that was life—the fate of most so she wasn't going to take it personally, just take it—accept it, and preserve those relationships of the past in their pristine state and not taint them with the present.

"We never think it's going to happen to us," Janie said in almost a whisper.

"What happens?" Morgan asked. Janie didn't answer but continued to stare out the window. Morgan reached over and gently placed her hand on Janie's slim arm. "Would you like to go sit outside in the courtyard?"

Janie lifted the covers, scooting her legs over the side of the bed.

"Do you want me to help you with your slippers?" Morgan asked.

Janie didn't want help. She stepped into the slippers that she found so flat, uncomfortable and unattractive yet had never voiced her dislike of the gifted attire. Morgan handed Janie her robe and the two walked arm in arm at a snail's pace. Without saying a word, they walked out the door, down the hall and through the glass doors to the back courtyard, at least that is what they

A Bible And A Fly Swatter 1977

referred to it as. Morgan moved the chairs to be side by side and the two made themselves comfortable.

"This courtyard gets a lot of sun," Morgan commented to get conversation going.

Janie smirked, turned to look at Morgan, and responded, "Courtyard? Let's be honest, this is a big slab of cement with a bunch of weeds that got lucky."

"Are you okay, Janie?" Janie seemed agitated and Morgan was concerned.

Janie shifted in her chair. She raised her feet to look at her slippers, stared at them for a minute then rested her feet back onto the cement and complained, "I would never buy these slippers."

"Nor would I," Morgan agreed.

"I would never let anyone tell me how to dress, what to wear," Janie firmly announced though in a mumble.

"I don't either, Janie," Morgan replied, knowing that something was definitely bothering Janie. She wanted to hear what was troubling her and weigh in, if she could—help, if she knew how, but Morgan had to leave to get to work. She didn't want to leave Janie in such a state and if Janie wanted to talk, or vent, Morgan wanted to be there to listen, but she couldn't; she had to go. "I'm going to have to get going, Janie; I need to get to work."

"Where do you work?" Janie asked.

"Samuel Pacific Imports, it's an import wine company. Beer too, but not much."

"A large company?"

"Yeah, but not where I work. I'm in a little office basically by myself. A salesman here and there but I'm usually by myself, well, with my dog. I answer the phone, take orders and most importantly, Janie," Morgan leaned toward Janie, squinted her eyes and said as if covertly, "I cover my bosses backside and I do a good job of it."

"It needs covering?" Janie was intrigued.

"He disappears a lot. To where? Only he knows. He's good at what he does, very good, but hard to find and not big on communication or sharing where he is or what he's doing."

"What does he do?" Janie wasn't stalling Morgan, she was genuinely curious.

- 33 -

"Sells wine, travels, makes deals. The quintessential sommelier, connoisseur and all that," she answered then added, "Janie, I have to run. Do you want me to walk with you back to your room?"

"No, I'll sit here on the slab," she answered, disgruntled, "and pray for a quake to split it open and take me." Janie looked at Morgan and smiled. "Come see me next time you come. Introduce me to your grandfather."

"I will," Morgan said, delighted to hear Janie's voice perk up a bit. She saw Alice watching them through the glass doors. She felt like she was leaving a baby chicken out in the open and the fox was already lying in wait, but she had to go. "I'll see you soon, Janie." She didn't have time to say good-bye to Aka.

Chapter 4
Samuel Pacific Imports

Morgan's boss left a message stating that he would be at the office until 2:00 p.m. He wanted Morgan to take over at that time and stay into the evening. Morgan doubted that he would be there until 2:00 but that is when she would show up due to his instructions. European associates of Samuel Pacific Imports had arrived at the headquarters and that's all that Morgan knew about the extended hours. Her boss Mr. Smith, Mr. Johan Smith—which George emphatically asserted was a "fake name"—informed that she needed to be at the office into the evening to do the usual: answer the phone, take orders and help make necessary connections and setups. She was happy to do it, happy to have the job. She was to be the constant fixture in that office where her boss chose not to be—that was her job, to do what she was told and to keep that office rolling and keep peace with the main office in Los Angeles.

The Northern California Samuel Pacific Imports office was located in a basement room below Buffalo Books, a large bookstore that employed George. One afternoon while waiting for George in the hallway, Morgan offered to help a well-dressed man move some boxes. He had just rented the basement office. She spent almost an hour helping this rather debonair, urbane individual who, in his business attire, looked totally out of place with the casual atmosphere of the bookstore. Another chance encounter with the handsome and sophisticated gentleman ended with Morgan acquiring a much better and steady job. She was now Mr. Johan Smith's faithful assistant, and faithful she was. She did what she was told, worked odd hours when requested and knew how to work with and around Mr. Smith's idiosyncrasies. She was allowed to bring OP to work with her—fully sanctioned by her boss—and when she worked late George often took OP home with him. It was an ideal setup for Morgan.

Samuel Pacific Imports did not, and would not, entertain associates at the basement office but the main office highly approved of the very low rent charged for the cement box. George referred to it as "the dungeon." It was a rather small room with cement walls and floor and had no windows. Mr. Smith took Morgan to a local antique store, made a few suggestions, then left leaving Morgan with a credit card and free rein to purchase whatever she deemed would make the office esthetically pleasing and comfortable—a project she thoroughly enjoyed.

Morgan added a few plants highlighted by grow lights, ornate standing lamps, a rich dark carved oak desk with an antique desk lamp. She hung framed pictures over the shattered holes in the cement wall that she managed to get a nail into. A thick wool rug from the Middle East added the warmth that the room so desperately needed. With OP's bed added to the corner, the office was complete and very much to both Morgan's and Mr. Smith's liking—though George still referred to it as *the dungeon.*

The dungeon became her home away from home. Most of Morgan's workday consisted of answering the phone and questions. It was definitely not a high-pressure job and only creative when others were hunting for Johan.

Occasionally one salesmen and one saleswoman from the area dropped by with orders instead of calling them in. Few others came to the office. The elusive boss made sudden, usually unannounced, appearances—always in a hurry to get somewhere else, wherever the "else" was, it was rarely shared. He typically seemed preoccupied as though he were expected somewhere and running late. He didn't mince words, in fact, he didn't speak much unless necessary. And, most impressive to Morgan, Mr. Smith was highly intelligent. Morgan took full advantage of his broad spectrum of knowledgeable. He surpassed any person Morgan had yet to meet when it came to facts and figures. Morgan could ask a question on any topic and Mr. Smith gave a quick and accurate answer—not too much detail, unless she needed it. He was like an information vending machine: Morgan put in the question and out came the answer—that quick and that simple.

Morgan pulled into the parking lot. As soon as OP saw George, her tail swatted Morgan's face like a car wash brush.

"So, you got Big Bird repaired; how's it running," George shouted.

"You have an alternative name for everything," Morgan yelled back.

"Well, it's big, it's yellow and you fly down the road in it."

Morgan walked over to George with OP arriving before her.

"It's running fine," she answered shaking her head. "And…*how are your lungs?"*

A Bible And A Fly Swatter 1977

"They're running fine," and he took a deep, exaggerated drag off the near spent cigarette.

George accompanied Morgan and OP into the building and to the stairs leading down to the office or to "the dungeon" as George persisted on calling it.

"So, do I have my big furry child tonight?"

"She'd love it and so would I, that's if you don't mind?"

"I'm off at 4:00," George informed.

"I'll be here into the night. So, anytime you want to come get her, we'll be down in the dungeon." Morgan headed down the stairs with OP while George headed back to the bookstore. She heard him say a loud hello to Benny before exiting the hallway which gave Morgan the heads up that Benny was on his way to the office.

"I'm just getting here, Benny," Morgan shouted up while unlocking the door. Benny looked a lot like a young Bob Dylan but lacking the confident mellow framework. He didn't drop by often but when he did he was never in a hurry to leave. Benny shot down the stairs at a gait that would rival a greyhound. He was restless, as though always attempting to burn off excess energy. At times it was aggravating for Morgan, like having a mosquito in the office. Every time she'd turn, he'd be in a different place or position. But it seemed to be just those hyper qualities that got Benny hired by Mr. Smith. Who could hit more places in a day than Benny?

Benny waited for Morgan to get settled in. He paced the office talking to and attempting to play with OP, who wasn't cooperating. OP watched him like a cat watches a mouse. She didn't pay the desired attention to her toy as Benny repeatedly tossed it then retrieved it each time himself. Morgan went about turning on lights and getting set up. She decided to wait for Benny to leave before she checked the messages and instead read the neatly folded note left by Johan.

"You have some orders?" she asked Benny who finally got the hint and gave up trying to get OP to retrieve her toy.

"Did your VW Thing come yellow or did you paint it yellow?" Benny asked in return.

"It was yellow when I bought it," Morgan answered and exhaled out of view. She knew the last thing Benny was going to tend to was business. He gave a dissertation on deep-rooted meanings behind the color one chooses for their car or their house. Then came a political rant followed by a critique of a new local restaurant. By the time he got around to giving Morgan his wine orders from several local establishments, Lacey had called in her orders gathered from the San Jose area. Immediately, Benny wanted to compare orders but Morgan rushed him along claiming she had several calls to make and needed to get to work. Benny hopped around the desk finishing a verbal list of restaurants he scheduled to visit the coming week then finally exiting out the door. Not ten minutes had passed when Benny popped his head back into the office.

"You gotta come see this," Benny said, sounding serious yet donning a crack of a smile.

"I have to finish my messages——-" she tried to explain but Benny interrupted, insisting that "you wouldn't want to miss *this!*" She knew the battle would take longer than leaving the desk to see the *"this"* so Morgan stopped the messages, turned off the machine and followed Benny out the door.

"What is it?" she asked several times as they made their way up the stairs and down the hall. She only received a shake of the head from Benny as he led her out to the parking lot where several bookstore employees were standing around a rolled-up rug by the Dumpster. Then, Benny filled her in: there was a man rolled up in the rug.

"Mafia style." George stepped up beside her. "Somebody pissed Vinnie off."

"Is it a man in there?" Morgan asked, observing the soles of a pair of shoes stacked horizontally within the hollow of the rug.

"Looks like it," George responded in his usual pococurante manner.

"Has somebody checked? Or called an ambulance?" she asked.

"Checked what?" Benny chimed in.

"Checked to see if he's alive; felt for a pulse," Morgan explained, a little annoyed by the indifference and distance displayed by the observing crowd. Evidently, no one had touched the man rolled up in the rug; no one had wanted to.

Morgan volunteered to reach in to feel if he was cold or warm and to establish a pulse, and to also see if there was a body attached to the pair of shoes.

To several *go-for-its, oh Gods* and a loud cowering *"eeeeuuuuw,"* Morgan knelt down and reached her hand past the shoe to the flesh of an ankle—cold, and no pulse. She retracted her hand and announced her findings to a captivated audience, "He's really cold and I don't feel any pulse." She reached her hand back in one more time to try again for a pulse, withdrew her hand and said, "I can't find a pulse. He's ice cold."

A Bible And A Fly Swatter 1977

"Dead," George bluntly announced.

Several onlookers stepped farther away from the rug at the sound of the word dead.

"Has anyone called the police?" Morgan asked.

"I'll go call them." Stacy headed back to the bookstore. She was the one who first noticed the shoes in the rug while dumping cover-less paperbacks into the Dumpster.

"Are you sure he's dead?" asked another.

"Well, why don't you pull him out and check yourself," George answered for Morgan. Several people went back to work replaced by new onlookers who gasped as they were enlightened to reason for the crowd. Stacy reappeared and announced to everyone still observing the encapsulated body that the police were on their way.

Benny was hunched over checking out the rug, not the body but the rug. And again someone inquired if the body within the rug was "really" dead. George sauntered over to the large tubular encasing and sat atop it, then proceeded to bounce the rug, enjoying the shock on the onlookers' faces.

"Yep, I think he's been put to sleep." George stood back up. Several others left but were soon replaced.

"Well, if he wasn't dead or injured before," Steve said to the air fully intending for George to hear him then left. He worked with George and found George not only cocky but insensitive and crass and jumped on any opportunity to turn an insult George's way

Everyone but George was standing a distance away speculating on the who and how of the matter. Another coworker from the bookstore asked, "You're sure he's dead?" and Morgan explained that she felt the poor soul's leg and it was cold, motionless and she couldn't find a pulse. He approached the rug. Morgan followed, assuming that he was going to confirm her findings by feeling the man's appendage himself. But he just stood bent at the waist staring at the soles of the man's shoes then again asked, "You sure he's dead?"

George sauntered over one more time and plopped down atop the rug proceeding to bounce with abandon. Morgan knew George well, knew how he found a perverse joy in shocking others while he kept his composure, but, this time, it was George who was shocked and lost his composure. He shot up like someone set a firecracker under his butt as the rug moved on it's own. All watched, eyes agape, as an older man struggled his way out of the rolled up rug. Unshaven and looking pissed off, he stared fixedly and angrily at George, glowered at those within his view then limped his way across the parking lot.

Everyone exchanged glances but George's expression was priceless for all who knew him and became fodder for jokes and laughter weeks after. Steve kicked himself for missing it.

Several police cars raced into the parking lot. Abandoned by the onlookers, even Benny, Morgan was left to explain: *"Where's the body?"* the officer rushed upon her. She reached her arm out and sheepishly said, "It went that way."

George's smiling face popped through the door.

"Well thanks for leaving me there to explain the dead man," Morgan said, trying not to smile or laugh herself. "I felt like an idiot."

"You confirmed him dead," George's smile grew bigger.

"And you resurrected him and he looked like he was going to *kill you.*"

George stepped into the office and shut the door behind him. "Where's the boss, *'Johan Smith'?*" he asked emphasizing what he thought to be a fictitious name.

"Now that's a familiar question," she answered. "Are you here to pick up the furry one?"

George didn't answer but instead informed Morgan that her friend, Jackie, had come into the bookstore, briefly, accompanied by a rather odd companion which Morgan knew immediately was her boyfriend by George's blunt description. Everyone seemed to be taken aback by the odd couple. Jackie was an attractive, rather voluptuous woman with erect posture that accentuated her large double endowment. She always drove a sporty car and wore stylish clothing and was outgoing most of the time. Her boyfriend, Buddy, was a very nice person and near impossible not to like. However, his exterior wasn't all that appealing: he slouched, his hair was usually a mess and when he wore anything stylish, you knew it was insisted upon or gifted by Jackie. But it was his teeth that captured everyone's attention.

"Those teeth!" George grimaced.

"Enough," Morgan responded. "He's a really nice person, okay. Maybe his family couldn't afford braces. Back off, George." And George said no more. He squeaked OP's toy until she awoke and headed for the door to George. "Don't forget to feed her," Morgan yelled as he shut the door behind them.

Mr. Smith informed, via his note, that he would be flying out of San Francisco to Los Angeles that evening, that he would be in Los Angeles for a day or so then "out of country" for a week, maybe two. He didn't indicate whether the "out of country" venture was business related nor did he indicate that she should keep his "out of country" status confidential though no one at the main office seemed to know that Johan was out of the country.

Nothing would be different except that Mr. Smith would not be stopping by the office for a week or so. There was always "petty cash" at the office in case Morgan needed anything (what Johan considered petty seemed substantial to Morgan).

George was very suspicious of Johan's activity. Morgan wasn't, she was just grateful to have the job. She was happy to tend to the orders, answer business related questions and insure the elusive Mr. Smith his privacy. There were a few out of the ordinary requests here and there and some office visitors that held little explanation, but most things plodded along at a predictable pace. Morgan did her job as requested. Mr. Smith paid her in cash, as she was "his" employee, his expense, separate from Samuel Pacific Imports. Morgan didn't care one way or the other. She had a job that was relatively easy, sometimes interesting, flexible, paid the bills and welcomed OP.

Chapter 5
Other Side of the Doors

Morgan walked into Sunny Acres and into a hallway disturbance. The staff had failed, once again, at keeping Albert dressed. He was heading toward the visiting area—the area kept well-lighted, clean and with a welcoming artificial scent—in the buff, displaying the most massive growth of pubic hair that Morgan had ever seen. It was hard not to stare at the abundant bush Albert had accumulated in his many years. Albert is a polite and an exceptionally quiet man—very unobtrusive, staying in the background and doing what he is told without objection. But when Albert removes his clothing, he looks like a man on death row who has just been found innocent and set free, as though he has taken control of his own life and he walks like he has purpose and pride. It was difficult for Morgan to watch as the staff grabbed and struggle with Albert, forcing him into a robe which he reacted to as if it were on fire. He writhed and cried and whatever sense of dignity he derived from his naked parade was quashed in agony.

"Hi grandpa," greeted Morgan. "How are you?" She handed Aka a book that she thought he might like. Aka liked to read, a lot. Aka looked up from his newspaper and held out his hand, not for the book, and Morgan inquired further, "What is it?"

"My teeth, Mokana. You have my teeth?" he asked, looking up at Morgan through his heavy black framed, thick glasses that needed cleaning.

"I didn't forget about your teeth, Grandpa; Jackie has them and she is going to drop them off, then she can visit with you."

Aka shook his head up and down in approval then they watched as the colonel was being guided to his bed by a middle-aged woman who they believed was a relative. She sat him down on the bed, his head hanging down and remaining down as he sat on the edge of the bed like an old and weathered stuffed animal. The woman looked over at Morgan and Aka, said hello and went about straightening the items on the table next to the colonel's bed which included a picture of the colonel in full military attire—looking strong, confident and handsome. With a nod and a half smile, she left the room. Immediately Aka looked up at Morgan. He shook his head from side to side; he knew what was coming. Watchful of the colonel, Morgan began telling Aka about Janie and asked if he would come visit with her and Janie in the courtyard. Then, like Aka anticipated, the colonel began to weep. When the colonel wept, there seemed to be no consoling him. He learned to weep quietly, as instructed by his family, so that he could stay at Sunny Acres. Aka waved Morgan to go. He would get back to his reading serenaded by the colonel and relieve Morgan of the obvious distress she received by the colonel's tears.

Morgan checked Janie's room but only her roommate was there, sitting on her bed staring at the ceiling. Morgan believed that she was sincerely waiting for it to open up to reveal Jesus, her savior, whom she spoke to regularly and loudly. Morgan checked the courtyard and found Janie with Xavier, one of Janie's favorite Sunny Acre employees. She had two: Xavier from Argentina and Lilly from the Philippines—both treated Janie, and the other residents, with respect and Janie greatly appreciated it. There were several residents and visitors in the courtyard including what appeared to be a gardener—or an employee who was appointed gardener by Alice. This lucky woman was pulling weeds in the afternoon sun while others in the courtyard chatted and watched.

"Hi Xavier." Morgan reached her hand out and Xavier responded, not by saying hello but by shaking her hand then excusing himself. "No, don't leave because of me," Morgan insisted.

"He's not off for another hour. Then he'll come back, you know, the volunteers' show later," Janie informed while offering Morgan a chair.

"What show?"

"Your Grandpa Aka didn't tell you about the show tonight?" Janie asked. "He's coming isn't he?"

"No, he didn't tell me anything and I don't know if he is going. He'll probably stay in bed and read," Morgan answered. "He's addicted to books like others are addicted to cigarettes, Janie. That's all he wants to do. I can hardly get him to leave his bed and I don't think the staff pushes him to get out of bed...probably because he's no bother while lying there.

"Looks like they are fixing up the courtyard or the garden. That will be an improvement," Morgan commented then went back to the topic of the show. "So tell me about the show."

Xavier was now helping the woman in the garden haul the weeds away. Everyone watched the unremarkable event as if it was a show itself. Janie explained that every now and then a group of volunteers came to Sunny Acres to entertain those so desperate for anything new. It was always a pleasure and tonight children from a dance school were coming to put on a show. It was the first event being held in the brand-new room with the hardwood floors. Sunny Acres existed in a rather old building. To raise the morale, spirits and fees, the owners were slowly giving the place a facelift. The new add-on was pristine, contemporary, with beautiful hardwood floors polished to a shine even the windows at Sunny Acres had not seen. It was built for the future, for years to come—the years most attending this evening's event would not see. It looked and smelled of newness and tonight's show was the room's debut.

"Will you be my guest, Morgan?" Janie asked. "The evening includes dinner."

"Yes, of course. If I'm allowed to come, that is."

"Friends and family. You're my friend, Morgan." Janie squeezed Morgan's arm and added, "You can be my family too." Janie's eyes searched for Morgan's reaction; she hoped that she wasn't imposing with such a remark, or feeling.

"Do you have family, Janie? Nearby?" Morgan asked. She pulled a stool over to rest her feet and make herself more comfortable then asked Janie if she also wanted a stool.

"I'm fine," Janie answered as she watched Xavier wheeling in potted plants, setting them at the rim of the small lawn area.

"Janie, I'm happy, honored, to be considered your friend and family." Then again she asked, "Do you have family nearby?"

"Do I have family nearby?" Janie repeated the question with an affected smile then lifted her arm, looked at the back of her hand and answered, "Right here, I have my grandmother's hands." Janie lowered her arm. "I could use Aunt Florence's big bottom to cushion my bones right now."

"Do you want me to get you a pillow?" Whatever it was that Janie was sitting upon was too thin to be of much comfort.

"I have their issued fake sheepskin. If I plop my old bottom on one of their pillows I'm sure it will send Alice into a rage, masked with politeness until you leave."

"Then I'll bring you one from home."

"Would you? That would be nice. Thank you so much, if it's not too much trouble." Janie added in a smirk, "Maybe that's their plan: keep us uncomfortable so we go back to bed…keep us hidden and out of the way."

"Sisters? Brothers? Children?" Morgan asked then quickly added, "I hope that you don't mind me asking you these personal questions. If you would rather that I don't, I'll shut up."

"No, no. I don't mind at all. Ask me anything you want, Morgan." Janie sounded very sincere. She added, "Do you have children, Morgan? I've never asked, I guess because you're so young but you might have a child."

"No, no, no. I don't. Well, a big black furry child named OP, my canine child," Moran answered. "Do you?

"No, no children at all." Janie paused. "I have been asked that question my entire life, Morgan. My entire life. Even now in my dying days."

"You're not dying, Janie," Morgan shot back, surprised at Janie's comment then added, "I'm sorry. It's none of my business. I shouldn't be asking you these questions."

"I've had to answer to the sin of not bearing children all my life." She turned to face Morgan and asked, "Do you plan to have children, Morgan?"

"Actually," Morgan thought for a second, "I don't think about it. It hasn't been in my plans. I guess I don't count it out but I don't count on it either."

"Things are different now," Janie responded. She appeared to Morgan to be reflecting as she spoke and Morgan was unsure if she should interrupt Janie's thoughts. She refrained from commenting.

"A world of orphans and abortions, yet my choosing not to have children bewildered their sense of normalcy. People are so curious why, as if I have committed some crime, crime against society, and they could find peace with it if they only knew why." Janie looked away and seemed to be with herself in thought again.

"I'm sorry if I brought up a sensitive subject, Janie," Morgan apologized once more.

"It's not sensitive, just annoying. Even Alice." Janie took an audible breath. "Alice likes to highlight the fact that I don't have visitors." Janie stopped herself, "Until you, that is. She asks me, 'Where're your children?'

"What do you say?"

A Bible And A Fly Swatter 1977

"Nothing the first hundred times then I made it look like I was about to cry and I confided to her that I had a child that was eaten by a shark on a fishing trip," Janie answered.

"Oh my God." Morgan looked shocked. "Is that true?"

Janie laughed. "No, no, dear. Like I said, I have no children. I just wanted to, possibly, shut Alice up, at least for the moment."

Morgan spontaneously laughed. "What did she say?"

"She stared at me for a while," Janie said. "She wanted to see if I was joking, I guess. She looked so serious. She was speechless for that moment. I wanted to laugh. I got her on that one. She hasn't mentioned my lack of a child since." Janie looked at Morgan with a satisfied grin.

"Have you ever been to South America, Morgan?" Janie changed the subject. "Xavier is from Argentina, or did I already mention that."

"I have hopes of seeing the world. My mother travels a lot...." And so went the conversation. Morgan was getting to know Janie little by little. She now knew that Janie did not have any real children, by choice—only the one that was eaten by a shark, by choice.

Residents and guests wheeled, walked and shuffled into the new room for the evening's entertainment. Aka preferred to stay in his room and read. Morgan made sure that George could care for OP and she attended with Janie. Not to anyone's surprise, Alice was busy pointing and commanding, decreeing herself Master of Ceremonies. She seemed to have everything under control and to her liking with the exception of Mr. Goldstein who was expressing his desire to also entertain the guests by play his saxophone, the saxophone Alice had confiscated and had yet to return to Mr. Goldstein.

Janie wanted Morgan to make sure that her roommate, Mrs. Schwab, did not sit anywhere near them. Janie wanted to enjoy, and wanted Morgan to enjoy, the evening's entertainment without having to listen to the endless requests shouted to Jesus by Mrs. Schwab during the performance.

"Here they come," Janie whispered to Morgan.

In came the little dancers in bright colors and shiny shoes. It wasn't ballet as Alice had anticipated the entertainment to be, but tap dancing. The cheerful and enthusiastic little entertainers donned downsized bowler hats and shoes as shiny as the floors—with metal taps. After a bright Hollywood-style introduction (and an exclamation to Jesus by Mrs. Schwab) the music started and the neophytes with professional hearts began waving their arms in the air and the swarm of shiny black shoes started flying across the newly polished floor—scuffing away at Alice's nice, new glossy hardwood floor. They were tapping to left, circling and tapping their way back to the right—leaving a trail of scuffs and scratches in their wake. The entire audience was physically and emotionally moved by their efforts with everyone smiling and clapping—everyone but Alice, who stood with her fists resting on her well-fed hips looking as if her shiny virgin floor was being raped before her eyes. All the while, the innocent dancers clanked, clattered and danced with devotion and fervor—grinding their little taps into the floor like nails on a chalkboard to Alice who winced and grimaced with confined fury.

The little tappers exited the room waving like Hollywood stars to their drooping fans. The evening was uplifting and a true joy to the residents and guests.

Morgan walked Janie to her room. She wrote her home and work phone numbers on a piece of paper and placed it in the empty drawer of the bare stand next to Janie's bed. There were no photographs, no books or cards displayed anywhere on Janie's half of the room. None of the things that made the room "hers" or homey. On the windowsill was a well-used fly swatter and that was it, at least from what Morgan could observe. Morgan left Janie sitting on her bed listening to Mrs. Schwab yell, loud enough for the heavens to hear, her heartfelt thank you to Jesus for the chocolates he left by her bed.

Morgan thought a lot about Janie on her drive home. She didn't have family visiting her; she didn't seem to enjoy or relate to the community chatter at Sunny Acres. Though Janie seemed weak and in need of assistance, she somehow didn't fit the environment. Aka was better suited to Sunny Acres than Janie. He was happy to lie there and read day in, day out. There was an aura of discontent around Janie at all times.

"Well here comes Mom," George yelled down from over the railing. OP wagged her tail and headed down the stairs to meet Morgan. OP was instant happiness to Morgan. That's all she felt when she saw OP, happiness and love. The world was OP's oyster and she seemed to find endless joy in what it had to offer. Morgan loved who OP was and loved how OP made her feel. She immediately wondered if Janie would be allowed a pet at Sunny Acres. Maybe even a fish would add to Janie's world.

A Bible And A Fly Swatter 1977

"OP! You crazy girl. Whatchoo got there?" Morgan leaned over to hug OP and realized that what she had was one of George's socks, balled at one end, hanging from her mouth. They sprinted up the stairs to the apartment. George followed them in and fell onto Morgan's couch, resting his feet on the antique trunk Morgan used for a coffee table. He flipped through a magazine while Morgan fed OP and talked to him about Janie and Sunny Acres.

"You can shoot me, Morgan," he yelled. "I give you my permission. Push me off a cliff. Pillow me in my sleep. Poison my bourbon, but don't ever let me end up in one of those places."

"I bet everyone has said that, George, that exact same thing," Morgan hollered back. "Yet, look where they end up." She joined George on the couch. "I think some are sort of out of it so maybe it doesn't matter but some look like they feel just as you do, particularly Janie...but that's where they ended up. It scares me; it feels like it's not a place to live out the latter years of your life but a place where you're put to die.

"There's a colonel who shares a room with grandpa Aka——-"

"He has to share a room with a stranger?" George interrupted.

"Yeah. I think everyone there has to share a room," Morgan answered. "This colonel sits on his bed and cries. Imagine what that man has seen, been through, and he ends up in Sunny Acres weeping his days away." She added with shame, "It seems so wrong. What a hero's end." She thought for a second. "I wonder if he now wishes he had died in the war. I guess I shouldn't say that."

"He's a colonel?" George asked.

"Yep. There's a picture of him in his uniform next to his bed."

"Remember that book about the guy in the mental hospital? I can't remember the name; it was really popular, written by that hippie guy."

"No. What book?"

"It doesn't matter. Anyway, he supposedly did his research at some veteran's hospital in Palo Alto or Menlo Park. Guess it's hellhole for vets there too."

"Where in Palo Alto?" Morgan asked. She had never heard of a veteran's hospital in Palo Alto. "At Stanford?"

"Not sure. There's some old veteran's hospital out there. My guess is that it's off somewhere not that visible to the public."

Morgan continued on about her concern for the colonel. "He represents a certain kind of strength. You know what I mean George? Those WWII soldiers are symbols of strength to America. Now this symbol spends his days

- 49 -

looking down, weeping quietly so that he doesn't get asked to leave." She exhaled. "It's sad, George; it really gets to me."

"So, whataya gunna do about it?' George asked, still observing and curious about the never before seen angst in his friend and neighbor.

"What *can I do* about it?" she questioned.

"Oh, you'll find something," George commented with a certain knowing.

She looked at him, tilted her head, not sure what he meant but George said nothing more about it. Instead, he changed the subject to an amusing story about Lorraine, one that Morgan, per usual, found more creepy than humorous.

George left and Morgan was haunted by his question: "So whataya gunna do about it?" *What could I do about it? Why would he say that?*

Jackie called regarding Aka's teeth. She couldn't find them.

"I don't remember if I put them in my pocket or in the glove compartment," Morgan responded. "Glove compartment, that sounds so outdated, huh? Like we put our gloves in there." Jackie laughed and Morgan continued in a playful snooty voice, "I'm sure I put them right next to your *driving gloves, Jacqueline, or your evening hand shoes.*"

"I can't find them, Morgan. Are you sure that you didn't take them with you or give them to the home? Or maybe, they're in your apartment somewhere."

"If I had them in the apartment I would have definitely noticed them, Jackie. It's not like they blend with the décor." She thought for a moment. "They have to be there somewhere, somewhere in your car. Just keep looking or keep an eye out for them. I'm sure they'll turn up," she said. "Now, there's another weird expression, keep an eye out." Again Jackie laughed and they chatted a bit before Morgan mentioned that her neighbor, George, saw her and Buddy at the bookstore.

"Yeah, we were there getting a book on fish," Jackie remembered in an upbeat voice.

"Are you getting a fish tank?"

"Buddy got goldfish," Jackie replied.

"Why would you need a book on fish if he got goldfish?" Morgan asked, puzzled. Goldfish were like having a plant, as long as they had water, and food now and then, they thrived.

"What do you mean?" Jackie responded in earnest.

"You can hardly kill goldfish. I mean, there's not really special care for goldfish is there?" Maybe Jackie knew something that Morgan wasn't aware of.

"One already died so he wanted to find out if he was doing something wrong or if the fish was sick and could pass it on to the other fish..." Jackie continued to explain, and Morgan smiled, thinking how Buddy truly was a nice and caring person.

"Jackie, do you know of a veteran's hospital in Palo Alto? I think it would be an old one, maybe one out of the way somewhere," Morgan asked.

"There's an old hospital, I *think* it's a veteran's hospital. It's old, has gates around it," Jackie recalled.

"Do you know where it is?"

"Yeah, I'm pretty sure it's off the freeway in a sort bad part of town. Why? Are you going to move Aka?" Jackie sounded concerned.

"Oh God no! George told me a little about it. I want to see it so can you give me directions?"

"Do you want to go check it out together?"

"Sure."

"Now?"

"What about tomorrow, Saturday? Unless you have plans?"

"Maybe Buddy would like to come," Jackie put out the hint.

"Sounds fine to me, but let's take my car so we won't be squished," Morgan suggested and the plan was made.

Morgan opened the closet door, bent down and passed through their secret passageway. She opened George's closet door and asked loud enough for George to hear her while in his bathroom, "Can you OP-sit tomorrow for a few hours?"

George yelled back, "Just send her on through in the morning and I'll take her with me to Rusty's." Rusty was George's best friend and very unlike George in disposition. He may have been easygoing like George, and generous, but Rusty was more serious and did not take pleasure in offending others as George seemed to. He could get rattled easily, unlike George. He lived in a beautiful house in Los Altos Hills on several acres with a swimming pool that was open for OP's swimming pleasure. Being a Newfoundland, OP was a denizen of the water and amusement to both George and Rusty.

"Will do, and thank you!" she shouted then scooted backward, bumping into OP as she tried to exit the closet door back into her own apartment.

OP was at the closet door before Morgan. George was on the telephone and laughing loud enough for OP to hear. Her tail was wagging as if she were joining in on whatever was so humorous. Morgan waited until George was off the telephone before she opened the closet door on George's side.

"George," she said through the cracked door.

"Come on in," he quickly responded.

"I got that call again last night, George," Morgan announced with a worried expression.

"The breather?" George started to play with OP.

"Yes. Creeps me out."

"Just hang up."

"I do, after I give 'em a piece of my mind."

"That's why he calls back, if it is a he. You give him something. You react, respond. You should just hang up immediately."

"It just gets me so mad. Whoever it is calls so late and I can't go back to sleep."

"Unplug the phone at night," George suggested as he twirled the sock and tossed it onto the couch for OP to retrieve.

"I probably should."

"Do you hear anything in the background?" he inquired.

"Ya know, I think I've heard a car, like maybe he's at a phone booth." Morgan changed the subject. "Are you going to be at Rusty's most of the day?"

"Yeah. We're going to watch the game. You can come to the house when you're done doing whatever it is you're doing," George offered then added, "What are you doing?"

"I'm going to go check out that veteran's hospital you talked about," she said. "I'm going with Jackie, and probably Buddy."

"Who's Buddy?"

"Her boyfriend, the guy you saw her with at the bookstore."

"Man, how'd he get a woman like her?' George questioned. "She's rich. Why not give the poor guy a gratuitous trip to the dentist, or orthodontist."

"Don't be mean."

"I'm not!"

George grabbed his head, but still laughed, after OP knocked over his coffee table on her trip to retrieve the sock.

Morgan heard Jackie drive up so she walked out onto the balcony walkway to wave hello. Buddy smiled up at Morgan and waved back. Buddy and Jackie looked as happy as usual as they hopped out of the little car, holding hands as they made their way up the stairway.

Morgan realized that leaving Jackie's costly car unattended at the complex while they were checking out the hospital was probably not a good idea and expressed her concern to Jackie while making coffee and offering them freshly made cheese blintzes.

"I think it will be fine here," Jackie responded without concern.

"I don't. George won't be home to keep an eye on it. There's another weird expression: 'keep an eye' on it," Morgan shook her head. "You know, those mini-monsters from next door, in the house," Morgan pointed in the direction, "drew all over my car."

"Drew on your car? Are you kidding?" Jackie was stunned, rethinking leaving her car in the driveway.

"I'm not kidding. The little monsters drew all over it."

"What did you do?"

"I tossed eggs at their car," Morgan replied.

"You did not."

"Oooooh, yes I did, and they thought that George did it."

"Seriously?" Her eyes opened wide.

"Yes, seriously. I was so mad. They took felt pens and drew all over my car. I knew that I couldn't get them, or their parents, to clean it off. I was pissed.

"They drove up and I yelled down to their parents. I told them what their kids did. They laughed, said something I couldn't understand and walked away so I went in and got a few eggs and hit their car with them. They haven't touched my car since but I don't trust leaving your car here unattended." Morgan set the coffees down on the trunk.

"Weren't you afraid that they would do something back?"

"No, not really. Anyways, they thought George did it and I think they're afraid of George." Morgan sat down across from Jackie and Buddy who were like conjoined twins on the couch. "They're afraid of OP too."

"Morgan," Buddy spoke up. "Do you mind if I turn on your TV?"

"Of course not, go ahead," and Buddy turned on the television which had his full attention while Jackie and Morgan chatted about various goings-on until it was time to go.

"I can stay here. You guys go," Buddy offered, more interested in the game on the television than the excursion.

"I guess if he's staying here he can watch out for your car and we can take my car," Morgan mentioned as they headed for the door.

"Buddy," Jackie tried to gain Buddy's attention. "I'll leave the keys here in case you need to use the car."

"Oh, and Buddy," Morgan said in a raised voice to get his momentary attention. "If the closet door opens and OP comes out, don't be alarmed; it's just George letting her back into the apartment." Buddy nodded without taking his eyes from the television and they were out the door.

Jackie was a bit reluctant to leave the Dino after Morgan's felt pen story. She knew that Buddy wasn't going to be paying attention to her parked car so she insisted that they drive the Dino to the hospital. Morgan agreed. Jackie retrieved the keys from Buddy and with another hard drop off the sidewalk, they were off.

"So, how are the goldfish doing?" Morgan asked and they kept conversations light on the drive down.

Jackie found the hospital, which was right where she had believed it to be.

"Do you want me to pull in?" Jackie asked.

"Yes, pull in. Pull up to the building on the left."

Jackie pulled up as instructed looking wholly uncomfortable. "What are you going to do?"

"Just park and I'll be right back."

"What are you going to do?" Jackie asked again. She parked the car and left it running.

"I'll be right back." Morgan hopped out of the car and disappeared through the glass doors. Jackie watched apprehensively.

Morgan walked across the beige tile floor, heels clicking and echoing through the empty hallway. There was no reception desk, no one there to greet or inquire who she was or what she wanted. Morgan opened the door to a large room that looked a lot like an oversized doctor's waiting room. Several men, both standing and sitting, turned to look at the intruder, motionless, except for one whose arms extended out as if he were reaching for something in front

A Bible And A Fly Swatter 1977

of him with both hands. He turned toward Morgan. His hands were opening and shutting as if squeezing some unseen object. He came within a few feet of Morgan with his pulsating hands when a uniformed employee shouted the man's name, *"Maurice,"* in a tone and volume that jolted Morgan and stopped the approaching man.

"What are you doing here?" the uniformed man asked Morgan, looking both perplexed and annoyed by her presence.

"This is the veteran's hospital, right?" Morgan asked.

"Are you looking for someone?"

Morgan didn't know what to say. She hardly knew herself why she was there other than out of curiosity. There was a moment of silence, then without thinking she blurted out, "I'm looking to volunteer." The offer to volunteer popped out of her mouth like an excuse. The man promptly escorted her out of the room and redirected her to another building as if it were a viable reason to be there—an option.

Jackie looked relieved when Morgan came through the doors.

"I need to go to another building." Morgan hurried. "Do you want to wait here or drive over to the other building? It's just right there. I should only be a few minutes." Before Jackie could answer Morgan said, "I'll just walk. I'll be right back." She rushed off ignoring Jackie's question-filled response.

The grounds were somewhat manicured with numerous buildings in a horseshoe configuration. It reminded Morgan of an old college campus—without visible students, or any people, for that matter, walking around. She headed up the walkway to the designated building, opened the large doors and, same as with the other building, entered a building with no reception area. She wandered about and quickly found an active cafeteria. People were chatting and eating and milling about; unlike the "waiting room" of the other building, it was an upbeat atmosphere. She went unnoticed at first as she watched the goings-on but Morgan looked out of place. A man with a somewhat agitated expression approached her and asked if she needed help. She told him that she was looking for the main office.

"Why are you looking for the *'main office'*?" he questioned, emphasizing the words *main office* as if no such thing actually existed within the complex.

"I want to volunteer," Morgan affirmed, now committed to the notion—she could think about it later.

"You want to volunteer in the cafeteria?" he asked, just as perplexed as he was by her request for the main office.

"No," she answered. "Well, maybe. Where would I find the office to sign up to volunteer here?"

He walked Morgan down several halls to an office where a single woman stood beside a desk. He said as if in jest, "This young lady would like to volunteer," giving a half smile to the woman then turned and left the office. There was an uncomfortable silence which Morgan felt compelled to break.

"My name is Morgan." The woman set the papers she was holding down on the desk and gave her full attention to Morgan. "My neighbor told me that the hospital might need volunteers. I think his grandfather was here. He said that it was a big hospital and that they could always use volunteers."

The woman stared at Morgan like one would stare at somebody else's coffee cup left on their desk. A few moments of silence passed and she asked, "What kind of volunteer work do you do?"

"Whatever you need. Whatever you think I'm capable of." Morgan stepped closer to the desk. "I work not far from here. My schedule is fairly open."

"Are you a student?"

"I hope to start college next year," Morgan lied but it seemed to make the woman a bit more at ease.

She shuffled a few papers around her desk then asked, "Do you know where Building D is?"

"No, but I'm sure I can find it," Morgan quickly answered, feeling like she had succeeded—the woman was going to direct her to where she could establish herself as a volunteer.

"Go out the main doors, turn right and follow along past this building. The large building behind this one is Building D. Go in there and find one of the nurses and tell her you're here to volunteer," she instructed and seemed as though she were merely contented to pass Morgan on to someone else.

Morgan could hear music coming from Jackie's parked car as she headed for Building D. She waved but Jackie didn't notice her. Jackie was staring back at the men who were staring at her through the glass doors—it was a mutual fish tank.

Morgan walked the distance to Building D, climbed the large cement steps and entered the oversized heavy doors. Again, there was no reception and the hunt for a nurse was on. She passed rooms where open doors revealed men in what looked like hospital beds. At the very end of the first hall, she spotted a nurse sitting on a desk smoking a cigarette. The nurse didn't notice her until she was almost *at* the desk.

"Hi," Morgan greeted. "My name is Morgan. I was sent here from the other building." Morgan turned slightly and pointed south to where the other building was located. "I'm here to volunteer." The woman looked baffled. From fear of rejection, Morgan rattled on, "I'm starting college next year and since I have an open schedule now and my neighbor told me that the hospital can always use volunteers I decided to come down and sign up. Anything that you need done; anyway that I can help out is fine with me. Just lead the way... or, let me know. I'm good at filing too." Morgan smiled, searching for a sign of acceptance.

"What is your name?" the nurse asked.

"Morgan." Morgan reached out her hand and the nurse obliged.

"Hold on, Morgan," she said then disappeared through a door returning with another woman. "This is Morgan. She was sent here to volunteer," the nurse said to the other woman.

"Who sent you?" the other woman asked Morgan but the nurse answered before Morgan got the chance.

"She was sent from the front building," the nurse answered. "Morgan." She looked at Morgan. "It's Morgan right?" Morgan shook her head to confirm. "Morgan wants to help out in any way she is needed." Again she looked at Morgan. "Is that right?" Again Morgan nodded her head in agreement.

The other woman looked at Morgan for a few seconds without saying a word. She was sizing her up—blunt and unimpressed as though Morgan were an annoyance she needed to get out of the way for the time being. She suggested to the nurse that she take Morgan to visit with John. Morgan wasn't asked or required to fill out any paperwork, just to follow the nurse who, during the walk to John, introduced herself as Anna. John was in the first room with the open door that Morgan had passed on her way in. She followed slightly behind as the nurse entered John's room.

"John," she said in a rather loud voice as if John might be hard of hearing. "You have company. Morgan is here to visit you." She smiled at both John and Morgan then left the room. Morgan was immediately uncomfortable. She didn't know what to say other than hello, which she did right away. John had

ZaneDoe

no arms and no legs and was not an old man as Morgan had anticipated. He looked at her without smiling which made her even more uncomfortable. Like a sudden dizziness, Morgan felt out of place and overwhelmed, hit with the realization that she had jumped into something blind and ill-equipped.

"Hello," John said in a very calm voice. "You're here to visit me?"

"I came to volunteer," she said nervously and feared what he might say next, like *"go away."*

"Well, that's nice of you but you're wasting your time here."

Morgan felt like running out the door and out of the building. She wasn't wanted there and who did she think she was to think that she was wanted or needed. *Oh God, what the hell am I doing?* She readied herself to apologize and scurry out of Building D never to return. Then he continued, "I have visitors, Morgan. Morgan is it?"

"Yes," she answered meekly

He continued, "But there are men here that never have visitors. They'd like someone to visit them, I'm sure. So thanks anyway, but you need to visit one of those men." He turned his head and stared back up at the ceiling as he had been doing when they entered the room.

"Okay. I will. Thank you." She exited the room with relief and stood outside the door by the wall so as not to be seen, pondering whether to abandon her impromptu decision to be a volunteer, turn right, race out of the building and into Jackie's waiting car—or turn left, go back to Anna and ask to visit someone else.

Morgan took a gigantic almost dizzying breath, held it and as she exhaled headed back to the desk where she assumed Anna would be, possibly finishing her cigarette. All the while feeling hesitant and unsure of her intentions for being there in the first place. This wasn't the first, nor likely to be the last, time Morgan jumped into something headfirst: she had only met Mr. Smith twice when she accepted a full-time job with him, quitting her present job to start the next day at Samuel Pacific Imports. Morgan tended to be led by feelings and not one to carefully think things out. The decision to get OP was not a practical one but made purely by the heart, and a decision she never regretted no matter what challenge OP's companionship presented. Morgan made what others thought to be impulsive and poor decisions but Morgan rarely regretted such decision so far in life, but did have a hard time explaining them to her mother who was constantly demanding some logical explanation.

- 58 -

A Bible And A Fly Swatter 1977

She saw Anna back at her desk still smoking a cigarette. A voice, a plea, came from one of the rooms as Morgan passed. She stopped to listen and looked at Anna, wondering if she also heard the man's plea. Anna paid no attention. Morgan decided to respond and entered the room where she heard the old man's voice. With great effort, a very thin and very pale old man tried to lift his arm only accomplishing a few inches. He voiced his plea again but Morgan couldn't understand him. She stepped up to the bed and leaned close to his face. He wanted water. There was a pitcher and a glass by his bed but he couldn't reach it and he appeared too weak to manage it even if he could. Morgan grabbed the pitcher. It was empty.

"I'll go get you some water. I'll be right back."

Morgan was volunteering.

Morgan took the pitcher to Anna and explained that the man in the room wanted water.

"You can get some water from there," she said, pointing to the water fountain.

Morgan filled the pitcher and rushed back to the room. She didn't stop to ask for permission to be in his room or to ask any questions. She poured the water into the glass that was on the bedside table and held the glass up to the man's mouth to help him drink. He drank and spilled, then drank some more. Morgan dabbed the water off of his chin with the corner of the sheet. When she placed the glass back on the table, he reached his hand as far as he was able. At first she thought that he wanted more water, however, he only wanted to touch her. He smiled, a toothless smile, and nodded, which she took as a thank you. His cold fingers were resting upon her forearm and he seemed relieved to have her there.

"I'm going to get a chair. I'll be right back," Morgan said. He gave another weak and sincere smile. She gently lifted his skeletal hand from her arm and placed it on the blanket. Morgan quickly dragged a chair over to the bed then sat down, placing her hand, which was warm, on his. "I'm going to sit and visit with you, if you don't mind," she said. "Can I tell you about my dog OP?" The old man relaxed and closed his eyes, and Morgan told him about adopting OP. She talked and talked and he appeared to have fallen asleep.

Jackie was waiting and Morgan knew that she should get going and she knew that she wanted to come back. She left the room and the "sleeping" man.

"Can I come back to visit. Is that going to be okay?" she asked Anna.

- 59 -

ZaneDoe

"If you want to…that will be fine." Anna looked up from her magazine. "Are you sure you want to volunteer here?"

"Yes, if you don't mind. When should I come?"

"Anytime, I guess. Whatever works into your schedule. But, Morgan, come to this building, D," she stressed. "Building D. You can volunteer visiting our men in Building D."

"Okay. I have someone waiting for me so I'm going to go but thank you, Anna. I'll be back. I'll see you soon…it was nice meeting you."

Anna gave a quick smile in response then her attention was back to the magazine. Morgan walked in a hurry toward the front doors, wondering why Anna was adamant that she visit only Building D. Morgan knew there were men in at least one other building and it was safe to assume, with so many buildings, that there were men in other buildings also.

As she approached the Dino she could see several men, patients, huddled around the glass doors facing the car. They seemed dazzled by either the Dino or by Jackie, Morgan couldn't tell. When she got closer, she could see a rigid and frightened Jackie.

"You okay?" Morgan asked while climbing onto the passenger's seat.

"Where the hell have you been?" Jackie demanded, still rigid and staring at the men staring at her.

"Let's go," Morgan requested as she tried to hold back a laugh at the collective stare down. "Do you want me to drive?" Morgan wondered why, if the Dino interested the men, that they didn't come out the door to see it. Jackie started the car, backed up slowly then exited the complex in silence.

"What the hell were you doing in there? Why were you taking so long? You had me worried. Those men were scaring me…" Jackie rattled on once away from the hospital grounds.

"I was just wanting to check things out, see what it was like for old soldiers there, and I ended up asking if I could volunteer at the hospital," Morgan explained.

"Volunteer doing what?"

"I wasn't sure but now I am. They need company, Jackie. They really, really do. I didn't see much but what little I did see, well, it looks like a lonely place, a really lonely place to be." She thought for a minute or so while Jackie waited to hear more. "You have to go inside and see it for yourself; it's hard to explain. It's more a feeling. You gotta go in there, Jackie."

- 60 -

A Bible And A Fly Swatter 1977

"Those guys," Jackie exclaimed. "I mean, I feel sorry for them but they were chilling me out. They sort of bunched up and just stared at me. Just stared, you know, no expression—just stared. I waved but they just stared back." Jackie seemed truly frightened by the men who would not cross the glass barrier.

"They were probably just looking at your car. I doubt they see many sports cars like this one around there," Morgan reassured. "They're men, of course they're going to be interest in a sports car and this one is unique."

"Well maybe. I don't know, they were scaring me, Morgan, and you just disappear." Jackie turned and drove toward downtown Palo Alto. "Wanna get something to eat?"

"What about Buddy back at my apartment?"

"Oh! I forgot. We can go pick him up and then get lunch," Jackie said while doing an illegal U-turn to unrestrained horns and headed to the freeway onramp.

"Let's pick up Buddy and go to Rusty's house. George is there with OP. They're watching the game so Buddy'll be happy then I can pick up OP. I'll take my car and you guys can follow...." It was a plan.

What Morgan hadn't planned on was Buddy inviting Lorraine into the apartment. There they sat on the couch, watching the game—at least Buddy was watching the game. Morgan couldn't be sure what Lorraine was doing in her apartment while the game held Buddy spellbound.

"I hate to rush you on out, Lorraine," Morgan lied, "but we have to meet some friends and we're running late." Jackie knew that Morgan was exaggerating and Buddy paid no attention. Morgan did indeed rush Lorraine out the door, watching through the curtains that Lorraine kept a steady pace back to her own apartment.

"Buddy," Morgan tried for his attention. "Yooohoo." He looked up. "Why was she in here? And, did she stay in the living room or did she roam around my apartment?"

"I think she used the bathroom," Buddy answered, torn between the blatantly irritated Morgan and the game.

"Why? What's wrong," Jackie asked.

"Let's just go; I'll tell you more about our lovely manager when we get to Rusty's." Morgan rushed them both out of the apartment. "I'll be right down," she shouted. Morgan shut all of the curtains then placed a glass of water behind the door before locking it to alert her to any unauthorized guest, such as Lorraine.

ZaneDoe

They pulled up to Rusty's impressive house and could hear the game playing on the television, which obviously pleased Buddy. Greetings and introductions were short due to the game and Jackie and Morgan joined OP by the pool. OP was soaking wet and tired; she only gave Morgan and Jackie a short wag then lumbered toward the lawn to lie down.

"What are these?" Jackie asked about one of the food selections on her plate.

"The boys' version of a cocktail weenie, I assume," Morgan answered and then began tales of Lorraine. She started with stories that George had passed along that had occurred long before Morgan moved in. They were good for a few laughs.

"Jackie," said Morgan, "I think, I'm almost sure, that I put Grandpa's teeth in the pocket of the jacket we bought in Half Moon Bay. Do you still have the jacket?"

"Didn't your grandfather take the jacket?"

"God, I don't remember…but if you can't find Aka's teeth, would you mind going to visit him and tell him yourself?"

"Why? Is he going to get mad and you want him to yell at me instead of you?" Jackie questioned with a laugh.

"No, he's too mellow. I just think he'd like your company. He said that he doesn't need his teeth for eating; he says that they just make him look good." She looked over at Jackie knowing that she would laugh, and she did. "If he cares about looking good, then he must care about others see him and therefore would like company. Make sense?"

"I'd like to visit him anyway," she said. "What can I bring him? Besides his teeth, that is."

"Anything to read. He loves to read. Magazines maybe," Morgan answered and the topics went from there. They relaxed and talked, amused by the sporadic bursts of hellish shouts at the television. Morgan pointed out, "For a game that is supposed to be so enjoyable, they sound like they are going to kill something."

"While they're busy with the game, let's take a dip," Jackie said in a mischievous voice, coaxing Morgan to go skinny-dipping. OP couldn't resist joining them, after she finished what was left on their plates—food better suited to the men and dogs as far as Morgan and Jackie were concerned.

- 62 -

Chapter 6
Fly Girl

"Hey, Mz. Janie," Morgan greeted.

Janie was sitting on the couch in the main room. She smiled back at Morgan. She wasn't reading a book or magazine nor looking out the window. Janie was just sitting by herself looking forward. It was a sad sight for Morgan.

"I wanted to introduce you to my grandfather, Aka, but he's asleep. He's usually reading but the book is on his chest and he's sound asleep."

"Sleep is good, Morgan," Janie commented. "So how are you?"

They talked awhile. Janie pointed out the improvements on the courtyard and they decided to move outside to enjoy the upgraded environment. Morgan brought chocolates, which Janie described as "like a drug" in the home. She also brought a cushion for Janie to sit on.

Morgan joked after handing Janie a small box of chocolates, "You mean I could become a chocolate dealer here and quit my job?"

"If you're not working for cash," Janie joked back.

They admired Xavier's hard work and admitted that it actually brought some cheer to the courtyard and some credibility to the home's name. In their dialogue of scattered topics, Morgan brought up her recent visit to the veterans hospital. She voiced her opinion regarding the fate of the veterans and described the dismal atmosphere in which the veterans existed. She told of the man with no arms and legs and of the man who pleaded for water.

Janie turned to face Morgan and looked at Morgan with such intensity that on a hunch, Morgan dared to ask if Janie might know someone at the veterans hospital. Janie stood up and said in a stern and determined voice, "I would like to show you something, Morgan."

"Of course," Morgan quickly responded then also stood up.

Janie looked purposeful, standing more erect than usual. Morgan sensed that Janie did not want her assistance on this trek so she refrained from offering her arm per usual. Janie said nothing on the way to the room, which was not the norm.

"Under my bed, tucked up at the head of the frame, there's a leather carry. Would you get that for me, Morgan."

Under the bed survived dust dinosaurs, a place Janie knew was safe, where something could be kept private. Tucked under the bed, a place that the cleaning staff had forsaken, Janie kept what appeared to be her only private possession. Morgan gently removed what looked to be an antique tooled leather clutch bag. The folded top was ornately tooled with images of leaves and fans. She handed it to Janie.

"If Alice comes in, I want you to take this with you. You can bring it back another time but pretend that it's yours, Morgan," Janie said in such a staid-laced manner that Morgan could, or would, not question the why of the request.

"Sure, of course," Morgan agreed without hesitation.

Janie opened the clutch. The edges of papers and photographs poked out from the compartments. Janie carefully pulled a photograph from the clutch and placed it in Morgan's hand. It was an old black and white photograph of young woman; she was smiling, beaming—as was Janie at that moment. This striking woman wore a heavy leather jacket lined with what looked like sheep's wool and a long scarf tucked into the front of the jacket, an aviator helmet and goggles atop her head. She was undoubtedly a beauty of her time. The smile on her face depicted undeniable satisfaction.

Morgan looked at the photograph and then at Janie, several times.

"Is this you?" Morgan was wowed by the prospect. "It is, isn't it?"

Janie gently nodded a yes then removed another photograph from the leather clutch and handed it to Morgan. It showed five women in full leather flight suits: fleece line jackets, leather pullover pants, heavy boots and goggles. Across the photograph, in black ink, were five names: Frances, Dorothy, Janie, Jo, Mary.

"Do you have more?" Morgan asked, excited and in awe. Janie pulled another photograph from the clutch. She paused a moment to look at it herself then handed the photograph to Morgan: two women in what looked like jump-suits were folding a blanket in front of a barrack style wood building.

"Is one of these women you?" she asked. Janie shook her head no.

"That's Frances and Mary." There was an air of respect in the way Janie said their names. She had one more photograph that she wanted to show Morgan: one woman was in the cockpit of an airplane and another woman was leaning against the outside of the airplane, both wore enormous smiles. *Fly Girls* was handwritten on this photograph.

"Is one of these, one of these woman, you?" Morgan asked of the women in the photograph.

"I'm ready to fly," Janie said in a soft voice, but the words seemed to soar. "It's a B-29." There was a spark, a life, in Janie's eyes that contradicted her physical condition. She gave a slight laugh. "Most of the men were afraid of that plane, Morgan."

"Why were they afraid of it?" Morgan naively asked; she knew nothing of planes and very little about WWII.

"Afraid to fly it. We women weren't." Janie raised her eyebrows and grinned with pride.

"You were a pilot. Wow, Janie—a pilot! That's fantastic. Wow! Amazing!" Morgan smiled as she stared down at the photograph with admiration, focused on Janie in the pilot's seat of the airplane.

Janie patted her hand, so delighted to share her proud past with one who openly appreciated it.

"You have to tell——" Morgan stopped mid sentence. Alice was guiding, more like pulling, Mrs. Schwab into the room. Morgan looked at Janie who nodded urgently for her to take the leather clutch. She placed the photographs back into the clutch and put it in her purse. Alice's maleficent presence extinguished the spark in Janie's eyes and she took on the posture of irritation and vulnerability at the same time.

"I'll visit with you later, Morgan," Janie said. "Can you help me to the bathroom please?"

"Of course."

Mrs. Schwab was talking to Jesus and Alice was moving about the room with seemingly no purpose. In a whisper, Morgan asked Janie why Alice was lingering in the room and Janie responded with one word, "control."

After Morgan was sure that Janie no longer wanted company and that she was safely where she wanted to be, she headed over to Aka's room. She found him enjoying a jar of baby food.

"Taste good, Grandpa?"

He patted the bed welcoming Morgan to sit down.

"Your friend brought me this," he said.

"What?" Morgan questioned.

ZaneDoe

"The one who had my teeth."

"Oooh, yes, Jackie." Morgan was glad to hear that Jackie had stopped by and was hopeful Aka received his teeth. "Did you get your teeth, Grandpa?"

Aka shook his head no, then gave a big toothless smile to emphasize the fact.

"I'm sorry, Grandpa. I guess she couldn't find them."

Aka looked up from his baby food jar and said, "If she finds them she oughta give 'em to her husband," referring to Buddy.

"So she brought her boyfriend with her." Morgan acknowledged and clarified that he was not yet her husband. "He's a really nice guy. Did you talk to him, Grandpa?"

Aka shrugged. Morgan didn't know what the shrug meant. She didn't press the response since Aka seemed to be more interested in finishing his jar of baby food than discussing anything.

"How many jars did she bring you?"

Aka opened the drawer in the table next to his bed displaying about a half dozen jars.

"Are you allowed to have them?" she asked.

Aka again shrugged a response.

"Well, if you need to hide them put them under the bed. I think that's a safe hiding place, one they don't bother with."

Aka nodded his head, yes.

"Grandpa," Morgan continued, "I'd like you to meet another resident here."

"Why?" Aka said between bites.

"Because she's a really nice person and an interesting person. And, she's my friend."

Aka laughed. "You have friends here?" He laughed again. "You need to get out more, Mokana."

"Will you come visit with us in the courtyard sometime?" she asked. Aka indicated a yes then opened the drawer and pulled out another jar of baby food.

"Peaches," he exclaimed with a smile.

Morgan was never quite sure if Aka enjoyed her visits or just tolerated them. He never appeared all that interested in her company. He seemed to prefer a book—and now, baby food.

- 66 -

A Bible And A Fly Swatter 1977

She inquired where the colonel was and Aka told her "they took him" but he didn't know where to or why. The colonel's area looked the same so it appeared that he would be coming back. His corner of the room was always heartbreaking to Morgan and she found it hard to look at. He looked so out of place in that room. Then, like a light bulb bursting in her head, she thought of Janie. Morgan got excited. Maybe Janie could brighten the colonel's existence there in the home. They shared military experience. Maybe that would make the colonel feel not so alone. She wondered if Janie knew about the colonel. Since Aka was more engaged with the baby food than conversation, Morgan cut the visit short and headed back to Janie's room, excited to tell her about the colonel. But Janie was asleep, or appeared to be. Janie had stated that sleep was a good thing for most at Sunny Acres so Morgan chose to save her news for the next visit.

The office was fairly quiet. There were no messages from Mr. Johan Smith. OP had a new chew bone and was succeeding in making the rock hard cylindrical piece of rawhide into a gummy blob. She took calls from Benny, Lacey and from individuals looking for Mr. Smith. Then she got the dreaded call: someone asking Morgan about a 1961 vintage Chateau Latour.

"Excuse me, Mr. Beaumont, do you mind, could you hold on for a few moments? We just received some packages that I need to sign for. Actually, can I call you back in a few minutes?" Morgan's voice was calm but Morgan wasn't. Mr. Beaumont sternly insisted on waiting on the phone as opposed to waiting for a callback. She set the receiver on the desk.

Morgan not only knew little if anything about wine, she didn't even much like it. She couldn't tell the difference between a Mouton Rothschild and a skid row favorite. There was no way that she could answer the potential customer's questions with even a hint of accuracy. Morgan raced up the stairs to find George.

"Excuse me, Steve. I'm trying to find George." Morgan tried to impart with the tone of her voice the dire urgency to find George immediately. Steve informed, with annoyance—since anything having to do with George rubbed Steve the wrong way—that George was taking a "leisurely cigarette break" out back.

"You know, next to where the dead guy was," he said and sauntered off.

- 67 -

ZaneDoe

"Thank you," she quickly responded and raced out the door at full speed, down the hall and out the back door almost smacking right into George mid puff.

"Oh please tell me that you know about a 1961 Latour," she pleaded.

"Why?" George responded, unruffled and not varying his stance.

"Oh George, just tell me if you know anything so I don't sound like an idiot. Quickly. *Please!*" she begged.

"Well, I doubt Mr. Johan Smith has what I believe you're referring to lying around the office or in those 'lightweight' boxes," George began. "I would think that you are wanting to know about a 1961 Chateau Latour from the Bordeaux region in France——-"

"Yes! Yes! That's what he said, Chateau Latour," Morgan interrupted. "Tell me anything you know about it so I can repeat it and sound like I know what I'm talking about."

"What does he specifically want to know?"

"He just said that he was calling to 'inquire about' so I don't really know so just tell me something to repeat to him." Her eyes opened wide. "Or, you could take the call as if you were one of our salesmen."

George laughed. "Well Morgan, I would just ask him what he wants to know about it and then have Johan deal with it. I can tell you this, it's a very expensive bottle of wine and I doubt that he's calling up to order a case."

"Why is it so expensive?" Morgan asked. "Seriously, tell me *something!*"

"Morgan, the man knows about the wine, that's not a wine you make a casual inquiry about. If Johan has it, I'd be duly impressed."

"So what do I tell him?"

"Tell him that you are familiar with the wine, that will make you sound knowledgeable but that Mr. Smith will need to speak to him about its availability. Just say that, nothing more."

"What color is the wine?" she asked.

"Deep ruby. Mulberry," he answered. "But trust me, he's not going to ask you what color the wine is."

"Thank you, thank you, thank you," Morgan's voice faded as she raced back to the office where OP let her know with a plaintive whimper as soon as she entered that her gooey, gummy rawhide was stuck against the wall behind the large potted plant.

- 68 -

A Bible And A Fly Swatter 1977

"Shhhhhhhhhhhhhh, *OP!*" to which OP barked indignation and pawed at the pot. Morgan dashed to retrieve the gummy rawhide glob, tossed it onto OP's bed and grabbed the receiver with her now wet fingers.

"Thank you for waiting and I apologize for the wait," she said, attempting to hide that she was out of breath.

"What was that?" he asked.

"What was what?"

"A dog barking? Is this the Samuel Pacific office?"

"Oh, I'm sorry. The deliveryman brings his dog with him. He's a really friendly dog. No one seems to mind," she explained then immediately brought the conversation back to the rare requested wine. She said exactly what George told her to say and that satisfied Mr. Beaumont. She assured that as soon as she touched base with Mr. Smith, she would have him return his call.

After hanging up, Morgan called Jackie who was typically home since she didn't work a regular job. She visited her housebound grandmother and often ran errands for her which Jackie's parents and grandmother deemed a job and gave Jackie a monthly salary for her trouble.

"Hello?" Jackie picked up on the second ring.

"Hi, this is Morgan, Jackie."

"Are you sure this is Morgan? Make OP bark," Jackie joked.

"Yeah, I'm at work. That's all I need is OP barking," she quipped. "I have to ask you about the baby food you brought Aka."

"Oh," Jackie gave a quick giggle. "Why, doesn't he like it? Is he not supposed to have it there?"

"He *loves* it. More than a baby...." Morgan told Jackie of her visit and how Aka was devouring the baby food. She thanked her for visiting Aka and for the gifts of pureed delicacies. They decided to sneak in jars on a regular basis, sort of compensation for losing his teeth. Aka didn't appear interested in getting a new set of teeth. Morgan wouldn't push the issue if Aka was happy without them. Jackie ended up finding Aka's teeth under the seat of her car. She cleaned them then placed them in a bag and then in the pocket of her sheepskin coat to return them to Aka. Unfortunately, some thief stole the coat from her car and now was in possession of Aka's teeth.

"So you brought Buddy with you," Morgan was curious if Buddy and Aka conversed. "Did he and Aka talk?"

- 69 -

"Buddy talked to Aka but it didn't seem like Aka was listening to him," Jackie answered. "He just kind of stared at him."

"It's not personal, I'm sure," Morgan assured though she was pretty sure Aka was fixated at Buddy's teeth. Buddy's teeth were slightly bucked and a bit mangled and it was hard not to stare at them when initially meeting Buddy.

"Maybe he was self-conscious about his teeth," Jackie wondered aloud.

"Or lack of," Morgan joked and Jackie laughed. She doubted Aka was self-conscious about not having teeth, particularly after focusing in on Buddy's protruding and mangled showing.

The conversation carried on about various topics until the door to the office opened. Morgan typically left the door unlocked during the afternoon hours only making sure that it was locked in the evening. Most knocked before opening the door but these two men in suits didn't. OP sat up which had the two men's attention immediately.

"Can I help you?" Morgan asked, holding on to the receiver. Jackie asked if her boss had shown up. Morgan didn't answer

"Is Johan Smith here?" one man asked while the other kept his eyes on OP.

Morgan surprised herself by the immediate distrust she had for the two men and by her flippant response. "Does it look like he's here?" The office was rather small and unless they truly believed that Mr. Smith was hiding behind the wine boxes or under the desk, it was obvious that no one else was in the office—no one else but OP who kept the men stationed at the doorway.

"Where can we find Mr. Smith?" the same man asked.

"I don't know but if you find him, please tell him that I may have an impressive sale," Morgan answered, keeping direct eye contact. Something inside told her to appear strong and ready as opposed to polite and accommodating. They reminded Morgan of agents of some kind: FBI, Secret Service. Regardless, they rubbed Morgan the wrong way and she wouldn't have told them where Johan was even if she knew.

"When will he be back?" was the next question.

"I have no idea," she answered. "Can I tell him who has come calling?"

The two men exchanged looks, a nonverbal exchange initiating their next move. Without a word, and with the one man still keeping his eyes on OP, they exited the office, closing the door behind them which Morgan believed was to assure that OP stayed in the office.

"Who was that?" Jackie eagerly asked.

"I don't know but they looked like Secret Service Agents."

"Secret Service Agents?"

"I don't know," Morgan answered with as much exclamation. "They just look like that, you know, that agent look: dark suits, no smiles. Really intense sort of cold eyes—the I-mean-business sort of look.

"Who knows what Johan is up to. No one can ever find him so it doesn't surprise me that someone is looking for him. I never know where he is." She added after a short pause, "You know, sometimes I wonder—he is too intelligent. He's too worldly, you know what I mean? He speaks five different languages, five that I know of, fluently. He's like an information machine—and he sells wine for a living?"

"That's *good* in the wine business, isn't it?" Jackie asked.

"I'm sure it helps. I don't know. I am probably way off base, influenced by George. I should just shut up. Next topic..." and they continued to talk about the light and simple.

"So, you selling wine now?" George asked. He was off work and stopped in to see if Morgan wanted him to take OP home. In truth, he wanted to take OP home—OP was his part-time dog.

Morgan smiled then asked, "Did you see those two men in dark suits?"

"No. Why?"

Morgan explained their sudden appearance at the office, emphasizing their somewhat menacing demeanor.

"Aaaaaah, looking for the elusive and mysterious Johan Smith." He didn't seem surprised or alerted by the visitors as Morgan was. "Now Johan, I believe—but Smith? That name combo just isn't right." George had one brief encounter with Johan and from that encounter on, George was suspicious. "This guy just doesn't add up, Morgan."

"Add up to what?" she asked then corrected herself while slapping her hand down on the desk for affect. "Never mind. Don't tell me. He's my boss and I like him and if he's an assassin with Interpol, I don't want to know."

George was amused by the gesture and the "assassin with Interpol" accusation. He said no more while he gathered up OP's squeak toy and OP and left the office for home. Morgan decided to stay longer at the office than usual hoping that Mr. Smith would call. She was eager to tell, or warn, him of the

ZaneDoe

two stoned-faced visitors in suits and about Mr. Beaumont's inquiry. But Mr. Smith never called. Before leaving, Morgan called the main office in Los Angeles by chance Johan was there. He wasn't, though the call allowed her to bring up the wine request for a Chateau Latour, 1961 which caused quite a stir at the main office. Morgan had no idea a bottle of wine could retail for so much money. She was careful not to reveal the potential buyer's name so that the sale, if there was a sale, would be credited to Mr. Smith, maybe even her. She made an excuse to quickly hang up the phone. The Los Angeles office called her right back. Morgan didn't pick up, though she heard them leaving a message on the answering machine as she locked the door behind her.

Morgan stood by Anna's desk awkwardly waiting for her to show up. Several men who appeared to be dressed in pajamas gathered near the end of the hall to take a look at Morgan. She smiled at them and waved which caused them to back up in unison. They now hid the majority of their pajama-clad bodies from view and peaked their heads around the corner to continue to watch Morgan. She was something new.

Eventually Anna strolled past the gathered men, lit cigarette in hand, only giving them a quick glance as she headed down the hallway to her desk and the waiting volunteer.

"You're back," Anna commented, looking neither pleased nor disappointed. Morgan would come to discover that Anna had the capacity to maintain an air of indifference in most all situations.

"I'm back. Ready to work, help, visit, whatever you need," Morgan answered, determined. "Do you want me to visit like last time?"

"Come with me." Anna grabbed a folder off her desk and headed down the hallway. "Do you smoke?" she asked Morgan.

"Sometimes, but I don't have any with me now," Morgan answered, assuming that Anna was going to ask for a cigarette.

"Well, you can smoke in here if you want." She stopped to make eye contact with Morgan as she stated, "But don't give cigarettes to the men. They'll ask you for them, but don't," her eyes squinted, "give them any."

"Okay," Morgan agreed and continued to dutifully follow Anna. "Are they not allowed to smoke?" she asked rather sheepishly. Anna was so adamant she almost feared to continue the subject.

- 72 -

A Bible And A Fly Swatter 1977

"Trust me," Anna said without losing her determined pace. She led Morgan to a large open room where a television sat sadly in the corner, one that looked like the ones displayed in thrift stores that weren't worth the ten dollar asking price. Scattered about the room were several men, some wearing what looked like pajamas, some in bathrobes and others were in well-worn khaki pants and undershirts. Some diverted their eyes when they saw Anna enter the room. The long sea-foam green drape was the chosen hiding place of one man in pajamas. It was at first glance a sad sight to Morgan and caught her off guard.

"Are these men soldiers?" Morgan corrected herself, "I mean vets?" To which, Anna, who had already stopped, turned her head and stared at her—pausing for an uncomfortable minute before answering.

"These are vets, alright. This hospital is all vets; didn't you know that?"

"I guess that was a stupid question. This is a veterans hospital," Morgan responded apologetically. She was taken aback by the scene. She wasn't sure what she expected but it wasn't what she was seeing so far. The men looked either frightened, bewildered or half not there. They didn't look like what Morgan expected "retired" soldiers to look like. "Would you like me to visit with the men in here?"

"Here, come with me." Anna walked Morgan over to a man sitting in a wheelchair by the window. He was smoking a cigarette by means of a hookah. His body was contorted and thin. He was very pale

"David, you have a visitor," Anna proclaimed rather loudly.

He turned his head and looked at Anna, then Morgan. His mouth opened, dropped open, and he spoke, "Aaaah waaaah taaaa…" Morgan could not understand him but figured that Anna knew what he was saying. She looked up at Anna expecting her to translate so that she would know what he had said. Instead, she announced to Morgan, in front of David, that he couldn't talk: "Don't worry. No one can understand a word he says. Just spend a little time with him," and Anna walked away.

Instead of looming over David by standing, Morgan pulled a chair over to sit down next to him. "Hi. My name is Morgan." She felt certain that he didn't understand her, otherwise why would Anna have said such a thing in front of David but she didn't know what else to do but talk, so that's what she did. "How are you?" It seemed like an absurd question once it came out of her mouth. She couldn't imagine one being much worse off than this man pretzeled into his wheelchair. David dropped open his mouth again and while

- 73 -

looking directly at Morgan repeated his former string of sounds, "Aaaaah waaaaaah taaaaaa goooooo aaaaah saaaaa da." He looked away from Morgan and glanced back out the window as he had been doing when she and Anna first approached.

Morgan pulled her chair closer to the window and looked out as David was doing. "It's beautiful out, isn't it?" she commented. David looked at her and repeated the sounds. Even with his unsteady head he managed to look directly into her eyes, then looked back out the window.

She noticed that the cigarette stuck into his hookah was at its end so she asked, "Would you like me to get you another cigarette?" David nodded, one nod, a yes. "I'll be right back." She was told not to give the men cigarettes so she headed off to find Anna to get permission and a cigarette to replenish his hookah.

"He is only allowed four cigarettes a day," Anna bluntly informed. She pulled a cigarette out of her own pack and gave it to Morgan. "Do you know how to put it into the hookah?"

"Yes. I'll just pull the old one out and put this one in."

Anna smiled. Morgan didn't know why Anna smiled, but Morgan smiled back then hurried down the hallway to return to David who was still staring out the window.

"Here's a cigarette," Morgan said as she pulled the finished cigarette out of the hookah and replaced it with the new one only to realize that she didn't have a match. "I forgot a match. I'll be right back." To what seemed to be entertainment to the others, Morgan raced off to get a match from Anna. As Anna retrieved matches for Morgan, she commented further on David's inability to communicate, how he just mumbled on and that Morgan should just ignore it and visit with him the best she could.

Morgan was off once more at a fast pace down the hallway and back to David.

"Okay, I have matches," she said and was surprised to see what appeared to be a smile from David in response. It was a one-sided lift of the corner of his mouth, but more than just his mouth, his eyes seemed to smile. She lit his cigarette and was fascinated by how this bent man in his hand-propelled wheelchair maneuvered the pipe's end to his lips. His hand swayed like an orchestra conductor but finally managed its way to David's mouth. He took a puff then looked at Morgan. There was recognition in his eyes. She wondered if it was

A Bible And A Fly Swatter 1977

just his body that was marred and his mind was fine. It was actually a scary thought for Morgan.

David stared back out the window.

"Can you see my car, the yellow VW Thing?" she asked and pointed to her bright-yellow car parked below. David leaned a bit forward. He appeared to be looking right at her car. He looked back at Morgan and lifted his eyebrows. Morgan was certain he understood her. She talked on, not sure that anything she was saying was of interest but that didn't stop her. She wanted to know about David, wanted to ask him questions instead of making herself and her life the central topic, but that didn't seem to be a possibility so she told David about her dog, her apartment and her job. All the while, the pajama-clad men huddled together—at a distance—and watched.

She left David as he was when she and Anna first approached, staring out the window. She was unsuccessful at locating Anna before leaving the building. She wanted to know more about David and she wanted to know if there was anything that she could bring the men: books, magazines, a radio—anything. She would need to find out on her next visit.

Morgan backed the VW Thing out of the parking space and drove slowly passed Building D, looking up to see if she could see David at the window. She could, and she waved as she continued down the drive. She saw Anna walking on the sidewalk engaged in a fairly animated conversation with the man from the cafeteria. Morgan drove by seemingly unnoticed.

Morgan couldn't stop thinking about David, and the other men. She wondered why they were still there: *Were they healed? Where they going home one day? Where were their families? Why wasn't anyone visiting them? Why was it so dark and depressing? Why had she never heard of this hospital all these years?*

Morgan was young and what the veterans hospital harbored exposed her to an existence previously unseen and unknown in her world.

"Mr. Smith——" Morgan was interrupted.

"You can call me Johan," something he had told Morgan more than once but *Mr. Smith* had become habit for Morgan.

"I'm too used to calling you Mr. Smith," she explained then continued with her original question. "Are you familiar with the veterans hospital, the old veterans hospital?"

"Yes, very. And you ask me this because?" Johan answered and asked.

- 75 -

ZaneDoe

"I started volunteering there. I just visit. I had never heard of the place. I didn't know it existed." She paused, reflecting to herself for a moment.

"Those buildings have been there some time," Johan commented. "I'm surprised that you weren't aware of the hospital's existence before now."

"No, I had no idea. I went there for the first time a few weeks ago." Then she added with a scowl, "It's so vacant."

"I doubt that," Mr. Smith said with certainty.

"I don't mean vacant as in no one there: Vacant as in hollow, lonely. It's sad, Mr. Smith. It's a sad place." Morgan shook her head, displaying confusing. "It's just, well, such an empty feeling when you walk in there. Sad and empty. I don't understand why the families aren't there or why they don't come and cheer the place up, why the place is so drab. You should see the TV they watch. I mean, you can hardly see anything on the screen—lines, fuzzy. I don't know. I'm not sure why I am bringing this up to you. I guess I just have had that place on my mind ever since my last visit and I can't seem to stop thinking about it and those men."

Mr. Smith gave a slight smile.

"Okay, I'll drop this topic." Morgan shook her head and waved her hands in front of her face as though tossing the thoughts from her mind then continued, "Anyways, I have two very important things to tell you," she announced. "Oh, do you want me to read the your messages first?"

"I prefer that you read them to me and then leave them on the desk for me," Mr. Smith replied. "But now you have my curiosity so what are the two very important things?"

She first told him of the phone call from Mr. Beaumont regarding the 1961 Chateau Latour, proud that she correctly recalled the name. This caught Mr. Smith's undivided attention. He put down the paperwork in his hands and listened to Morgan tell of Mr. Beaumont's inquiry and of the brief conversation with the Los Angeles office.

"So what is, pray tell, the second thing that you want to tell me?"

"Before that, I just want to know if that wine sells, do I get a commission? I know that I didn't sell the wine, but I did make sure that this office gets the sale. I didn't let the L.A. office know who wanted the wine." Morgan questioned and made her case.

Mr. Smith had no objection; if a bottle of 1961 Chateau Latour sold Morgan would get a commission. He didn't state how much or what percentage but she wasn't concerned about the amount. She was actually curious if she would receive commission the same as the salespeople; it would be a bit of an inspiration to learn about the wines and a new undertaking at the office.

"Now, what was the second thing?" Mr. Smith insisted.

Morgan first apologized for not behaving as professional as Mr. Smith may have wanted or expected then she proceeded to tell him about the two stern-faced men in suits. She described how they looked and how they asked where they could find him. She told him of her somewhat flippant responses and justified her attitude by the fact that she didn't trust these men from the get-go.

Mr. Smith wanted to know not only the day and exact time of their visit but a more detailed description of the two men including if she could precisely describe their shoes. She could describe the two men in fairly good detail, but had not noticed anything in particular about their shoes. Though Morgan wanted to ask *Why the shoes?* she didn't and did her best to describe what little she did remember about the men's shoes—they were dark and "business-like."

Mr. Smith listened but had little to say about the two men. He informed Morgan that he would need to use the office that evening and that he would like her to close up the office by 3:00, but, before closing, "Please go over to Bailers and pick up a pasty or two and chips for me. Leave them on the desk with napkins."

"Do you want me to get you something to drink?"

"No, thank you, just the food please," and Mr. Smith actually smiled.

"George!" Morgan gave a subdued holler across the bookstore.

George stepped down from the ladder and met her at the door.

"I'm going to pick up some pasties for Mr. Smith; do you want me to get one for you or bring some home?"

"Pasties," George repeated. "Sounds like you're going to a strip joint."

"British joint," she replied. "Do want any?"

"Is your Mr. Johan Smith at the office?"

"No, not now. But he was," she answered. "He asked me to get him some pasties then I can take off. He needs to work so I'm going home after I pick up his food."

"Then get some and bring it home; I'll eat 'em there..." George and Morgan talked for a bit longer under the watchful eyes of Steve, which only made George talk all the more then promptly excuse himself for a cigarette break. To the owners of Buffalo Books, George could do no wrong. To Steve, George got away with murder. George would always chat with customers—he was well-read and well-informed and shared his knowledge at a leisurely pace and the owners appreciated it. Steve was a pointer. He pointed to where a customer could find information and often that pointing finger was aimed at George.

Morgan arrived at home before George. She had time to walk OP, make a few phone calls and relax before George popped through the closet door for a pasty.

"Where's my pasty?"

"I even got you a beer, Sir George," Morgan announced knowing that it would please him.

"You got a beer from Bailers? A British beer?" George took his seat with OP by his side.

"No, I grabbed some of the samples in the office."

"The mystery man sells beer too?"

"I thought you knew that—wine and imported beer." She took a deep breath. "I have two, maybe three things I want to tell you about...." She set the plated pasties and chips on the table along with two beers.

"Hey, you're not old enough to drink, young lady," George taunted and took a bite of his pasty. "Aaah, aaah! It's hot! Fuck! Thanks for the warning." George wiggled and blew air over his tongue.

"I heated them up, sorry." Then Morgan responded to his comment regarding her underage status. "Yes, I am old enough." She jetted her face to his. "Do you want to see my fake ID?" to which George laughed, opened his beer and sucked the cold fluid over his burned tongue.

Morgan told of her visit to the veterans hospital. She explained how the setting was not like a hospital but more like a rest home though not nearly as cheerful. She hoped that George could better enlighten her on that hospital.

"These are guys that need long-term care, sort of like the rest home. I don't think it's a short stay once you enter one of those hospitals. They deal with more than physical maladies...." George explained to the best of his knowledge what information he had about a veterans hospital. Morgan listened with reserved questions. She wasn't sure what to make of the whole situation and felt it best to change the subject for the time being.

A Bible And A Fly Swatter 1977

"I want to show you something, something that Janie gave me, or handed to me to care for for the time being." Morgan got up and retrieved the leather clutch with the photographs from her bedroom. She respectfully asked George to wash his hands then come sit on the couch with her to view the photographs since she didn't want to chance getting food or drink on them. He agreed.

George carefully took the photograph from Morgan.

"She was a W. A. S. P., " George announced with an expression that indicated he was wowed.

"What do you mean, a *wasp?*" Morgan was perplexed.

"To be exact: Women Airforce Service Pilots. You know, they flew planes during World War II. I'm impressed, Janie was a pilot." George reached for another photograph and asked, "How old is she?"

"I don't know. I'm not good at guessing ages."

George stared off from the photograph that he had been admiring. Morgan knew that he was calculating or figuring something, so she quietly waited.

"She'd be in her sixties, I'm guessing. I'm pretty sure that the WASPs were in 1943 or 44. That's kind of young to be in a rest home. Are you sure these photographs are of her?" George continued to examine the photographs.

"Sixties is old. She's old, George. She's not as old as Aka. I'm just guessing that she's seventy, maybe; I don't know." Morgan thought for a moment. "It's 1977 and World War II was in 1945, right?"

"So if your friend is seventy years old, she would have been in her thirties when she was a pilot," George calculated. "That could be."

"She has a hard time walking but doesn't use a wheelchair," Morgan explained. "She sometimes complains that her back hurts her. Maybe she has an injury and that's why she is in a rest home early." Morgan tried to remember if Janie had said anything specific about her health or age and she was sure that she hadn't.

George talked more about the women pilots of WWII and Morgan listened with awe and fascination while they admired Janie's photographs, both acknowledging that Janie's role was a significant part of history.

Morgan returned the clutch to her dresser-drawer for safekeeping and she and George headed back to the kitchen table to finish their pasties. George commented on the open curtain and window in the kitchen and that even the living-room curtains were open, "Is nutcase away?" Morgan typically kept them closed unless she was certain that Lorraine was gone from the complex.

"Oh...my...God," Morgan exclaimed, gaping each word—she suddenly remembered an event that she had neglected to tell George. "The other night when I got home, late, Lorraine was up against the fence. You know, the fence at the bottom of the stairs that's covered with ivy. She was just standing there—-"

"Doing what?" George questioned rather loudly. He looked at Morgan as though he were about to laugh.

"Not funny, George. She looked like a zombie."

But George gave a hearty laugh anyway.

"OP ran off to the ivy, the ground cover, you know where all the dogs go," Morgan explained, again interrupted by a comment.

"You mean where all the dogs *go* so their owners don't have to pick it up," he uttered with an accusatory tone.

Morgan smiled. "Yeah, that's the spot." He was right. The large patch of overgrown groundcover hid well whatever passed through it. She never recalled seeing anyone cleaning the contents of that hearty spread—she knew that she never had. Then she broke into a laugh herself. "You know, those guys downstairs hide their *apartment key there!*"

"In the ivy or that patch of whatever?" George asked. Morgan nodded yes and he shook his head the other way with a huge grin. "Great, reach in for the key and come up with a gift from OP."

"Anyways, I was going up the stairs," Morgan continued, "and thought that I saw something as I passed at the bottom. So halfway up I turned to check and there she was. Just standing there, pushed back up against the fence, pushed into the ivy just staring at me." Morgan mimed a shudder.

"What'd she say when you saw her?" George was still smiling.

"Nothing. I said her name, 'Lorraine?' then waited for her to say something. But she didn't. It was really spooky. OP went up the other side and I could hear her on the walk so I continued going up the stairs and just rushed into my apartment and locked the door behind me. I'm going to get a deadbolt put on that door. If it hadn't been so late, I would have scooted into your apartment or hollered for you to come over."

"Did she have her gun?" George asked half in jest.

Morgan tossed up her arms as to indicate *stop!* "Oh my God. Oh my God. Don't even say that! We need to change this subject."

George agreed. He could see where he found Lorraine humorously weird, Morgan found her sincerely scary. Morgan left for the bedroom to change her clothes; she hadn't been in the room but a few minutes when George shouted, "Hey Morgan, you've got company."

"Who?" she yelled back.

"Take a guess."

Morgan rushed from the bedroom to the kitchen where she saw Lorraine peering through the kitchen window. She was on her way to Morgan's front door.

"Oh fuck," Morgan exclaimed in irritation. "Come on OP, come," she commanded in a whisper while grabbing OP's collar and rushing her into the bedroom.

Morgan answered the gentle knock on the door, intentionally not opening the screen door.

"Yes?"

"Have you see a black bear around here?" Lorraine asked, perfectly serious.

"A bear? Like a bear in the woods bear?"

"I saw a black bear. I want to know if you saw it," she answered. "You were out that night."

Morgan shook her head no, bewildered by the question. Lorraine stood at the other side of the screen door in silence. Morgan guessed that she wanted to be invited in and that the silence was pause for the invite. But Morgan had no intention of inviting Lorraine into her apartment.

"I haven't seen a black bear around here. If I do I'll let you know."

Lorraine turned, without a word, and headed back down the walkway to her apartment.

"We have bears! We have bears!" George waved his hands in the air and waved his head in play. "Where's my shotgun! We've got bears...."

It was such an absurd claim but it got Morgan thinking.

"Oh George, I think we have *a* big black OP bear and Madame Dementia thinks she's *a wild bear roaming the apartment complex.*"

"Cherry Locks and The Big Black Bears." George laughed. "Maybe she was by the fence in the dark the other night bear-hunting."

"Oh God. *Not funny*, George," Morgan shot back. She paused in thought. "Oh my God, maybe you're right. Now that *really* scares me. But she's seen OP. She knows that I have a large black dog. But then there couldn't be a bear around here. Could there?"

ZaneDoe

"No, there's no bear around here. Just keep OP out of her view; I'll help you, just keep OP away from her and keep you away from her too for that matter. She's nuts; we both know that. Who knows what she might do, what she's capable of. God help you if you wear that black fuzzy coat at night." George laughed again then chastised, "I warned you when you moved in to keep away from her."

"Would you close the kitchen curtains so I can let OP out of the bedroom?"

George shut the curtains and the window.

"Another beer?" George inquired.

"Sure, in the fridge." Then Morgan asked, "Does Dan know that she is off-center?"

"He'd have to." George thought again. "Well, Dan is stoned a lot of the time so maybe she seems normal to him."

"He's stoned? Are you kidding? As in weed? Isn't he an attorney?" she asked in true surprise as she headed to the bathroom.

"I think he just does real estate now but it's beyond weed, Miss Naive, waaaay beyond weed," George hollered loud enough for her to hear through the bathroom door.

"So the landlord uses drugs and the apartment manager is a mental case," Morgan shouted back. "No wonder they fell for the teacup Newfoundland." George loved the teacup Newfoundland dupe and repeated it in his raspy smoker's laugh.

They spent the next few hours talking about the veterans hospital with George continually veering the topic back to Janie. She was a legend in George's eyes and he wanted to meet her.

"You will, George; I'll be seeing her tomorrow if you want to come. I'd be happy to introduce you, " Morgan invited but the next day was not a good time for George.

They were chatting away when Morgan noticed that it was getting dark and she needed to take OP for a walk. George accompanied her to help ease her worries about Lorraine. They ended up walking OP a few blocks to the park, which they normally would never do since some unsavory types tended to hang out there, however, it seemed safer than traipsing around the complex with Lorraine on the hunt for a vagabond "black bear." George got into more detail about the missions of the women pilots in World War II as they meandered

- 82 -

around the park waiting for OP to finish her business. The more he talked, the more Morgan was impressed with Janie beyond her already admirable feelings for her.

"Janie." Morgan sat down next to her. "I have your clutch and photographs in my purse. Would you like me to put them back under your bed?" she asked, ready to hide them while Alice was out of the building.

"No, Morgan. I would rather you had them for safekeeping." She was relieved to have them in Morgan's care, someone she trusted.

"Janie, were you a W. A. S. P.?"

"You know about the W. A. S. P.s? I'm surprised," she paused, "and pleased."

"1945?" Morgan inquired, hoping to appear at least a tad bit knowledgeable.

"It was before that for me, Morgan. I was in England for a while, flying planes there. Have you been to England, Morgan?"

"No, I haven't been anywhere, really. I plan to see places in the future but for now, I don't do much traveling."

Janie continued, "England was beautiful, even in wartime."

Were our soldiers in England? Morgan was confused and embarrassed that she knew very little about the war. She had a hundred questions she wanted to ask Janie but her intent for this visit was to introduce Janie to Aka.

"I'd love for you to meet my grandfather, Aka." Morgan stood up from the bed. "Please?"

"Yes, yes. Of course."

"He's Hawaiian, or mostly Hawaiian. I actually don't think any full-blood Hawaiians exist anymore or have existed for some time, at least according to my grandmother."

"So you're part Hawaiian," Janie commented. "So that's why you have that hair."

"That hair?" Morgan laughed.

"Your thick black hair; it must come from the Hawaiian side," Janie figured.

"I think it's from the Spanish side, but who knows. I look like my father and he's

Spanish, right off the boat from Spain."

- 83 -

Janie got to her feet.

She listened to Morgan warn about the colonel as they strolled to Aka's room. She told how it broke her heart to hear him cry and how Aka appeared to be able to ignore the sounds of his poorly veiled pain but it was hard for her to ignore them. Realizing that the colonel and Janie more than likely shared the same war and possibly they could strike up a friendship, she felt excited. Janie felt it from her.

"What?" she stopped to ask Morgan.

"What, what?" Morgan responded with a smile displaying such joy that it made Janie not only more perplexed but caused her to give a quick chortle and shake of her head as they continued on their way to Aka's room.

Aka was buried in a book. "Surprise, surprise," Morgan announced their arrival. He looked up, set his book on his lap and waved his hand hello. "Grandpa this is my friend Janie," she said as they made their way to Aka's bedside. Morgan pulled the chair from the wall for Janie. Aka just stared.

"Hello," Janie's voice was sweet.

Behind Janie's back Morgan gave Aka the wide-eyed reprimand in an attempt to persuade the antisocial Aka to be more sociable for the moment. Aka acknowledged her silent but exaggerated hint and put his book on the bedside table.

"Where you from?" Aka asked, which Morgan felt was a rude beginning but evidently Janie didn't. She responded immediately with enthusiasm.

"From many places, sir."

"Sir?" Aka laughed aloud.

"I believe Morgan said that you were from Hawaii."

"So, Mokana has been talking about me," he said looking up at Morgan.

"Mokana is my Hawaiian name," Morgan quickly explained. Conversation started up so easily between Janie and Aka, quick and animated. Morgan stepped away. She looked over at the colonel's side of the room. His belongings were positioned the same; everything looked untouched, frozen in place. The only thing missing was the colonel. She couldn't help herself and interrupted their conversation to ask, "Grandpa, where is the colonel?"

"Some medical problem," Aka answered.

"Is he coming back?"

Aka shrugged; he didn't know, which didn't surprise Morgan since Aka kept glued to a book, newspaper or magazine most of his waking hours.

- 84 -

A Bible And A Fly Swatter 1977

"I'm sorry for interrupting. I'll be right back." Morgan excused herself to use the bathroom. When she returned Janie and Aka were talking about Hawaii, talking and not taking much notice that she had returned. Morgan politely excused herself once more; she needed to pick up OP and get back to the Samuel Pacific Imports office. It didn't appear that she would be missed, which was very encouraging for Morgan.

Morgan found a note left by George on the kitchen table. He had taken OP to Rusty's house for a swim and would meet up with her at Samuel Pacific Imports. Morgan once again thanked her lucky stars for the blessing of her neighbor and friend. She loved OP and wished that she could afford a house with a yard but she couldn't and she was no more willing to give up OP than she would be to give up a child. She was determined to one day find that house with a yard, one day, but until then she would continue to find a way to manage a roof over her head with her humungous loveable companion. George was helping to make her situation relatively easy for the first time in the two years that Morgan had been out on her own with OP.

She made a sandwich to take to work and was off.

Jackie's Dino was sitting in the parking lot at Samuel Pacific Imports when Morgan arrived. It wasn't Buddy in the passenger's seat but some other older man.

Jackie got out of her car bubbling up with enthusiasm as soon as Morgan pulled in.

"What's up?" Morgan asked immediately.

"I want you to meet Ronnie," she said and looked at Morgan as if she should be just as excited about the prospect.

"Ronnie?" Morgan crunched her eyebrows together. "You mean Dr. Ronald Ketchum? The 'other man'?"

"Come meet him," Jackie insisted.

"Jackie, I feel weird. I really don't want to." Morgan was adamant.

"Why?"

Though Jackie's response seemed innocent and candid, Morgan was puzzled by it and retorted, "*Jackie*, come on. I like Buddy. I'd feel like a traitor. You do whatever you want, but I'm not comfortable with it." Jackie just stared with disappointment as though Morgan's response was wholly unexpected. Morgan explained further, "Jackie, the guy is married, has kids. He's supposed to

- 85 -

be some upstanding Stanford doctor. I think it's shitty." Jackie's eyes opened wider. "I'm sorry, Jackie, but I do. And, let me add that Buddy adores you, as you already know. He has no idea. He thinks you're an angel, maybe a misunderstood angel but he believes in you." Morgan looked right into Jackie's eyes. "*You* know that. Don't get me in the middle by having me meet this guy, okay?" Jackie stepped back as Morgan opened the car door. "I have to get to the office, just call me later."

Jackie removed the shocked expression from her face before heading back to her waiting lover. She made an excuse to Ronnie for Morgan's quick departure.

"Wow, this is a shock," Morgan exclaimed when discovering Mr. Smith sitting at the office desk. "It's good to see you. Do you want me to come back later or tomorrow so you can work?"

Mr. Smith looked up at Morgan as she closed the door behind her and responded, "So, I can't work with you here?"

"Well, there's only one desk and George will be dropping OP off in a while and you might not enjoy working with me and OP here."

"Why?"

She hung her purse on the antique iron hook that she found at a flea market and so proudly managed to get nailed into the stubborn cement wall. Morgan sat down in the chair farthest from the desk then answered, "Because what work I do here, unless you have something else for me to do, is done at the desk and OP occupies her time here either playing with a squeak toy, and I emphasize squeak, or sleeping which includes snoring, rather loud snoring—not an atmosphere that I imagine you'd enjoy working in." She kept to herself the fact that OP would probably still be wet from swimming in Rusty's pool and the scent of a wet-dog would permeate the office—quickly.

Mr. Smith smiled, a sight not often seen.

"I'll be leaving shortly." He put his closely-guarded pen back inside the pocket of his suit jacket and leaned back in the desk chair, now facing Morgan. "I might have a commission check for you."

"Oh God." Morgan grinned like the Cheshire Cat. "You mean Mr. Beaumont bought that bottle of wine, that really expensive, mega-dollar bottle of wine?"

"Let's say he bought that wine and more."

- 86 -

Mr. Smith reached for his briefcase then stood up, pulled a suitcase from the other side of the desk and placed it by the chair. "The office is yours," he said.

"Any special instructions, or same old, same old?" Morgan asked, rising from her chair as well.

"I would like you to keep the office door locked when you're here from now on," Mr. Smith instructed. He nodded his head toward the door. "I had a fisheye put in. Use that before opening the door." He ran his hand through his hair, picked up the suitcase and in his usual erect somewhat regal posture headed for the door.

"Any special instructions?" Morgan asked again before he left.

"I'll call you if I do. Lock the door behind me."

Morgan checked-out the new peephole. She could see the distorted back-half of Mr. Smith as he made his way up the stairs. There was an added dead-bolt which Johan didn't mention. The key to the deadbolt was lying by the phone properly identified by a tag. She was certain that the new peephole and deadbolt were a result of the two unexpected and unexplained visitors although she had no idea why.

Morgan was on the phone. She didn't hear anyone come down the stairs but she noticed the door handle move, then came several knocks on the door. She quickly wrapped up the conversation with Benny and made her way to the peephole. It was George. He noticed the new peephole and was bouncing his head to-and-fro at the fisheye. Morgan unlocked and opened the door.

"What the fuck is this?" George chided. "Door locked. Peephole. *Paranoia!*" He stepped into the office with OP who pushed past him to Morgan, wagging her tail and exercising her vocal cords. She was still wet to the touch.

"Johan had it put in," she answered. "Notice the deadbolt too?"

OP romped around the office looking for her chew bone. She stopped to sniff the new stack of boxes left by Mr. Smith and began to scratch at them with her paw.

"OP, stop it," Morgan raised her voice to get OP's attention. OP looked up, but just for a few seconds, then continued to sniff the boxes and paw at them. George watched OP with lifted eyebrows. She quickly responded to his innuendo of suspicion. "They probably have imported food of some kind." She exhaled and added, "That's all I need is for OP to break open the boxes and devour some outrageously expensive caviar or some rare hundred-year-old salami or something." Again she yelled for OP to leave the boxes alone.

"I'll move them on top of the others." George pointed to the boxes of wine that were stacked on the other side of the office. "This way if you have to leave her in here she won't be tempted." George anticipated lifting boxes with some weight but they were light, too light to contain bottles of wine or beer. "Well, these don't contain wine or beer my lady," he commented while relocating the boxes. "Maybe some featherweight thousand-year-old imported salami that Johan is black-marketing in Atherton.

"So, why does Mr. Smith have boxes marked wine that are too light to contain wine?"

"He just has other things boxed in the used wine boxes. Look who's paranoid now?" Morgan shot back.

George placed the second box atop the first.

"You sound so sinister every time you refer to anything having to do with Johan," Morgan uttered as she watched George emphasize just how light the boxes were. She felt that George's constant skepticism about most everyone and everything was used for humor sake but his suspicions regarding Mr. Smith seemed serious and were beginning to irritate Morgan. She held a great deal of respect for Mr. Smith and he gave her a job with the freedom and pay she only dreamed of at this early stage in her working experience. "You know George, I wish you would quit acting like Johan is some Mafia man or criminal or assassin. He's my boss and I really do like him."

"*Soooo?*" George stood in front of Morgan. "Why the deadbolt and peephole?"

"I'm not saying anything; you'll only rag on about Mr. Smith even more."

"Aaaah, so there is something you know is suspicious and won't tell me," George smiled, and Morgan changed the subject.

"You should come with me to the veterans hospital. You should volunteer with me."

George responded with sarcasm, "You've only been there a couple of times now you're the volunteer advocate?"

"Advocate?" She continued, "No, honestly, you should come see this place, see those men. It's sad; it's lonely and sad there. They need visitors. Something."

"Oh, I know what's coming next," George said while rolling his eyes.

"What?" Morgan was commenting from her heart and she wanted him to take this matter serious.

George knew that she was serious and he was familiar with the rather reprehensible state of affairs at the veterans hospital. The roll of his eyes was to indicate that he knew Morgan would soon be emotionally and otherwise involved at the hospital and that he wouldn't be the only one that she would be coercing to join her in her crusade—whatever it might be. Whether it was that George knew Morgan well or that he just knew her type, he often was one step ahead of Morgan as her young life was unfolding. So he said what he knew he would eventually be saying: he would join her on a visit to the veterans hospital.

And with his friend once again smiling and jovial, pleased with his response, George left for the bookstore.

Chapter 7
Jump for Joyce

Janie wasn't sitting on the couch in the visitors' area when Morgan walked in so she glimpsed through the glass doors but Janie wasn't in the courtyard either. Morgan checked her room and the hallways but no Janie. She continued on her way to visit Aka. As she approached the door, she heard Janie's voice inside the room.

Janie was sitting at Aka's bedside in a chair pulled up close to the bed. She was showing Aka something too small for Morgan to determine what it was but it appeared to be a piece of jewelry. Aka handed it back to Janie. Morgan could see that it was a round silver pin. Janie held it up to her chest, as if that is where the pin belonged. Morgan watched for a minute or so, unnoticed by either Janie or Aka. The colonel was still not back in his side of the room—they were alone and seemed to be having a cheery visit so Morgan decided to quietly leave. OP was waiting in the car so it was going to be a short visit to start with and she also was eager to get back home and check out her new answering machine.

Johan had given Morgan the dual cassette answering machine from the office when he purchased an updated version. She now had upgraded from the Ansafone (which George insisted was named so due to the origin and accent of the inventor) to the Phone-Mate and wanted to see if she set it up correctly and if she had any messages. Not everyone had an answering machine in 1977. And, not everyone was comfortable when leaving messages on these newfangled machines which became entertainment in itself.

"Hi Morgan." Sandy sounded a bit reserved as she was being recorded. "Ah, oh, okay. I'm being recorded now aren't I? Ummm, well, I called to tell you," then she giggled. "This feels weird talking to a machine. Okay." Another giggle. "Oh well, I called to tell you." She stopped again. "How long do I have to talk on this thing? Is it still recording?"

Most said a word or two then hung up, usually, "Hello. Morgan? Hello," not familiar with the concept of leaving an entire message.

The answering machine was working as it was supposed to and she had a message from Jackie: "I called to tell you that Buddy and I will go to that hospital with you to visit the soldiers if you still want us to. What do you do there?" There was a short pause. "Is this still recording? Morgan, was that your voice on the, this, machine? Oh, I'm hanging up. Call me back."

Morgan had been working on getting friends to commit to a visit at the hospital.

George heard Morgan listening to her answering machine and popped through the closet door with a grin on his face so big that it made Morgan not only suspicious but made her grin too.

"*What?*" she asked to prompt the explanation behind the massive grin and George burst out laughing, which of course made Morgan laugh too. "Come on, *tell me!*" she prodded.

George plopped onto the couch and continued to laugh, shaking his head and bobbing his shoulders. Every time he began to speak in an attempt to give Morgan an explanation, he couldn't help himself, he burst out laughing. Morgan continued to listen to her messages while George cycled through his laughter and was finally able to tell her the story: The two guys that live downstairs below Lorraine, who Morgan had seen several times but never met, had invited George over to meet their bird, Andrew. George was pleased with the invite since he had lived next to the mystery men for over a year but hardly knew them. He grabbed a bottle of wine and headed down to meet Andrew and his proud parents, Thomas and Charles. They had a turntable on a stand next to Andrew's cage that was playing a "*Teach Your Bird to Talk*" record that repeated, in a soothing voice, the same phrases over and over: "Hello. How are you? Hello. How are you? Hello. How are you…Where is the kitty? Where is the kitty?"

So there the three sat, chatting over wine and homemade zucchini cake, finally getting to know each other, against the background sounds of the record attempting to brainwash Andrew into repeating phrases. Suddenly, all conversation stopped as the three heard the sounds of Lorraine exiting her apartment and descending the stairs which ended by the front door of their apartment. Then came the dreaded knock on the door. Charles shook his head and Thomas put his finger to lips to emphasize the need for continued silence since they had no intention on responding to the knocking, which had become par for the course with the apartment tenants.

"Hello. How are you?" said the record.

Loudly, but mimicking the calm of the teaching voice, Lorraine responded, "I'm fine."

"Hello. How are you?"

"I'm fine. How are you?" asked Lorraine.

"Hello. How are you?"

"I'm fine," Lorraine answered again.

"Hello. How are you?"

"I'm fine," she again answered but not quite as calm as before.

"Hello. How are you?"

"I said I'm fine," she responded while George, Thomas and Charles muffled their laughter. The record continued to repeat the question and Lorraine continued to answer.

"Where is the kitty?"

"I don't know!" Lorraine sounded annoyed.

"Where is the kitty?"

"I don't know where your cat is," Lorraine exclaimed at full volume.

George whispered, "Do you have a cat?" Thomas shook his head no.

The three drank their wine, listened and laughed, wondering just how long this would go on. Long enough that Thomas had to creep into the bedroom to let out his laughter. It finally ended with Lorraine shouting some obscenities, slamming the screen door and stomping off. They scurried to the window and saw her cross the driveway and head down the sidewalk. All agreed that she was scary but amusingly so.

George kept laughing and telling Morgan that she should have been there.

"I guess you had to be there," she said. "You know, George, I don't find her very funny anymore. I find her sort of like a ticking time-bomb. She really scares me."

"Aaah, she's just half brain dead."

To Morgan, Lorraine was a scary kind of stupid.

"Oh come on," George laughed. "She was repeatedly answering the same question. I mean, how funny is that?"

"More crazy than funny, George."

"But it's funny!"

- 93 -

"Jackie and Buddy are going to go to the hospital to visit," Morgan changed the subject. "I can still count on you too, right?"

George stood up from the couch and headed to the closet with spurts of laughter. "I can't believe you don't find that hysterical. What a fucking nut case she is."

"You'll go to the hospital, right? You said that you would."

"Yeah, yeah," he responded to the question then added before vanishing into the closet, "That was funny. You'd have laughed you ass off if you were there."

Morgan watched George bend down to squeeze through the passage-way to his apartment. He could benefit from losing a few pounds, particularly around the middle. Other than walking to the corner store and walking OP, Morgan never saw George do much besides sit or stand with a drink in one hand and a cigarette in the other.

Morgan had been visiting David for over three months. Each time she arrived, David would be sitting by the window, most often staring out. She discovered that the string of contorted words that he had been offering to all who would listen was "I want to go outside." She asked Anna if she could take David outside but the request was denied.

"I promise that I'll be careful," Morgan implored Anna.

"It's against the rules," Anna responded with indifference.

"Well, who takes them out when they go out?"

Anna stopped filing the edge of her fingernail and looked at Morgan. "They don't." She held eye contact with Morgan a few seconds longer then went back to filing her pinky nail.

"They don't?" Morgan wasn't sure she understood Anna correctly. Surely these men left the building from time to time. "You mean they don't go out-side? At all?" Anna merely shook her head, confirming that they did not go out *at all.* Morgan didn't know how to respond to what sounded like an intentional and admitted torturous existence for these men. Not only was David's request to go outside ignored due to a lack of communication but anyone's desire to go outside was ignored by policy. There were a few minutes of strained silence, silence that hid Morgan's shock and silence that hid Anna's brief guilt. Then Morgan broke the silence. "How do I get permission to take David outside, just a walk around the grounds?"

A Bible And A Fly Swatter 1977

"You don't, Morgan." Anna sounded a bit annoyed.

"Anna, there has to be somebody that can give me permission." She was resolute. "What about when the other men have visitors? Don't they go outside or go out to eat or somewhere?"

Anna said nothing and gave no immediate response. However, Morgan had a feeling that Anna wasn't ignoring her but pondering the predicament.

"Morgan, you have a lot to learn about this place and these men. How often have you seen anybody here visiting while you're here?" Anna looked directly at Morgan while waiting for her to answer.

Morgan thought for a few seconds then said, "Never. Now that you ask, never."

Anna tilted her head forward with a nod then went back to filing her nails. As Morgan turned to leave Anna added, "You could try going to the office you went to when you came here the first time. Go there. Ask them if you can take David out for a roll."

"I *will*," Morgan stated with commitment.

And on her next visit she did ask. And, they told her that she wasn't a nurse nor a staff member, but a volunteer of her own doing and she would not be allowed to remove a patient from the building. To her inquiry about Anna taking David out to visit the sun, she was told that Anna and the other staff members were too busy with their own work. Morgan wanted to bring up the fact that Anna spent a good deal of her time smoking, doing her nails and reading magazines but she knew better. Morgan thanked both of the rather stern individuals for their time and left back to Building D.

Anna immediately wanted to know what transpired. Morgan was surprised at her seemingly sincere interest. She told her the conversation and Anna seemed disappointed that Morgan hadn't succeeded in getting permission to take David outside. Morgan had anticipated more of a "I told you so" reaction from Anna.

"Anna, can I be direct with you?" Morgan asked, and only asked because she did feel some sympathy from Anna for the barren existence of the men on her floor.

"Yes, go ahead," Anna said, displaying genuine interest.

"I'd go out of my mind living like this, never having visitors, never going out, never going anywhere——-"

Anna interrupted. "Haven't you noticed," she said flippantly referring to the fact that the majority of the men on her floor where considered out of their minds.

"Well, even if I wasn't out of my mind when I got here, I sure would be if I had to live like this." Then Morgan backpedaled in case she had insulted Anna's care. "I know there are reasons for the rules and I know the men are cared for but there's no entertainment but that fuzzy TV. And all David says, or what he says the most, is how he wants to go outside. It's hard to listen to that and not be able to help him with something so easy to do. You know what I mean?

"I've got a few others who will come visit, if that's okay." Morgan had already asked if it were okay to bring others to visit and understood the lack of objection to be permission, though no one had come so far.

"Oh, I know what you mean, Morgan. I know exactly what you mean. So, young lady," Anna said with a glint in her eyes. "Do you play the guitar?"

"No. Why?"

"Well, learn and come entertain them," Anna said very matter of fact.

"I don't but I know others that do. So I can bring someone to entertain, not just to visit?" Morgan asked, excited by the open door Anna was presenting.

"Go for it," Anna answered then wrote down something on a piece of paper and handed it to Morgan. It was her name and home phone number. "Call me and we can talk."

Morgan left that day fueled with enthusiasm and determined to follow through.

Morgan was thrilled to hear Johan's message on the answering machine. She jumped up and hopped around the desk shaking her hands as though she were shaking rattles in the air and exclaimed, "Yes! Yes!" Mr. Smith gave her the amount of her commission check and instructed her to fill in the amount on one of the pre-signed checks in the drawer. She ran out the door and up stairs to Buffalo Books—with OP trailing behind—to tell George about her monetary bonus. Stacy told her that George was dumping cover-less paper-backs in the Dumpster. She grabbed OP's collar and headed out the back door to the Dumpster. George was filtering through the books to see which ones he wanted to take home.

"I got a commission check, a *big* commission check," she hollered, waving her arms. OP wagged her tail and barked repeatedly—because inflamed humans were exciting.

George responded in his usual nonchalant manner. "Well rich girl, you want some free books?" Morgan shook her head with disappointment at his meager reaction. "Hey, they throw all these books away. It's a waste. Come check 'em out and see if there are any that you want."

"Then don't toss them away. Give them to a thrift store or something," she suggested. "If you're not going to get excited for me then I'm going to have to go call other people that will." Morgan left with OP back to the office. She noticed when descending the stairs that the office door was closed. She knew that she had left it open in her hurry to find George. Morgan grabbed on to OP's collar and opened the door with OP entering first. The two men in suits turned and stepped back at the sight of OP. Morgan left the door open behind her and kept a hold on OP's collar.

"Can I help you?" Morgan asked, making sure this time she took in every detail of these men, including their shoes.

"The door was open. We're looking for Mr. Johan Smith," said the one with the longer black hair.

"Yes, it was open but then shut. Are you looking for Mr. Smith in the desk?" Morgan said sternly but cautiously. These two men rubbed her the wrong way from the get-go. She walked with OP around to the back of the desk and the two men moved in unison away from the desk. "What do you want?" she asked, still holding onto OP and taking note of their attire. She noticed that the man with the lighter and shorter hair had a nose that looked like it had been broken.

"Where is Mr. Smith?" the man with the dark hair asked.

"Who are you?" Morgan answered with her own question. He didn't answer and again asked where Mr. Smith was. "First tell me who you are." OP felt the irritation and tension coming from Morgan and let out a bass bark at the man with dark hair. "Tell me your names and I'll tell Mr. Smith that you came by." The two men looked at each other without saying anything. "If you're not going to tell me who you are then you need to leave," Morgan said abruptly then looked down at OP as if to confirm that OP would backup her request. They shuffled on their feet a bit then proceeded to exit the office without saying another word. Morgan leaned forward to see if she could get a better look at the men's shoes and noticed that the man with light hair had additions to the heel and sole of his left shoe, as if his left leg was shorter than his right. As soon as they were halfway up the stairs, Morgan let go of OP's collar and rushed to close and double lock the office door.

Morgan called the main office in Los Angeles to try to locate Johan. She wanted to tell him right away about the two men returning to the office. He not only wasn't there but they wanted to know if she knew where he might be. Per usual, Morgan responded as though she knew that Mr. Smith was on the road taking care of business for Samuel Pacific Imports and only wondered if he happened to have stopped by the main office. In truth, she had no idea where Mr. Smith was or what business he was taking care of. Morgan conveniently brought up the Chateau Latour sale in hopes of getting a bit of praise, but none was given.

After hanging up, she called Buffalo Books for George. Steve answered and was customarily annoyed but dutifully summoned George to the phone. Morgan told George of two men's visit and asked if he could quickly go outside and see if they were still around and if he could find out what car they were driving. George gladly complied, telling Steve that he was taking a cigarette break, another cigarette break. Most bookstores in the 1970's allowed employees and patrons to sit down and enjoy a cigarette in the store but not Buffalo Books. One of the owners implemented a new policy that not only denied smoking in the store but also in the back offices or hallway, therefore, cigarette breaks were given liberally to comply with the new policy.

A knock at the door had Morgan rushing to look through the peephole. It was George. She quickly opened the door. "I'm on the phone. Did you see them?" George told her no and said that he'd talk to her at home and headed back up the stairs. She locked the door, instructed OP to get her chew bone and get back to her bed.

Morgan busied herself on the phone returning calls regarding Samuel Pacific Imports matters before she began her quest for entertainment. She first called Jackie, explaining her search for entertainment for the men at the hospital.

Jackie had always wanted to start an official band. She believed this was an opportunity to get the guys together and perform. She was excited at the prospect. Morgan was annoyed by it.

"You can't drag an electric band up there, Jackie. You'd probably scare the hell out of them."

But Jackie was convinced that it was a great idea; she even had the name for the band, Vitamin K. Morgan immediately laughed at the name and was surprised at what offense Jackie took to her laughter. Morgan thought the name was ridiculous and sounded like something from *Sesame Street*, nevertheless, Jackie was serious. This wasn't going as Morgan had hoped and she soon got off the topic then off the phone.

Janet kept coming to mind. She knew that her boyfriend not only had purchased a mail-order art school package for Janet, but Rocky also had bought her a guitar and one would assume lessons to go along with it. Morgan mulled over why Janet just kept coming to mind when she wasn't even sure if she could play the guitar much less sing. She'd have to call her and see how the guitar was coming along and solicit her talents, if she had any. Janet still lived at home with her parents who were elderly, having Janet, their only child, very late in life. Morgan assumed that she remained at home because of their age. Morgan had met them several times; they were so welcoming and pleasant that Morgan could see why Janet would not be in any hurry to leave.

Janet was as friendly and as good-natured as ever. She not only told Morgan that she could now play the guitar but that she also wrote her own songs. And, she would be happy to come to the hospital to perform for the men. Morgan told her that everything was in the beginning stage and that she would touch base with her regarding the date and time once she got the approval from Anna. Since Janet didn't work, her schedule was open which was a bonus for Morgan. She hung up the phone feeling even more inspired and enthusiastic about bringing some entertainment, and hopefully, joy to the veterans at the hospital.

Within the hour Jackie had called the office. She told Morgan that Buddy had slides from his backpacking trip with his brother and suggested the veterans might enjoy seeing them.

Morgan was silent while she pondered the offer then burst forth with, "I think it's a great idea but I'll have to run it by Anna, the nurse, first."

"Why do you have to run it by her? Aren't you in charge of entertainment?"

It amused Morgan how Jackie always jumped to conclusions, manufacturing situations or one's status greater than it actually was. It was automatic for Jackie. When Morgan was sent to the Wall Street Journal office for a temporary clerical job through a temp agency, Jackie concluded that Morgan would be negotiating stocks for clients with the big guys—shouting from a desk with paper in one hand and a phone in the other. She had a childlike perception that was almost charming and amused Morgan. "No, I'm in charge of finding the entertainment but I have no authority. I have to okay the entertainment with Anna."

"Ooooooh. Okay. Well let us know."

"Does Buddy have a portable screen?"

"If he doesn't, his brother probably does and I'm sure we can use it."

"That's great," Morgan said and with gratitude added, "Thanks so much. I bet they'd love seeing the outdoors, lakes, the mountains, all of that. I think it will be great. I'll let you know." Morgan had no idea that Buddy backpacked. She found it hard to imagine. "I didn't know Buddy backpacked."

"His brother does, a lot. Sometimes Buddy goes with him," Jackie responded. "Buddy is a really good photographer."

"I can't wait to see the pictures, or slides," Morgan commented though thinking to herself that with Jackie a "really good photographer" might mean that an entire roll came out okay.

As Morgan walked to her VW Thing parked with the top down, she saw Mr. Smith pull up on the side street. She put OP in the car and ran to catch up with him. She wanted to tell him about the two men. He got out of his car and the two stood on the sidewalk as she described the encounter.

"They were both wearing suits, dark suits, and the taller one had black hair and it was longer. He was wearing dress shoes, nicer but normal men's dress shoes. But the other guy, well he had light hair and it was regular short hair but his left shoe had sort of a lift on it, something that made it thicker than the other shoe; you know, as if his left leg was shorter than his right so he had to add on a layer to his shoe, like an added sole, and his shoes were more like lace up boots," she explained while catching her breath. "And the one with the lift on his shoe, his nose looked like it had been broken. You know how a fighter's nose sometimes looks?"

Mr. Smith nodded a yes.

"Well, it looked like that. It was sort of wide and crooked." Mr. Smith said nothing. Morgan continued, "I asked them their names several times but they wouldn't answer then I told them that they needed to leave if they were not going to identify themselves then OP barked at the guy with dark hair." This information made Mr. Smith smile. "Mr. Smith?"

"Johan," he corrected.

"That doesn't come natural for me, but okay, Johan, do you know who these men are?"

"I think I do," he answered yet Morgan was certain that he knew exactly who these men were.

"They sort of scare me. I know that they're afraid of OP so I feel safe with OP there but——-"

"Don't worry about them," Johan cut in. "Keep the door locked. Just keep the door locked when you're there at all times. It's a good idea to do that anyway. Keep the door locked and if someone makes you uncomfortable keep OP by your side. Don't answer the door if you're not comfortable. It's up to you, Morgan." Then Johan wished Morgan a nice weekend as he proceeded to the office.

She ran back across the street and into the parking lot to a barking OP. It was Friday, payday, where she retrieved her weekly check from Johan's large-folder checkbook. He filled out the checks and left them there for her to rip off one by one. She also had her commission check and Morgan was eager to get to the bank before they closed otherwise she would have pressed Johan for more information about the men in suits.

Morgan called Anna at her home and found Anna much more animated than when at the hospital. She told Anna that she had both a woman who sang and played the guitar and a slide show of the "great outdoors" to entertain the men. Anna believed that it would be best to start out with the slide show and have the singer at another time. She wanted to see how the men reacted to strangers and an event out of the usual. And, she firmly indicated that she wanted Morgan and her friends to be subtle when approaching the building and setting up. If the men reacted poorly to the strangers and event, she wanted them to quietly and calmly remove themselves. Morgan agreed to her terms.

Morgan got the impression that Anna had not obtained permission to provide entertainment for the men. She didn't want to ask or even bring up the possible fact that the entertainment might be breaking the rules; she just wanted to make sure it happened. Morgan would be discreet, and pray that the men reacted positively to their efforts. She immediately called Jackie.

ZaneDoe

It was Sunday afternoon and the majority of the office staff was gone, which is how Morgan believed Anna wanted it. Still, Morgan, Jackie, Buddy and George (who Morgan insisted come along) parked by the side of the building and quickly entered Building D with their equipment. Once Anna was aware of their presence, she led them to the common room to set up. Morgan made her way to David and excitedly told him of her surprise before returning to join the others. Morgan turned back to look at David, who had his head partially resting on his own shoulder, watching the newcomers. Like a passenger strapped in a car without gas, David was parked by the window and there he lived his days. She jogged back to get him.

"You ready?" Morgan asked as she grabbed onto the handles of his wheelchair. She had the feeling that David was perpetually ready, and waiting to experience life and time away from the window.

Most of the other men occupying the common area scattered—some behind the long and weathered drapes, some stood up against the wall like magnets on a refrigerator and some remained seated without much reaction. Jackie seemed preoccupied by the frightened men and worried to Morgan and George that they wouldn't come near enough to see the slide show.

"Don't worry about it," George casually advised. "Let's just get this set up."

Morgan was grateful that George honored her request, or nagging, since Buddy seemed perplexed by the slide projector and, like with Jackie, taken aback by the surroundings and behavior of the men. Anna and George moved tables, set up the screen, arranged chairs a comfortable distance from the visitors so that the men might meander over to a chair and enjoy the show.

"This might take some doing," Anna said to George, and he knew exactly what she meant. She didn't anticipate that the men would readily make their way to the chairs, so she added some incentive. "I'll be right back." Anna left while George finished setting up. Morgan stood a distance from the individual men while she explained in a calm and unobtrusive manner that they had a slide show that she knew they would "really enjoy." Buddy and Jackie stood side by side, still taking in the dismal ambiance, looking like unwelcome guests at a party.

Anna returned with bowls and bags of chips, popcorn and pretzels. "Here." She handed them to Jackie and Buddy indicating that they fill them and place them on the tables next to the chairs.

- 102 -

A Bible And A Fly Swatter 1977

Morgan saw Anna in a whole new light.

George turned to Anna. "Ready if you are."

"Anna," Morgan stepped up. "Do you have a radio so we can play some music in the background?" She did and agreed that music might be better than having a stranger shouting a narrative during the slide show.

With the radio tuned to a classical station and David up front by the projector in eager anticipation, George got the show started with instructions from Anna to take his time. Moving along at a relaxed pace suited George just fine. He lit his cigarette. Anna lit hers and Morgan placed a newly-lighted cigarette in David's hookah.

George let each slide sit on the screen for a considerable amount of time. It was hard to tell if it was the lure of the slide show or the lure of the snacks but slowly the men made their way to the chairs, some remained standing. They gave equal time to watching both the slide show and the strangers. When Buddy responded to a staring veteran with a generous friendly smile, the veteran's eyes opened a bit wider and he zoomed in on Buddy's teeth. Buddy kept smiling, the vet kept staring and George and Morgan quickly looked away to hide their pursed-lipped refrain.

Jackie was right, Buddy was a "really good photographer." The angles, the depth of field, the composition and subject matter were all professionally executed. Morgan and George were both surprised and impressed and praised Buddy accordingly, as did Anna.

Morgan leaned toward David and whispered, "Are you enjoying the slide show?"

David responded, in a tangle of words that only Morgan could clearly— at that point—understand. He enjoyed every minute and wished that he was "eeun sa pu shur." She thought the show for David might be both a blessing and a curse, that he loved what he saw yet it only deeply reminded him of what he was missing.

George stood only a few feet away, looking on as David and Morgan interacted. Morgan's expression changed. George knew that something was brewing, that whatever David said had stirred something within her. And, he was right: Morgan was even more determined to take David outdoors, but now she set her sights beyond the hospital grounds.

To everyone's delight, the slide show was a success. Anna was pleased, and nervous. She did not get permission for this event. Though she enthusiastically was partaking in the event, she was nonetheless preoccupied the majority of the time with getting caught along with her desire to insure that this would not be the last event.

George noticed Anna's vacillating expressions of worry and delight. "Between a rock and a hard place," he commented to Anna out of earshot of the others. She gave him a steady look, a tight-lipped smile and continued to pull the chairs back to their original stations.

George hurried everyone along and had the long screen tucked under one arm and the projector in his other hand. Buddy picked up the box of slides and when Jackie finished carrying the bowls back to Anna's desk, they followed George out the door.

"Anna," Morgan said. "I don't want to push things but I just have a question or a request actually."

"What's that?" Anna asked, still busy putting the bowls and remaining snacks into bags to take home.

"Can I please move David to another window. You know, so he can have another view?"

Anna smiled. "Of course. Pull the drapes back on the north side. You know which ones I'm talking about?"

"Not really. Not sure which side is north," Morgan sheepishly answered.

"Not the drapes where Ernie hides but the ones to the left."

"Oh, okay," Morgan replied. "Thanks." She rushed off.

Dust powdered off the drapes and they smelled musty. Ample housing of spiders still active and those long-gone attached from the back of the drapes to the window and the wall. She shook the drapes then dragged a chair to hold them back away from the window. And, with David's permission, she wheeled him over to the new location, promising to come back and clean the glass. David's strained yet striking smile reassured Morgan that she had made the right move. Morgan headed for the doors looking back to see David's head zigzagging about the window, taking in the new view.

"No Aka, I think you would have really enjoyed it," Morgan insisted. She told Aka of the slide show at the veterans hospital and he listened but shook his head as though to say, *not for me.* "Why do you think you wouldn't have liked it?" she asked, puzzled by his reaction. *It's not like it is a step down from your daily activities,* Morgan thought to herself.

- 104 -

"You're showing slides in the nut ward," Aka answered.

"*It's not a nut ward*, Grandpa!" Morgan said, taken aback at Aka's comment. "These men are our soldiers, our veterans. They've been through war. You know that. I've heard a few of their stories, Grandpa. They should never be called nuts."

Aka looked up from his newspaper. "I know, Mokana. I know." He gave her a toothless smile. "It's a good thing you go there."

"I would really like you to go with me sometime." She solicited, "We're going to have entertainment on Sundays. There are snacks, and music and it's fun, Grandpa. It's a nice way to spend a Sunday. It's not every Sunday but some other Sunday. Would you come with me?"

"Your friend," Aka said. He was looking at the doorway. Morgan turned to look also. Janie was making her way through the doorway, slowly with a smile on her face, the kind of smile Morgan had yet to see on Janie. She looked very happy, unsteady on her feet, but smiling and making her way without use of a cane or walker.

"Janie!" Morgan exclaimed, delighted to see her. She walked over to assist Janie the rest of the way then offered her a chair, which Janie gratefully accepted. Morgan told Janie about the slide show but Morgan's enthusiasm was met with a complete change of expression on Janie's face. Morgan did not understand her expression and was not sure what to say. She rode out the momentary silence then asked Janie if something was wrong. Janie looked at Aka and Aka looked back down at his newspaper.

"I would love it if you would come to the next event there, Janie," Morgan invited. Still Janie said nothing. "I would love to have both you and Aka come to the next event." She wasn't going to give up. "I'm in charge of the entertainment and it will be fun," she said like an angry parent says when demanding to a resistant child that some event will be fun.

Morgan was at a complete loss and she pondered on her ride home as to why both Aka and Janie had such resistance to her invitation, one she was certain that they would both enjoy. She wished that she could be a bug on the wall and hear what they said after she left.

When she pulled onto the driveway, she saw George sitting with OP in front of his apartment and she rushed out of the car.

"George," she said in a subdued yell. "Why do you have OP out front? What about Lorraine?"

George just smiled. She quickly made her way up the stairs. OP wagged her tail and gave out a bark, which made Morgan even more nervous and George laugh.

"Don't worry," George reassured and followed with an explanation, "Lorraine went to a 'beauty'," said with a snicker, "salon and came home with bright-red hair, not her usual unnatural red but this neon red. She asked me what I thought."

"What'd you say?"

"I asked if she actually paid to make it that color. I guessed she wasn't too happy about the color herself. She went back to her apartment, grabbed that purse and headed off down the sidewalk. I think she went back to the salon."

"Oh God, I hope she didn't bring her gun," Morgan commented, half serious.

"She won't be back for some time."

"Did it really look bad?"

"Like florescent cotton candy."

Morgan unlocked her front door and invited George in as OP pushed through before her.

"Anna called you," George informed.

"How do you know that? Are you answering my phone now while you raid the fridge?"

"Maybe you should turn down the volume on your answering machine."

They discussed the event at the veterans hospital again, cogitating possibilities for the next event. George said that he had no talents to offer. Morgan claimed the same.

"Does Rusty do anything, I mean does he have any talents that would be good for the hospital?" Morgan inquired, trying to pool talents from their friends but if she couldn't find any, she would not hesitate to hire talent for the men.

"Tap dancing," George answered with a straight face, unlike Morgan.

"Are you serious? Rusty tap dances?" Her smile turned to a chuckle as she placed Rusty dancing in the common room at the hospital in her mind; *it could work.*

"Yeah, I'm serious, top hat and all."

"Are you serious?"

A Bible And A Fly Swatter 1977

"I told you I am. He's been in shows. And, he'll probably be glad to entertain for the veterans," George said without cracking a smile which convinced Morgan that he was indeed telling the truth. "Just don't tell him how depressing the place is. He's got that 'I'm a dancer,' Hollywood image of himself when it comes to tap dancing. Don't tell him anything but you'd looooove to see him dance for an event. Leave out the drooling men hiding behind the curtains and shit—"

Morgan cut him off, "*George!*"

Morgan coyly asked Mr. Smith, "You wouldn't want to come to the veterans hospital, would you?"

She had talked about the hospital and the men to Mr. Smith whenever he had a minute or so to listen and he encouraged her efforts.

"When?"

"You mean you would?" Morgan blurted out, astonished that she didn't get "the look" and an immediate "no."

"Again I ask, when? And, Morgan, is there a reason why are you asking me in particular?" Mr. Smith always spoke with a certain distance—businesslike. He rarely spoke with emotion. He had a syllogistic shell that seemed impossible to crack.

"Well, this woman, Janet, plays the guitar and writes her own music and she's going to entertain the soldiers on Sunday. I think you'd enjoy it."

"They would be referred to as veterans, I'm sure."

"I call them soldiers. Veterans, soldiers—same thing, at least in my opinion."

"This coming Sunday?" Mr. Smith asked then quickly added before she could answer, "I have a commitment this coming Sunday."

"Oh good, because it's the next Sunday."

"So, is this Janet a professional?"

"No, but she's gorgeous," Morgan answered in truth and hoping that such a feature might encourage him to attend. "She really is beautiful. Maybe not the brightest light on the Christmas tree but she's stunningly beautiful."

Morgan wanted people to visit. She wanted people to see how these men were existing and she wanted the men to see something new and different, believing it would brighten their lives. People were important to Morgan and always added to the quality of her life. She wholeheartedly believed it was the

- 107 -

same for everyone. To Morgan, loneliness was a kin to inhumane punishment and one that few deserved.

"Do you know where the hospital is, Mr. Smith?" She corrected herself, "I mean Johan?"

"Yes."

"Oh, that's right. I forgot. It's me who didn't know about or where the hospital was. So, Sunday around one o'clock in Building D. It's on the right side, a big old square building. It's three stories high, gray cement-looking building. You won't see my car, the VW Thing, because I park on the far side of the building but I can park it out front if you like."

"No need. I'm not promising that I will be there, Morgan."

"It would be great if you showed up. I think those men need to see people, people outside of the hospital. If they won't let me take them outside into the world, then maybe I can bring some of the outside world in to them..." and Morgan talked on and Mr. Smith seemed to actually be giving her his full attention.

"Aka, I'll pick you up. You and Janie," Morgan insisted.

"You taking me out on the town with no teeth?" Aka said, knowing that such a comment would rattle a bit of guilt in Morgan, which of course it did but failed to cause her to let up. She hounded Aka until he agreed to visit the veterans hospital then left to work her hounding magic on Janie.

With permission, of sorts, to take Aka on an outing and with Janie agreeing that she would go no matter what, Morgan left Sunny Acres enthused and happy.

George was napping so Morgan shouted from the open closet door to wake him.

"Oh man, I just got to sleep," George moaned.

"You can go back to sleep but you have to promise me that you will come on Sunday to the hospital first," Morgan beseeched.

"Why?" George sat up. "Can't that guy figure out how to work the projector?"

"No, that's not why. We're not showing slides. Janet's going to play the guitar and sing. You gotta come"

"Why?"

A Bible And A Fly Swatter 1977

Morgan got up from her kneeling position and walked over to sit next to George. OP followed, pushing the door open so far and so hard that it hit a chair with a loud bang. George called OP over to the couch with a smile. Morgan noticed how OP kindled something in George that no one else seemed able to. No matter what OP did, no matter what OP damaged or destroyed, and no matter what time of day or night, OP solicited a good reaction in George—a laugh, a smile, a burst of aberrant energy. And OP felt it.

Morgan explained, or pleaded, "Because I want you there and because the more people that are there the better."

"Why?" George asked, though his attention was mostly on OP as he tossed her a tug toy.

"Oh come on, George. It's definitely going to be more festive with lots of people, for one, but also because Janet is going to play the guitar and sing and it might be awkward if the men all scatter or hide. It's not like she's going to be in a coffeehouse. It can be uncomfortable if you're not used to the place. It's hardly an upbeat environment." She waited for George to respond. He was listening but it was more fun tugging at the other end of a toy with OP than it was listening to Morgan plead her case. She continued. "Aka and Janie are going to come and even Mr. Smith might come. I know Anna found you helpful. We have to give Janet an audience of some kind in case the men hide from her." To that comment George laughed.

"Okay, okay, okay. I'll be there," George committed. "Can we take OP?"

"That's a good idea; maybe I can in the future. Do you think I can leave her at Rusty's for that Sunday?"

"Yeah, it's Sunday. I'll call him. If Rusty wants to come, then you can leave her in his backyard. She can't get out." George often took OP with him to Rusty's. OP loved the large backyard, mostly the swimming pool and Rusty reveled in the fact that OP scared his excessively nosey neighbor who, though the entire yard was enclosed with a tall wood fence, found where the knots in the fence had fallen out—or had been pushed—to peep. It was a win-win situation.

"You have two dads, don't ya girl, don't ya..." George said as he roughhoused with OP. With George's wild hair, they looked like two animals playing on the couch.

Morgan left OP with George and went back to her apartment to call Anna. They talked like friends instead of the previous supervisor to volunteer

- 109 -

communication. She informed Morgan that the man Morgan first attempted to visit, who had no arms or legs, had been transferred. He had been a minor concern for Anna due to his relatively new status. Though she didn't come right out and say it, it was safe to assume that the Sunday entertainment was definitely an unauthorized event. There were few who would be capable of reporting or complaining about the event other than the man with no legs or arms, and he was now gone. She agreed with Morgan that providing an unwavering audience for the entertainer would be a good idea. She wanted to have a few events to see how the men reacted before she petitioned for permission. "Not too many cars if you can help it," Anna requested. That was fine. Aka, Janie, Janet and George would be riding with Morgan. She had yet to ask Jackie and Buddy if they wanted to join the festivities.

George just got back from taking OP to Rusty's. He put on an ironed shirt and shoes other than his hiking boots then popped through the closet door, per usual.

"So, I take it the two old ones in the car are Aka and Janie?"

"Wow, an ironed shirt." Morgan took notice, not missing the change of shoes either. Then she answered his question, "Yes, that's Janie and Grandpa Aka. The stairs are too much for them." She had the top down on the VW Thing, assuming that Aka and Janie would enjoy it—and she was right.

"So, we're picking up the singer and her guitar, right?" George asked in a way that was obvious that there would be a follow-up, therefore, Morgan just responded with a glance and a nod. "So, am I supposed to sit on one of the old folks' lap?"

Morgan gave an embarrassed chuckle. George was right. It was a tight fit, something she hadn't given much thought to. "Do you mind driving, George?" If George drove, Janet could sit in the front with her guitar and Morgan could sit in the back between Janie and Aka.

"Sure," he answered. "I think Rusty might show up."

"Excellent. I hope he does—the more the better." Morgan thought for a second then asked, "Do you think they liked us there, George? The soldiers?"

"I think you might be projecting what you like," he answered, "or what *you* would want. This interruption is disrupting the status quo for these guys and might rattle a few." George held out his hand for the car keys. She tossed the keys to him without comment. "You're doing a good thing. Just see what happens."

As Morgan closed and locked the front door, she noticed Lorraine standing like a palace guard at the other side of the walkway. Morgan guided her eyes in Lorraine's direction at George. He whispered, "Let's get the fuck out of here before it follows us." They pretended not to see Lorraine and quickly made their way down the stairs and to the VW Thing with Janie and Aka waiting patiently and looking cheerful.

George came with Morgan to knock on Janet's door. He was to carry her guitar and anything else she might need help with. Both Morgan and George had the same reaction to Janet as she opened the door, but for different reasons. Janet was well-endowed and her blouse was hardly hiding the fact. She was wearing a denim skirt the size of a tube top and high-heeled boots. Janet's hair was rather large for her petite and beautiful face, and seemed particularly big this day. Janet looked exaggerated and Morgan felt the attire inappropriate for the event but didn't know what to say: she didn't want to offend Janet in any way nor did she want to lose the expected and only entertainment for the Sunday event.

Janet wanted to bring her amplifier. Morgan had the handy excuse that there was no room in the car and insisted that she bring just the guitar and leave the other equipment behind. With Janet walking ahead of them, George gave Morgan a look that she had to ignore for many reasons.

Janet and her guitar fit onto the front seat with little problem. Morgan introduced Aka and Janie and after the cordial introduction, both Aka and Janie lifted their eyebrows to Morgan in recognition of Janet's notable outfit.

Rocky had provided Janet with a guitar that had every impressive bell and whistle that an acoustic guitar could possibly have; Morgan just hoped that the outcome of her lessons were as impressive. If not, Janet's alluring good looks and provocative attire might be entertainment enough. As they drove to the hospital Morgan kept thinking that she should race in first to warn Anna about Janet's outfit, hoping that it would be acceptable and no problem. So, when they arrived she did just that.

Anna was amused, much to Morgan's relief. Morgan ran back to help Janie and Aka out of the car and up the stairs to the heavy front doors but George had beat her to it.

- 111 -

Janet had impact before even opening her guitar case. Ernie didn't wait for the festivities to begin or for any coaxing to come out from behind the security of his drape. He was standing freestyle fixated on Janet as were several other previously staid inhabitants. Janet wasn't taken aback by the somber surroundings but delighted with her potential audience and once set up, she worked the room like a celebrity. It was Janie who seemed taken aback. George immediately retrieved a chair for both Janie and Aka. Aka nodded and thanked him, but Janie, stymied, said nothing.

"Whataya think?" Morgan asked David as she rolled him to be next to her for the show. David's head waved as he responded but the only word Morgan truly could make out was "pretty" which she assumed was in reference to Janet.

"Are you comfortable, Janie?" Morgan asked. "Do you want me to get a seat cushion?" Janie looked up at Morgan but still said nothing. "Would you like something to drink? Coffee?" Janie merely shook her head, no, without making eye contact.

Morgan's concerns were divided. She wanted the event to go smoothly, to entertain and brighten the men's dreary world yet obviously something was significantly bothering Janie. Morgan couldn't divert her efforts from the event to Janie at that moment.

The chairs were set up, a little closer than they were at the previous event. The snacks were set on the tables which were also placed closer to the entertainment than they had been during the slide show. Jackie and Buddy made a welcomed appearance. Anna made sure that all of the lamps were turned on by the center of the common room which brightened up the staging area. At first Anna placed a stool for Janet to use as she played but in regard to the length of her skirt, she removed it and hoped that Janet would be able to play standing. Janet was fine with standing during her performance.

Janet tuned her guitar and hummed a bit in preparation. She lit up the small stage and her audience with her smile, enthusiasm and striking pose before she even sang a note. The anticipation was palpable—for varying reasons. Janet introduced her song and strummed her guitar for a minute or so. All faces with a gamut of expressions were on Janet. Then Janet took her hum into vocals—a gainsay to the rhythmic sounds of her guitar playing. Janet knew how to play the guitar well enough, but her vocals needed some fine tuning. Other

A Bible And A Fly Swatter 1977

than a few cross glances from the visiting audience, her strained, high-pitched and off-key vocals did not distract from her devoted performance.

At the end of Janet's first song, George began to clap and the others quickly joined in. The large room with its hard surfaces and high ceilings caused an echoing of clapping hands that made it sound as if Janet were performing in an auditorium and the applause was intoxicating to her. Janet smiled to a giggle then did her high-pitched gasp—it's what she did when she was truly excited. Janet's reaction to her first round of applause was contagious; she was ecstatic and began clapping herself. She glowed and giggled, and a performer was born. She waved to several men, which elicited reactions from a blank stare to hearty reciprocation.

Janet had prepared to sing several songs from her first songbook, and one by one she was going to get through them all. Anna put a break in the performance by calling for an "intermission." She hoped that the men might choose to mingle.

Morgan observed Janie staring at David, intently, several times during Janet's performance. She realized that she had failed to introduce them. She turned David's wheelchair around so that his angled head could view Janie.

"Janie," Morgan said, "this is my friend, David. David, this is my friend, Janie." David's head wobbled and zigzagged as he focused his attention on Janie who had not taken her eyes off of him. She didn't look at his hookah, as most people did when first introduced to David, maybe to keep from staring at him while he bobbed and twitched to find himself a workable position. She was looking at David as one looks at a photograph instead of a person. David formulated what was his version of a smile.

"Where is the lady's room," Janie asked as she pulled herself up from the chair.

"It's by the nurses' desk," Morgan answered. "Let me help you, take you."

Janie put her arm through Morgan's, she stopped for a few seconds to look at Aka, who was engaged in conversation with George and didn't pay attention to her, then continued on with the help of Morgan.

"Where are you going?" Jackie hollered.

"To the bathroom," Morgan yelled back.

"I'm coming." Jackie caught up walking side by side with them to the bathroom. Once there, Janie asked to have a few moments of privacy. Both Jackie and Morgan wondered, at first, what exactly she was referring to. There was only one toilet in the bathroom; it was meant for one person. Janie didn't wait for a response. She closed the bathroom door behind her.

"Let's walk out into the hall a ways," Morgan requested and stepped away from the bathroom door. Jackie thought that they should be close to the bathroom door in case Janie needed help but followed Morgan into the hall anyway. Jackie talked about her lover, Dr. Ketchum and Morgan listened with feigned interest. Soon Anna approached to let them know that Janet was ready to do her second set—or attempt to finish her list of first songs.

"You go ahead, Jackie. I'm going to wait for Janie."

"I'll wait with you."

"No, go ahead." The look on Morgan's face told Jackie that she would prefer that she goes back to the common room and leave her to wait for Janie alone. Morgan watched as Jackie hurried down the hallway with Anna, her mind pondered Janie's peculiar behavior: *Was the trip too much for her? Was she not feeling well? Were the surroundings upsetting to her?* Something was wrong and yet Morgan felt it an inappropriate time to delve into the root of Janie's apparent distress.

The look on Janie's face as she shuffled her way out of the bathroom confirmed that something was indeed wrong. Morgan reached to assist Janie and asked, "What's wrong Janie?" Then quickly added, "Is there something I can do?" Janie gave a partial smile and shook her head no. The subject was dropped and they slowly made their way back to join the second half of the show in progress, with one big surprise: Johan was standing by a pillar with his eyes glued on Janet.

Morgan whispered into Janie's ear, "That's my boss Mr. Smith, Johan."

Janie stopped, took a look and responded, "Handsome."

Morgan agreed.

Some of the men who were previously standing at a distance were now either seated or standing by a pillar among the visitors. Anna stood with her arms folded across her chest, leaning against the wall with an expression that radiated triumph. The show was a success. Most of the men were mingling, in their own individual ways—and that might be just standing ten feet away instead of thirty.

Janet brought to light that these pajama, undershirt and khaki or bathrobe clad residents were indeed men; they were no doubt of the male species—transfixed on the female attributes of the entertainer no different from the nonresident males sitting before her. This good-hearted, rather tone-deaf entertainer for the day brought out a vitality in the room that Anna longed for but never knew how to bring about. She never imagined during her employment at the hospital that she would experience what she was seeing before her this day.

When Janet finished an upbeat tune, Abe hollered and jumped up and down, cavorting about in front of the little stage. It was an Abe no one had experienced before and though he had Janet's name incorrect, yelling praise to "Joyce," his animated response caused Mr. Edwards to do, with surprising exuberance, a little dance to the beat of Abe's pleas, "Again, Joyce. Sing, Joyce. Sing, Joyce, sing…." And she did.

George was loving it. His shoulders hardly stopped bobbing from subdued laughter the entire performance. The event was a success, achieving what both Morgan and Anna were striving for—entertainment that would bring the men out of their shells and open the door to socializing with those outside of the facility. Anna was happy. Until now, it appeared that no one wanted to take the time or effort to extend a hand from the outside world. Morgan too was happy and feeling exhilarated until she spotted the horrific change of expression on George's face.

Without due warning, there stood Rusty with Lorraine by his side. Rusty was a welcome sight but Lorraine certainly was *not*. With dropped jaws, Morgan and George locked eyes, both realizing that Rusty must have come to the apartment to find George with intent on attending the Sunday event and Lorraine somehow got herself invited along.

Anna leaned into George and asked, "Is there a problem?"

"Yeah, the loon with the radioactive hair," George responded, still looking in shock.

Morgan quickly joined Anna and George. "I'm going to kill Rusty, George."

"What's wrong with her, or her being here?" Anna was puzzled by the alarm this single individual had instantaneously caused. George and Morgan turned to look at Anna in unison but only George responded.

"Let us count the ways."

"She's our apartment manager, Anna." Morgan wanted to explain but there wasn't the time.

ZaneDoe

"To say that she is unstable is like saying the 1906 earthquake was just a little shaky," George added.

Morgan noticed that she was gripping onto her purse, the purse that typically concealed her gun. She immediately pointed it out to George. Rusty was heading toward George with Lorraine in tow. George's eyes pierced through Rusty; he clenched his lips tight in an effort to say nothing.

Rusty stood before them. Lorraine had already taken her own path, right to the men standing by the table of snacks. With Lorraine out of earshot, George proceeded to rake Rusty over the coals for bringing Lorraine to the hospital. Morgan and Anna just listened, trying at times not to laugh as George so aptly described Lorraine's character. He stood up and whispered into Rusty's ear the likelihood that a loaded gun was in Lorraine's purse.

"What the fuck?" Rusty's eyes shot open.

Neither George nor Morgan wanted Anna to know that Lorraine may have a gun. It was best to wrap up the day's event, with alacrity, and get Lorraine out of there as quickly as possible and that's just what all three went about doing. Anna followed their lead but was still not convinced that Lorraine was a true emergency. Lorraine was talking to the men and it appeared that several were talking back. Mr. Edwards was not verbally responding but evidently was intrigued by Lorraine's hair.

Janet was shining like a star as she packed up with the help of Johan. Johan walked alongside Janet carrying her guitar as she waved good-bye to scattered fans. Morgan hurried about helping Anna move chairs and clean up but still taking notice of the interactions in the common room: Janie was sitting next to David, staring at him one moment then looking at the floor the next. Aka was sitting next to a resident along with Jackie and Buddy where it appeared that Buddy was doing all the talking. Rusty was helping with the chairs yet keeping an eye on Lorraine; the prospect of her having a gun in her purse had him on edge.

Morgan said her usual verbose good-bye to David while moving him to the window of his choice. She was pleasantly surprised that Janie held onto the handle of his wheelchair and walked along with them. She noticed Janie's hand move onto David's shoulder, hesitate for a few seconds then she gripped back onto the handle of the wheelchair until Morgan offered her arm as support when leaving.

A Bible And A Fly Swatter 1977

George waved to get Rusty's attention. He pointed to Lorraine, expressing his desire for Rusty to gather up Lorraine and take her with him. But Rusty protested; he was not happy about chauffeuring a gun-wielding temperamental, "middle-aged basket case." They kept their eyes on Lorraine as George reminded Rusty that *he* brought her; there was no room in Morgan's vehicle and no one was going to volunteer to give Lorraine a ride home since no one would be "stupid enough to bring her in the first place."

Lorraine stood in front of three men sitting on the couch. She was talking, shaking her head and they were quietly listening. She opened her purse and searched inside. Rusty's eyes again shot open and George stood up, shouting, *"Lorraine!"* from across the room so loud that he caught everyone's attention. She turned toward George holding a hairbrush in her hand and waved a hello. George summoned her and she promptly excused herself to the men whose attention she had held and strutted her way to George like a properly retired runway model. George smiled at Rusty; Rusty grimaced and George hurried off.

Chapter 8
A Tapping Success

Several months and many more events took place in the common room at the hospital. Anna believed that it was only a matter of time before someone discovered the secret Sundays. She decided to request a meeting to introduce the "concept" of ongoing events taking place in Building D for the men. A meeting was set up. She at first intended on keeping the unauthorized events secret, presenting it as a concept but she ultimately decided to add an event to her presentation. She was nervous and worried for days that bringing to light any activity not sanctioned by the powers that be, no matter how dubious and often those changed, would not only jeopardize her job but cause the clandestine days of entertainment and happiness to end forever.

"Don't worry, Anna," George reassured.

"But I am," Anna said taking a deep breath. "It's not only about my job but if I lose my job everything will go back to how it was and that's not a good thing, George. If they reject the entertainment for the men, then I don't know how I can do anything about it." Anna was troubled. "Those men deserve these events. They live in nothingness, George. Rarely does anyone even visit them. This is the best thing that has happened to them since I've been there." Anna's fear and stress were blatantly evident and George wanted to help ease her worries.

"Seriously, you don't need to worry." He gave a quick laugh then asked, "How well do you know Morgan?"

"Why?"

"Because if you know Morgan, then you know if they don't allow these men these couple of hours of harmless enjoyment that she will find a way to turn it around. She's got that fire, Anna, and so do you. And," he said with knowing commitment, "I'll be there right alongside her and make sure that the public knows what stark and depressing lives our American heroes are forced to live in this hospital. Your eleemosynary activities for these men won't go unappreciated to the general public. Don't worry."

"Eleemosynary?" she questioned.

ZaneDoe

"Charitable," George answered then felt brave enough to asked Anna out for a drink. He wanted to meet Anna at the establishment of her choice and tactfully avoided having to pick her up. For the first time, George was a bit uncomfortable about his car, embarrassed actually. He had a beat-to-hell 1962 convertible Volkswagen Beetle. The top looked like an angry cat sought revenge on it. The engine was strong, the gas mileage was good and it sufficed for a reliable vehicle for George and with the front passenger's seat missing, OP fit in it just fine. He hadn't cared what anybody thought about his car, until now. The exterior and interior were a wreck, but it ran and that's all George cared about, until this minute. Suddenly his "shit-mobile" didn't seem so satisfactory.

Anna agreed to meet George for a drink at Scuttlebutt, a rather small and uncelebrated local bar that, though it has been around for at least fifty years, was still not well-know. The bartender was grumpy but the clientele was friendly. George would park his car around the block and walk to the bar.

Anna's presentation went remarkably well with two of the administrators asking to attend the next planned event. She told them only of the slide show but described the response to the slide show more along the lines of the men's response to Janet's performance. Several in the meeting objected with their expressions—why create any more work, or change what is working, for them. But the two newest arrivals in the administrative flock seemed relatively impressed and wanted to witness an event and the men's reactions themselves. Now Anna just had to touch base with Morgan to make sure that they had entertainment that would be both pleasing to the men and to the administrators.

"I want to take the colonel to the hospital for one of the shows, Aka," Morgan informed, hoping Aka would help with the endeavor.

Aka looked up from his book. "He's back, Mokana."

"You mean he's back in the room again?"

Aka nodded a yes.

"Where's he been?"

"I think he's been sick," Aka said. "He went to visit some relative and got sick but," he looked up at Morgan with disappointment, "he's back now."

"I want Janie to meet him. When do you think he'll be back in the room?"

- 120 -

A Bible And A Fly Swatter 1977

Aka shrugged. He wasn't all that excited about having a roommate again. He liked having the room to himself. He liked turning on his light in the middle of the night to read and he wasn't looking forward to the colonel's tear-filled serenades. Morgan kissed Aka on the cheek good-bye and left to join Janie on the patio.

"So, Morgan," Janie said while staring at Xavier, "why don't you marry Xavier so he can stay in this country." She looked over at Morgan, eyebrows raised. "He's a really nice man." She paused, "And, quite handsome, wouldn't you say?"

"Why? Is he going to be deported?" Morgan asked, sure that some issue related to Xavier was on her mind.

"I hope not," she replied then asked, "Well, how are you today young lady?"

"Fine. I wanted to tell you that the colonel is back in Aka's room and I'd love for him to meet you and you to meet him. I really want to take him to the hospital to one of the shows." Morgan shifted in the chair. "Are these new cushions?"

"Look nice but they feel awful." Janie shook her head. "They're cheap."

"I guess they just try to save money where they can," Morgan said, not wanting to perpetuate any of the negatives that stressed Janie in her current abode.

"Well, it's not cheap to live here, if you call this living. I think you'd be very, very surprised, Morgan, just how much this *life of luxury*," she said while shaking her head back and forth with a strained look on her face, "is costing me."

With a degree of uneasiness Morgan dared to ask, "Do you *have* to live here, Janie?" To which Janie gave out a stifled laugh, turned in her chair to look at Morgan once again.

"Oh dear, dear, dear," said with an unabashed smile, "would I live here if I didn't have to?"

"Sorry," Morgan said swiftly and uncomfortably.

Janie reached over and patted Morgan on her arm. "Oh, don't apologize. It is one long story. But my dear, I could live at the Moana for what it costs to live here."

Morgan had to ask. "Moana Hotel, as in Hawaii?"

The conversation was interrupted when Xavier stepped up beside Janie.

- 121 -

"Good afternoon Miss Janie." Xavier always presented himself as mellow and happy. "How do you like garden?"

"I love how the garden is coming along, Xavier," she answered in a pleasant and welcoming voice. She truly cared for Xavier. He was one of the few things that she liked about Sunny Acres. "Have I introduced you to Morgan, Xavier?" She had but Xavier removed his glove and extended his hand to Morgan as if it were the first time. They exchanged hellos, smiles and then there was silence.

"I better get back to work, Miss Janie." Xavier smiled once again at Morgan then went on his way. Both Morgan and Janie watched Xavier as he disappeared down the walkway.

"He is a good young man," Janie said. "Now what were we saying, Morgan?"

"You said the Moana Hotel. Were you referring to the Moana Hotel in Honolulu?"

"Oh yes," she now remembered Morgan's question. "Yes, in Waikiki. Have you been there, Morgan?"

"Yeah, I'm familiar with it. When were you there?"

"Way before you were born."

"You do know that Aka grew up in Hawaii. He surfed. Did you know that? Did he tell you about his past at all?"

Janie's eyes suddenly got intense. Alice was thumping down the walkway toward the patio at a fast pace. "Running of the bull," Janie noted. Morgan looked over to see Alice heading their way. She always had an angry expression on her face and Morgan had the feeling that when Alice approached that she was about to be chastised for one thing or the other even though she didn't live there, nor did she do much of anything but sit and talk when she was there. Alice didn't stop when she reached Janie and Morgan but charged by as though she were off to catch some other criminal at the home.

"Did Aka talk to you about Hawaii?" she asked again.

"Of course, Morgan. He's all Hawaiian, plain to see. We talked quite a bit about Hawaii. I was there, living there. It was too short of a stay. Aka has me remembering those days." Janie's expression returned to a pleasant and relaxed state. "I can remember my apartment like it was yesterday: Kerr Apartments on Liliuokalani Avenue in Honolulu—how's that for remembering?" She smiled. "I have so many wonderful memories and evenings at the Moana

Hotel, Morgan. They had entertainment there most every night: hula dancers in the Banyan Court, Hawaiian concerts. Dances, lots of dances." Janie seemed to step back into that world as she spoke. "The Islanders, that was their name. I'm pretty sure that was their name. Yes, I'm sure that was their name. The Islanders played at the Moana. I remember the yachts at the harbor——-" She unexpectedly left memory lane, looked at Morgan and emphasized, "That's before the attack of course." After a few moments of silence Janie continued to rattle off memories as though she were ordering them off a menu. "...I played tennis; I danced at the Royal Hawaiian...I met Hilo Hattie, well, actually, her name was Clara if I recall correctly. She was full of energy, so energetic and smart, very a smart lady.

"I met so many people, so many good people. It was easy to meet people then. I walked on the beach at night. I never worried; I was safe. It was a good time, good years. I had a good life there." Janie was quiet for a minute or so then again turned to look Morgan directly in the eyes. "What is David's, the David at the hospital, what is his last name?"

Morgan thought for a minute. Surely Anna had mentioned his last name or she had seen it somewhere. She thought hard.

"I honestly don't know. I don't think his last name was ever mentioned and I never asked." She didn't know George's last name until she noticed it on a piece of mail sitting on his table.

Janie looked out over Xavier's new garden and dropped the subject of Hawaii. Morgan's mind was on last names—specifically people actively in her life whose last name she didn't know dashed through her head.

"Wow, was I always like this?" she asked herself aloud.

"Like what?"

"I don't know the last name of a lot of people that I know, people that I talk to all the time—I don't know their last name and, I don't think that they know mine either. That just seems weird to me, now that I think of it."

"Morgan, I don't know your last name, and do you know mine?"
Both grinned.

"Your last name is Sampson; I know your last name," Morgan rebutted.
"And your last name is?"

"Killington, though I think about changing it."

"To what? And why?"

"Not sure, but I have never liked the 'killing' part of the name. Morgan Killington sounds like '*Morgan's killing them*' to me."

"You're being silly," Janie proclaimed then asked, "Will you find out David's last name for me, Morgan?"

"Of course I will." Morgan was eager to accommodate such a simple request. Naturally, Morgan assumed that Janie believed that she might know David. She wanted to ask her about it, however, Janie looked so very content as though her mind was once again reflecting on her Hawaiian memories and Morgan didn't want to disturb Janie's momentary state of what almost appeared to be bliss. She put her feet up and enjoyed the sun and silence.

Then, out of the blue Janie said, "I own a house, Morgan. A duplex." Of course Morgan wanted to ask right off why she didn't live there instead of Sunny Acres but, again, she felt it best to refrain from asking questions and to just listen to Janie. She looked in deep thought as she continued, "Some of my relatives," she paused, "are renting it out. I think one lives in one and they are renting the other out. I'm really not sure." She again turned to face Morgan. "The duplex has a very nice yard. I don't know what shape it's in now; I hope it's in good shape, that they saved my garden. They are renting it so they must be keeping it in good shape to get the money they're getting each month. Maybe they are renting both out. I really don't know."

"Would you like me to go over and check on it?" Morgan asked and Janie answered with, "I worry about Xavier."

Morgan was aware of Janie's concerns about Xavier; she expressed them often. Xavier loved America and had no desire to go back to Argentina. From what Morgan gathered, he was in America lacking a green card. Before their discussion of either Janie's duplex or Xavier's predicament could continue, Albert came nobly through the glass doors in his birthday suit. He proudly sauntered over to admire Xavier's new flowerbed making Janie and Morgan smile in unison and silently hope that Albert would have his time in the garden before Alice sent her henchmen to extinguish his enchanted moment. They stifled their giggles as Albert bent over to smell a flower. He looked so happy as he moved from flower to flower like a chubby bumblebee.

Alice brashly came through the patio doors smiling; she was giving relatives of a prospective resident the tour—making sure they saw the pleasant patio with the newly landscaped and charming garden. There was Albert, the unexpected pink statuary that smacked the smile right off Alice's face.

A Bible And A Fly Swatter 1977

"Oh, I can't watch this, Morgan." Janie had a sorrowful look on her face.

"Neither can I," Morgan agreed and reached for Janie's arm to help her out of her chair. The two rushed to get as far away from the soon-to-come unpleasant and heart-wrenching scene.

"No, no. We can't have the girl, Janet. That's not going to work. We have to think of something else," Anna worried. She set a date for the next event and was on a quest to find the perfect entertainment that would assure the events could continue. "The high muckamucks will be there."

"Muckamucks?" Morgan questioned.

"Mucketymucks, big-wigs, VIPs—whatever you want to call them. They'll decide whether we can continue these events for the men. Now that they know I've been doing them, it will be near impossible to continue if they disapprove."

Morgan could hear George hammering on his screen door through her kitchen window and swore she was also hearing the hammering through the receiver.

"Where are you?" she asked. Anna didn't answer but continued on about the type of entertainment that would be appropriate for the next event. Morgan listened more carefully and there was no doubt that she was hearing the hammering sounds through the receiver. Anna was at George's apartment. Morgan thought it would be funny to pop through the closet door into George's apartment and surprise her.

"I'm sorry, Anna, can you hold on a minute? I have to check on OP."

"Of course."

Morgan quietly opened her closet door, crawled through and exited out of George's closet door with a bang.

Anna screamed, leaped backward, dropping the phone then hitting the bookcase (giving George and Morgan a good laugh at Anna's expense).

"Busted," exclaimed George with a grin. Anna wanted their budding relationship to be kept private.

"I'll go hang the phone up," Morgan said, "unless you want to keep talking on the phone."

Anna beamed a guilty smile.

"Yeah, you do that," George chimed in. "Come back over and let OP through."

- 125 -

Anna looked stunned as she watched Morgan bend down to exit through George's closet.

"I'll explain later," George responded to Anna's bewilderment. George continued his repair on the screen door and Anna waited for Morgan to return. This time she returned through the front door with OP by her side.

The two sat side by side on George's couch meandering down a short road of entertainment possibilities at their disposal. None were seeming too promising.

"We need something entertaining and wholesome." Anna was frustrated and Morgan was impressed at how important this was to Anna.

Morgan shouted out to George, "George, what talent does Rusty have again?"

He poked his head past the door. "What?"

"What talent does Rusty have? You know, like for entertainment, maybe at the hospital."

"He does theater and dances."

"Like tap dancing?"

"Musical stuff dancing." George scrunched up his face. "You're not going to ask Rusty to tap dance around for the soldiers are you?" The way George posed the question made both Morgan and Anna laugh and Morgan waved George on. The two then went back to hashing over convincing therapeutic entertainment. Suddenly Morgan leaped from the couch and yelled.

"I got it! I got it!" She got the attention of even OP as she waved her arms in the air. "I know the perfect entertainment—*perfect!*"

Anna demanded, "Tell me!"

"Nope, I'll show you," she responded, ebullient and sincerely pleased with herself. "Come on, OP." She headed for the door, eager to get her plans in motion but George pushed her back into the apartment and rushed in behind her, slamming and locking the door. He pumped his hands up and down imploring silence with a look of urgency on his face. Anna was immediately concerned.

"Lorraine?" Morgan whispered. George nodded confirmation. Seeing the worry on Anna's face, she quietly stepped back to the couch. "It's our nutcase apartment manager. You know, the one who showed up at the hospital with the red hair. When she comes knocking, it's best to pretend that no one is home. Trust me, she's somewhat amusing at first but the humor wears off quickly."

A Bible And A Fly Swatter 1977

Morgan mouthed to George that she was going back to her apartment. She grabbed OP by the collar and disappeared through the closet door only to find Lorraine peering through her kitchen window—watching Morgan exit from the tiny closet followed by OP. This sight would certainly have been a curious one to the average person, but Lorraine wasn't average. Morgan waved and headed for the bedroom, hoping Lorraine would remove herself from the window and head off to somewhere else. She did; she headed for Morgan's front door. Leaving OP in the bedroom, Morgan answered the door.

Lorraine was there because she wanted to go back to the hospital. She rather liked the attention of her captive audience. She wanted to go back.

"Well, when they have another show Rusty will be going again. I'm sure he wouldn't mind giving you a ride." She looked past Lorraine and waved. "I think Thomas is signaling to you." He wasn't; he wasn't even there but it worked. Lorraine rushed off to the downstairs apartment.

"Jesus? Jesus, I just can't remember. I'm sorry," shouted Mrs. Schwab to the ceiling.

Morgan stepped into the room. Mrs. Schwab's initial expression was one of delight at seeing someone come through the door but quickly turned to profound disappointment. Morgan smiled at her anyway then made her way over to Janie's bed.

"I think she was expecting Jesus," Janie explained.

"So, has she ever seen Jesus come through that door?" Morgan whispered. "Or said that she saw Jesus?"

"Uhhah. Yes. According to Mrs. Schwab Jesus comes through that door a lot." Janie looked at Morgan with raised eyebrows and added, "Maybe Alice is the anti-Christ, whatdayathink?" Then she asked, "Are you here to visit Aka?"

"Yes and to look into some other matter. I just wanted to stop by and say hello to you while I'm here. And, ask you if you'd like to go back to the hospital sometime. I think the entertainment is going to be a regular thing, at least I hope it is."

"Yes," she said, "I would love to. Please, I would really love to go back. I enjoyed myself, Morgan."

Mrs. Schwab started back up yelling to Jesus which motivated Morgan to be on her way. Janie tried pressing a pillow around her ears but eventually grew tired of listening to her roommate and got up to read a magazine in the guest area.

Much to her surprise, Janie saw Morgan talking with Xavier in the garden. Curious, she stopped to watch for a minute or so. The conversation was quite animated. Janie was intrigued. Yet, instead of putting her nose where she felt it didn't belong—and to avoid letting either Morgan or Xavier know that she was peeping from the other side of the doors—Janie took the magazine back to her room to read.

There was a muffled knock coming from the closet. Morgan opened her closet door and answered the knock with a "Yes?"

"Are you up for company?" George asked.

"My, aren't you being polite——-" Morgan was interrupted by the door abruptly opening wider exposing Anna by George's side. George had Anna with him and he didn't want Morgan to say something that he would regret Anna hearing (Morgan and George exchanged sarcasm on a regular basis—most not intended for others' ears). "Yes, come on over. You can use the front door," she said, thinking that it might be easier for Anna. Anna was in her thirties and to Morgan that was the brink of middle age, but they were already crawling their way through the door to her apartment so she just stepped back allowing them entry. OP was quick to greet them.

"So what do I owe this late night visit?" Morgan said in jest. "Would you like some coffee?" Anna did but George made a quick closet exit to retrieve his own kind of beverage.

"Saturday, Morgan. It's this Saturday," Anna announced with worried excitement. "You're sure that you have everything under control now? I'm really having to trust you."

"I have it perfectly under control and you are going to love it but I do have a question for you," she said, "besides if you want cream or sugar or both."

"Both please. Ask away."

"Do you think it would be okay to bring Janie, or anyone else? I mean, on the day with 'the judges' being there?" Morgan worried that bringing anyone who wasn't affiliated with the hospital might be frowned upon and might hurt the chances of the entertainment becoming a sanctioned event.

"Oh, I hadn't thought of that. I don't know. Who did you want to bring?"

"Just Janie, but I can justify Janie if need be."

A Bible And A Fly Swatter 1977

"Justify?" Anna asked then took a sip of her coffee.

"I can say that she's with the entertainment."

George was now standing by the table with his sidekick glass of bourbon. "Janie is with the entertainment? Huh...so you're getting entertainment from Sunny Acres?" George questioned with a laugh.

"Well, sort of. And don't laugh. Everyone is going to love it," Morgan's reply was smug.

"George, I don't think you should be there or anyone, except Janie if you have a good excuse for her being there." Anna was concerned. She realized that she had put everything in Morgan's hands and hadn't thought much about the particulars and neglecting the particulars could doom the cause. "What about the food, the snacks?" she added.

"Well, that's where I can come in," George chimed in. "I'll bring the food and I'll help set up whatever needs to be set up."

"But if I didn't get permission to have others there—" Anna's worry was cut off by George.

"I'm your boyfriend, ya know. The boyfriend. So, I'm carrying the crap up and do the dirty work—par for the course. It'll be Janie and me, that's all. And Morgan already has permission to be there...."

It was settled and all three moved to the living room to visit but before Morgan could settle in for what was sure to be a long visit she needed to walk OP. She left George to pick the music and out the door she went with OP. OP took off ahead of her and was squatting in the ivy before Morgan was halfway down the stairs. The brief outing was made even shorter when Lorraine stepped out of her front door and onto the walkway as OP was sniffing her way down the ivy. Morgan called for her in a hushed voice. Eventually OP responded and joined Morgan under the staircase, waiting for Lorraine to disappear.

After several minutes, she stepped out onto the driveway telling OP to "stay" so she could check for Lorraine. She was standing at the railing staring out toward the street. She had toilet paper wrapped around her coifed hair held on with large silver clips.

"Hi Lorraine," Morgan yelled. "Out to see the full moon?"

"Is that you, Morgan?

"Yes, it's me," she answered.

"No, I'm not looking for the moon," she said in a stern voice.

"Enjoying the stars?"

"No," she said, still staring forward. There was about thirty seconds of silence when Lorraine added, "Sometimes the bears come down to go through garbage cans."

"There are no bears here in the city, Lorraine," Morgan shouted back and Lorraine talked on about seeing one herself.

Morgan listened and pondered whether to officially introduce OP, to bring her upstairs and show Lorraine what Morgan believed she was mistaking for a bear but Lorraine had seen OP several times before. And, Morgan couldn't be certain that Lorraine didn't have her gun with her and how she would react to the sight of OP.

"Well, if I see a bear out here, Lorraine, I'll let you know," she shouted over Lorraine's talk, hoping to cut the encounter short.

Lorraine did another visual survey of the area then went back into her apartment. Morgan grabbed OP's collar and bolted up the stairs.

"Aaaah, I heard *the deranged* one talking," George commented as Morgan rushed through the front door.

"She was standing on the walkway with toilet paper wrapped around her head looking for a bear." Morgan took a deep breath and collapsed onto the chair.

"A bear?" Anna was baffled. Thus flowed the stories of Lorraine which explained their degree of panic and concern when Lorraine made an appearance at the hospital and also made for an entertaining evening, for Anna.

The chairs were lined up. Anna was nervously setting out the refreshments with George dutifully by her side. The three dignitaries were standing side by side watching, with amazement: the previously sedate and antisocial patients were mingling, obviously enthused and eager for the coming entertainment.

"The king and queens are looking pretty pleased so far," George mumbled to Anna. She glanced over quickly but did not respond. She still didn't know what entertainment Morgan had organized and when asked by those who would be judging this event, she merely told them that it was a surprise that all would definitely enjoy—and she prayed that she was right.

Morgan showed up with Janie on her arm. The crossing was slow since Janie left her cane behind. She helped Janie to a chair then made her way to Anna and George.

A Bible And A Fly Swatter 1977

"Hi guys," she said with a smile that beamed all was okay.

"Is she the entertainment?" George asked referring to Janie.

"Oh Morgan," Anna worried.

"Janie?" Morgan questioned. "Well, she could be. She was a W. A. S. P., a pilot in WWII so she fits right in here and I'm sure she has one hell of a lot of good stories to entertain with but nope, she's not today's entertainment— maybe next time.

"Okay, we need a large area cleared at the front. Maybe it would be better to put the chairs sort of in a circle," Morgan continued then looked up at George. "George help me rearrange the chairs."

Anna cut in, "So where is the entertainment?"

"Actually, Miss Worrywart, they are outside getting ready and will be coming up any minute."

"Outside where?"

"Go look out the window past the desk," Morgan instructed and Anna scurried off. She raced down the hallway so fast that she slid into the window when trying to stop. Unaffected, Anna watched through the window from above as the group of children, with the help of several adults, readied themselves in their costumes. The smile on Anna's face couldn't have shined any brighter. Morgan had arranged for the little dancers who performed at Sunny Acres to come and perform for the veterans. Anna watched, though she felt she should be in the common room helping, she was glued to the charming view below her. She couldn't take her eyes off the children in their simulated sailor costumes who began marching single file to the entrance of the building.

George met Anna in the hallway. "Oh George," she said, smiling and looking as though holding back tears.

"What's wrong?" George placed his hand on her shoulder, he would have embraced her if they weren't at the hospital; he knew such a display would make Anna uncomfortable.

"Oh, George," she repeated. "They are just darling. Oh Morgan, God bless her." Anna assumed George was aware of the pending entertainers, but he wasn't. He had no idea what she was talking about. She brushed past him when she saw the children entering the building with their chaperones close at hand directing them toward Morgan's waving hand. The "judges" lit up like proud parents would as the little parade passed by.

- 131 -

Everyone took their seats, even the men who typically hung onto the security of the drapes. The judges remained standing, observing from the back. The introduction was brief; the arm on the turntable was lowered onto the album and the little sailors tapped their hearts out. Due to the acoustics of the common room, the little tappers sounded like an orchestra of playing spoons. The dancers seemed to like all the noise their little shoes were making and they stomped all the harder.

The dancers did three routines and then one little girl sang "God Bless America," touching every heart in the room, even evoking a few tears, and having most up on their feet through the song.

The audience was wild about the entertainment and the fervent applause trumpeted that the event was a huge success. The little dancers took their bows and promptly left, not staying to enjoy the refreshments. Morgan and Anna speculated that the environment might have frightened them a bit, but they did an exceptional job, pleasing all who attended and helping Anna and Morgan to achieve their goal. The judges gave a thumbs up then left themselves.

Morgan leaned forward and told Janie that David's last name was Mundt. Janie repeated the name then spelled it, spelled it correctly. "Yep, that's it," Morgan confirmed. "I'll be back." She left to join Anna at her desk.

"Yeeeeeeeesssss!" Anna shouted, not caring who heard her. "We did it; we did it; we did it, Morgan!" She jumped up and down a few times then wrapped her arms around Morgan to thank her. Of course Morgan was just as pleased but she was at that moment taken aback at how mistaken she was about Anna, how she had initially misjudged Anna's concern for the men on her floor. Anna cared, deeply cared.

"Where's George," Anna asked and Morgan told her that he was talking with some of the men, well, listening actually. They decided to go back into the common room and join the others. As they turned the corner Morgan stopped short, and grabbed for Anna's arm to stop her also. Morgan directed Anna's attention to David. There was Janie sitting in a chair pulled up next to David's wheelchair, her hands holding David's left hand. She was leaning into him as close as it was possible. David held the mouthpiece to his hookah limp in his right hand as oppose to the clenched grip he demonstrated at all times.

George saw the two standing at a distance and hurried to join them. "What's up?"

"Look at Janie and David," Morgan said nodding her head their way.

A Bible And A Fly Swatter 1977

George saw Janie get up on her own and offered her assistance but she shooed him away. She stubbornly made her way to David to sit herself down in the chair next to him. Once George saw that she was seated safely, he moved on to the snack table to munch on the hardly touched array and talk to whomever was interested in chatting with him.

Anna and Morgan watched together, but only Morgan was truly affected by the scene.

"She asked me what David's last name was," Morgan commented.

"So that's why you asked. I wonder why she wanted to know?" Anna was now curious herself.

Janie's hand reached for David's face. Her fingers gently moved across his cheek as David's head swayed a response. Janie pulled David's free hand up to her face, leaning down to meet it. All but Morgan and Anna were preoccupied leaving David and Janie alone and they were truly in a world of their own.

"Let's go see what's up," George urged.

"No," Morgan shot back in a whisper. "Don't interrupt them. Please don't."

"Come on, my dear, let's go have a smoke." George put his arm around Anna's shoulder and the two left down the hallway to Anna's desk.

Morgan took a few steps back to sit against the shelf along the wall with her eyes still fixed on Janie and David. It looked as though David was trying to shake the mouthpiece from his right hand when Janie reached over to remove it from between his fingers, placing it behind the hookah. Again she stroked his face. David's hand made a gallant effort to reach for Janie. She stood, bent at the waist, pitched forward as she took David's arm, pulling it toward her chest and rested her face against it. Janie stroked and caressed David while he fought his unruly body to respond. Morgan couldn't take her eyes off them.

"We have to wrap this up, my tiny young neighbor," George proclaimed into Morgan's ear in a low voice.

"George, this is unbelievable." Her focus was still on Janie and David. "Just look at them, George."

"Maybe you should go over there and see what's up," he implored. Anna was off work shortly and they had plans.

"Okay," she said," maybe I will; maybe I *should*." And with hesitation, and at a slow and guarded pace, Morgan approached Janie and David. She stood a short distance away and waited for one of them to acknowledge her presence before she spoke. David's zigzagging head strained to look directly at Morgan. She stepped closer. His eyes were glossy yet looked bright and alive as if they were seeing something Morgan didn't, or couldn't. Again David's mouth opened to speak and he managed to drag out words that Morgan couldn't understand but evidently Janie already tuned into David's unique speak, and she did. She pulled herself away from him, leaned back into her chair to also look at Morgan.

"I'm sorry to interrupt." Morgan said, unsure what else to say at such a moment. The joy between Janie and David was unmistakable.

Janie smiled up at Morgan and whispered, "David says 'thank you'." Morgan looked at David then back at Janie as Janie continued, "This is my old friend David Mundt, Morgan." There was a sound or sense of relief to Janie's voice. She turned back to take in the company of her long lost friend as though nothing else mattered and repeated while staring into David's eyes, "My old and very dear friend, David Mundt."

Morgan didn't know what to say but knew that she wanted to give them more time. "I'm going to get things packed up and then I'll be back," was all she could think to say. She took a few steps then turned back to ask, "David, do you want a cigarette?" He responded with a contorted grin and a shaky nod, yes.

Eventually, Anna insisted that it was time to go with the staff for the next shift having already arrived.

Morgan strolled back to David and Janie. Though against the rules, Morgan placed another lighted cigarette into his hookah and gave him a kiss on the cheek. She stepped away while Janie said her good-bye. Once Janie rose from the chair, Morgan stepped back and they locked arms as the two made their way to Anna and George waiting by the front doors.

Chapter 9
The Men Are Back

"So, Simon," she asked already knowing the answer, "does Mom know that you're living at the beach house?" Morgan knew how he would latch onto the opportunity to use the house as if it were his own the minute her mother purchased it. It was just a matter of time, and, Simon wasted none of it. He liked to take credit for others' hard work and money as though the fruits of their labor deserved to be his own. The new beach house would help provide Simon with the desired image he so longed for but failed to attain on his own.

"What difference does it make; they aren't going to be back for months now," Simon snapped back.

"Well, that's true. I guess OP and I could come stay there too until they get back. OP would looooove," she extended and emphasized the sentiment, "running on the beach."

"What do you want, Morgan?" Simon responded with peeve. "I'm having guests. I gotta go."

"Having guests" meant that Simon was having people over that he would be attempting to impress for one reason or the other. Friends were people he already knew, and knew him. Guests were people he was trying win over. Simon could be gracious and charming beyond notion if he saw an outcome that would be to his own benefit. He was a lazy opportunist, and he knew it— though great effort was made to keep that fact carefully hidden from others. And once anyone actually got to know Simon, they became painfully aware of his ability to manipulate people and circumstances to his advantage—no matter whom it may hurt in the process. Simon lied, he manipulated and made others feel that he was doing them the favor.

"That's okay. OP and I won't bother you and your guests when we're there; we have our own things to do." Morgan was smiling from the inside out. She knew Simon was gritting his teeth, steaming by the thought of her showing up to stay at the beach house, particularly if she brought OP with her. "So maybe next weekend. I think I'll invite George, my neighbor. Maybe we could stay longer than the weekend. I'll have to talk to Mr. Smith about getting time

ZaneDoe

off." Simon hung the phone up and Morgan burst out laughing, and when the phone rang a minute later, even though the caller didn't leave a message, she knew it was Simon calling to thwart her plans for a stay at the beach house. Though Morgan was curious about what excuse and what temperament he would use, she wasn't going to give him the chance or satisfaction to dissuade her...with a touch of trepidation that he might succeed.

"Yoooohooooo," came George's call through the closed closet door.

Morgan leaned over from the kitchen chair and opened the door shouting back, "Come on over" which he did immediately.

"We're going to the movies. Wanna come?"

"You and Anna?"

"Yeah, me and Anna. Would like to join us?" he asked again.

"George, sit down for a minute," she implored. "I have to tell you this."

"Let me go get a drink and I'll be all ears."

As George readied himself to crouch down to their thoroughfare Morgan questioned,

"You can't listen without a drink?"

"Oh, I can, but," he answered with a smile, "do I *want* to?" And George disappeared through the closet door returning with drink in hand. He plopped down onto a vacant chair and proclaimed, "I'm ready—all ears, a clear mind and some time to spare."

"You know, I can hardly believe this myself, this thing with Janie and David. Janie knows David; she knew him from back in Hawaii, way back, in the 1940's." She hesitated for a second. "I think they were more than just friends."

"What are the odds on this one. Talk about fate...." George pondered aloud the chances of such an encounter. He pulled the pack of cigarettes from his shirt pocket and Morgan promptly reached for an empty can of dog food. She set it on the table to be used as an ashtray. George picked it up to look inside, took a whiff, grimaced then set it back down.

"Yeah, like a cigarette smells better," Morgan sneered.

"Continue," he said.

"Well, I sort of have to read between the lines because behind Janie's deep-rooted smile—" George cut her off.

"*Deep rooted?*" he mimicked with a laugh.

"Yes, *deep rooted.*" Morgan explained, "She has a smile like it comes from way deep inside, not like her usual smiles."

- 136 -

A Bible And A Fly Swatter 1977

"Okay, what about her *'deep-rooted'* smile?"

"Cut it out." Morgan felt George was making light of what she was saying. To Morgan this was a monumental event, a serendipitous reunion of the heart. "Can you imagine being in love with someone and believing that they were dead. This was way back, Pearl Harbor time. Then finding them after all those years? And, finding him in a wheelchair like that? Come on, George; it's like something out of the movies."

"Hey, I'm not saying it's not remarkable, Morgan. Lighten up. I'm listening. I'm serious. Now continue. I'm sure there's more to this."

"No! OP no!" Conversation stopped for a few seconds replaced with laughter as they listened to Anna scold OP for who-knows-what.

Morgan took a deep breath. "When I first introduced David to her at the hospital she kept staring at him. She asked me at the rest home what his last name was. I thought that was odd but I didn't question it. Then, at the last event with the little dancers, I told her his last name and it confirmed it for her, that it was David from Hawaii, from her past.

"I've only known Janie for a few months—"

"You've known her longer than a few months," George interrupted.

"Yeah, true. God, time really is going by fast, but whatever, I have never seen her look like this. Janie hates Sunny Acres. She's there because she has to be. I guess there's no one to take care of her or help her. She doesn't have kids and she never married. She's pleasant enough but she always has this certain expression, this sort of sadness mixed with anger or resentment or something about her. Or maybe it's frustration."

"Maybe it's contempt," added George.

"Why contempt? Isn't contempt and anger the same thing?"

"Somewhat. Maybe she has contempt for those running the place, for whomever put her there or won't help her. Think about it. If Janie ended up at Sunny Acres because no one would or could help her then, unless she has some miraculous change in her condition—whatever that might be—then she's doomed. She's looking to die there."

Morgan hadn't given much thought about the finality of Sunny Acres and how Janie was more than likely doomed to finish out her life there at Sunny Acres. Maybe so for Aka also. Morgan said nothing. The new insight was emotionally stifling.

- 137 -

"That's probably the awful truth, Morgan. Fuck, I'd resent anyone who stuck me in that vacuous chamber to finish out my life. Go on," George encouraged. Morgan looked stunned by the sudden reality and he wanted to bring her out of it.

"Well, now I really want to make sure that Janie goes to the hospital with me regularly since I can't take David out of the hospital."

"Why?" George finished his drink then lit another cigarette. "Why can't you take David out of the hospital?"

"Ask Anna," she smirked. "Themz da rulz."

"Rules have been known to be broken, young lady..." and that's all George had to say to put Morgan at ease and a grin back on her face that beamed a spirited agreement.

"Come on, let's go back to my apartment before OP does Anna in." George grinned and they ducked into the closet one after the other.

Anna, George and Morgan looked up in unison as Rusty flung the screen door open. They heard Lorraine shout to Rusty in the background. His face twitched as she spoke. The three waited in silence. Rusty looked as though he was about to burst a verbal hot air balloon.

He stepped inside and shut the door behind him then began: "I am never, *fucking, never,* offering that woman a ride again," he said rolling back his eyes. *"Never!"*

"Why, what happened," Anna innocently asked while Morgan and George knowingly grinned at each other, eager to hear the newest fiasco.

"Where do I fucking start..." and Rusty burst forth with Lorraine's craziness—nothing that would surprise either George or Morgan.

Rusty told of how Lorraine begged him to take her to Rhodes department store. He chastised himself for actually accompanying her inside the store—he should have known better. Lorraine, donning clown-like make-up and with her wild-red hair stacked high on her head, stomped through the aisles at the department store with Rusty in tow. She was at a determined pace stopping only at the cosmetic counter (shouting along the way—in anything but a dainty or appropriate indoor voice—for Rusty to "hurry the hell up"). Well-mannered Rusty lamentably followed as ordered arriving at the cosmetic counter and standing sheepishly alongside Lorraine. There was an attractive, "very attractive," and tastefully groomed clerk arranging a display behind the cosmetic counter. Like a truck driver yelling at someone who cut him off, Lorraine demanded to smell "a bottle of your Anus Anus," with a delayed and gruff "please."

George and Morgan were now full-out laughing.

"Anus, Anus?" Anna innocently asked.

Anna was aghast while Morgan and George bobbed up and down with laughter.

"It's Anais," Rusty clarified.

"Like Anais Nin, the author?" George said mid-laugh.

"Oh, the perfume Anais Anais," Anna recalled. "Oh my God. She said Anus, Anus?"

"Eau de Anus..." George snorted a laugh. He and Morgan were beside themselves with digs and laughter but Rusty still wasn't amused. Rusty accompanied Lorraine to the shoe department and when the salesman came to assist she merely complained for all to hear about her aching feet, the high prices and then removed her shoes, that is when Rusty walked away to stand by the exit and wait.

"And that was just at the one store." Rusty sounded exhausted.

"Then why did you go into other stores or even give her a ride?" George scolded. "You knew better. I warned you. Stay away from her. I'm surprised that you gave her a ride or spent any time with her now that you know she carries a gun in her purse."

"She carries a gun in her purse?" Anna looked horrified. George and Morgan looked at each other, knowing an explanation was expected but how does one explain Lorraine.

"You have to live here, Anna," George said

"Well, I'm glad that I don't!" Anna retorted.

Morgan wondered if Anna's comment was hurtful to George since he had fallen for Anna hard and fast and had voiced to Morgan how nice it would be to have her there all the time. She was a few years older than George, and seemed to suit George perfectly in every way.

Morgan chimed in. "Lorraine isn't something one can explain. She's something you have to experience to believe—not to understand, mind you, because there's no understanding Lorraine but to believe her ways you have to live around her. The guys downstairs actually hide from her but she hasn't hurt anyone. She's just the free entertainment around here..." and though not intended, this led into a barrage of Lorraine stories. Morgan and George were never shy of Lorraine stories, they had the exponential growth factor and never seized to entertain when shared.

Rusty decided to join them at the movies. They shot up to Rusty's house to drop off OP and all four spent an enjoyable evening together. All four got along so well and it was so easy to be together. Morgan not only loved George, but she grew to love Anna and Rusty also.

"So, where's 'Mr. *Johan* Smith'" George asked, with his usual emphasis on Johan's name as though fictitious. Morgan walked back to the desk. "You going to keep this door locked all the time?"

"Sure am," she answered. "After those two guys came here. I would say that they were either Mafia or C. I. A. by the looks of them."

"Who does Mr. Smith say they are?"

"He doesn't but," Morgan's eyes opened wide and her tone stepped up a few beats. "Johan called me this morning and guess what I thought I heard in the background?"

"Do tell," George said as he stepped into the office and closed the door behind him—and locked it.

"You know that gaspy giggle Janet has?" she asked, sure that observant George didn't miss Janet's distinctive cackle.

"Yeah?"

Morgan continued, "He was telling me about, well, first of all, he was calling from Spain. He was giving me a list of wines to give to Lacey and Benny and while he was talking I swear I heard that excited sound she makes in the background."

"Did you say anything?"

"No, of course not; it's not my business. Anyways, I'm too intimidated by Johan to ask him a personal question like that. But, George, will you call her house and ask for her?"

"Why?"

"So I can see if she's home or out of town."

"Then why don't you call?"

"Because I don't want her to know that I know that she is out of town if her parents say she's out of town, you know; they'll tell her I called."

"But what if she isn't out of town, then what?" George asked.

"Just say you were calling about the hospital, about her playing for the vets."

"Like you just said, it's really none of your business. You're just being nosey."

"So?" Morgan wrinkled her brow. "Will you call?" George shook his head no. "Come on, George; I'm dying to know, nosey or not."

"Why?"

"Not to bash Janet or anything, but Mr. Smith, well, I see him as very sophisticated, sort of the opposite of Janet. The sommelier, the continental man, the elitist—"

George cut in. "All that goes out the window when thinking below the belt."

"I guess. They would make a good-looking couple, don't you think?"

"I don't think about it," George cracked and changed the subject. "I came down here to pick up my over-sized child and to tell you that Anna has everything worked out. You just show up with Janie and the entertainment and we, as in Anna and I, will take care of the rest."

"Oh God, thank you so much, George." She felt like hugging him but she knew that would make him uncomfortable. "You're a good friend—a good neighbor and a good friend."

"And a good dad to the furry one," he quickly responded to change the direction of the conversation. "Come on, OP. Let's go.

"Don't forget to deadbolt the door behind me," George teased.

It wasn't long before both Benny and Lacey had knocked on the door, there to drop off orders and, of course, Benny wanted to know where Johan was. Benny never stuck to business at hand, there was always some other topic, issue or opinion he would feel compelled to expound upon. Mr. Smith's location was none of Benny's business and he had been told that more than once which Morgan believed made Johan's whereabouts even more desirable to Benny.

"Benny, I don't know where he is at the moment and if I did, unless he told me to inform you, I wouldn't tell you anyways," Morgan announced in a lighthearted manner.

"It's anyway, not anyways," Benny corrected for the fiftieth time.

"Whatever," Morgan shook her head. She had calls to make and had no interest in listening to Benny for any extended amount of time. She knew with

ZaneDoe

George gone that the possibility of being interrupted and someone saving her from Benny was slim to none.

"As Mr. Smith's employee, I believe that he should be more accessible..." he began. "I have questions—-" Morgan cut him off.

"Then ask me and when he calls in I will relay them for you."

"I should be able to speak directly to—" Again she cut him off.

"No you shouldn't, Benny; that's my job. I am the go-between for Mr. Smith," she insisted. She had worked for Johan long enough to know how he liked his office to function, and that was without him and without him being bothered. "Mr. Smith travels a lot. He pays me so he can go about his business without interruptions, Benny." Morgan's explanation didn't satisfy Benny's sense of entitlement to direct contact with Mr. Smith so they went around and around until a knock at the door halted the discourse. Benny moved to answer the door and Morgan quickly stopped him.

"I'll get it." She stepped from behind the desk and hurried to the door. Morgan leaned into the peephole then held her breath. She hesitated, not sure whether to open the door.

Catching her indecision, Benny whispered, "Who is it?"

Morgan stared at Benny as the visitors knocked again. She then waved Benny over to look through the peephole. He took a look. Then, again in a whisper, asked who the two men were. Morgan put her finger to her mouth to shush Benny. The doorknob shook as the visitors tested it. Morgan and Benny looked at each other, Morgan with her eyes opened wider and her lips pursed. They waited in silence until the two men in suits walked away from the door. She listened as they climbed the steps.

"What's going on?"

"They're the reason I have the door locked, but don't ask me who they are. I don't know who they are but they've come here looking for Johan."

"Menacing," Benny said, "and I've seen them around here, Morgan. I've seen them on the main street."

"They look like, well, I don't know, like some secret service or something." Morgan moved back to her desk with Benny at her heels. "They don't smile. They're scary looking. Pushy."

"So what do they want?"

"Johan," she answered.

"For what?"

"I don't have a clue but when I told Johan about them coming here, he knew who they were." Anticipating Benny's next question she added, "And no, he didn't tell me who they were but he had the locks and peephole in the next day."

"Intrigue," Benny joked.

Morgan realized that she had probably said too much already and she needed to find a way to end the conversation or topic. She insisted to Benny that she had an appointment and needed to finish up some work before leaving. Benny left but hadn't been gone long when he was on the phone to Morgan.

"Those two men are in the parking lot by your car, Morgan. Just standing a little bit away from where your car is parked," Benny informed. "They know you're there. I think they're waiting for you. Do you want me to come back?"

Morgan acted unaffected by the two men by her car, feeling guilty that she got Benny involved. She told him that she wasn't concerned, changed the subject quickly then hung up. Truth being, she was very afraid; she was there alone. George had OP and George was meeting Anna at the park so she couldn't call him to come back. She called Jackie. Jackie wasn't home. Then she called Rusty, but there was no answer there either. She thought about calling Clark and telling him that her car was having a problem. He was a car ambulance. He would rush to the scene like the automobile EMT. He lived for such calls. She decided to call Steve upstairs at Buffalo Books and ask him if he wouldn't mind walking her to her car.

"Steve, two strange men were knocking on the office door. I looked through the peephole and they were just so scary looking. I have to leave the office and I'm afraid to walk to my car alone," she explained. Steve was happy to oblige. He was taking over a task that would have normally been designated for George—*he* was needed instead of George and that was a boost to his ego no matter what the purpose.

Morgan rounded the corner with Steve by her side. The two men turned so that their backs faced Morgan and Steve. Morgan asked Steve to get into the car; she would drive him around to the front of the store leading the two men to believe that she did not drive off alone. She dropped off Steve and took off for home using a different route.

Morgan quickly pulled into the driveway and hurried up the stairs to her apartment. Once inside, she locked the door behind her, something she was getting used to doing with Lorraine on the loose. Per usual, Morgan was seduced by the blinking light on her answering machine—its heart was beating. There were few mechanical objects she loved as much as her answering machine and couldn't imagine life now without it. She had a message from Randy responding to her request that he perform for the veterans at the upcoming Sunday event. She called him back immediately.

"So you will do it?" she questioned with such delight that he would understand that a no would cause major disappointment.

"Yeah, I mean if you think they'd like to watch some guy dancing," Rusty answered, his doubt unquestionable.

"Oh, I have the best idea, Rusty…."

They came to an agreement and Morgan even promised that Lorraine would not be there. The next message was from Johan. He said that he would call her after office hours. She let the machine answer each call to keep the line open, to make sure she didn't get involved in a conversation and miss Johan's call. When she heard Johan's voice, Morgan dashed for the phone to pick up. She was eager to tell him about the reappearance of the two sinister looking men.

Morgan told about the two men arriving at the office while Benny was there and how Benny had seen the men on the main street of town before. Mr. Smith inquired if she had been keeping regular hours.

"Yes, I would say I do. If I have a vet appointment for OP or sometimes things happen or come up but mostly I'm there each day about the same time, maybe only fifteen or twenty minutes late at times." She worried that she may have been upstairs or out in the parking lot with George while he took his break or perhaps walking OP and missed Johan when he called. He had no response so she added, "Benny was complaining——" Johan let out a trifle laugh. Morgan continued, "He was complaining that he didn't have direct contact with you. Say, if he wanted to ask you a question or if he was having a problem. I told him to just relay the question or problem to me and I would make sure and pass it along to you. I told him that you hired me so that you could do your business without being bothered, I mean interrupted." Johan still gave no response. "I hope I said what you would want me to say."

"Do you think that you could work in that office with Benny there?" Mr. Smith asked.

- 144 -

A Bible And A Fly Swatter 1977

"Oh God," she blurted out then paused: of course she *could* yet there was no question in her mind that she didn't want to. But if that's what Johan wanted, then of course she would do it. "Yeah, I could work with Benny in the office. I can still bring OP to work with me if Benny is there, right?"

"Yes, yes, of course. There may be a time here or there where having your dog at the office won't be appropriate but I'll give you fair warning and it would only be for a day or two. But don't concern yourself with that."

"Thank you." Morgan sounded relieved.

"No, don't worry. I'm glad that you have your big dog there with you," Johan added.

"So, Mr. Smith——-" Morgan started but was cut off.

"Johan," he corrected for the umpteenth time.

"I'm sorry." She continued, "What about those two men. Why would they be waiting by my car?"

Johan didn't answer her question but requested that she get him Benny's phone number.

"We're having another entertainment thing at the hospital if you're going to be around, Johan," Morgan hinted.

"What did you come up with for entertainment?" he asked, sounding as though he was sincerely interested.

"Well," she thought she would test his response, "they really loved Janet but I called her house and her mother said that she was on vacation." She paused to allow Johan to comment on Janet's whereabouts, but he didn't so she continued. "So, I think Rusty is going to dance. You know, tap dance, well, not the corny tap dance stuff. You have to come see it. I know the guys are going to love it...." She talked on a bit, pausing here and there for Johan to speak, which he didn't. She listened carefully to his side of the line to see if she could catch sounds of Janet. She didn't. Although, someone had turned on music in the background and Debby Boone's "You Light Up My Life" was hardly Johan's taste in music.

The next day at work, Morgan barely settled in when Johan called. He obtained Benny's phone number from Morgan and promised to get back to her before noon, "You're time." And, per usual, Mr. Smith kept his word (he had yet to break it) and called right before noon.

"Benny's going to be working out of the office with you, Morgan," he started. Morgan was simulating banging her head against a wall from the

- 145 -

thought while not letting on to Johan of her displeasure at the news. "I know that the office is small but I'm sure you'll know how to arrange it so everything works. You will need another desk."

"There's an older office desk, kind of ugly though, but there's a desk in the back of Buffalo Books that George asked me if I wanted. Do you want me to take it?" Morgan asked, cringing a bit at the thought of how it would look in the little office. She had put quite a bit of labor into creating the look she liked for the cement room and that desk would be a blight on her decorative efforts.

"If you don't mind. That would work."

There were a few seconds of silence on both ends.

"You do mind," Johan said.

"No, it's fine," she lied.

"I'm going to find another office. We need a better office, a better location."

"But, Johan, if we move to a regular office complex am I still going to be able to bring OP to work with me?" Morgan worried that if she couldn't bring OP with her then she would need to find another job. There was no yard at the apartment complex and even if there was, her landlord believed that she had a teacup Newfoundland.

"I already told you. I already addressed that concern. Your dog, OP right?, can be at the office." Johan dropped the subject of OP and went on to Benny's presence and job at the office. Morgan's responsibilities would remain the same. In fact, Johan specifically stated that when he called that he did not want to speak to Benny unless he, himself, requested it.

"You do know that Benny is a real, ah, you know, chatter-er?" Morgan wasn't sure if Johan knew what she was going to have to endure having Benny in the office. She knew that he was aware of Benny's hyper personality but did he know how Benny found the need to pontificate on a subject ad nauseam.

"Ignore him," Johan bluntly responded. That was something Johan had no problem doing—responding bluntly and ignoring people. Johan could comfortably answer a question with a cold stare. That was near impossible for Morgan. For the sake of her job, and sanity, Morgan would find a way to deal with Benny's chatter.

Janie requested that Morgan put the top down on the VW Thing. Morgan was happy to do so; she took notice how flying down the freeway with the top down suited Janie. She didn't flinch as the wind whipped wisps of hair in and out of her face or tugged and wobbled her loose skin. She also didn't speak much when the top was down, she just sat erect, staring forward. Janie intrigued Morgan. As Janie sat there braving the wind, Morgan could easily imagine her a pilot. She wondered if Janie was equally remembering those days. Janie hadn't lived an ordinary life and Morgan imagined those memories must support Janie as she lives her sedate life at Sunny Acres.

Morgan parked the car as close to the front of Building D as possible and helped Janie descend the fair distance from the seat to the street. Arm in arm they headed for the front doors but were intercepted by Anna and George; they seemed to come from out of nowhere.

"We'll take it from here," George said playfully and he and Anna whisked Janie from Morgan with urgency and smiles. The expression on Janie's face said that she was both trusting and excited.

Morgan continued on by herself into building D, wondering exactly what surprise Anna and George had cooked up. Rusty met her as she came through the door; he was looking dapper and from another era, an era well-suited for the residents: fedora hat, suit pants, vest, long-sleeve dress shirt and tap shoes.

"How do I look?"

"You look great, Rusty. You really do."

The snacks were already on the tables, the stage was set and someone had strung little lights around the staging area. At the back of the stage were two large artificial palm trees.

"This is *wonderful!*" Morgan was ecstatic. "This looks so nice and *you* look so nice. You look perfect. Did you get the big band music okay?"

Rusty grabbed Morgan's hand. He showed her that he had the music and turntable set and ready to go then he led her over to the window at the back of the room. She leaned forward across the wide shelf-base of the window and saw through the filmy glass a scene that confirmed Anna and George as angels: under the tree, sitting propped up on a blanket sprawled out atop the grass, was David. Another blanket covered his lap. He was wearing a Hawaiian shirt and a lei around his neck. On his one side was a picnic basket and on the other, holding his hand, was Janie, also wearing a lei.

"Pretty nice, huh?" Rusty commented in a whisper.

"Oh my God, Rusty." Morgan was tearing up and couldn't find any other words at the moment. She never felt such love for two friends as she was feeling for George and Anna at that moment.

It was hard to pull away from witnessing this very personal and private reunion.

"Happy?" George asked as he shuffled up behind the spectators at the window.

Morgan turned and hugged George so tightly that he japed a protest.

"That is so wonderful. You and Anna are so wonderful, George. My God, it's perfect…" she gushed on, "…and the leis, they are perfect, so perfect. And the Hawaiian shirt. Oh God, George, you guys did everything so perfect…." Morgan carried on with praise for what Anna and George had created for the long-lost friends.

"Let's give 'em their privacy." George grabbed Morgan's arm and the three headed back to wait with the others for the entertainment to start.

Anna was standing by the turntable. Morgan and Anna exchanged triumphant smiles and Anna was ready to drop the arm and get the show on the road.

"Ready," shouted Rusty, poised on the stage with his hand grasping the fedora tilted down over his eyes. Anna had turned the volume up to the highest the speakers could handle; she set the needle on the album and "Boogie Woogie Bugle Boy" blared across the room to the delight of everyone. Rusty may have started the dance but it wasn't a solo performance for long. The common room came alive with the footsteps of another era. The music wafted out the window Anna opened so that Janie and David could hear and enjoy the tunes of their time.

Chapter 10
Adventures of The New Office

Buffalo Books was quite a different bookstore for its time. It not only had a very large and eclectic book selection but Buffalo Books offered two couches and several chairs for their customers—contemporary and homey at the same time. It wasn't uncommon to find a dog at the foot of a customer relaxing and reading on one of the couches or chairs and most passersby believed that the cat curled up at front window was a prop. John and Ruth gave birth to a business that was a reflection of them, of their style—easy going, respectful and welcoming—a respite of sorts for customers as well as a successful business. Buffalo Books' popularity was rapidly increasing yet there was no intention of changing the casual atmosphere, only improving upon it if a means came to mind.

They had a small office behind the counter where a door led to a storage room which opened through another door to another larger storage room. The second storage room contained odds and ends of furniture and cardboard advertising displays. Mr. Smith arranged to rent that second storage room as the new office; it was much larger than the cement office and had a window. Morgan was delighted to discover the news from both John and Ruth who dropped by to meet OP and officially welcome Morgan and OP to their new office upstairs.

"Oh, that's wonderful," Morgan exclaimed with sincere exultation. "When do I start moving up there?"

"Anytime you want I guess; we moved out the furniture and it's all yours. We have the key for you. You have a separate door, two actually. One opens to the parking lot, but we never use that door; it's got a heavy security bar on it but it can be used if you like," John explained and Ruth set the keys down on Morgan's desk. "It looks like your phone is going in right away, today. Don't know how Smith arranges this stuff but the phone company called us and they're coming right out."

"Then I'm going to start the move now." She hesitated to ask, but only for a minute, "Is George really busy today?"

ZaneDoe

"Yeah. He can help you. So can Steve if you need him. We're going to be at the store most of the day and we can give you a hand too."

"Oh, that's great. I'll start packing and then I'll be up to take a look around to see how things will go, or fit. And, I know I have a window." Morgan was excited.

"Yeah, you have a window." John looked around. "You don't have a window in here," he observed.

"Smith said to leave the metal desk in there for you," John added. "And, he even paid us for that old piece of crap." Ruth gave him a disapproving look for the latter comment; she was happy to get paid for the desk which she thought was a fine and functional desk, not a piece of crap. In large, John didn't filter his comments and that's why Ruth was the side of the partnership who dealt with customers and worked the floor.

"Mr. Smith told me about the desk; it's for Benny to use."

"Who's Benny?" Ruth inquired.

"He's one of the salesman." Morgan refrained from added personal commentary. "Mr. Smith wants him to now work in the office. He's always worked through this office but since Mr. Smith is gone most of the time and I think he's going to be doing a lot more traveling and thought Benny could help out more if he had a desk here in the office. That's the reason for getting a bigger office.

"So, you both have never met Benny?" she asked. They shook their heads, no. "Well, he's the opposite of Steve, is one way to put it."

"What do you mean?" Ruth asked and Morgan worried her description might have sounded offensive.

"Well, you know how Steve is more quiet? He really listens to the customers. He's not in their face but helpful," Morgan delicately explained and Ruth nodded in agreement. Morgan continued, "Benny is just the opposite. Benny is sort of in your face and he expresses his opinions whether wanted or not. It can be wearing so I'm going to put his desk, tactfully, as far away from mine as possible." Morgan grinned and Ruth and John reciprocated.

"We'll see you soon and just call or come up if you need help moving," Ruth said as they headed for the door.

"Yeah, and we'll tell Smith so he'll send us our moving fees," John added in jest and Ruth gave him a good swat to the arm.

A Bible And A Fly Swatter 1977

Morgan considered calling Benny and making him help with the move but then she wanted everything in place as she liked it with his desk at a distance so she tossed that idea out. She locked the door behind her and ran upstairs to check out the particulars of the new office space. She cut through the bookstore instead of using the key to the hallway door. When she saw George she informed, "John and Ruth said you can help me move to the new office." And then teased, "They said that it was okay if Steve helped us."

"Hey, that could be fun for me." George walked Morgan to the new office space. "Twice the size, if not more, than the dungeon."

And it was. Morgan could see the layout in an instant and was eager to get the move started.

"Do you want Steve to help, seriously?" she asked George.

"Yeah, he'd be a lot of help. Do you have books that he can move *one at a time!* No, we'd have to rush him to the hospital at the first sign of a paper cut. I can help you by myself."

"So, OP will still be in the office right?"

"Yep. Mr. Smith guaranteed it."

"And how does our big black child take to Benny, cocaine boy."

"You really think so?" Morgan stopped and questioned.

"No, let's just call him a talkative, moody, neurotic with a sinus problem. So, we're putting the rug in first, right?" George stood with his hands on his hips perusing the new office space.

"I'll get things packed up but yeah, the rug first."

By the end of the day, and with George's sporadic help, and maneuvering around the telephone man in his too-tight jumpsuit, the office was set up and ready for work. OP's bed was closer to Morgan's desk than before and out of Benny's view.

The first incoming call was from Benny. Mr. Smith had explained everything to him and Benny was ready to occupy *his* new office. Morgan quickly reminded Benny that he was sharing *her* office.

"Your office?" Benny questioned which immediately annoyed Morgan.

"Well, it's the Samuel Pacific Imports office," she snapped back bluntly, as Johan had instructed. And, it worked. Benny's tone changed and he pleasantly informed her that he would see her the next morning.

"What time do you get there?" he asked

- 151 -

ZaneDoe

Oh shit, screamed in her head. She got there when she chose to get there. "I'll be here about 9:30."

"Isn't that late for an office?" But he didn't wait for an answer. "See you at 9:30."

She wasn't making a second set of keys for Benny until Johan instructed her to do so but she suspected that Benny would harp on this matter. She knew Benny was going to harp on a lot of matters, most of which will have nothing to do with his job. The peace and quiet of the office was enjoying its last day. At least Morgan was happy with its appearance and the added space allowed her to bring a few more decorative items and perhaps with the window, she could add a very *LARGE ficus* tree, placed tactfully in the area between her desk and Benny's. Yes, that idea was a winner and she was on a mission that night to find one.

With OP and George by her side, and the top down on Bigbird (as George called it), the hunt was on. She normally purchased her plants at a nursery in the Half Moon Bay area since they always gave her such great deals but there was no time for that. She would have to fork out the money and pay the regular price for such a room-dividing tree.

"Naaah, don't worry. Good old Mr. Johan Smith will reimburse you," George commented as he looked at the price tag hanging from the tree.

"I'm not sure how to ask him since this is just something that I want and is not necessary for the office," Morgan worried. She felt that three hundred dollars for a *ficus* tree was way out of her personal office budget and a lot to ask Johan to pay for what would be deemed an unnecessary decorative piece.

"Oh come on, Morgan. Yes it's necessary and three hundred dollars is nothing for Smith. That's nothing. He'll be happy that you're happy. Let's buy it. Put it on my card and when he pays you, you pay me."

"Are you sure?"

"Of course," and George walked off to find a store clerk to help them move the tree to the VW Thing.

With OP squished up against the plant in the back seat, giving it the sniffing of its life, they were off back to the office to strategically place the plant. It seemed easiest to get this gigantic leafy lifesaver in through the door opening out to the parking lot. Morgan opened the door from the inside and she and George struggled to lift, drag and spin the tree into place.

- 152 -

A Bible And A Fly Swatter 1977

"This is so perfect, soooooo perfect." Morgan was all smiles. "George, go sit at Benny's desk." He did. "Can you see me?"

"Can you see me?" he retorted.

"No!" she screamed with delight.

"Okay, mission accomplished. Let's go. Let's lock up and get out of here."

George exited through the door to the parking lot. Morgan quickly locked the door behind him, lowering the heavy bar back in place. She locked the front door then hurried to catch up with George, excited about the new leafy office screen. When she climbed onto the drivers seat, George informed her that the men in the dark suits had arrived and most likely saw him leave the new office.

Without looking around Morgan asked, "Are they still in the parking lot?"

"They're in the parking lot across by the restaurant."

"How would they know it's the new office?"

"Because they can see in when the door was open and it looks like the old office, you know, same furniture. You ought to have Smith move the peephole door over."

"He already did, George. I'm surprised you didn't notice." Morgan added, "Do you think Ruth and John would mind if I left the doors open so that your office area could actually see into my office? OP won't come out and bother anybody."

"Do you really want to sit here and discuss this now with scar face and his buddy watching us?" George lit a cigarette.

"Do you want to follow them?" Morgan asked.

"No. Leave this espionage caper to old Mr. Smith."

"He's not old," she corrected.

"To the young svelte and handsome Mr. Smith. How's that?"

She started the Thing and slowly backed up so that her headlights shown brightly on the duo's dark car sitting alone in the parking lot of the closed restaurant.

"Don't start anything, Morgan. Just pull out of here and let's get home," George insisted.

She drove slow enough to keep the lights focused on their car for an uncomfortable amount of time, at least for George, then she pulled onto the street going in the opposite direction from how she would normally drive home. "I

- 153 -

don't trust these guys and I don't want them to know where we live. I'm going to take a very long detour."

"Not to scare you, but I got the feeling if they wanted to know where you live they'd know but it's fine with me, whatever way you wanna detour home but let's get outta here." George, who exhibited little worry about much of anything, seemed concerned about the two men—they had him on edge. He suspected that the Northern California Samuel Pacific Imports office was doing business other than import wine, even if the wine company didn't know it. George believed that Mr. Smith was involved in other ventures which accounted for his stealthy behavior and Morgan was just too trusting and innocent to pick up on the covert goings-on. "You need to tell Mr. Smith about spotting these guys here at night and that they probably know about the new office."

"I will," she agreed. "He should call me tonight or tomorrow morning and I'll let him know."

"And tell him he owes you for the green monstrosity in the middle of the office."

Morgan laughed. Laughing was normal, a constant, when spending time with George.

It appeared that the dark car containing the two men was indeed following them. Morgan pulled into the Stanford campus and onto the narrow roads reserved for bicyclist and the landscaping staff. She soon lost them or whomever it was following close behind. They made it home and Morgan was certain that they had not been followed only to confront another unwanted guest—Lorraine. There she stood against the railing, not with a drink in her hand but a bottle.

"Is that for drinking or throwing," George questioned as they slowly pulled up the driveway.

"Good point and I'm not going to find out either." Morgan stopped the car, put it in reverse and pulled back out onto the road and drove off.

"Let's pick up Rusty and go get a pizza," George suggested.

Rusty was home and preferred to make the pizza himself. He was an excellent cook. George always said that he'd make someone a good wife. "He cooks, cleans and dances."

"You know, Lorraine could have mistaken OP for the bear she's been hunting and tossed that bottle right at her," Morgan noted as they sat down to eat.

A Bible And A Fly Swatter 1977

"Lorraine could mistake someone in a dark coat for the bear she's been hunting and clobbered them with a bottle," George replied.

"Man, that lady is scary," Rusty commented with such passion that it made George and Morgan laugh aloud. "Why are you laughing. I'd move out of that place. She's crazy enough to make me leave if I lived there. Why does anyone put up with it?"

"OP, Rusty. I have a Newfoundland who weighs more than I do. I don't know any place that I can afford that accepts a dog her size and I can't afford to rent a house with a yard," Morgan answered first. Then George corrected.

"The landlord doesn't know that OP is her actual size, remember?"

"But Lorraine has seen her and we're still living there."

"That's true, but she thinks OP is a bear," George grinned.

"I don't know, she thinks I have a bear in my apartment? I know that she's seen OP through the kitchen window."

"I'd get out of there," Rusty chimed in.

"It's relatively cheap. Not too far from my job and Lorraine can be good for a laugh—free entertainment." George added, "I think the guys down stairs are gay."

"So what, they are willing to live under a crazy woman with a gun because they're gay. That doesn't make sense," Rusty emphatically responded.

"They have a large bird that talks and squawks. Not many apartments are going to allow a loud bird," Morgan defended. "They have a large bird and I have a large dog, not that the landlord knows that I have a large dog. All I know is that the landlord thinks I have a teacup Newfoundland and I'm getting by with it so I'm staying."

"But what about your contract. Isn't it in there and if they find out she's not a teacup you'll lose your apartment."

"I think I'm covered." Morgan took another bite of pizza then explained, "When I signed the new contract I conveniently left out the word teacup so she's accurately and officially on the contract. I'll worry about it if Dan ever calls me on it, until then, we have our OP passageway and life goes on."

Rusty looked George's way. "I'd get the hell out of there."

George took another swig of beer, held up his pizza and just laughed.

Morgan and George ended up staying late at Rusty's, watching OP enjoy the pool and playing cards using the much coveted Famous Amos cookies as poker chips.

"Hi, Johan." Morgan was relieved that he called. "Yes, I was just going out the door but I'm so glad that you caught me before I left." She asked if she should make a key to the office for Benny and was relieved when Johan responded with an emphatic *"No!"*

Morgan explained, in a tactful way, how and why she purchased a large *ficus* tree—making sure to bring up the fact that she couldn't make it to her usual nursery and the cost was much higher than she intended. Without worry, Johan instructed her to take money from the petty cash to cover the cost of the tree. Then, quickly before Johan insisted that he needed to go, she told him about the two men in suits who appeared to be watching her and George as they brought the tree into the office the night before. She told of how she believed that they had followed her when she left the office and of how she was able to lose them by taking unofficial roads on the Stanford campus.

Johan asked about the car they were driving but Morgan didn't know the makes of cars very well: all she could tell him was that the car was dark and had Jaguar look to it.

"Thank you for telling me this," Johan said with no display of concern.

"Telling you about the men?" she attempted to clarify.

"About everything."

Morgan hoped that Johan would explain the who and why of the two men but wasn't surprised when he offered no explanation.

"Are you going to come to the office and see how you like it?"

"Morgan, I know that I'll like it," then Johan instructed, "Keep the office door locked, same as before."

Morgan rushed to say, "I asked George if I could leave the side door open that opens out to the Buffalo Books office during the day. You know, so they can see what is going on in the office and I can walk right into their office if anything uncomfortable happens like those two men showing up."

"You leave the side door open to the bookstore while you're in the office from now on; that's a good idea." He paused. "That might keep Benny more business-like too. I'll see you when I get to town. Good-bye, Morgan." He hung up before she could respond.

Morgan called to OP and grabbed her purse. As she locked the door behind her, she could hear the phone ringing. She stopped for a second, pondering whether to run in and answer it but OP was already heading down the stairs so she decided to skip answering the phone and continued on her way.

A Bible And A Fly Swatter 1977

Morgan arrived a little after nine o'clock. The staff had already arrived at Buffalo Books, however, they didn't open their doors until ten o'clock. She felt agitated from the get-go and had a bad mood rising. She wasn't sure why she suddenly felt out of sorts. There was no reason to be in a bad mood. She used her key to open the hallway door entrance to the new office and found Benny standing inside.

"Well, you finally arrived," Benny immediately blurted out while OP brushed past him in search of her chew bone and to give the new office a proper Hoovering.

"So, Benny," she took a deep breath, this was a glimpse of things to come and an answer to the root of her bad mood, "how did you get in the office if you weren't issued a key?" she asked, though certain she already knew the answer.

"Through the bookstore," he said, matter-of-factly.

"Okay Benny, here's rule number one: Do not enter the office unless I am here," Morgan said while exhaling. "Mr. Smith is very adamant about his rules and no one, except for Mr. Smith, is to be in this office without me being here."

"Why?"

"You can ask Mr. Smith that question if you like, but I suggest that you don't and you just follow his rules."

Again, Benny asked why.

"My guess it's because he can't be here regularly so to keep things as he wants them—so he has strict rules. Whatever his reasons, Benny, I don't really care; I do as he tells me and no one is to be in this office without me here. Is that going to be a problem for you?"

Benny answered loudly as though responding to a superior in the military, "No Ma'am" then he changed it back down to ask, "Does your dog come with you to the office every day?"

"She's on the payroll, Benny, so you're going to have to get used to it."

"Is she really? Is she a guard dog or something?" he asked in all seriousness.

Morgan lied a response, "Yes, she's a guard dog. She's my protection and Mr. Smith is happy to have her here. I work alone." Morgan added with subdued frustration, "Well, used to.

"I'm here at all times of the day and night depending on what's going on so OP is here with me." She smiled. "Try approaching me fast and see what happens."

All Morgan knew from experience with OP was if Benny quickly approached Morgan OP might look up. Maybe she'd stand up if she thought Benny had something to eat or it was time to go. OP's guard dog abilities had never been tested and Morgan wasn't actually sure what OP would do if she seriously needed protection—it was OP's appearance that Morgan relied upon for protection, but Benny didn't need to know that. She wasn't about to debate with Benny the presence of OP in the office regardless of how he felt: Morgan was already in a foul mood and any kind of discourse about OP would not have a happy ending.

Benny turned away and stood by the window looking out over the back parking lot.

"So, you found your desk alright." Morgan wanted to confirm that the desk he had dropped his jacket on was his.

"This is my desk? Why this desk?" He stepped over to it. "I can't see you with that big tree in the way," he commented further.

Morgan ignored his questions. She walked directly to her desk, which she thought was no doubt obvious to Benny *her desk*, and causally announced that Mr. Smith had called that morning expressing his desire for Benny extend his territory to the East Bay then Morgan got right to business. Once OP found her chew bone, she did several circles then settled down on her bed.

"He wants me to do the East Bay and not Lacey?" Benny questioned.

"It appears so. Do you have the current list of imported wines? If you don't, I have a copy." She hoped that her hint was taken: *Take your wine list and hit the streets. Do not linger about the office, at least not today.* Unfortunately, Benny was typically too hyper and hints bounced off Benny like raindrops on a speeding wiper.

There was a light knock on the door leading into the bookstore. Morgan jumped up to answer. It was George.

"Good morning," he said and nodded to Benny. From behind his back he pulled out a new toy and tossed it across the office to OP who was already wagging her tail at the sight of George. The toy hit the floor with a squeak. OP didn't bother to stand but scooted on her stomach to grab the new toy in her mouth, leaving her glob of a chew bone behind. It had a rather loud squeak with

A Bible And A Fly Swatter 1977

excited OP. She moved the toy around in her mouth with spurts of squeaks until she positioned it just right and every chew produced a squeak.

Morgan smiled. George smiled bigger and left, leaving the door to the bookstore open. Benny walked over to shut it and Morgan quickly and firmly explained that the door was to be left open during working hours: another rule that didn't seem to sit well with Benny.

"Why?" he asked.

"Because Mr. Smith says so," was as far as Morgan was going to explain. She was surprised just how much Benny's presence in the office and his questions were aggravating her. She took several veiled deep breaths to try to calm herself and noticed Benny staring at OP. Two sounds were now coming from the squeak toy—one a high-pitched short squeak as OP bit down and a more muffled elongated sucking-sound of a squeak as OP released. These went from intermittent to consecutive, and, from a bit distracting to quite amusing for Morgan as Benny's visible disapproval and agitation grew.

"Okay, that's about enough of that toy," Benny exclaimed from across the room. Both Morgan and OP ignored him. She saw him out of the corner of her vision crane his neck past the *ficus* tree so that he could make eye contact. Still, she ignored him. After the guard dog introduction, Morgan doubted Benny would approach OP to take the squeak toy away.

Ruth stuck her head through the doorway. "Someone got a new toy," she said with a grin and left. If the toy had been annoying Ruth, then Morgan would have taken it away from OP but Ruth seemed amused so she would let OP squeak it to her heart's desire, hopeful that it would help encourage Benny to be out the door making sales.

It didn't take much longer of the nonstop squeaking before Benny gathered his wine list and a wine box and left the office.

George leaned through the doorway. "Your friend with the little white car is here, here with the boyfriend with the bad teeth."

"Oh, Jackie and Buddy!" Morgan was glad for the news. "Is it okay if I cut through the store's office?"

"Of course." George headed back to work as Morgan made her way to find her friends.

"Hey!" Jackie said with excitement and reached to hug Morgan. Buddy wrapped his bottom lip over his top teeth in a type of smile she hadn't seen from him before.

ZaneDoe

"My office has moved—" she started to explain when Jackie cut in.

"To where?"

"Oh, just down the hall, right next to the bookstore. It's the door next to the hallway entrance to the bookstore," she said. "Come by when you're done here and visit, okay?"

"Okay, we'll see you in a bit.," Jackie confirmed and Morgan rushed behind the counter and back into the new office where OP had abandoned the squeak toy for the jellied chew.

It wasn't long before Jackie and Buddy were knocking on the office door. Morgan was delighted for their company since Jackie's effervescence and Buddy's kind naivete were certain to lighten her mood.

"Oh, I love the big tree. Did you get that at Hassum's?" Jackie asked as she stroked the *ficus* like a pet.

"No, I had to get it pretty quickly so I just went to a local place and thank God I didn't have to pay for it."

"Expensive?"

"Very, but Johan didn't seem to mind."

Buddy was petting OP with more interest than usual and both Morgan and Jackie took notice. Jackie informed that Buddy was planning to get a cat, though she believed he really wanted a dog.

"You're getting a cat, Buddy?" Morgan asked, mostly to include him in the conversation. It made her uncomfortable to be talking about him as though he weren't there, which often happened with Jackie, but before he could answer Jackie chimed in.

"That's why we were at the bookstore. He wanted to get a book on cats," she explained. Just like with the goldfish, Morgan wondered why he needed a book on cats; it was pretty basic—you give them love, food and toys, and a catbox.

"Did you guys find a good book?" Morgan asked, more to Buddy than Jackie.

"Several," Jackie answered.

Buddy still hadn't participated in the conversation.

"Well, guess who I have to share an office with now?" Morgan changed the subject.

"Johan? A new employee?" Jackie guessed.

"*Benny!* Hyper Benny. That's why I got the tree to separate us."

- 160 -

A Bible And A Fly Swatter 1977

"Oh, so that's his desk by the window." Jackie laughed when realizing that the tree created a leafy wall between the two desks. "Will he be here all the time or a lot?"

"God, I hope not. He's like Little Benny Question Box.; he can drive you nuts."

Buddy spoke up. "I think he's a powder freak."

"Yeah, you're not the only one who has made that comment," Morgan responded.

"You mean cocaine?" Jackie asked and both Buddy and Morgan nodded a yes. "I thought he was just sort of neurotic, but he's really friendly, don't you think?"

"I'm used to being in here alone, working alone. It's just going to be odd having him here," Morgan lamented. "I think Mr. Smith plans on him selling over the phone, here in the office; this is going to be a mini-hell for me if he does."

Buddy was staring out the window. "There's a cat, maybe a kitten, in the parking lot," he said with a new energy in his voice.

"I bet it's a stray, Buddy...good chance it needs a home. Do you want to go check it out?" Morgan witnessed a lot of cats and kittens by the Dumpster which she was certain were strays and hoped that Buddy would choose to give one a home.

"It's gone," he replied.

"Let's go look for it..." and Morgan convinced the two to help her search the parking lot for the kitten which ended up with Jackie and Morgan doing the hunting and Buddy standing by the Dumpster looking lost himself. This seemed to be a pattern, others doing and Buddy standing on the sideline: books, television, movies or watching others in real life. Morgan was beginning to believe that Buddy was most comfortable in life as an observer, as one who ponders and plans but seldom does.

"Excuse me." Morgan waved and hollered to Xavier. "Janie's not in her room and she's not in the courtyard." Xavier raised his arm and pointed past Morgan. She turned to see Janie walking from the hallway in her direction. Morgan met her halfway.

"I couldn't find you."

ZaneDoe

"I was daring, young lady. I actually walked out the front door, on my own and without permission." She walked with her usual caution. Morgan followed and sat alongside her on the couch.

"Speaking of escaping, would you like to go to the next event at the veteran's hospital with me?"

Janie placed her hand on Morgan's leg and gave it a light and affectionate squeeze then replied, eyes and mouth smiling, "You and your friends have made me very happy, Morgan...thank you." It was clearly not necessary to ask Janie if she wanted to go; it was a given.

Morgan wished that she could make Aka as happy; he seemed fairly indifferent about most things, Morgan included.

"I'll let them know up front that I'll be here to pick you up if you like. I need to get going. I stopped by to see Aka and to see if you wanted to go on Sunday. There's a delivery coming to the office so I have to be there and need to go."

"You work in the evening?"

"Sometimes. Mr. Smith left a message on my machine at home that a delivery was expected today. It wasn't there when I left so I suspect it's going to be there late. They just leave it at the bookstore for me," Morgan explained. "He doesn't like deliveries sitting outside the door or even to have them left at the bookstore. He likes the boxes safe in the office so I'll just head back."

"That's a long drive for you."

"No, not really. But even if it were, I don't mind. I can't complain," Morgan answered in a hurry then gave Janie a quick hug and was off, only stopping briefly to inform the current staff at the desk that she would be taking Janie on an outing come Sunday.

"You want to come with me?" she asked George though he looked so relaxed she doubted he would get off the couch. His feet were up and a glass of bourbon rested in his hand. Morgan stood at the door waiting for an answer. Then she heard Lorraine's door open and she shot into George's apartment quietly shutting and locking the door behind her.

"What?" George sat upright.

"Just Lorraine," Morgan warned. "*And, your curtains are open.*" Before Lorraine made it to George's living-room window, like two children running from

- 162 -

A Bible And A Fly Swatter 1977

a bully, George and Morgan, with OP right behind, scurried to the closet door and made their way into Morgan's apartment where the curtains were shut tight.

"Do you always keep your kitchen curtains closed?" George whispered.

"I do now."

They could hear Lorraine descending the side stairs by Morgan's apartment.

"She's probably on her way to that store so she'll be back in a few."

"Do you want to go back to the office with me? I have to pick up some delivery and put it in the office. We can go get a bite to eat while were down there." Morgan always enjoyed George's company and tried for his company whenever she could. "Unless you have plans with Anna or something."

"Nah, no plans. Sure I'll go," he replied with a bit of enthusiasm; he was hungry mostly. "So, what's the important delivery?"

"I have no idea—something that Johan doesn't want sitting in the hallway or at the bookstore," she answered then added after observing George's squinting eyes, "He doesn't like packages for the business left outside the office. It's probably expensive wine or something."

"Has he ever opened one of those boxes in front of you?"

"No, but that doesn't mean anything."

"Let's go before Lorraine gets back from the store." They rushed out the front door, raced down the stairs with OP vying for the lead and hopped into the VW Thing. They passed Lorraine as she exited the corner store, bagged bottle in hand.

They talked and laughed the entire ride while OP enjoyed the open air and her audience. She gave an entertaining bark to some children who yelled and waved to her at a stoplight. OP's size often commanded an audience.

The boxes were by the side door inside the bookstore.

"These are far too light, again, to be bottles of highly-guarded expensive wine, my innocent friend," George proclaimed as he helped carry the boxes into the Samuel Pacific Imports office.

"Oh well," was Morgan's only response. She had no desire to engage further in George's speculations.

"George," Ruth hollered into the hallway.

"Yes?" George stepped back so that they could see each other.

"When you get a moment, come see what we just got in." Ruth was excited.

George leaned into the office, "be right back."

Morgan lifted each box to stack out of the way in the corner. They *were* too light to be bottles of anything. They were too light to be literature. There was nothing that she was aware of that Samuel Pacific Imports carried that would take up a box that size and be that lightweight. It was none of her business but it did give credence to George's suspicions.

George walked through the door with a long narrow box.

"What's that?"

"Scrabble," George beamed. "Let's play."

Ruth and John solicited and respected George's input for the store and selling board games was one of George's suggestions. He had also recommended that they set up a table and chairs with a chess set available for customers along with extending the store hours into the evening and having live acoustic music on Friday or Saturday evenings. Morgan had suggested that they serve coffee, tea or wine. The coffee and tea were being taken into consideration. Ruth and John seriously considered all their suggestions.

"Has OP eaten?" Morgan asked before they got too involved in any activity.

"Of course she's eaten." George turned to OP, "Haven't you eaten, girl." And OP let out a loud bark, the way she usually responded to George's questions.

"Okay, then let's play," and Morgan cleared off her desk then grabbed Benny's chair to set on the other side of the desk for George.

"Let the games begin," George announced playfully.

"You know I am only willing to play you because I know you have had at least one glass of bourbon, otherwise forget it. You're knowledge of words is far too advanced for me. I already know that you dumb down your vocabulary when you talk to me." The proclamation amused George and he laughed as he set up the game.

"Who's going to win?" asked John who was holding on to the doorframe and leaning halfway through the door.

"I already know, John," Morgan promptly responded. "George. Without a doubt, George."

"I wouldn't be too sure, Morgan. Have fun guys," and John disappeared back in to the bookstore.

- 164 -

A Bible And A Fly Swatter 1977

George briefly explained the game of Scrabble to Morgan to make sure she understood the rules and they started what would turn into hours of play.

The lights went out and the bookstore closed.

"Urbane?" Morgan had heard the word, or thought she had. "I guess I have to trust you. What does it mean?"

"The opposite of Lorraine," he answered using a common reference point.

"We shouldn't be playing this without a dictionary, George," Morgan complained. "You could make up words and I wouldn't know the difference."

They took a break to bring something to eat back to the office. A little later they took another break. George decided to go for a short walk with OP and he came back with news.

"Johan's buddies are sitting in their car by the park," George announced and OP went back to her bed and back to sleep. Morgan headed for the window to see for herself "You won't see them. They're in the dark. But they'll be able to see you for sure."

"This is getting too weird. I'm tired of this and I'm calling Johan. I don't care how late it is or what time it is in Spain. He needs to know that these guys are hanging around here." She rewound the answering machine tape searching for the last number that Johan left.

"Don't you erase the messages after you listen to them?" George asked.

"No. I don't at home either. I like to keep them."

"For what?"

"You should hear some of my messages at home; they're really funny. I just like to keep them."

George turned on a lamp and turned off the bright overhead lights.

"I found it," and Morgan jotted down the phone number. She called. The number was to a hotel in Spain and Morgan was told that the Smiths have checked out. She knew of no other number to call at the moment.

"Should we just close up and leave?" She asked George, uncertain whether to leave or stay locked in the office until the two men left. It occurred to her that maybe there was something in the office that they were after. "What do they want?"

"Why don't we finish this game and maybe they'll have left by the time we're done."

"Johan wouldn't put me in a dangerous situation."

ZaneDoe

"Well, he lets you have OP in the office...never know."

"What do you mean? You mean you think he let's me have OP in the office because he knows it's dangerous to be here?" Morgan questioned with a bit of irritation. "I doubt it, George. I've had OP here since day one——" She was interrupted by the sound of someone outside the door. She no longer had the sound of footsteps on the stairs to give warning that someone was approaching the office. She looked at George. The doorknob turned. George was twirling a tile in his hand and watching the knob. The door opened and George leaped from his chair.

It was Mr. Smith.

"*Oh my God, Mr. Smith. Oh my God!*" Morgan took a grand inhale while she swung her hand up to her heart. "You scared the hell out of me."

"Why are you here so late?" Mr. Smith commented in a low calm voice, unruffled by the extreme reaction to his presence. He shut the door and walked over to Benny's desk to set his things down. Morgan quickly locked the door. Johan looked around the office. "This looks nice, very nice, Morgan."

"You know George," she said. George lifted his hand as to salute and nodded his head. "We were playing Scrabble. I came to move the delivered packages into the office and we decided to play a board game that Ruth just got in at the bookstore, but Johan, those men are here, *now!*"

"Those two men are sitting in their car across from the parking lot, in the dark," George added curtly. He suspected that Mr. Smith was, intentionally or not, putting Morgan in the middle of some unsavory goings-on.

"That's why I turned the lights out, Mr. Smith," Morgan explained.

"Johan," he once again corrected.

"Johan."

"You saw them?" Mr. Smith asked George.

"Yep. They can see the parking lot, the building, but you can't see them unless you're down on the street," George answered while he began collecting the tiles and putting the game away.

"I was afraid to leave." Morgan hesitated. "I don't know what they want and they just scare me."

"I'm going to pull my car around to the back parking lot. I'd like you to, the two of you, to stay in the office until I get back." It was a soft-spoken order and Mr. Smith waited until Morgan nodded before he left the office, keys in hand.

- 166 -

A Bible And A Fly Swatter 1977

"I can never get these things to fit back in the box right."

Morgan could sense that George was bothered, if not angry.

Johan pulled his car into a very obvious parking space. He took his time exiting his car leaving the car door open while he entered the building from the side door and walked back into the office.

"After I leave, then you lockup okay?" Johan instructed, looking at Morgan directly.

"You mean lock up and go home?" she questioned and Johan confirmed. He put on his jacket, picked up one of the newly delivered boxes, placed his briefcase atop it and left the office out the back door that exited into the parking lot, making himself very visible. Morgan, with George by her side, watched out the window. Johan placed the box on the front passenger's seat, moving at a leisurely pace. He climbed into his car, slowly, then drove out of the parking lot. Morgan and George watched the two men pull out onto the street; their headlights remained off. A few minutes later, while both of the cars were out of sight, they heard the screeching of car tires but had no idea if the sound was related to Johan and the two men.

"Let's lock up and get the fuck outta here like the boss instructed." George spun away from the window. "But...I sure would like to open one of these boxes. How 'bout you?" he said in optimism, pausing alongside the boxes.

"No," she curtly answered and hurried OP out the door.

Morgan was full of speculation on the drive home. George remained fairly quiet but was enjoying her ballad of what-ifs.

"Here, Madame, give me your arm and let me help you into the limo," Morgan played as she assisted Janie onto the high step of the VW Thing.

"And quite a limo it is, my dear." Janie was pleased to be out and about and excited to be on her way to see David. Janie wanted to feel the life around her so Morgan took the top down on the Thing. Janie loved the feel of the wind against her face, her body, and even enjoyed when it rained into the open car. As they pulled away from the front of Sunny Acres, both noticed Alice glaring through the glass doors. Instead of being pleased that a resident was getting away for an enjoyable outing, she looked as though Janie were an escapee.

They weren't far into the ride to the veterans hospital when Janie asked, "Do you believe in God, Morgan?"

ZaneDoe

Morgan gave Janie a quick glance, curious as to the origin of the question then answered, "I didn't used to. I really, really didn't but yes, I do now. At one time I was a diehard atheist, Janie. I loved taking on the opposition too. I'd argue with anybody—anybody: strangers in a restaurant, classmates, family, you name it. I challenged anybody to prove to me that there was a god."

"At such a young age," Janie noted.

"What do you mean?"

"To be an antagonistic atheist at such a young age. What would make you that way?"

"What would make me an atheist? An antagonistic atheist? " She again looked at Janie. "Well, a lot of things but mostly, no one can prove there is a God. At least not that I know of."

"You're not an atheist now?" Janie asked to confirm.

"I'm not, so if you were planning on converting me, Janie, it's too late."

Janie had her eyes partially closed and seemed to be enjoying the wind and sun on her face. Morgan decided to just ask, "So, what brings up this topic?"

"What made you go from an atheist to a believer, Morgan?"

"Sort of a long story. One trip. One trip where I got lost, but it's a long story."

"Can you tell me?"

"Of course, but it might not be that interesting to anyone else but me." Morgan began thinking about the inscrutable series of events that changed her belief and life as they continued their drive in silence.

Janie spoke up, "I would love to hear every detail, if you'd like to share them."

"You really want to know?" Morgan didn't want to bore Janie. "I could give you the short version."

"I would rather hear the long version, and every detail." Janie turned in her seat and looked at Morgan. "Will you take me to the harbor, Morgan."

"The harbor? You mean the harbor in Redwood City?"

"Any harbor; it doesn't matter."

"Sure." Morgan was a little taken aback. "We're early anyways." (It didn't matter how many times Benny corrected her use of the "word" *anyways* Morgan still used it, but now with intention).

- 168 -

A Bible And A Fly Swatter 1977

"I'd love a cup of coffee," Janie informed. Her voice was so calm, so relaxed. So content.

"So would I." Morgan changed lanes on the freeway and headed for the Redwood City harbor where there were sailing boats, houseboats and at least one or two yachts plus an indoor/outdoor café.

Morgan and Janie strolled arm in arm to the outdoor seating of the café.

"Cream in your coffee?" Morgan asked.

"Yes, please. And sugar," Janie answered in a voice that resonated confidence, a calm strength instead of a tempered resentment or frustration so often displayed at Sunny Acres.

"Would you like something to eat? Maybe a donut or something?" Morgan asked. Janie shook her head no. Her focus was on the life around her and she looked so relieved and gratified that it was hard for Morgan to take her eyes off Janie.

Morgan watched Janie as she waited at the counter for the coffees. Seeing Janie with David was seeing her in a completely different light but this again was a Janie she had not witnessed before. She looked so comfortable, like she belonged, that she was in her element and as though when they finished their coffee, Janie would wave good-bye as she walked back to her houseboat—not back to the confines of a rest home. It felt particularly wrong to Morgan to take her back to Sunny Acres when seeing her like this.

"Your coffees," the server said for the third time.

"Oh, sorry." Morgan's mind was on Janie. "Thank you." She balanced the very full coffee cups in one hand as she grabbed onto the railing carefully descended the stairs to the outdoor tables.

Without saying anything, she placed the coffees on the table. Morgan was sitting with a longtime friend who she regularly had coffee with at the harbor, that's what it felt like. Together, in silence, they breathed in the bay air, watched and listened to both boats and birds. In due time Janie insisted Morgan tell the story of her conversion, from beginning to end. Morgan still didn't know why Janie wanted to hear this particular story but she would certainly share it with her friend if she cared to listen.

"Well, to start with, how does someone prove the existence of God anyways. If you believe, I guess there's a turning point from where one accepts on faith and one truly knows. You know what I mean?" Morgan looked at Janie who was staring out at the swaying boats on the water.

ZaneDoe

"Go on, I'm listening." Janie's eyes were taking in the beauty about her while she listened to Morgan's journey from believer to atheist and back again. "Okay, it was way out in the mountains outside of Monterey...."

Morgan was baptized Catholic, attended public elementary school and faithfully went to catechism every Tuesday. She made her first communion and by age twelve was confirmed. She went to confession at least once a month and to church every Sunday as required, doily pinned atop of her head and all—she did her religious duties willingly.

Morgan's mother decided to send her to parochial high school. She didn't mind catechism, *surely it was the same*, so she had no objection. It wasn't long before the gaping difference between attending catechism one day a week and attending an all-girls school ruled by nuns became alarmingly obvious. The oversized blue plaid wool skirt, the bland white blouse with every button tightly fastened, the skinny blue sweater with the tiny and shiny pearl buttons and the huge white shoes was the uniform that caused ulcerous embarrassment at the ego-tender age of fourteen. She ran to and from school via the creek route to avoid being seen by former classmates from the public school, which in turn caused Morgan to be fined by the hall patrol on a regular basis for having dirt on what were supposed to be perpetually white shoes—shoes that were referred to as "clodhoppers."

By mid year Morgan was a constant figure in detention—unsolicited classroom questions from a curious mind only added to her time. She was even required to come in on numerous Saturdays to pick weeds and haul garbage to satisfy further punitive requirements. Morgan was near burned at the stake for her choice of outfits on "Free Dress Day," something that would have hardly been noticed at a public school. Morgan was having a very difficult time and she never adjusted to the sting of the ruler whether on her skin or that of a classmate's.

For Morgan, the nuns had altogether lost any angelic qualities she had previously attributed to them and became dictators in black robes. They disappointed and angered her and Morgan soon took pleasure in playing the devil's advocate in more ways than one. Mostly, she fearlessly debated their religious teachings and the frustrated and flustered nuns excused her from the classroom, prolonging her detention duties.

- 170 -

A Bible And A Fly Swatter 1977

By year's end, Morgan's mother was informed that it would be best for all concerned to *not* enroll Morgan back at Holy Cross High School come the next year. Morgan returned to public school. However, she fiercely maintained her campaign against theology. She would take on any religion and anyone willing (and some not so willing) who would engage the topic. She thoroughly enjoyed the bravado of the debate of an existence of a god and felt herself articulate and confident in her steadfast position. She doubted that she shook anybody's religious foundation but she knew that no one could sway her belief that there was undeniably a lack of any profound proof that a god existed. Her mantra: *"God? Prove it!"* And, nobody could. *"I win."*

Shortly after graduation, Morgan was invited to join some friends on a backpacking trip. Though she had never taken on such an adventure before, Morgan enthusiastically accepted. She would have no idea until it was too late just how inadequately prepared she was in most every way for such an outing. In her naivete, Morgan was ready and eager when her friends showed up. For all to see, she proudly tossed her well-packed backpack into the van. Possibly believing that Morgan was no tenderfoot, no one spoke up to inform Morgan that her outdated canvass backpack and flannel lined sleeping bag were sub-standard backpacking gear at best.

It was a long winding drive through the back roads of a mountainous area unfamiliar to Morgan. Eventually Rich pulled the van over and everyone piled out, put on their backpacks and headed off leaving the vehicle locked and parked on the side of the road. Like a trail of ants, with Morgan lagging behind, they walked a little over a mile on the serpentine road until they reached a very steep, tree-filled mountainside. This was "the shortcut," according to Chris. Morgan felt like she was stepping onto an inevitable avalanche but she obediently followed.

They all grabbed onto the skinny trees slanting upward which helped stop them from a tailspin to the bottom though still sliding most of the way down. When they all finally hit bottom, relatively unscathed, Morgan assumed that their ultimate destination would either be at the bottom of the decline or close by. Much to her dismay, they continued to hike. They were now in an area with snow. She was having a hard time keeping up but had the company of Lee's dog, Roger. Roger would run off the path to sniff and investigate but always returned. It was getting colder and Morgan worried that Roger's short hair wouldn't keep him warm in such weather.

- 171 -

They ultimately reached an area that the others deemed the campsite. Morgan didn't find anything special about the area to warrant the miles or to even repute it a desirable campsite. She tossed her pack onto the ground and plopped atop to rest. To her amazement, the others set out to do more hiking and some fishing. Morgan was beat and stayed behind at the camp, as did Roger. While she rested and tried to warm her feet, Roger chewed a log into a twig.

By nightfall Morgan was freezing cold with a flurry of light snow only added to her misery. No one had a tent where she could take refuge and unlike the others, she didn't have the warm down-filled sleeping bag or the "space blanket" or the foam mat or the special socks nor any of the other wise-outdoor gear designated for such conditions that her campmates were savvy enough to possess. Morgan had the outdated camping gear she borrowed from her mother. The sleeping bag was lined with flannel and had pictures of happy deer jumping over logs and was meant for inside a tent in summer conditions. She recalled sleeping in that very same sleeping bag as a child.

Morgan was freezing and from the looks of it, so was Roger. He was curled up on a blanket under some low branches and looked to be shaking from her vantagepoint. She called him over. He hesitated at first, as if it were too cold to even get up, but eventually obeyed. Morgan unzipped her sleeping bag and coaxed Roger to cover. Even with Roger curled up next to her, she could not get warm or anywhere near it. Morgan was too cold to sleep, and if shaking meant that Roger was awake, then he wasn't sleeping either. She lay awake through the night, freezing, angry and determined to leave the next morning.

At the first stirring of the others, Morgan made her announcement that she was leaving. She informed Lee that Roger had slept in her sleeping bag with her and that he shook most of the night. She felt it was best that Roger go back with her. If they gave her the keys to the van, she would take him home with her and be back to pick them up whatever day they wanted her to return. The others tried to convince Morgan to stay and expressed their concern about her ability to find her way back through the mountains and to the road where the van was parked. And, if she could, would she be able to find her way out and back to the same spot to pick them up.

Morgan blew off their concerns and assured them that she could find her way both to the car and back to the road to pick them up. Rich finally acquiesced and tossed her the keys to the van wherein Morgan promptly rolled up her rather heavy sleeping bag as tight as possible, attached it to her backpack

A Bible And A Fly Swatter 1977

and hoisted it onto her back. She called to Roger, who followed without delay as though eager to leave himself and they were off as the others watched in partial disbelief.

She started out confidant in her direction but after a lengthy hike and numerous path choices, Morgan was unsure she was heading in the correct direction. The snow had covered traits of their trek in to camp. She could follow her own tracks back to the campsite but not only was that quite a distance, she had no desire to spend another night in the freezing cold, nor did she want Roger to suffer the same fate. With Roger continually racing off in different directions, always returning to wherever she may be, she continued on though growing more tired, and frustrated, and more sure that she had strayed from the original route in.

Quite unexpectedly, she walked into the path of a wild boar—a cute outdoor pig this was not! With the size of that boar, they had little chance if it decided to attack. Morgan quickly grabbed Roger's collar to turn his head away from the boar, hoping to keep Roger from barking or showing any sign of aggression to prevent a confrontation. She held onto Roger and froze in place. Fortunately, the boar chose to trot off in another direction. With Morgan's adrenaline inspired renewed strength, she began hiking at full speed.

The snow was getting deeper making the trek far more strenuous and convincing Morgan that she was definitely heading in the wrong direction. She was relieved to eventually see what appeared to be a cabin in the distance. Morgan changed directions and headed toward the cabin where she hoped to find help or at least directions to a main road. After slogging through the heavy snow for what seemed like an eternity, she finally got close enough to see that what looked like a cabin from a distance was in fact a rundown shack. Directly outside the door, stretched between two trees, was the furless skin of what she presumed was a rather large animal though its shape resembled too much that of a human. Pulling Roger alongside her, Morgan did double time back to the cover of the forest, hoping that she had gone unnoticed. Once back in the woods, she kept her pace until her fatigued body could go no farther. With Roger by her side, she sat down to rest.

Periodically, Morgan could hear gunfire in the distance. The encounter with the boar led her to believe that she was hearing shots from boar hunters. At times the gunshots seemed too close for comfort and Morgan would call out for fear that she or Roger might be mistaken for game and become some hunter's accidental target. No one answered her calls, just more gunfire.

Daylight was rapidly leaving and Morgan had no flashlight which meant that she would have to try to find her way in the dark if she couldn't find the main road and her way out quickly. The backpack and sleeping bag felt off-centered and progressively heavier to the point that she wanted to dump it; leave it behind, but she couldn't.

Morgan resorted to counting her steps one at a time to keep going. She would count out fifty steps then stop to rest. She was exhausted and getting colder and more frightened as time passed. Accepting that she was lost, Morgan decided to surrender her inept sense of direction to the better sense of the dog. Morgan followed Roger's lead. Though he took excursions up the side of a hill to chase a squirrel or to sniff a rock, Roger acted as if he knew the way. She realized too late that she should have followed him all along. He led her to the base of where the group slid down on their journey in—the "shortcut." Morgan recognized it right away, there was no question that it was the same place. It was so steep that the narrow trees grew out of its side at a forty-five degree angle. It looked as though a tremendous wind had blown them upward and that's how they remained. To climb to the top seemed a daunting prospect, an almost unattainable task, particularly in her weakened state, but it was the only way she knew to get to the road where the van was parked.

Roger immediately started up the slope at an angle. Morgan followed, sliding down two steps for every three. To make any progress, she had to grab on to one of the narrow trees, pull herself up, wedge her foot into the V at the base of the tree, (clutching with all her strength to hold herself and her backpack in place) then step back out onto the loose dirt and do her best to make it to another tree. She would need to repeat this process up the entire mountain side.

She hadn't gotten far when her arms began to quiver. Morgan's whole body was aching and her legs felt stiff and heavy. She took a good look upward at the distance she would need to cover in order to reach the road and honestly doubted that she would be able to accomplish the task but she continued nonetheless. Morgan grabbed on to and straddled another skinny tree.

A couple more trees and Morgan needed to rest. To accommodate the small space, she had to remove the backpack. She bent forward as far as she could and was able, though difficult to maneuver in such a tight space, to remove it. As she pulled the backpack to the front, she lost her grip. Quickly

A Bible And A Fly Swatter 1977

out of reach, she watched the backpack tumble down the near vertical terrain landing at the base where she had started her climb. The backpack not only contained her food, water, clothing and money, but also the keys to the van. Morgan knew, without a doubt, that she did not have the strength to make the descent to retrieve her backpack then restart the climb. She questioned whether she could even make it to the top from where she sat.

Roger was now struggling to make headway in the loose soil. He was sliding backward and sideways and Morgan couldn't reach him to help.

In tears and frustration she said aloud, *"God, please help me. Get us out of here!"*

Morgan tried to stop her useless crying but for those few minutes, she couldn't.

Again she pleaded, *"God, please, help me!"* Not thinking about or remembering for those few moments, that there was no proof of a God, and she knew it.

Morgan wiped her tears. "There's no *God.*"

With a deep breath, she prepared to continue her laborious climb. She looked up and around to locate Roger but she couldn't see him; it was now dark. She called out to him feeling guilty for insisting that Roger go with her—if he was hurt, it was her fault. Morgan gathered her strength, pulled herself up and stepped back onto the mountainside in reach of another tree. Again, she would pull herself up, rest against the tree, then step onto the unstable ground sliding back, digging her boots into the soft dirt to hoist her tired body to the next available tree where she would steady herself at its base. It looked as though this climb would take all night.

Morgan had only progressed a short distance when Roger began barking. She yelled to Roger and tried to hurry the task of pulling herself from tree to tree, but she couldn't go any faster. As she lifted her head in search of the closest tree she could make no sense of what she saw—no sense at all. She stood grasping onto the same skinny tree, confused. She looked down from where she had climbed. This was beyond reason or logic: Morgan wasn't at the first quarter of this near insurmountable climb any longer; she was at the top, just below Roger who was standing on the edge of the road barking down at her. Where she was irrefutably not even close to being half the way up this long, very steep obstacle of a climb, she was now only a few yards from the top.

Morgan dug her boots into the loose dirt and with newly gained strength pulled herself up by several trees and was onto the road. She lay there with her legs half dangling over the edge, both baffled and elated. It was but a few minutes staring up at the stars trying to make sense of what just happened when she was interrupted by another extraordinary occurrence. An old red truck came easing its way up the narrow dirt road. Morgan sat up and reached for Roger's collar as the truck slowly came to a stop beside them.

"You need a ride?" came a gentle voice from the open window of the driver's side . Morgan stood up, holding on to Roger's collar and just stared at the priest behind the wheel of the old truck.

"Can my dog ride also?" she asked, still stunned.

The priest smiled. "Of course."

Morgan needed that ride—she was weak from fatigue; it was dark and she had no idea just how far the van actually was.

Roger hopped onto the bed of the truck while she climbed onto the passenger's seat . The cab was warm and comfortable and the priest's smile was more than welcoming; it was almost familiar. She explained her situation as they slowly made their way down the bumpy dirt road until they came upon the van parked on the side. The priest pulled up alongside the van and Morgan climbed out of the truck.

"Perhaps you'll find a spare key in the wheel well," he said, composed and calm and generous in a way Morgan couldn't explain.

"I'll check." Hidden in a magnetic holder tucked up in the wheel well was a spare key just as he suggested. The van started right up and Morgan followed the red truck through and out of the mountains to a main road where the truck disappeared.

"God? Prove it." He did.

Janie waited a few seconds to make sure that Morgan's story was complete. When Morgan looked directly at her she then asked, "Did you know that there is a monastery out that way?"

"No, I didn't. I didn't think there was anything out there." Morgan heard and saw no activity during her time in those mountains other than the hunters' gunshots.

"I'm sure that's where your priest came from." Janie then asked, "Did you believe, or do you believe, that God sent the priest?"

"Yes and even more so, how did I get from near the bottom of that mountain to the top," Morgan answered. "I didn't climb it. There is no other explanation and, even more than anything, Janie, the feelings that came over me, well, that was my proof. I can't explain it in any way that anyone will understand. I just know. It wasn't me who got me out of there."

Janie took another sip of coffee.

"Are you hungry?" Morgan asked.

"I'm fine, Morgan. Just fine." And Janie did look just fine. Happy. Comfortable and at peace.

"Did you tell your friends what happened?" Janie inquired.

"No way; I haven't told anybody this. I mean, no one cares anyways but I can't prove it so why say anything."

"So this was your path back to God?"

"Yeah, or His path for me," Morgan answered then asked, "Do you believe there is a God or something around you?"

Janie donned a huge grin and added, "Well, look who I bed next to!" And with that arcane bit of fact both snickered to a full-blown laugh. They laughed like two schoolgirls not caring about the attention their boisterous laughter was drawing.

It began to sprinkle. Before continuing on to the hospital, Janie and Morgan took a walk around the harbor.

"Can I ask about the entertainment?"

"I think it's a slide show of Buddy's trip to Hawaii, or something like that. I know that not as many people will be there today since George, Randy and the nutcase, you know, Lorraine——-"

"The tall lady with the sort of red hair?" Janie questioned.

"'Sort of red,'" Morgan laughed. "That's a good way of putting it. Yeah, she's our apartment manager if you can believe that."

"The men seem to like her." Janie was always observant.

"Well, if they only have to deal with her for a short time every now and then she's probably an entertaining curiosity but try living next to her...." And Morgan gave Janie a summary of what she and George dealt with on a regular basis, which of course, had Janie taken aback with a burst of a giggle here and there.

Much to Morgan's shock, Lorraine *was* there. She was floating around the common room among the men as though hosting her own party. Anna informed Morgan that the men found Lorraine entertaining and that Lorraine showed up on her own via a taxicab. She even brought pastries.

"But how did she know that the event was taking place?" Morgan inquired with anguish.

"Now, that I don't know."

"There's David, Morgan," Janie interrupted. They let the topic of Lorraine rest and continued on with the day's event. It was hard not to notice how animated and cheerful Lorraine was throughout the event. Though her physical presentation was the usual garish display, Lorraine's behavior could be viewed as close to normal.

Anna and Morgan discussed plans for a special reunion for Janie and David. They conjectured up scenarios that would be pleasing to both Janie and David.

"The beach," Morgan suggested to Anna. "The beach, like in Hawaii where they met."

"Well, I can care for David outside of this place but there's no way he could be absent and it would go unnoticed. I'd have to do some heavy bribing."

They sat on Anna's desk in silence and thought.

"There has to be a way, Anna."

"If you think of one, let me know. I'm up to giving anything workable a try."

The sound of loud music played in the background as they sat upon Anna's desk brainstorming.

"They're alive, Morgan. They're finally alive," Anna uttered in one of the sweetest voices Morgan had ever heard from Anna. She looked at Anna's face and realized the nurse who initially appeared so indifferent to the men in Building D was anything but. Morgan supposed her nonchalant manner was how she coped and saved her own heart while keeping her job.

"I can't help but wonder about the other buildings, Anna," Morgan responded.

"I know." She shook her head. "But we can't push it; at least not now. For now, Morgan, let's just focus on what we got going here."

"You're right, you're right...okay, let's figure this reunion out...."

"Don't bother getting here before me, Benny," she said with a sense of torture as she unlocked the office door. "John or Ruth aren't going to let you in the other door either. I told you that I would be here at 9:30 and you shouldn't expect me to be here any earlier than that."

"I think an office should be open before 9:30," Benny responded and he followed her through the door.

"Not in this business." Morgan put her purse down on the desk. "Have you ever called in an order before noon?

"I have to go get OP."

"You're going home already to get your dog?" Benny asked with obvious disapproval.

"No, she's at the park with George, across the street."

"Oh, okay."

"And, Benny, if I needed to leave to go get OP somewhere, I'd go.

"So Benny, what you are going to be doing in the office since what you do, or what your job is, is selling wine to businesses door to door so to speak." She waited at the doorway for an answer.

"It saves me time and effort to do some calling first. . . ." Benny's explanation was as widespread as usual and expected. He answered more than what was asked. She listened politely. Nothing he said that he needed to do in the office he couldn't do at home. She excused herself and hurried off to retrieve OP.

Benny was making calls while Morgan was answering calls. Morgan wanted so badly to give OP the squeak toy while Benny was in the office but he was making business calls so she limited OP to the gooey chew.

And so went the workdays at the Samuel Pacific Imports office. Benny often tried to engage Morgan in conversation or to get her to chime in on a topic of interest to *him* but she became good at appearing too busy to chat, even if she was talking to a dial tone.

While pretending to be occupied with Samuel Pacific Imports paperwork as Benny repeatedly craned his head past the *ficus* tree to see if she was still busy, it came to Morgan that she had access to the beach house. Simon may not like it, but too bad. She had a place at the beach where she could take Janie and David. The idea ignited sparks and Morgan was on a mission.

"You're pretty busy over there," commented Benny. "You making us all rich?"

"Actually, I think Lacey is making us rich; these are her orders."

Benny's face shifted. Morgan tried not to smile. She looked back down at the piece of paper that had a song Jackie had written on it.

"So, her sales are up?"

- 179 -

ZaneDoe

"They're always pretty good but she's been hitting more restaurants lately and having some pretty good success with it."

"What restaurants?"

"Ones in her territory, Benny," she answered.

Benny grabbed the phonebook, looked through it for about fifteen minutes. "I'm going to take this with me," he said then, much to Morgan's relief, was on his way out of the office with phonebook in hand.

"Jackie, this is Morgan."

"I know it's you, Morgan," she said per usual, but saying "This is Morgan" was habit for Morgan so it wasn't going to change.

"How good are you at acting? Can you be put in a tense situation and act your way out of it or through it?"

"Yes, yes. You know me; I love it. What do you want me to do?" Jackie was excited at the prospect; it was a form of drama so right down Jackie's alley.

Morgan finished her conversation with the more-than-willing Jackie then called Anna to reveal her well thought-out plan.

"I don't think we even have anything like that, Morgan," Anna said after listening to Morgan's detailed plan.

"Then how do the men leave the hospital?"

"You know, I don't know. I can't say that I have ever seen it, at least not with the old men," Anna answered in earnest.

They agreed to meet after work to discuss the matter further, both wanting George's input. Morgan believed her perspicacious plan would no doubt work without much, if any, problem. *Who kept tabs on these men?* Other than the nurses, it appeared to Morgan that no one knew whether they were there or not there, awake or asleep, dead or alive. She knew her plan would work—at least at that hospital.

Chapter II
The Escape

"Hi. Yes, I'm here to pick up David Mundt," Jackie said to the stone-faced nurse's assistant. "I have the paperwork right here." She placed the filled-out form that Anna and Morgan contrived onto the desk. "What's your name?"

"My name's Deborah," she answered as she picked up the paper.

"Dee Bore Ah?" Jackie enunciated.

"Yes, not Deb Or Ah. It's pronounced Dee Bore Ah," she insisted. "Everybody gets it wrong and I hate when people call me the name *Debbie*."

"I think Dee Bore Ah is nice, unique," Jackie responded, eager to get on with the plan and to avoid conflict of any kind. "Is David ready?"

"Wouldn't Anna take care of that?" Deborah said with a touch of annoyance.

"Oh, well I spoke to Anna and she said that David would be ready so if you could point me to his room I'll go ahead and get him and be on my way," Jackie quickly said in one breath.

Deborah walked Jackie almost to the door of David's room. She stopped just short, pointed, then turned and walked away. Jackie watched Deborah disappear around the corner before she popped her head through the doorway. David was in his wheelchair, hookah in place and a bag that was to suffice for a suitcase on his lap.

"Hi David." And with a gigantic smile Jackie added, "I'm here to steal you away. Now remember, I'm your great-niece Jackie." It failed to register with Jackie that it didn't matter. Not only was no one going to question David, they couldn't understand him even if they did. "Are you ready?"

David labored to lift his chin in acknowledgement. He was more than ready. Jackie grabbed onto the handles of the wheelchair and they were off, at a speed not necessary but for Jackie it was. She struggled, smashing and banging not only herself but the wheelchair as she tried to get out the heavy front doors. Once out, "It's a beautiful day isn't it?" Jackie exclaimed and Jackie continued to talk not noticing David's tears. "Morgan and Anna, oh and George, are waiting for you around the corner. They parked on the other side of the building. ..."

George borrowed Rusty's VW bus—the perfect getaway vehicle in every way. It not only had enough room to accommodate David's wheelchair, but Rusty had a portable ramp which he used to load his equipment into the van and that ramp made easy access for David's wheelchair. He had palm fronds Hawaiian print material for the seat cushions in rich browns and greens. Parts of the interior were covered with an actual bamboo material—all professionally done, and a custom interior that only added to the ambiance of the excursion.

There was an excitement in the air. David was hurried into the van. George hopped onto the driver's seat, Jackie onto the passenger's seat and Anna sat in the back next to David.

"You can light up if you like," George offered loudly to David.

"Do you want a cigarette?" Anna asked.

David's head moved in such a way that was not a common nod of a no but Anna understood what it meant. Anna had placed David's necessities in the van's closet, secured his wheelchair against the side and they were off—not at the speed they would have liked but at the best speed the VW bus could offer.

"Just don't pay attention, Grandpa," Morgan hurriedly instructed. "Don't even look her way." Alice was by the front window. Morgan arrived at Sunny Acres early when the place was the busiest intentionally. She had arranged to take Aka and Janie for the weekend. Janie had two sisters who were her caretakers of sorts but due to the fact that Janie held the purse strings, Janie was still in charge, at least where she could be. All seemed to be in order but one never knew with Alice at the helm.

"Let's get on our way," added Janie. She too was worried about the Alice factor.

"Are you kidnapping me again, Mokana?" Aka said in jest and turned to look at Janie, though she had no idea what he was referring to other than a pleasant wisecrack.

Janie and Aka sat on the backseats and Morgan stacked their weekend bags on the front seat. She had the top down as Janie preferred but this time she brought several blankets in case it got cold as they crossed through the mountains to the coast. Morgan saw Alice heading toward the front door and she backed the car up, turned the radio on at full volume and took off out of

A Bible And A Fly Swatter 1977

the parking lot so there was no way for Alice to catch up nor for them to hear her. They were off. Noting the sluggishness of the VW bus, they timed it so that Morgan would arrive well before George.

Morgan turned the radio down once she was away from Sunny Acres but it was difficult to talk with Janie and Aka from the driver's seat so Aka and Janie talked with each other and Morgan turned the radio back up.

It was a beautiful warm day. Janie and Aka didn't use the cover of the blankets until they reached the chill of the fog when approaching the coast. The smell of the sea intensified and was delightful as they drove down the road and pulled up to the front of the beach house. The driveway was exceptionally steep and Morgan felt it would be difficult for Aka and Janie to exit the car at that grade. She hopped out of the car and quickly ran to the side of the garage to peer through the window for Simon's car. It wasn't there.

"Hold on," Morgan instructed. "I'm going to go inside and open the garage then pull in there so you guys can get out there. I'll be right back."

Morgan took the key from under the flowerpot. The house was damp with a chill. She flipped the thermostat up then hurried to the inside door leading to the garage. Morgan pushed the button to the garage door opener and as the door wobbled its way along the track she raced back out the front door. She carefully backed the VW Thing into the garage and left the door open so George could see it when he arrived.

"It's a bit chilly in the house but it'll warm up quickly," Morgan said as she helped Janie and Aka out of the car. "We can make a fire in the fireplace and that'll help warm the place up."

"Aye," came a shout from across the street. It was Steve. Steve was in his mid twenties and still lived with his parents, but who could blame him—a house on the beach rent-free. Steve had very little interest in anything in life but surfing though he didn't have the look and carriage of a typical surfer: His hair was black; he slouched, was thin and didn't don the typical healthy outdoor or rustic ambiance of most surfers. He had an attitude and manner as if everything in life bored him and most everything was an effort, even normal conversation.

"Hi Steve," Morgan shouted back with a quick wave then continued on into the house with Janie and Aka. The beach house was a multi-level structure. The garage was on the middle level. Stairs led down to a lower level which was still up from the yard with an extended deck. Rather steep stairs led to an

- 183 -

upper level where the kitchen, dining room, living room and a large deck were located. There were stairs that led from that level up to the master bedroom which also had an enclosed deck facing the ocean.

"Let me help you," she said and reached under Janie's arm. Janie held onto the railing and the two slowly and carefully made their way up the stairs. Morgan intended on going right back down the stairs to help Aka but discovered him on their heels as they reached the top. "I would have helped you, Grandpa!"

"I don't need your help, Mokana. Now move."

Morgan assisted Janie to the living room, which was a couple of steps up from the dining room. Janie relaxed down into the comfortable couch situated across from the fireplace. Aka headed straight for the sliding glass doors leading out to the back deck. He began fiddling with the lock trying to figure out how to open the door. Since the wood for the fireplace was stacked on the back deck, Morgan used it as an excuse to open the door for Aka without appearing to be giving him any kind of aid. Aka walked strait for the railing. He stood looking out over the golf course, looking from side to side, breathing deep and saying nothing. Morgan grabbed a couple pieces of firewood and waited, but it looked as though Aka preferred to be left where he was, to be left alone. Morgan went back into the house, sliding the screen door shut behind her.

She had the fireplace ablaze in no time and the warmth was quickly permeating the living room. Morgan and Janie sat and chatted while waiting for George and the others to arrive. In the back of Morgan's mind was the makeup of the house and how she would arrange the sleeping and maneuvering of all concerned particularly with David and his wheelchair—all the special needs of each guest. Morgan hadn't given it much thought prior. All Morgan wanted was to get them to the beach house, the details were something she'd worry about later. That later had arrived.

George pulled up to the front of the house and parked on the street. Morgan ran down the stairs when she heard the comic beep of the VW bus. She saw Steve watching the arrival as he was doing something with a bicycle wheel on his front porch.

"Give me instructions," George said as he rounded the bus.

Anna opened the sliding door and hopped down.

"Hey David," Morgan said with joy. "You made it." She turned to George and Anna. "We have two sets of stairs but we can manage," she said with an

A Bible And A Fly Swatter 1977

optimistic grin. Jackie finally exited the passengers seat. She was gathering her belongings and looked like an encumbered tourist. She looked at Morgan with a self-satisfied and happy face—she had pulled it off just as she had promised. Morgan leaned in to give Jackie a hug and whispered, "Good job and thank you."

Anna gathered up belongings while George attached the ramp to get David out of the bus.

"Aahhm hurh," David said as his chair slowing descended the ramp.

"Yes, and it's going to be fun, David," Morgan responded. "Janie's in the house, and so is Aka, my grandfather. You'll like him."

Steve was now standing on the walkway off his porch so as to get a better look, not at the scene but a better look at Jackie and Jackie took notice. George carefully rolled the wheelchair down the steep driveway with the help of Anna and into the garage. It was no problem lifting the chair through the door but the stairs leading to the living room and Janie were another story. Even David acknowledged with his eyes the obstacle before them.

"We can lift the chair and push," Morgan suggested. She watched Anna and George exchange looks of doubt. "I'll get Steve to help."

"Who's Steve," asked Anna.

"He's a neighbor. He's out front," she answered briskly then turned to exit through the garage door where Jackie stood listening.

"The guy in his front yard?" Jackie asked, referring to the dark-haired guy with whom she had been exchanging glances.

"Yeah. We need some added muscle here."

Jackie immediately put her things down and demanded, "You stay here; I'll go get him." And Jackie jogged out of the garage and up the driveway before Morgan could disagree or question her. Morgan watched through the garage window as Steve walked across his lawn to greet Jackie. He not only nodded a yes to Jackie but the typically sluggardly Steve moved at a pace Morgan had not seen previously. The two cantered back to the house with Steve ready to help. Morgan watched Jackie as Jackie stood staring at Steve while he helped transport David in his wheelchair up the steep stairs to the waiting Janie. Morgan recognized that look in Jackie's eyes.

"Let's just get the chair up those few steps to the living room," Morgan instructed and with ease George and Steve moved the wheelchair up the few steps. Janie bent down, lifted David's hand and kissed it. Morgan opened the drapes on both sides of the living room giving view to treetops and the dewy groomed lawns of the golf course. She peeked out onto the back deck to check on Aka. He was sitting in a chair taking in the view.

"Is Aka here?" asked Jackie

"Yeah, he's on the back deck. Let's go say hi," Morgan answered and suggested.

"Grandpa," Morgan said in a low voice. He seemed to be in his own world. "Jackie is here to say hi." She stepped out onto the deck. Jackie followed. So did Steve. "You remember Jackie, right?"

Aka turned in his chair looking up with a somewhat bothered expression on his face. He only glanced at Jackie then looked at Steve. "Who's this?" Aka asked while fixing his eyes on Steve. Morgan and Jackie turned to look at Steve, both curious why Aka focused in on Steve immediately. Steve just stood there, looking bored as usual.

"This is our neighbor, Mom's neighbor, Steve." Morgan stepped aside giving a full view of Steve. "Steve this is my grandfather, Aka." Steve only nodded his head and with effort lifted his hand in a sedate greeting. There was silence as Aka continued to look at Steve as though he were some kind of oddity—Morgan would agree. Morgan quickly added, "Grandpa, Steve surfs." Then she turned to Steve and said in a near whisper, "Aka was a well-know surfer long ago, you know, when surfboards were huge and made of wood—-" she stopped. She was going to add a little of his Hawaiian origins but when she saw Steve's face come to life she stopped. He walked past Morgan and Jackie then reached his hand out to shake Aka's hand. Aka didn't reciprocate. He just turned in his chair back to facing the golf course. Undaunted, Steve pulled a chair up next to Aka, facing the chair toward the golf course, and sat down. The two sat in their chairs staring out in the same direction, as though Morgan and Jackie were no longer there. Morgan looked over at Jackie who looked like she was about to laugh as she observed the silent two in their chairs. Morgan shrugged and she and Jackie went back into the house to join the others.

"The Senator Hotel, I think. Hotel Street," Janie laughed. David's head bobbed and out came a string of sounds directed at Janie making the joy on her face from laughter even brighter. "Oh yes, the bull pens." She patted his hand, still laughing.

"Bull pens?" Morgan questioned as she, with Jackie following behind, stepped up to the living room to join them. "Don't tell me you were a bull fighter too," she joked.

- 186 -

A Bible And A Fly Swatter 1977

"Oh no, dear, this was a different sort of bull pen," Janie answered with a grin and looked back at David as though "bull pen" was an inside joke. Morgan dropped the subject.

"Are you hungry?" Morgan asked.

"Are you hungry?" Janie asked David in response and again indistinguishable sounds came from David to Janie. She looked up at Morgan standing by the fireplace. "Yes, we're a bit hungry, Morgan. I can help you."

"No, Janie. You stay there. Anything you guys want in particular?" she asked while glancing for Anna. She didn't know what David could or couldn't have to eat. She didn't recall seeing David eat before.

Janie asked David what he wanted "for lunch" while Morgan asked Jackie if she knew where George and Anna were.

"You surprise us," Janie said.

"I'll see what's here and if there isn't anything good I'll take a quick drive down to Piggy's Market."

"Piggy's Market?" Jackie questioned.

"Oh, wait till you taste their cookies, piggy cookies. I'm going to have to go pick some up," Morgan declared with a grin and left the living room to find Anna and George. They were on the lower level of the house standing on the bottom deck.

"Anna," Morgan interrupted. "I'm going to make lunch but I don't know what David can or can't eat," she whispered.

"Man, this place is nice," George interjected. "I could live here."

"I'm going to go to Piggy's Market to pick some stuff up for lunch and dinner and so on. Do you want to come and show me what to get?" she asked Anna.

"Get whatever you want. David's food just needs to be cut up into small pieces or he can do softer foods easy like Jell-O," Anna answered.

"Anna," Morgan added, "what about, you know, going to the bathroom and stuff. I don't know any of that for David. I never even thought about it. Should—-"

Anna quickly interrupted, "Well I have. Don't worry about it, Morgan. It's my job. I'll take care of it."

"There are several bedrooms on the bottom floor and one bathroom and upstairs there's a master bedroom with a larger bathroom. Would the master bedroom be best for David?"

- 187 -

Anna reached over and hugged Morgan and Morgan wasn't sure why.

"The bedroom upstairs might be best. More privacy I would imagine," Anna said.

"Okay, it's yours. Or David's."

Jackie stepped up to the sliding doors next to Morgan.

"Well, we're going to go to Piggy's. Do you guys want to come?" Morgan asked but she saw that they were happy kicked-back on the deck and said, "Okay, never mind. See ya in a bit."

Morgan ran upstairs to ask Aka if there was anything that he wanted from the store, remembering that he didn't have teeth. She didn't want to bring up his new favorite food, baby food, in front of his company, Steve. And, wasn't sure if he would be comfortable eating baby food in the presence of the others. But, Aka turned with no reserve and requested, "Get me that food in a jar, Mokana. And, bananas. And pudding. Can you get me pudding?"

"Of course, Grandpa," she answered. "Anything else?"

"Ice cream," he added.

"What kind?"

"All kinds," Aka answered with a smile then turned back to face the golf course. He and Steve were now sitting with their feet up against the railing, which looked much more comfortable for Steve than Aka. Morgan didn't ask Steve if he wanted anything from the store. She wouldn't have gotten it anyway. Morgan wasn't all that fond of Steve, in fact, she and Simon referred to Steve as The Sloth in a not so affectionate way. She looked over to the next-door neighbor's house, surprised that Claire hadn't made an appearance on her same-level deck to see who these strangers were.

Claire lost her only son in the Vietnam War and since that tragedy she didn't leave the house very often but was very aware of the goings-on around the sanctity of her home. Simon had ingratiated himself into Claire's life, not so much out of the kindness of his heart but to make sure that she didn't find complaint with him and his parties. It also made him look all the more the resident, the good neighbor and the owner of the beachside abode.

"You wanna go with me?" Morgan asked Jackie naturally assuming that she would say yes, but she didn't. Jackie chose to stay at the house, which surprised Morgan. As she descended the stairs, Morgan hollered to George and Anna to ask if they wanted anything special. They didn't want anything , ex-

A Bible And A Fly Swatter 1977

cept maybe to be left alone. Morgan grabbed a jacket and took off in the VW Thing by herself.

She had a few memories stirred as she made her way down the winding road to Piggy's Market. It was a fine line whether they were actually good or not, but past romances were like that and she just let the emotional notes play.

Piggy's Market had the usual one or two cars parked in front. The old small store with its rustic wood exterior looked like a hobbit's house. It gave the appearance that it had been hollowed out of the trunk of a huge redwood tree. Tall trees surrounded and loomed over it almost hiding the little store from public view, but the locals were faithful and if Piggy's sold nothing but cigarettes and Piggy cookies the market would survive.

"It's been a long time, Morgan," commented the clerk and owner, Mike. "Are you here visiting Simon?"

"Hi Mike," she answered a bit annoyed at his presumption that the beach house was Simon's. "Nooooo, not visiting Simon. Simon actually doesn't live here, Mike, but he does come stay at our mother's beach house a lot, it seems. Actually, I'm here with some friends for the weekend. And," she continued, "I'm here to pick up dinner, and lots of Piggy cookies of course." She then proceeded on her way to search for edibles to suit everyone at the house, everyone but Steve who she hoped would be gone by the time she got back.

Mike brought out a fresh batch of piggy cookies and yelled across the store, "How many did you want, Morgan?"

With her arms full, Morgan turned and yelled back, "Two dozen if you have that many, Mike."

"We don't have the big fancy grocery carts, Morgan, but we have baskets. Why don't you use a basket. No charge." Mike grabbed a handbasket and carried it over to Morgan. She placed the items huddled in her arms into the basket which filled it. "I'll take this to the counter. Come get another basket, Morgan," Mike insisted. With a smile he added, "Come get two or three and fill 'em all up."

"Do you have two dozen piggy cookies?" Morgan asked as she scanned the available baby foods in jars.

"You bet."

Morgan retrieved another basket, filled it and as Mike suggested, filled a third handbasket.

"I'm done, Mike."

"Be right there." Mike hurried to the counter. They chatted as he checked the items through he register. "Lots of napkins and baby food. I know what that means. Yours?"

Morgan grinned. "No, no baby for this girl. OP is enough for now."

"So where's that horse?"

"She's staying at a friend's back home. He has a swimming pool so OP is in waterdog heaven."

Mike helped carry the groceries to Morgan's car, making the same comment as he had twenty times before: "The Nazis would be pissed to see that you paint their car yellow. Don't wanna piss off the Nazis do you, Morgan?" At first Morgan had no idea what he was talking about, in fact, she took offense to the remark. She thought he was implying that she had some affiliation with Nazis. But Mike always said it lighthearted as though some kind of joke yet Morgan was at a loss. She would smile and flip off a comment, not really getting Mike's meaning. That was until Simon informed her that her VW Thing had its birth as a Nazi vehicle during WWII. She hated the thought, but loved the vehicle.

"That's exactly why I painted it yellow, Mike, to piss off the Nazis," she answered as they mutually smiled and she pulled out of the parking space. Mike waved and disappeared into his hobbit-house market.

Morgan got everything from baby food to eggs to pumpkin pie. She believed she had purchased enough to last the weekend. Morgan knew with Anna, Jackie and George they'd come up with meals to please everyone.

As she drove back to the house, Simon came to mind. She had given him clear warning that she was planning a weekend with friends at the beach house. She didn't know if he considerately made himself absent for the weekend or if he was just out and would be coming back to an unexpected full house. The latter was the most likely. Simon functioned in an air of entitlement which often made him selfish and rude and Morgan wanted to make sure that he didn't make anyone feel unwanted or uncomfortable. She wanted to confront him before he even entered the house and had the chance to make anyone feel as though they were trespassing on his territory. As she pulled up to the steep driveway she saw that she was too late. Simon's car was in the garage.

Morgan parked in front of Claire's house and rushed in carrying only one bag of groceries. There at the top of the stairs, standing in the dining room, was Simon looking indignant which immediately sparked anger in Morgan. She reached the top of the stairs. No one was talking. Per usual, Simon was able to change a happy gregarious atmosphere to uncomfortable, fraught with tension. Morgan placed the groceries on the dining-room table while smiling at everyone.

"This is my brother, Simon," she said in the most upbeat manner possible. "I take it you have made introductions and have met already." Morgan took a deep breath and in a cheery voice asked George if he could get the remainder of the groceries out of the car. George jumped up and Anna accompanied him.

Simon said nothing. He glared at Morgan then turned and walked up the stairs to the master bedroom. His displeasure was obvious to all, all but Aka who was still on the back deck staring out over the golf course. In a buoyant and merry manner Morgan emptied the grocery bag and put the items away, trying her best to not display to the others that she was affected by Simon. When she finished putting the groceries away, she sprinted up the stairs to the master bedroom. Fortunately, the door was unlocked.

Morgan closed the door behind her and approached Simon who was standing on the front deck to the master bedroom. He turned immediately when he heard Morgan and was heading straight at her with his mouth open ready to speak his mind of which Morgan couldn't have cared less. She stepped out onto the deck and closed the sliding door behind her to try her best to make sure no one in the house would hear them.

"Who are these people?" Simon asked with his entire face furrowed with displeasure. "You get them from some institute or something." Simon thought himself biting but with wit and humor. Simon was only negative and self-centered.

"Do you mean the people in the living room?" Morgan questioned with refrain.

"Yeah, and the old guy on the deck," Simon responded in peeve.

Morgan shook her head. "The 'old guy on the deck' is Grandpa, *your* grandfather, Simon. That's Aka. You don't even recognize your own grandfather. Or doesn't he have enough to offer for you to bother with him."

Simon glared straight at her, turned away but quickly turned back. "What are they *doing here?*"

"The same thing you're doing here, Simon. They're enjoying Mom's beach house." Morgan could feel herself winding up and she was ready to hit

ZaneDoe

him with several poignant facts if he were not compliant and gracious to her guests.

"Well Morgan, too bad," he said looking directly at her like a dog trying to establish dominance and he proceeded to inform her that he was planning for company that evening and they would have to either go or stay down stairs while he entertained. "This was already arranged and I'm not changing my plans."

Morgan's heart was racing. At first, she could say nothing. She felt like crying. Not because Simon hurt her feelings or that he was unduly cold—she was used to that—but because she didn't want anything ruining this weekend, this holiday, this event for Janie, David and Aka. And because it was hurtful to feel love for someone so selfish as her brother. She could only stare at Simon, at first with nothing to say; she was stymied in emotion but when Simon attempted to pass her to go back into the house Morgan snapped to. Righteously bellicose and thinking clearly.

"You need to get your things and leave, Simon. You need to walk out of here politely and not come back until Monday. Take your company and go elsewhere or I'm going to have to have a talk with Grandma Killington because I am sure she still wonders what happened to her cat, the cat she loved so much. You know, the one that you weren't so fond of."

"What are you talking about, Morgan." Simon looked uncomfortable; he knew exactly what she was talking about.

"Oh, and that emergency money hidden in her house," she reminded. Morgan caught Simon taking money that their grandmother had hidden in case of an emergency. He claimed to Morgan that she wouldn't notice it gone because he was going to put it back right away. He promised that he was only borrowing it briefly and assured Morgan that he would replace it shortly—as he made a quick exit. "Maybe I should remind her too that you still owe her three-thousand dollars for those supposed car repairs while in Portland. Then there is the college money. And since you basically weren't even attending college," Morgan grinned. Simon had taken one art class, which he never finished, at a community college—a college that was basically free.

"Or maybe I should let Mom know. Mom wouldn't be too happy to know that you borrowed money from Grandma *for college* and never paid her back." She gave Simon a steady stare to make sure that he knew that she wasn't playing around. Morgan rarely confronted Simon even when she wholly disagreed

A Bible And A Fly Swatter 1977

with him or his actions. She wanted to keep the peace. And, it would only hurt Grandma Killington if she knew Simon's lies. He borrowed money from Grandma Killington more than once and to the best of Morgan's knowledge he had yet to pay any of it back. When it came to free or easy money Simon had few scruples, and he would cross the line without hesitation only rationalization. But Simon cleaned up nicely and few suspected his unconscionable soul.

Simon stood there saying nothing, a bit in shock. Morgan had never done this to him before. Morgan believed he was deciding whether she would actually expose his past acts which would without a doubt cause turmoil with Simon and the family.

"You're so full of shit, Morgan." He said it as if he were doubting his own claim. Morgan could see that Simon was uncertain and worried.

"You're not going to ruin this weekend, Simon. You don't know how much it took and how much it means for this weekend to happen, and happen smoothly. I'm not going to let anyone or anything ruin this weekend. I don't care if you hate me from now through eternity. You're not ruining this weekend, Simon."

Simon turned his back to Morgan.

"You leave us to our planned weekend, Simon, and I'll shut up. And if you don't, then, believe me, I won't." They stood there in silence until Simon turned around.

"You're really a bitch, Morgan," he said in a low voice.

"Oh, you haven't seen 'bitch,' Simon. You wanna see 'bitch' then go out there and be an asshole and you'll see beyond 'bitch.' I know your scams and the bullshit you pull on people and if you think I don't, you're naïve—not me. I've always stepped back and kept silent, whether I should have or not but if you do anything to fuck up this weekend, Simon, trust me I'll make sure you're sorry. In fact, I'll make sure I come stay at *Mom's*" beach house on a regular basis, friends, dog and all."

Simon looked around, as if he were thinking, making a decision. To Morgan there was no decision. If he didn't leave, she would pull more pressure out of the bag. Simon looked at her and seemed to know it.

"Okay, okay. I'll go. But leave my stuff alone."

Morgan stepped aside and Simon slid the glass door open to the bedroom. He gathered up a few things from the closet and bathroom then headed for the bedroom door, stopping with his hand on the door handle. "I'll be back on Monday, Monday night."

"Why don't you say hello to Grandpa before you leave," Morgan suggested.

"Is that request backed by another threat?" he quipped.

"No; it just would be a nice thing for you to do. You don't even visit him at the rest home."

Simon grinned. "That's right." He opened the door and walked down both sets of stairs exiting through the garage door. Not a word to anyone. Morgan heard his car back up the driveway and race off down the street. She took in a huge breath, held it, then exhaled slowly to calm herself, shook her whole body as if shaking off the Simon-encounter and made her way down the stairs to join the others.

Lunch consisted of a small snack for everyone. No one was very hungry. Steve planted himself next to Aka and seemed to have no intention of leaving, though he was much more pleasant than Morgan had ever recalled. Periodically, she would peak out the window to see if Aka and Steve were conversing but it appeared not, though it didn't seem that Aka minded Steve's bland company. They sat on the deck in apparent silence while everyone else gathered by the fire and socialized—talking, sharing stories and laughing. David's eccentric laugh was pure joy, to everyone, but especially to Morgan.

Eventually Anna needed to care to the needs of David, excusing them both with the help of George and Steve in getting David up the stairs to the master bedroom. Conversations continued with Morgan proudly telling the story of how she adopted OP which sparked her need to give Rusty a call to check on OP.

After dinner Jackie felt the need to help Steve carry the empty salad bowl back to his house—she was gone for over an hour. Morgan was cleaning up the kitchen and chatting with Janie who was leisurely sitting in a chair by the counter. George took a walk on the golf course with Anna. David was taking a nap in the master bedroom.

Jackie popped through the door full of enthusiasm.

"Don't tell me, you did most of the talking," Morgan commented; she couldn't imagine Steve carrying on a two-way conversation for an entire hour. Jackie just laughed and inquired about David's whereabouts.

"He's taking a nap."

A Bible And A Fly Swatter 1977

"Oh, that's good," and Jackie smiled at Janie.

"Steve's not good for much, at least in my opinion, but his added muscle power with David's chair sure helped." Lifting David in his wheelchair up any of the stairs turned out to be more difficult than anticipated and Steve's assistance was almost a necessity.

"Do you want me to go get him so he can come back and help with David's chair again?" Jackie asked with a sense of delight that was a bit too blatant for Morgan.

"Well, don't get too excited, Jackie—Bride of Buddy," Morgan gibed. "We're going to have dessert upstairs on the front deck so David doesn't have to go back down the stairs then up again, at least for tonight. We can hangout on the deck for the evening." She turned to Janie. "There's a freestanding fireplace on the deck; I should get a fire going in it."

"That would be lovely, Morgan." Janie's voice was calm yet filled with emotion and life. She was so much a part of everything taking place, not a sedate-being on the sidelines. It was a constant reminder to Morgan how she didn't want to take Janie back to Sunny Acres. It was hard to believe that Janie had only been a part of her life for a very short time. She felt so close to Janie and their serendipitous meeting brought about a relationship that went beyond just friends. Janie was like family to Morgan. Seeing Janie this relaxed and happy meant the world to Morgan. She looked back over at Jackie.

"Maybe Steve would be willing to come back tomorrow and help."

"What time?" Jackie asked in an instant.

"What time what?"

"What time do you want Steve to be here to help?" Jackie clarified.

Morgan laughed, shook her head and looked at Janie then joked, "Another notch on your Guatemalan belt?"

"What?" Jackie didn't get the joke. She sensed Morgan was flinging a dig her way but she didn't understand it. Jackie was fond of wearing peasant blouses, she found them to be a casual sexy and her leather Guatemalan belt always accompanied a peasant blouse. "I don't get it."

"What time do you think you want to get up, Janie? When do you think everyone will want to be up?" Morgan asked.

"Well, Morgan, what will we be doing tomorrow?"

"Anything you want, actually"

"I'll leave all of that up to you, dear."

ZaneDoe

"I think about nine and we'll be ready to head out somewhere, sound good?" Morgan queried.

"That sounds like a good time; you know us old-timers tend to get up early," Janie responded while Jackie looked on, eager to make contact with Steve again.

"Okay then ask Steve if he'll drop by tomorrow around nine to help out." Jackie headed down the stairs like a dog chasing a ball.

"Whataya think Janie?" Morgan lifted her eyebrows at Janie and Janie smiled back.

"She's not married, is she?" Janie asked.

"No. I think I introduced her boyfriend to you. Maybe not. Oh well." And the subject was changed.

As soon as Anna announced that David was ready, Morgan grabbed some newspaper and wood from the back deck and headed to the upper deck to get a fire going. David was already on the master bedroom deck waiting for the others. Anna had taken the liberty to borrow one of Simon's sweaters and it looked quite handsome on David; she combed his hair differently as well. With insufficient muscle control, David's facial expression didn't vary much, but somehow, David looked decidedly different. He no longer looked the prisoner of his chair as he sat on the deck waiting for the others to gather.

Aka, Anna, George, Jackie and Janie made their way to the deck to join them with Janie proudly sitting by David's side. As others fed themselves their choice of ice cream, Janie fed David his. Morgan offered coffee and George offered wine. Wine it was. At first Morgan worried if it was okay for David to have wine, but when Anna voiced no objection she didn't give it another thought. All David needed was a straw and Anna brought plenty.

Morgan noticed Jackie repeatedly looking over in the direction of Steve's house. She knew Jackie didn't like to be without a man but thought she could go two or three days. She didn't see what Jackie saw in The Sloth; he was the epitome of boring in Morgan's eyes.

"Morgan," Jackie said to get her attention. "Aka and Steve talked about surfing."

"Yeah, Mokana. That boy is going to take me surfing tomorrow," Aka announced.

Morgan and Jackie locked eyes in mutual worried surprise.

A Bible And A Fly Swatter 1977

"Surfing, Grandpa? You mean you're going to watch him surf or you're going to go surfing too?"

"Yeah," Aka answered then dug back into his ice cream.

"Would anybody like more ice cream?" Morgan asked. Aka immediately lifted his bowl while the others declined. Morgan grabbed his near empty bowl and nodded for Jackie to follow her. Once in the kitchen she turned to Jackie with wide-eyes and her mouth agape.

"Don't worry, Morgan; I'll go with them," Jackie said in haste. "I'll make sure everything is okay."

"Jackie, let me get you Steve's number and call him and ask him what the hell he's doing. Aka will do it. Aka will surf and he'll probably drown." Morgan shook her head in frustration. "That's crazy. Call him and ask him what he's up to." Morgan found Steve's phone number and asked Jackie to use the downstairs phone. "When you find out then tell me in private. Obviously Aka wants to go." In farce she added in a sweet voice, "*I'm sorry Mom, I took Grandpa to the beach house and drowned him.*"

Morgan brought Aka his bowl of ice cream and sat back down with the others. The fire was going well and giving off just the right amount of heat. It was a beautiful night and the smell of the Pacific Ocean added to the ambiance and stirred memories for most, separate but beautiful.

George was mindful to keep David's hookah replenished. Soon Jackie rejoined them looking pleased, which Morgan knew was brought on by her telephone call and put Morgan's worries to rest for the moment. They sat on the deck and talked, telling stories and jokes. Aka loved the jokes, whether very funny or not, which had both George and Jackie firing off jokes at record speed. Morgan couldn't stop watching David, and as she saw him now, it was hard to imagine him back in that hospital. She didn't want to take him back there nor take Janie back to Sunny Acres.

Eventually the topic of what to do the next day was broached. Each looked to Morgan to set the plans. She wanted this weekend and was determined to make it happen but she really didn't invest in a plan beyond getting David, Aka and Janie away from their respective homes.

"Let me think," she said. A ride through the mountains came to mind and she was sure that David and Janie would enjoy it. She was pretty sure that Aka had his mind and will set on surfing since he announced "I'm going surf-

ZaneDoe

ing" several times. Each time he said it Morgan cringed inside having yet to talk to Jackie to see what the "surfing" was actually all about.

"Okay, Aka, we'll all go surfing tomorrow," George joyfully chimed.

Morgan looked around to see the others' response. David raised his chin as though he was all for the idea. She noticed a rather large chocolate ice cream stain on the front of Simon's sweater, Simon's purchased-to-impress sweater. She would hand wash the stained area, not for Simon but for David. She fully intended on giving David the sweater; it looked so debonair and fitting on him.

Morgan looked at each person sitting on the deck and a feeling rushed through her that about brought her to tears. She deeply cherished each one and each for different reasons. She once heard Mike from Piggy's Market yell out to a customer, "You can't always pick your family but you can always pick your friends." She had picked her friends well.

Morgan made her way up the stairs stepping on the rim of her mother's bathrobe every other step. It was too long but cozy all the same. She wanted to get the coffee started so it would be ready when everyone awoke but Anna, George and Aka were already on the deck, already sipping hot coffee as golfers chatted, shouted and swore below them. She poured herself a cup and joined them on the deck.

"Where's Janie and David?" she wondered aloud.

"In their room," George answered.

"I'm going to go in and help David get ready in a bit," Anna contributed.

Morgan was so pleased that David and Janie had so much private time together and wanted to comment on the fact but not in front of Aka.

"I'm going surfing, Mokana," Aka stated. No good morning or how are you, just reassurance that he was indeed going surfing. Jackie already informed Morgan that Steve and Aka had a mutually exhilarating exchange of surfing stories which naturally ended in their mutual craving to go surfing. According to Jackie, Aka's experience was the issue for Steve, not his age. Steve didn't see Aka as having *been* a surfer but *as* a surfer. She said that Steve claimed Aka asked him several times about the surfing at the local beach, the beach right down the road and so close to the house, and Steve offered to take him so he could see for himself. Morgan wasn't sure what to make of it but since all were willing to join Aka and Steve at the beach, she felt they could keep the excursion safe

- 198 -

A Bible And A Fly Swatter 1977

for Aka. He was going, there was no stopping him so she could only respect Aka's determination.

"I know, Grandpa." Then she asked, "Does Steve have a wetsuit for you, Grandpa? The water's not warm here like in Hawaii." Aka didn't answer but George whispered, "Good point." Morgan waited for Aka to address the wetsuit issue but he continued to sip his coffee and said nothing. She decided to call Steve, or ask Jackie to.

"Well, I'll make pancakes with bananas and walnuts if that sounds good to everyone," Morgan declared as she got up to leave the deck.

"That sounds great," Anna responded. "Do you want help?"

"No, I can handle it but are banana pancakes okay for David?" Morgan asked and Anna smiled and nodded yes.

Before starting breakfast, Morgan went back downstairs to find Jackie. No Jackie. She darted up the stairs to inquire with Anna and George and was told by George, "Check out front." She did. There was Jackie sitting under a tree with Steve, talking. Jackie talking and Steve looking like a sloth taking an undeserved nap. Morgan made sure that her robe was closed properly before approaching the two to ask Steve about a wetsuit for Aka.

"I have an extra," Steve said with effort.

"Yeah Steve, but look at your size and look at Aka. Are you going to cut the legs off so they'll fit?" she asked, annoyed by Steve's lethargic attitude."

Steve actually chuckled then responded, "It'll fit."

She felt it a waste to continue the topic with Steve and would have to trust that he knew what he was doing. She had no other choice. This might be Aka's last chance to ever surf again in his life and she wasn't going to ruin it for him. Morgan informed them that she was making banana pancakes if they were interested then headed back to the house. Midway she remembered that they would need Steve's help getting David down the stairs so she turned around and yelled, "Don't forget to stick around Steve; we really need your help with the wheelchair." She waited for a response. It took a minute but Steve waved his hand in acknowledgement and Morgan continued on to make breakfast.

Careful, careful, careful Morgan repeatedly thought to herself as George and Steve maneuvered David down the stairs. George had backed the bus down the steep driveway into the garage. With the ramp in place, it took but a minute to roll David into the bus and they were ready to go. Janie and Anna climbed into the bus after David and George hopped onto the driver's seat. Steve left for home with Jackie in tow. He would load up his vehicle and meet them at the beach. Aka rode with Morgan in the VW Thing.

"I wish OP was here with us, Grandpa," Morgan said. "She loves the beach; she loves the water."

"Why isn't she here, Mokana?"

"There wasn't room in the cars."

"Well, okay, we bring her next time," Aka said.

Morgan beamed with gratification. She smiled from the inside out and confirmed, "Yeah, next time." She was delighted that Aka looked to a "next time."

Aka was living his dream, and he wasn't drowning. David, with his hookah, was a hit with the few locals who gathered to take on the waves or bask in the sun. The very un-athletic Jackie unabashedly stripped down to her bikini and attempted to ride the waves, with absolutely no success but she impressed Steve—which Morgan believed was the impetus for the attempt at surfing in the first place. Janie strolled at the corner of the water with Morgan, letting her feet feel the surf as David looked on. George and Anna had time to themselves—sitting on the rocks letting the ocean spray and cool them. Morgan was exultant. The only thing missing to make the day perfection was OP, but like Aka said, "Next time."

Steve helped George lift David in his chair up to the master bedroom. Anna followed to attend to David. Steve left for home to take a shower, promising that he would return to share a meal with everyone and again help transport David. Aka wanted to soak in a hot bath so June rushed to shower first.

Morgan whispered, "Do you think you could help Aka?" to George.

"From what I've seen so far, don't think he's going to let me help him with a bath," George responded, accurately.

"Yeah, that's probably true."

"If he can take on the Pacific I'm sure he can take on a tub," George added.

"Guess so," Morgan agreed then made the sign of the cross.

A Bible And A Fly Swatter 1977

"Hey Morgan," Anna called down from the slightly opened door of the master bedroom.

"Yes?"

"There are some nice shirts——-" before she could finish Morgan yelled back.

"Take whichever one you want. Take two, three. Sweater, shirt, whatever you want. Please do, take 'em."

"There is a great hat——"

Again, before she could finish Morgan responded, "It's David's."

"Thank you," Anna said cheerfully and closed the door.

George and Morgan began pulling food from the refrigerator and cupboards.

"Buffet style?" George asked.

"Sounds good to me."

"I don't think Anna is too fond of your brother Simon," George commented as they prepared the table which they had managed to lift up the stairs and over the railing to the living room. Morgan wanted the ambiance of a fire going in the fireplace and to have the panoramic views the living-room windows offered.

"I don't blame her," Morgan quickly acknowledged. "Simon's full of himself. He doesn't do for anyone unless he's getting something out of it. Most people don't see that until they've dealt with him for a while. He turns on the contrived charm and plays people. Most people don't pick up on it because he doesn't have that...you know, that handsome sort of playboy look to him. He comes off initially as so non-threatening so people don't have their guard up. Anna's perceptive." She turned to look George directly in the eyes. "Seriously, I wouldn't put much of anything past Simon. No one wants to think that way about their own brother but...I already know he's capable of some pretty cold-hearted crap, stuff I don't even like to repeat." Then she smiled at George. "But I would have if he didn't leave."

"So, he'll be real happy about his clothes disappearing." George laughed.

"I always kept my mouth shut about Simon, George. Always. I never said anything to *anyone*. He knew that and counted on it. But now, well, that's over after his shitty behavior in front of David and Janie. He pushes me and I'm pushing back but I've got the big guns. He had nothing on me but I have more than he cares to know on him." She took a deep breath, held it then relaxed.

- 201 -

"He didn't even take a second to say hello to his own grandfather. I'm done with him, George. Done with him. He plays others, now I'll play him."

George grinned.

"David'll be leaving here with some new duds, and that's great," Morgan said with an even bigger grin than George.

"Duds?" George mimicked and the subject changed while they prepared the lunch buffet, which included a variety of baby foods for Aka..

"Oh, George," Morgan said excitedly, "we should *roast marshmallows*."

"In the fireplace?"

"Yeah. I'll run down and get some after lunch."

"More like an early dinner than lunch, Morgan," George observed.

"Since when did you get picky about the title of a meal?"

"You...or we, are sort of sporadic about eating, ya know," George said with a more serious tone. "But I'm sure Janie and David, and even Aka are used to eating at particular times."

"Oh God, you're right. I didn't even think of that," she said with wide-eyed guilt.

"Probably doesn't matter much under the circumstances—they're having a great time—but something to keep in mind, maybe." George added, "Don't worry about it; this might be a welcome change. I should have kept my observation to myself."

"Yeah right, like that will ever happen."

Aka came up the stairs with his hair still wet. He combed his hair straight back, something Morgan hadn't seen before. It was flattering on him. Perhaps that's how he combed his hair back in his surfing days. He was wearing the same pants and shirt. Morgan thought that he had a change of clothes in his bag but maybe not.

"Grandpa?"

"That's me," he perked.

"If you need another shirt we have plenty...here, at the house. I can get you one," Morgan offered.

"You have plenty of shirts?" Aka questioned, wondering why there would be an abundance of shirts at the beach house. He didn't see Simon during his brief scowling appearance and had no idea that Simon was living there.

"Would you like one?" she asked enthusiastically. "Nice, clean, ironed." She could hear George chuckling in the background.

A Bible And A Fly Swatter 1977

"Okay, Mokana. Get me a nice clean shirt," Aka said and headed through the kitchen to the back deck to take chosen seat.

Morgan tapped on the door to the master bedroom. "May I come in?"

Anna opened the door. "Yes, of course. We are ready for lunch now."

"I need a shirt for Aka," Morgan informed with a smile and headed to the closet. She emerged with two IZOD tennis shirts that had never seen a court—a blue one and a white one.

"I'm going to see what color he likes." Morgan trotted down the stairs and out to the deck. Aka liked them both but wanted to wear the white one.

"Here, go ahead and put this one on and I'll fold the other one up and put it on your bed," she said. "They're yours, Grandpa."

Steve arrived in the arm of Jackie. They ascended the stairs as though heading to the altar.

"Great. Good timing," Morgan announced when she saw Steve. "David's ready."

George and Steve were getting the hang of it and it seemed less of a chore getting David's wheelchair down the steps this time. They lifted him up the several steps to the living room where Janie greeted David first with a glorious smile then a hug. David looked dapper in his crisp Ivy League shirt, pullover sweater and stylish fedora—it made his usual dark trousers look appropriate and part of his style instead of issued. George pushed David to the table where Janie immediately went about helping him with his selections. Janie was responding to David, to his elongated and tortured syllables unrecognizable as words to most but that now seemed as ordinary as listening to someone speaking another language. By Janie's remarks Morgan could tell that they were discussing his new clothing, the hat in particular. Evidently, David wore such a hat at the time Janie knew him during their shared past. Morgan still wasn't sure if the past they shared was one of romance but whatever it was it was deeply meaningful to both.

Jackie called out to Aka for lunch. He proudly walked through the door and up the stairs to the living room, grabbed a plate and filled it with an array of soft foods. With his hair slicked back, a gleam in his eyes and a white shirt that accentuated his brown skin, Aka once again looked the Hawaiian man. The Hawaiian surfer, strong and proud—not the toothless, listless aging man lying in bed with a book propped up before him, or escaping his surroundings in sleep.

ZaneDoe

With everyone taking a seat and their plates filled, they waited for Morgan to say something. "Let's eat" perhaps. Morgan really didn't have anything to say but she looked at them individually then from the heart came, "I am so happy to have all of you here with me." Even the man of inertia, Steve, the individual she previously found so annoying was a positive and integral part of the success of this joyous day.

"Cards?" Morgan responded to George's suggestion. "Yes, perfect; let's play cards. Whataya think?" She scanned the faces of approval.

Anna and Jackie cleared the table as Morgan tried to find a deck of cards in the house. There were none, at least none that she could find.

"I'll go next door and ask Claire," she announced then raced down the stairs. Surely Steve would have a deck of cards at his house but Morgan could borrow a deck from Claire before Steve made it across the street. She was enjoying his contribution to the day but Steve still remained a devoted sloth.

"Hi," Morgan said. Claire stood at the open door, smiling. Claire looked tired and lost, but that is how she appeared every time Morgan encountered her so Morgan didn't give it much note. She was never unkempt. Though she rarely left the house, Claire still had her hair done at that salon once a week, along with her nails. She had a husband but Morgan never saw him, or traces of him.

"Hello Morgan," Claire said. "Would you like to come in?" and she stepped away from the door to allow Morgan passage.

"Thank you" Morgan said as she stepped through the door. "How are you, Claire?"

"I'm fine, just fine and you?" Before Morgan could answer Claire commented, "I see that you have company this weekend. Simon must be enjoying the company."

"Yeah, I have some friends over for the weekend. In fact, not just friends but my grandfather is here too for the weekend. We wanted to play cards but I can't find any so I wondered if you had a deck we could borrow."

"Oh, of course I have cards, somewhere around here." Claire stepped over to the cabinet by the kitchen and opened a drawer. "Do you play Bridge, Morgan?" She shuffled a few things around then pulled out an unopened deck of cards.

"No. My mother plays it. I think we're going to play poker."

"Simon must be happy to have you both here visiting." Claire spoke with such sweet innocence. She truly didn't know the real Simon. She had no idea that the beach house was not actually Simon's honest residence.

"Well, Claire, not really," Morgan raised her eyebrows and said in a pleasant voice while hiding her aggravation with Simon's misleading and self-serving image. She decided against saying anymore, instead, she dropped the subject of Simon and made an effort to convince Claire to come over to join the card game and have coffee and desert. At first Claire resisted but Morgan remained casually adamant.

"I'd love for you to meet my grandfather; he's Mom's dad. I know she'd love for you to meet him." Morgan knew that wasn't true but it sounded good and added a bit of neighborly pressure. Claire couldn't say that she wasn't dressed appropriately to go out because she was always dressed as if she were expecting company or ready to go out. "Please?" Morgan begged, "Pretty please?"

"Can I bring something?" Claire asked, her voice had a surprisingly cheerful quality to it. "I have a pineapple upside-down cake. Can I bring it over, Morgan?"

The cake wasn't needed, in fact Morgan had no idea what an "upside-down cake" was but to refuse the cake would put a shadow on Claire's social efforts.

"That would be great, thank you. I'm sure everyone will love it." Claire handed Morgan the playing cards. "I'm going to get the table set up so come on over as soon as you can, or if you're ready now just come with me."

"I'll be right over, Morgan; you go ahead."

Morgan headed for the door. "You don't need to knock, just come right in."

She raced across the yard and dashed up the stairs. Morgan wanted to get the table set up and also wanted to fill the others in regarding Claire. She wanted them to know that Claire coming for a visit was a rarity and therefore truly a special occasion and it was important that Claire feel comfortable. Morgan briefly added that Claire was rather reclusive since the loss of her son in Vietnam. There was a short silence after the information about Claire was disclosed.

They went about getting another chair for the table and the dishes and silverware set up for desert. As Morgan was getting things in order she wondered what kind of relationship, if any, Claire had with Steve. She decided to go downstairs and out front to meet up with Steve and Jackie before they came

ZaneDoe

back in the house. She wanted to let Jackie know about Claire but also wanted to find out if Steve had any conflicts with Claire, though a conflict would take effort so it could be beyond Steve's scope of activities. Claire definitely took precedence over Steve in Morgan's eyes so she needed to know.

They approached, Jackie all smiles.

"Steve, quick question for you," Morgan said. And, he said nothing back. "You get along with our neighbor Claire right?"

"Yeah," he answered.

"Excellent." Morgan looked at Jackie. "Claire is going to play cards with us. She rarely goes out of her house so this is pretty special and I want to make sure that she has a really good time."

"Of course, of course," Jackie quickly responded.

Morgan whispered to Jackie, "She lost her son in the Vietnam War," as they walked on to the house. "She basically has become a recluse since then so coming over is sort of a big deal, but I don't want to make a big deal out of it, I just really want her to feel comfortable. She's never come over before…."

Playing cards ended up being even more fun than Morgan had expected and lasted longer than anyone expected.

The entire weekend went beautifully and Morgan got to know Aka like never before. The return back to Sunny Acres and the hospital was not sad as Morgan had anticipated. The return was lively and felt like it was the beginning not the end of their adventures and time away together.

Chapter 12
Surrounded in Photography

"You pay to pray," George questioned with his usual sarcastic tone.

"I guess," Morgan replied while adding water to OP's kibble. "You lit a candle and then kneeled down in front of the candles and said your pray. There were ten-cent candles and dollar candles."

"What was the difference, besides the price?"

"The ten-cent candles were small and the dollar candles were big," she answered.

"So. . ." George started.

"Hold on." Morgan yelled through the closet doors again for OP to come from George's apartment. "OP, come on. Time to eat."

OP barreled through the closet knocking the vacuum cleaner aside like it was a light-weight broom.

"There's my girl." George patted OP on her thick black coat as she rushed out of the closet door to her food bowl.

"This is how I believed it worked when I was little," Morgan took a deep breath, knowing George was going to be critical, and proceeded to explain, "if you lit a ten-cent candle then an angel would listen to you and take your pray or message to God. But, if you lit the dollar candle then God Himself would listen to you."

George laughed, as she expected he would.

"In fact, if I had a special request I used to steal money from those newspaper stands or from the Macy's bag thing——-"

"What?" George interrupted.

"You know when you go into Macy's they have that big square pillar where you put in a quarter and get a carry bag," Morgan said, "well, my little fingers were small enough to fit in the slot so I could pull quarters out. I could slip my finger in the slot and pull up a quarter. Same with the newspaper machine. I could get my finger in the slot and pull out coins."

"You stole money, a sin, to talk to God through a candle?"

ZaneDoe

"That was the plan." Morgan knew it sounded absurd to George but it made perfect sense to her as a child. "I thought it was important at times that God heard me. Like I saw an old man in San Francisco once with no legs. He was on the sidewalk; I can still see him in my mind. I saw him when my mom stopped at a stoplight. I was young, maybe eight years old, I think. I thought if I lit a big candle and prayed for him then God would help him but I didn't have any money. I could see the change in the newspaper stand that was at the store next to the church, so, I stuck my little finger in and took out enough for a big candle."

"So God would grow new legs on the old man?"

"I don't know; I was just a kid. God worked miracles so why not and I thought that I had direct access to God because I could get a dollar for a big candle anytime I wanted to."

"The start of a life of crime: the Catholic Church," George commented with a smirk.

"I never took the money except to light a candle. I think I got ten cents a week allowance if I did garbage duty so funds weren't flowing. I even used to make change in the collection basket when my mom gave me a dollar to put in the basket. I thought that the church had enough money because everything had gold on it. I thought a dollar was too much so I would put in a dollar and took out change. I had to hold on to the basket because the guy would try to pull it away before I could get my change." Morgan smiled as she remembered then added, "Hey, I quit Brownies because I didn't think I was getting my money's worth out of the five cent weekly dues. And, convinced my friend that her five cents a week could be better spent and she quit too.

"So, George, you never went to any kind of church as a kid?"

Morgan's telephone quacked.

"Saved by the quack," George joked.

"I know, I have to get rid of that phone. I really am going to get rid of that phone." She only used the duck phone because she didn't want to hurt Simon's feelings but now Simon's feelings were quite low on her list of considerations.

"Hello," Morgan answered before the answering machine could pick up. "Hey...yes, we pulled it off perfectly; I loved it—great time!...No way?... Wait, George is here. Tell him okay." She handed the duck body to George and watched George's expression as he listened to Anna tell of how Lorraine showed up at the hospital and was at that moment engaging the men.

A Bible And A Fly Swatter 1977

Both Morgan and George had taken the day off and were just casually hanging out talking, pondering and laughing which was their typical exchange. So far it had been a Lorraine-free day. Now they knew why.

George gave out a hearty laugh, looked at Morgan then he began to laugh even harder. Morgan was eager to hear what else Anna was adding to the fact that Lorraine was there that was making George laugh so hard.

"You can open your front door and let the air blow through the screen door since Ding-a-ling is away," George commented as he hung up the phone.

"Should we go down there?" Morgan worried though smiling as the light poured into the living room through the open door.

"Anna says she's acting normal and the men seem to be enjoying her company, according to Anna," George answered void of concern.

"It's Lorraine, George. She may be packin'," Morgan cracked. "Some guy says the wrong thing and it turns into a massacre. Anyways, she can't just show up down there anytime she feels like it; she might wreck everything. You know what I mean?"

"Not really."

"I had to fill out a form to be a volunteer. You know, I had to get permission. I don't want Anna to get in trouble or to have them get upset about people just showing up and have everything we've worked for ruined. Particularly if it's Lorraine, the loon, who is just showing up, that might ruin *everything*."

George just grinned.

"What was so funny, George?"

"Anna said that she was dressed completely different, that she looked like an airline stewardess from the fifties," George answered keeping his broad smile.

"*What?*"

"Yeah, Anna says she's got some blue outfit on, like an airline stewardess, and her hair is in a 'twist' or something."

"In a twist? You mean like a French twist style?"

"I guess, hell I don't know but it all sounds pretty funny." George was still grinning. "She said that she's acting like a stewardess too—going up and down addressing the men like she's on an airplane, but they seem to enjoy the crazy person so I guess all is well."

"I'm going to call Anna and see if she wants us to come down," Morgan announced, very serious, very concerned, unlike George.

"For this, I'm going to go fix a drink. I'll be back," and George headed for the closet.

"You can use the front door, no cherry-headed nutcase to catch you for the time being." But George chose the comfort of their passageway.

"It feels sort of empty not to have OP in the car with me," Morgan said. She stepped on the gas, pulling onto the freeway toward the veteran's hospital.

"Have you ever been away from OP this long?" George asked. Rusty took OP for the weekend to make things easier for the getaway and then decided to visit his uncle in Sausalito early Monday morning, taking OP with him. Wisely, he didn't mention to Morgan that he would be taking OP sailing with them on the San Francisco Bay. Fun for OP, but the worry would have been too much for Morgan; she would have never given permission. If Morris and the Anglin brothers, in all their desperation, couldn't survive the rough waters of the San Francisco Bay then what chance would OP have if she fell overboard.

"Yeah, but I still miss her...."

They pulled the car around to the back of the building to park so that the highly recognizable car would not be easily seen by Lorraine. Morgan looked up. David was at the window, wearing the unintentional generosity of Simon upon his head and watched as Morgan and George scurried across the lawn toward the front doors.

"So if we're going to the first floor but have to go up stairs, then what's in between the ground and the first floor?" Morgan asked as they climbed the stairs to the front doors. George didn't answer, but rushed through the doors taking his place beside a pillar so that he could watch without being seen. He hoped all was well, that Morgan could put her worries to rest and they could leave *without* Lorraine. Morgan took her place beside him.

There was Lorraine, standing in front of a row of sitting men. She was wearing a white blouse, navy-blue fitted jacket with a matching navy-blue skirt. She wore a cap upon her vibrant-hued hair that was pulled up and back in a heavily-clamped twist. Morgan couldn't tell if it was an actual stewardess's cap or a military cap of some kind. If the men's chairs were lined up one behind the other, it would look like child's play, like they were playing airplane with Lorraine as the stewardess and the men as the passengers. With David at the far end by the window in his wheelchair, he could be the pilot.

A Bible And A Fly Swatter 1977

Both watched and tried desperately to hear what she was saying to the men but couldn't. She was bending at the waist, leaning into the "passenger" with an unfamiliar smile on her face. She stood upright, took a few steps back then kicked her foot up as though kicking a ball off behind her, followed by a raised eyebrow smile while several of the men let out a laugh. All but David were giving their attention to Lorraine, even those not seated in her imaginary airplane.

"I don't see a purse?" Morgan whispered.

"Maybe Anna has it." No sooner did George finish this short sentence when Anna came around the corner from the hall on the opposite side of the building. She briefly stopped by David with smile then continued on past Lorraine and the men only noticing George and Morgan once she stepped into the hall leading to her desk. Cautiously Anna turned on her heels to make her way to her friends.

"Oh God, Anna, is this going to be a problem?" Morgan fretted. "Is she going to fuck everything up?"

"Did she leave a purse with you?" George jumped in.

Anna's attention went to George first. "Good to see you." She had truly taken to George; he was kind, considerate and so very entertaining to Anna and she loved spending time with him. She answered, "No, no purse. She didn't even come to the desk. I just found her here. Others, the other employees, I guess think she is supposed to be here. No one has said anything."

"Anna, is she going to mess everything up?"

"I hope not," Anna meekly responded. "I'm not sure what to do about her myself." She glanced over at Lorraine then back at Morgan. "What's with the uniform?"

"Good question," George snickered, still watching Lorraine with her captive audience.

"The men seem to like her," Anna pleasantly added.

"She's a nut case, Anna. Seriously," Morgan said. "I could kill Rusty for ever bringing her down here. How the hell did she get down here today?"

"Commandeered a school bus?" George joked. "What if you tell her that she can only come on a certain day and just make sure that it's a day that others are here so she doesn't think she's in control."

"Why should she be here at all, George," Morgan was adamant. "She's a loose cannon, to say the least."

"Well, the men seem to like her, Morgan," Anna kindly informed. "They're glad to have the company. They don't shy away from her; they really seem to like her."

The hushed conversation went on for some time. George somewhat indifferent, Anna somewhat in favor of Lorraine's visits and Morgan horrified by Lorraine's hazardous potential.

"I have to get back to my desk," Anna proclaimed, rubbed George's shoulder and quickly left the two to discuss Lorraine.

"Should we hang out and see how she gets home?" Morgan quietly asked George.

"Hell no," his voice stern. "I'm not taking a chance she sees us and we end up having to give her a ride. She found her way here; she'll find her way back." George continued to stare at the bizarre stewardess. "Maybe they still use electric shock treatment here and they can give it a whirl on nutcase while she's here."

"Good thing Anna isn't hearing you accusing them of using shock treatment. I think she feels bad enough about this place."

"I'd put my money on it's still in use here."

Morgan whispered, "Should we go?"

George watched the imaginary airline stewardess for a few moments before answering. "Scrabble?"

"Gin?"

"Pente?"

"Gin for money?"

"Scrabble for money?"

"No way am I playing Scrabble for money with you," Morgan quietly protested. "Do you have a game?"

"We can drive by Buffalo Books and I'll pick one up," George said in a hush. He pulled Morgan's arm to follow and the two walked along the wall to the front doors unseen by Lorraine as planned.

Both gave a hearty wave to David as they passed by the window; the wobble of David's head confirmed they were seen.

Morgan pulled up to the back door to the bookstore but didn't park. "I'm going to go pick up some empanadas," she said. George nodded and hopped out of the car.

Enrique's was just around the corner. It was a fairly new restaurant and the owner, Enrique, was always there. Enrique didn't look like an Enrique: Enrique was black with an accent that Morgan, with her lack of worldliness, couldn't place. He was friendly without smiling, a smooth talker. He made Morgan nervous, not because of his ability to seemingly always sell her more food than she intended to buy, that was admirable when it came to business, but it was her own inability to say no to the parade of empanadas Enrique had to offer that made Morgan so uncomfortable. Enrique always had a new empanada that she "moost" try—one, two, three that she must try, "Dey so fahry gewd," he would insist with his gentle voice and unyielding gaze. Morgan was amazed at what Enrique would stick in an empanada—from bananas and chocolate to a variety of meats and vegetables. It seemed like anything could be cooked within its dough and Enrique had a way of making it delicious.

Oh shit, Morgan cringed. The restaurant was near empty. An eager Enrique was standing at the counter. She would have quickly backed out the door but he saw her come in. He fixed his eyes on her as she pressed a smile on her face and stopped before the sandwich board menu. She was only pretending to read the days' offering—she knew Enrique was going to rehash the menu and then some and wondered if he did this to every customer or did he just sense her defect. At least she wasn't being convinced to buy something that she wouldn't enjoy.

Morgan blared her horn as a car cut in front of her preventing her from turning into the parking lot. She instead pulled up to the sidewalk parking on the street beside the parking lot. She could still see George leave the building and with the bright-yellow car, he more than likely would see her. She waited, with the smell of the warm empanadas tempting her. One empanada Enrique convinced her to buy of the five was filled with a fried plantain, a sour cream sauce and spicy raisins. She pulled it out to take another appetizing whiff. With her nose at the empanada, Morgan noticed Johan's car in the parking lot. It was parked on the far side, not where he usually parked. It appeared that Johan was sitting in the car. Morgan felt she should see if he needed anything even if it was her day off. She placed the empanada back into the carryout box and grabbed her purse but stopped. Johan stepped out from his car as another car pulled up alongside him. The passenger side window rolled down and Johan began talking to whoever was seated in the car. Morgan was a bit

ZaneDoe

sidetracked by the car itself, a forest-green MGB GT, a car on her must-have list. Her eyes temporarily fixed on the little green beauty when the passenger door opened. Her eyes widened when she saw that it was Benny. Johan took a few steps back and Benny walked past him to the back of the car. He lifted the hatch, bent forward into the car then stood back upright, facing Johan and handing him what looked like a black satchel. From her peripheral vision she saw that George was cutting across the parking lot; she waved for him to hurry. George cocked his head, looking somewhat bewildered, waved the game he was holding then quickened his pace.

"What's up?" George asked as he hopped onto the front seat.

Morgan nodded in the direction of Johan. "Something's up. Check that out."

They sat lower in their seats and watched.

With the driver's side door open, Johan sat sideways on the seat of his shiny black Porsche. She couldn't see what he was doing but whatever it was it had to do with the satchel and Benny was intently watching.

"Let's go." George was eager to get on their way. He reached over and put the Scrabble game on the back seat.

"Just seems odd, doesn't it? Why are they parked at the far side of the parking lot?"

"Who cares, Morgan. I got the game." George extended his nose over the takeout box from Enrique's. "You got the food; it's a day off, let's get out of here."

Morgan agreed but she was undeniably curious and sound of the VW Thing starting was very conspicuous.

"Here, have a empanada. Let's just eat one and wait for them to go. I don't want to draw their attention this way."

"Then we don't haaaave foooood for the gaaaaaame," George kidded a whiny complaint.

"Trust me, I have enough empanadas," Morgan replied, rolling her eyes.

George opened the box and grabbed two. "Why'd you get so many?"

"Because I'm a wimp."

She took one of the empanadas and a napkin then scooted back down on the seat. "Sort of slide down more, okay?" she instructed George.

They watched Benny again go to the back of the MGB. He appeared to be rummaging through something in the back, but without removing any-

- 214 -

thing from the car he closed the hatch and returned to Johan's car. Johan shut the door to his car, backed up leaving Benny standing as he drove off. Benny returned to the MGB and a few minutes later that car also took off out of the parking lot. Whoever was driving the MGB was still a mystery and no one seemed to notice Morgan's car.

"So, what do you think that was all about?" George asked, straightening his posture and wiping off crumbs from the empanada.

"I don't know. I didn't think he was friends with Benny," she said while starting up the car. "Maybe it was business, but then why wouldn't they meet in the office?"

She pulled out into traffic.

"Why not ask one of them?"

"You always say that, George, 'Ask him'. You really don't know Johan very well. Asking personal questions is *not* okay. Why do you think he likes *me* working in his office—it's rare I ask any personal questions. I do what I'm told and I don't even question that."

"I thought it was because you're cheap to hire," George said with raised eyebrows and half a smile.

"Probably that too." She smiled back. "But he likes that I don't ask questions—unlike you. Actually, George, he pays me a decent salary, particularly since it's cash. Anyways, let's get home. Let's enjoy a few games of Scrabble with the curtains open before Looney Tunes gets back..."

Morgan, with the help of Anna, tried to convince Lorraine that she could only show up at the hospital on event days, however, Lorraine appeared oblivious until Morgan informed her that the hospital had hired security guards and unauthorized visits would be dealt with sternly. That bit of information seemed to wake Lorraine up out of her fog and she agreed to come only on event days—and, Anna or Morgan would let her know when those event days were taking place.

Events continued on a regular basis. Every now and then someone from the main office would attend. Occasionally Morgan would invite Lorraine and surprisingly, and for reasons they could only theorize about, she acted close to normal when attending the events. She was fond of wearing her pseudo-airline stewardess outfit and she always acted the attentive hostess. Lorraine loved to dance, which was entertaining in many ways to most. But the entertainer

- 215 -

ZaneDoe

extraordinaire for the men still was Janet. She had yet to come back and they often asked about "Joyce," wanting to know when she was coming to sing for them.

"She's on vacation," Morgan would repeatedly reply to Janet's admiring fans, "I'm sure she'll come here as soon as she gets back."

"Sooooo, where's your office buddy?" George asked as he strolled into the Samuel Pacific Imports office from Buffalo Books.

Morgan looked up and OP got up.

"Aaaaah, here just in time to take OP for a walk."

"Sounds good to me; I could use a break."

"You know, something is up, George. Benny is rarely here and he was supposed to be here a lot, not that I want him here, and when he's here he doesn't say all that much."

"That's a good thing, right?"

"Yeah, but it's not like Benny, not the Benny I know. He's not on the phone making sales calls either when he's here."

"So what does he do?" George asked as he picked up OP's leash.

"He comes in, grabs boxes usually, tells me he'll call me with orders."

"Nothing odd about that, right?"

"For Benny? Yes; he *always* talks, brings up some topic that has nothing to do with work and goes on and on. And I intentionally said 'anyways' about fifty times and he didn't correct me once and he *always* makes a point to correct my grammar.

"So why did Johan put in a desk for him if he's never going to be here?"

George started for the door with OP in the lead.

"And," Morgan continued a little louder, "I haven't heard much from Johan for weeks, in fact, I think I've talked to him twice in two months. *And,* Janet is missing in action."

"You suspected she was with our Mr. Johan Smith." George stood by the door waiting for Morgan to finish.

"Yeah, but after all this time you think it wouldn't be a secret. *Come on.* When I call her house her mother still says she's on vacation. Vacation from what? She doesn't work."

"What does she say when you ask where she is?"

- 216 -

A Bible And A Fly Swatter 1977

"'Out of town, Morgan. I'll tell her you called,'" Morgan mimicked her shaky voice. "Then she doesn't say anything else. It's like she wants to get off the phone and she's sort of a chatter, a talker."

"As are you, Morgan. I'll walk OP. Be back," and George left out the hallway door shutting it behind him.

It's what Janie said David wanted: he wanted to be around cameras; he wanted to be around photography.

The blatant and rude stares were something Morgan wasn't prepared for. Jackie, once again the willing accomplice, took the gawking of employees and customers in stride but Morgan began to fume. Intrigued by all that was offered in the enormous store, Jackie wandered off while Morgan kept a close eye on Janie and David and continued giving disapproving glares at those gawkers who happened to glance her way.

Rusty and Morgan found the largest photography store in the Bay Area: it was spacious and held sections that were akin to a museum. One was able to tour the store hardly noticed due to the size and, once greeted, the employees were too preoccupied flipping cameras and lenses every which way between each other and ardent customers to pester the causal patron. Shoppers moved about unfettered and enchanted with the enormity of their surroundings which made this store emerge the perfect venue to allow David to immerse himself in everything photography at his own pace. Next door was a restaurant which made the location all the better.

Rusty, Morgan and Jackie, with the help of Anna of course, escorted David out of the hospital and up the ramp into Rusty's van where they whisked him away to a place they felt he could comfortably lose himself in the world of photography with Janie by his side.

"How's it going?" Rusty stepped up alongside Morgan.

"These people are fucking rude, Rusty. They actually *stop* and stare. Just stare straight at David like he's some kind of float going by," Morgan raged between her teeth.

"How many people see a guy rolling around with a hookah, Morgan... let it go." Rusty watched Janie and David for a few minutes. "They're doing fine. Look at them—they couldn't care less who's staring at them." Rusty smiled and added, "Should I go stick a joint in his hookah?"

Morgan realized that Rusty was right. The stares from strangers were of no concern to either David or Janie. They were moving about unhampered, conversing and enjoying themselves. She wondered what they were talking about. She envied Janie's ear for David's unique language and was impressed by Janie's ability to push David along since she often used a cane in order to move herself around.

Eventually Janie did look tired and a bit strained. She began to look like a miner pushing a full load in a coal cart, yet still appeared to be enjoying every molasses step. In due time Janie sat herself down and Morgan took that opportunity to join them. David's static sounds told Janie that he wanted to show Morgan some things, many things. Janie rose and looped her arm through Morgan's. Morgan pushed David's chair as Janie guided the way to the special pieces David wanted to share—some old, some new and most Morgan could only feign knowing their function: it was a lens, but the significance of the lens was a mystery to Morgan. A bit like accompanying a child going through their toy box, one toy would bring great joy to the child's face though it appears like any other toy to the onlooker. This was David's colossal toy box and Morgan was the naïve onlooker.

When David had had his fill, they all agreed to go next door for a bite to eat. According to Janie, David was looking forward to a cup of coffee.

Not only was it frustrating finding a parking space due to the fact that all the handicap spaces with the needed extra space and close location were taken by able-bodied drivers who preferred the convenience of a handicapped designated space, but the restaurant was not set up physically or psychologically for a chaired patron. The looks on the faces of the staff and nearby customers alone screamed their lack of preparedness for this customer on wheels. After the whispers, the calling of the manager and unnecessary panic, they moved a few plant stands and other pieces of furniture out of the way and led the party to a table at the back of the restaurant by the kitchen doors.

"No. No," Morgan spoke up. "Nope. We would like a table by the window so we can see the water," she insisted, posed like a cat about to pounce. "Right over there. We'll take a table over there."

There were a few seconds of silence before Rusty began turning David's chair to leave the undesirable location for a table by the window. The keeper of the menus quickly positioned herself ahead of the others and reluctantly guided them to a new location, looking to Morgan for approval before divvying out the menus—perplexed when handing David his, she placed it on the table in front of him.

Everyone ordered lunch. David only wanted coffee with lots of sugar and cream. It was important to David to hold and drink his coffee on his own—a task not made easy when the waitress, who refused to make eye contact, set a cup filled to the brim before him. Janie sipped off the top and carefully handed the cup on the saucer into David's assisted yet shaky grip. He managed a tight hold on the cup, spilling coffee onto the saucer, himself and Janie but he also spilled coffee into his mouth with great satisfaction.

Morgan discreetly watched, pondering just how long had it been since David had been in a restaurant, drinking a cup of coffee on his own.

David's eyes lifted, making contact with the others. They sparkled. His sense of accomplishment and joy was contagious. He may as well have set foot atop Mount Everest with Janie his Sherpa.

They rushed David through the front doors where Anna immediately joined them.

"How was your day out?" she asked David and he quickly responded with a mild contort of his face and a waving head. "I'll call you later," she said to Morgan. Anna needed to get David to his room for routine care.

"Talk to you later," Morgan responded as she and Rusty rushed back out the door. Rusty helped Janie out of the van and into the VW Thing. He left to give Jackie a ride home. Morgan rushed off in the opposite direction.

After such a long day Morgan expected Janie to be tired, eager to get back to Sunny Acres to rest, however, she was anything but. She may have physically been worn by the day but her spirits compensated and she insisted on climbing the stairs to Morgan's apartment to meet OP.

George knew Janie would get a kick out of seeing him and OP popping out of the closet, plus, though he hadn't seen Lorraine all day, he didn't want to take the chance by using the front door. Their introduction was an immediate love-fest with Janie hugging OP as if she were her own dog that she hadn't seen in weeks. Janie told of an encounter with a Newfoundland while in England and Morgan shared her story of adopting OP. OP didn't leave Janie's side once during her entire visit. When it was time to leave, all four climbed into the Thing with Janie and OP sharing the backseats.

Morgan kept looking in her rearview mirror at Janie. She didn't want to take her back to Sunny Acres and Alice; it felt deeply wrong. Yet, Janie looked happy.

Chapter 13
Life Moves On

"Yeeees?" Mrs. Schwab answered softly as she stared up at the ceiling from her bed.

Janie walked over and sat down beside her. Mrs. Schwab immediately reached for Janie's hand. Janie set the Bible down on the bed allowing her to hold Mrs. Schwab's hand within hers.

"I have something for you, Mrs. Schwab. It's very special, and very, very important," Janie said slowly and in a low voice.

Mrs. Schwab sat up, giving Janie her full attention. "Alright. What is it, Miss Janie?"

"This is very, very important, Mrs. Schwab," Janie emphasized.

"The Bible?" she asked, noticing the Bible tied in a ribbon sitting next to Janie. Like a schoolgirl whispering to another in class she added, "A gift of Jesus."

"Yes," Janie said with surprise; she knew the perfect way to make sure her plan succeeded. According to Mrs. Schwab, Jesus made regular visits to the room. She insisted that Jesus brought her everything from chocolates to her new slippers. "This was a gift from Jesus."

"Oh my Jesus," Mrs. Schwab exclaimed placing her hands over her heart. "Jesus left the Bible for me?"

"Jesus brought the Bible for you to give to Morgan," Janie explained. "You know Morgan...the young girl who comes to visit me?"

"Jesus was *here*," Mrs. Schwab confirmed with elation.

"Yes, he was here while you were out of the room——-"

"Was I in the bathroom, Janie?" Mrs. Schwab interrupted.

"No, you were somewhere else." Janie worried that Mrs. Schwab was so enamored with Jesus's visit that she wasn't listening to the mission so she spoke a bit louder. "He brought *this* Bible for Morgan, Mrs. Schwab. This Bible is for Morgan, Morgan only, and *no one else*. That's what Jesus said. That's what Jesus wants. He wants you to give this Bible to Morgan. Do you understand?"

"I understand, Janie; this Bible is for Morgan," she said, easing Janie's worries.

"And Jesus wants you to hide this Bible." Janie picked up the Bible. "Until you can safely give it to Morgan, you must keep it hidden. No one else is to get it, Mrs. Schwab. It's very, very important." She looked directly into her eyes. "He wants *you* to keep this Bible safe, to hide it until you can give to Morgan. Only Morgan and no one else."

Mrs. Schwab shouted up to the ceiling, "I will, Jesus. I will care for this gift for Morgan."

"Shhhhhh," Janie hushed Mrs. Schwab. "It's a secret, Mrs. Schwab. You have to keep the Bible a secret until you give it to Morgan..." and Janie reiterated the importance of fulfilling Jesus's request for secrecy. Mrs. Schwab understood and took her mission to heart.

Morgan had taken a couple of days off from work. Death was new to Morgan. She had yet to lose anyone close to her, anyone that she loved so dearly. David's death was sudden, unexpected and she was unprepared in every way to deal with the loss of someone she not only loved so much but was such an integral part of her life, who had enlightened, inspired and gave her Morgan's life a new direction.

Someone began knocking on Morgan's front door. She listened to the knocking, waited, giving thought as to whether she wanted to see or talk to anyone. She sat on the couch just staring at the door, until she heard a bark.

"George, why didn't you come through *our* door?" Morgan asked bewildered as she held open the door for both George and OP.

"I don't know," George answered. In truth, he knew Morgan had been crying on and off for days and he wanted to give her her privacy. The typically energetic, curious and always on the go neighbor sat alone with the curtains closed. The answering machine picked up every call he heard through their thin walls.

Morgan immediately went to the kitchen to get OP her food. She offered George an imported beer she had gotten from the office.

"How are you doing?" George asked in a tone rarely heard. The insouciant, mixed with sarcasm, was his usual temperament on most all occasions but he stepped out of character to displayed serious concern for Morgan's newfound bereavement. He had never seen her like this.

A Bible And A Fly Swatter 1977

They sat down on the couch while OP ate at an audible speed.

"Does Janie know?" she asked.

"Sure, yes," George answered. "Anna took care of that too."

"I should have," Morgan said in a whisper.

"No, you shouldn't have. Anna is experienced in these matters, Morgan. You're not. Let her handle things."

She looked over at George and asked a question she really didn't want to ask but had to. "What do they do with him? Where did they take him? He has no family, right?"

George scooted over next to her, put his arm around her and let Morgan cry into the comfort of his chest.

Eventually Anna showed up at Morgan's door. She knew when George failed to answer that he would be with Morgan. Both agreed to keep all unpleasantness regarding David's death hidden from Morgan. Anna herself was told to take a day off after she responded unfavorably to a coworker's comment referring to David's passing as "a burden gone." Anna realized that she may have felt the same way not that long ago but she had since seen the men in a different light. And, she was more determined than ever to ensure that they never be put back in the dark.

Morgan returned to work and was actually grateful for the distraction of her workday routine. She was at her desk preparing to respond to messages when interrupted by a light knock on the door. As instructed, Morgan looked through the peephole before opening the office door. There, on the other side of the distorted view of the peephole, was Janet—smiling.

"Hey Janet. Come in," Morgan welcomed. Janet was alone and though Janet regularly looked happy, this time she was radiant. Morgan desperately wanted to ask where she had been but since she was more than likely with Johan, she decided against it. "Here, have a seat." She immediately informed Janet that the men at the hospital missed her and were eager to see her perform again.

"Ooh, they do?" Janet asked, wonderstruck and pleased. "Can I go back?"

"Yes, yes, of course. We'd all love it," Morgan answered but was more focused on Janet's peculiar manner—she sat down in an odd way. She couldn't help but ask, "Are you okay, Janet?"

"I'm pregnant, Morgan," she answered with obvious joy at her news.

ZaneDoe

Morgan had a gamut of questions—How many months? Is Johan the father? Are you going to marry him? Does anyone else know?—but kept them to herself. She offered her congratulations then asked how she was feeling.

"Wonderful, but thirsty," she answered with a giggle.

"Oh God, I don't have anything here to drink but I can get you some water," Morgan offered.

Another knock at the door had Morgan certain that Johan had arrived behind Janet, though he usually used his key. She quickly opened the door to George and OP. Janet's eyes popped open when she saw the size of Morgan's dog.

"She's friendly," Morgan instantly assured then ordered OP to her bed to ease Janet's worry.

"Wow, is that OP?" Janet asked, her eyes still fixed on the gigantic canine. "I thought she was a little dog."

"She's harmless, Janet. You remember George, right?" Morgan asked, getting the focus off of OP.

"Hi George," Janet quickly said with a smile.

"Hi there, Janet." George turned to Morgan. "I have to get back to work." He looked back at Janet. "Nice to see you again." And George scurried out the door giving Morgan a wink on his way out.

As she shut and locked the door it donned on Morgan that Janet has never been to the office before, nor had Morgan told her where the office was. It was obvious Johan was attached to her presence at the office so Morgan now felt comfortable to broach the topic of Janet and Johan.

It was a bit like tapping the side of an overfilled water-glass; it didn't take much for Janet to spill every detail (which Morgan was certain would not have been sanctioned by Johan). Janet beamed every nuance of their relationship including their adventures in Spain. She had been to Paris, most of all, she had gone shopping in Paris. Chatty Janet claimed that Johan was a good listener, to which Morgan smiled to herself. Since the day Johan offered Janet a ride home from her performance at the veterans hospital, they became inseparable. Morgan wanted to ask about Rocky but refrained; Janet was happy, pregnant and Rocky had to be out of the picture completely by now.

"Where's Johan?" Morgan had to ask.

"He's outside, taking care of some business," she offered. "I thought that I would come up and see you, say hello."

A Bible And A Fly Swatter 1977

"Well I'm glad that you did..." and the two continued to talk until Johan made his appearance. As Morgan had expected, he didn't say much—a hello, a few questions about orders. Morgan wanted to ask about Benny's lack of office time but decided against bringing up any topic that took the luster from Janet's moment. Janet and Morgan visited for a little while longer while Johan patiently waited. The duo exited into the hallway: Janet undeniably beautiful and Mr. Smith still the constant enigma.

"Your mother was here," George informed.

Morgan pulled the key from her front door. "Oh God. Did you talk to her?"

"Yeah."

"Come on in."

George followed in behind OP and made himself comfortable on the couch.

"You have a message from your mom on the machine too."

Morgan looked at the trusty Phone-Mate to see its glowing red heart beating. "What did she say to you?"

"She just asked when you'd be home," George answered then added, "She didn't look happy."

"It's probably because of Grandpa...I wonder if she went to see him?"

"You mean she wouldn't go see him?"

OP began pawing at the closet door indicating she wanted to go into George's apartment which bewildered Morgan and made George laugh aloud.

"I was feeding her bacon; go ahead and let her back in."

Morgan opened the closet door, crawled through to open George's door and let OP through then backed up to a standing position and continued her conversation with George.

"So your mother wouldn't go see your grandfather?" George continued.

"I kind of doubt it. They have no relationship that I know of. Something must have happened long ago. I never knew him growing up, actually. I didn't even know he existed." Morgan joined George on the couch. "I don't think she cares about him or even likes him. I wasn't even introduced to Aka officially."

"What?"

"Oh, it's a long story but I don't think my grandmother had a good relationship with him—he's *her* husband—and I don't think my mother likes him much less loves him or wants to be around him but I don't have a clue what he did or supposedly did. And, I don't ask; it's just better that way and I doubt she would tell me anyways."

Morgan's mother did not visit Aka, but Steve did. Their budding friendship was in full bloom with Steve making repeated visits to Sunny Acres: Aka was a true surfer, a classic, a relic and one to be admired in Steve's opinion. Aka rode a board cut from wood that was almost twice his height. Steve felt privileged to be sharing time with Aka, a living legend. Steve couldn't care less that Alice glowered at his presence—Steve glowered right back. In fact, Steve's slow, steady, expressionless manner seemed to unnerve Alice. He never introduced himself when entering Sunny Acres nor explained his relationship to Aka to the staff. Nothing was said when Steve swooped right in at a snail's pace and escorted Aka out of Sunny Acres and off to a movie theater so they could watch a surfing film featuring an old friend of Aka's named Rabbit. Steve never stopped at the front desk to ask permission to visit, or permission to take Aka out: *he just did it*. Maybe the truth was, that no one challenged Alice hence her illusion of absolute power and domain over Sunny Acres. Unknowingly, Steve challenged Alice and Alice stepped aside.

Simon was in a silent tizzy as he packed up his belongings at the beach house. His mother had the nerve to decide to move in to her own house on a permanent basis. Even if she were to invite him to stay at the beach house with her, Simon couldn't keep his well-orchestrated image alive while rooming with his mother at what would be clearly her home. The beach house was at least an hour away from Leilani's mother's residence and after spending close to six months in travel with her mother, she needed a break. She expressed to Morgan that she had never experienced the truly "whiney and negative side of Grandma" until this extended trip together and she direly needed time away from her. She even inquired about Morgan setting up an answering machine for her at the beach house so she could avoid her mother's calls.

"You know Simon thinks of the beach house as his?" Morgan tattled.

"What?" Her mother responded in a question, affirming to Morgan that she did not know that Simon was living at the beach house, along with chosen guests.

"I didn't think you knew, Mom. Simon has been living at the beach house."

A Bible And A Fly Swatter 1977

"I asked him to come and check on the house, honey. I'm sure he stayed a couple of days. You can too," she explained.

"I know, but that's not what I mean. I just thought you should know; Simon was living there full time, like it was his place. I'm sure that's what he led everyone to believe...and, Mom, I didn't care that he lived there but I came one weekend to bring Aka for a visit and he was a real asshole." Morgan could feel the old anger still build in her just by thinking of how rude Simon was to those she loved.

"Don't call your brother that name," she lightly scolded. "You brought Grandpa here?" She asked, overtly surprised.

"I brought him with a few of my friends. It was really nice, Mom. But Simon wasn't. He was rude."

"What do you mean by rude, was he rude to Grandpa?" Her tone changed.

"He was rude to everyone and he didn't even go say hello to Grandpa," Morgan explained.

"Who else was here?"

"Just a couple of friends of mine. We came for two days. Oh, and I have to tell you, Claire came over and played cards with us."

"Claire! Well, I'm glad to hear that. I'm glad that you invited her, but why was Simon rude? He wasn't rude to Claire was he?"

Morgan shook her head and rolled her eyes. Her mother didn't know the real Simon. Just because Leilani was his mother, it didn't make her exempt from being used and manipulated by Simon for Simon's gain. They talked a bit more about Morgan's weekend visit at the beach house then said good-bye.

Morgan's mother was back home and Morgan was back to work and back to participating in the hospital events. David's passing was painful and it took awhile before Morgan felt comfortable to continue with the Sunday events. Passing the empty window and to be in the common room among the laughs and chatter without David was too difficult at first but eventually Morgan could make it through a Sunday without staring at the empty window-side with inevitable tears. Janie no longer attended the entertainment at the hospital. Morgan didn't push for her to attend: if it was painful for her, she could only imagine how painful it would be for Janie whose relationship went back years with David.

Janet had a baby girl, Althena. She liked bringing the screaming (*"She's going to be a singer like me"*) little one swaddled in pink to the office. Morgan got the impression that with Johan gone so often for extended amounts of time, that Janet was bored and a trip to the Samuel Pacific Imports office was her getaway. OP was fascinated by what to her was an interactive toy. She'd nudge the baby and the baby would giggle or scream and that was a quality toy to OP. Sometimes Janet would bring lunch. Sometimes she would stay for hours. When or if Althena fell asleep, Janet was eager to help out at the office and Morgan could always find things for her to do.

Benny quit. He never stopped by with his resignation, nor did he call Morgan with any information: she was informed by Johan that Benny was no longer working for Samuel Pacific Imports.

"Why?" Morgan naturally asked.

Johan looked at Morgan, smiled and said, "I gathered that you would prefer not to have Benny working in the office with you, correct?"

He was correct, but Benny was rarely there to start with. Johan had previously insisted that Benny have a desk in the office, that the doors be locked at all times and that Morgan no longer work in the evenings. Johan leaves town, which is highly usual, then returns with a pregnant Janet. It only took several months for everything to change: Johan a father; no longer the reminder to keep the doors locked; Morgan back to working some evenings and Benny suddenly no longer works for Samuel Pacific Imports. Add to this, the eleven o'clock news: Morgan and George were at Rusty's house watching the television while Rusty made his famous pizza in the kitchen. They were discussing the merits of jogging, shouting back and forth, until the eleven o'clock news displayed a car being towed up the side of a cliff by the ocean. They sat, silent, stunned, watching as the familiar vehicle dangled at the side of the cliff. Though a Rolls Royce Silver Shadow was not a rare car, it certainly wasn't one seen often in their area. Where Morgan believed that the two mystery men were driving a black Jaguar, George got a good look at the car in daylight and it was a Rolls Royce Silver Shadow.

"I thought it was black?"

"It looks dark at night," George answered, keeping his eyes on the television screen. "Yeah, that's it. Astrakhan. I'm sure that's it. Yeah, I'd bet money that's it."

A Bible And A Fly Swatter 1977

The newscaster gave little detail other than the vehicle had driven off the coastal Highway I, over the cliff at Half Moon Bay, and was spotted sticking out from the surf. Nothing was said about anyone being inside the car. They naturally sought out the newspaper for further details but the paper gave nothing more than what was reported on the news. And, come the next day the story was over—not another word about a Rolls Royce found sticking out of shore at Half Moon Bay.

Morgan didn't know how to put the pieces together. George absolutely had a theory regarding the sequence of unexplained events but Morgan would have no part of it. She not only adamantly discredited George's hypothesis, she refused to listen further after he made claimed that Johan "got rid of" the two men and his former ways now that he was a father. George had his well-calculated suspicions down in logical order but Morgan refused to listen. She just wanted life to go on as usual—no more kicks to the gut. Too many changes happening too fast. David's passing was quite enough for Morgan to handle still.

Chapter 14
Reunion?

Janie sat on her bed while Morgan sat on the side of the bed using Janie's fly swatter to silence the annoying buzzing about them.

"You're pretty good at that, Morgan," Janie lightheartedly commented.

"Oh, I hate flies, Janie. Imagine what they walk on then they land on your food or your cup where you put your mouth," she said, shuddering her shoulders. "They land on you then you swat them and they come right back to the same spot, like rubbing it in that you missed them. I can't even relax if there's a fly buzzing around my apartment."

Smack. She got one. "Are they getting in through this window...but it has a screen on it..."

"They get in where the screen is loose, Morgan. Here, hand me that," Janie said and reached for the swatter. Whack, whack.

"*Wow!* You're good." Morgan grinned. "And fast."

"I get a lot of practice," she said with pride and disappointment. "Too bad they don't make it a competition here. I could win something."

They chatted for a while then decided to visit Aka together. Aka and the colonel were both in the room. Much to Morgan's surprise, the colonel looked almost happy. She greeted him and he responded with a quiet hello and a smile, a genuine smile. She decided to take this opportunity to introduce Janie to the colonel. It was a pleasant exchange. They didn't make conversation but the greeting was cheery and sincere.

"Hi Grandpa," Morgan said to Aka who was sitting in the chair by his bed reading.

"Hello Aka," Janie said and turned leaving the colonel sitting on his bed.

Morgan wanted to ask about the change in the colonel but it would have to wait for a more private venue. They talked a little then Morgan asked Aka if he would like to join them out on the patio. He agreed, which was another change Morgan didn't expect.

As they walked their way to the patio Aka asked about Leilani, "Your mother is back?"

ZaneDoe

"Yes. Did she stop by?" Morgan wondered how he knew she was back since there seemed to be no communication between them.

"Steve told me," Aka answered.

"Steve?" Morgan was perplexed; Steve certainly would know since he lived only a few doors down from the beach house but she had no idea that Steve was in contact with Aka.

"We're friends, Mokana. Becoming good friends. He visits me."

"Here, at Sunny Acres?" she asked, sure that Steve hadn't come all the way to Sunny Acres to see Aka.

"Yes, here. Sunny Acres." Aka laughed.

"Mooooorgan?"

All three stopped, turned to see who had called to Morgan.

It was Mrs. Schwab. She was returning to her room when she saw Morgan. She was excited. She had the gift from Jesus for Morgan under her bed and she was eager to complete her mission. She walked as if her feet were frozen, in sort of a shuffle but this was a hurried shuffle aimed straight at Morgan. Janie stepped behind Morgan and with exaggerated posturing shook her head and hands indicating an unmistakable no to Mrs. Schwab. But she was focused on Morgan, not on Janie. Then Janie stepped in front of Morgan, whispering, "I'll take care of this," and intercepted Mrs. Schwab. Janie reached her head up to Mrs. Schwab's cheek and strictly said, "No, not now. Jesus wanted you to give Morgan the Bible alone. No one else is supposed to be around, Mrs. Schwab. Now is not the time."

It was difficult to ascertain if Mrs. Schwab truly understood, however, she did not argue with Janie but followed her lead as she walked her back to their room.

"You two go on," Janie shouted back to Aka and Morgan, and they did. They made themselves comfortable and waited for Janie to join them. This gave Morgan the opportunity to ask about the change in the colonel but Aka didn't have an answer. All he knew was that the colonel came back to the room and the crying spells stopped. He began to read, just like Aka, and the two became very suitable roommates.

"Maybe they doped him up, Mokana." Aka smiled.

"Do they offer you drugs, pills, Grandpa?"

"I spit 'em." He laughed triumphantly.

- 232 -

A Bible And A Fly Swatter 1977

Morgan took a chance and invited Aka to the beach house. It was a Saturday and Morgan's mother was expecting her, just her. Morgan would have brought Janie also but for reasons Janie would not divulge she didn't want to go. In fact, Janie seemed a bit distant and where she had been enthusiastic about any excursion outside of Sunny Acres with Morgan, she had begun declining invitations. Morgan spent more time with Janie at the home where Janie seemed more content—although her wit about Sunny Acres was still intact. She was less energetic than usual and sometimes seemed to drift off. Morgan attributed the changes to the passing of David.

The ride to the beach house was very pleasant. They kept the top down on the Thing. OP sat in the back taking in and loving the barrage of scents blowing her way. Aka insisted on visiting Steve at some point on their visit to the coast. Depending upon how the encounter went, they would stay a few hours, the whole day or overnight.

Morgan pulled up to the front of house. The garage door was open and her mother's Thunderbird was parked inside. It only took a few minutes for Morgan's mother to exit the open garage and head up the driveway to greet her and OP. Morgan waved and with a big smile she waved back, still making her way up the steep driveway to Morgan's car.

"Oh, OP," she said.

OP was standing and her large body hid the surprise guest, but not for long. She approached the car and Aka turned in her direction. The smile dropped from her face. Morgan quickly exited the car, gave her mother a hug and proceeded to the passenger's door to help Aka out of the car. OP darted past Aka and Morgan to the front yard.

"Hello Leilani." Aka was demure, anxious yet beseeching.

She looked at Morgan, her lips pursed tightly together. Morgan at once looked away.

"Doesn't Grandpa look nice, Mom?" Morgan tried to break the tension. And, he did look nice in Simon's shirt, new pants and shoes...and his hair slicked back which is how he wore it since his day of surfing.

"How are you, Dad?" Leilani asked with little if any sincerity.

"Real good, Leilani. Real good," Aka answered in all sincerity. He smiled, hesitant, then looked to Morgan.

"OP!" Leilani yelled as OP whipped her front yard hose around like she was in a struggle with a wild snake.

- 233 -

OP provided a great distraction for what was an awkward and tension-filled reunion for Leilani and Aka. The damage to the hose and her muddy feet opened conversation as they settled in at the kitchen table. Leilani made coffee and Morgan did her best to keep conversation flowing, even if it were just between her mother and herself. Aka sat quietly with his eyes hardly leaving his daughter who he had not spent any time with in many years—too many years. Leilani never looked directly at her father. He was like the elephant in the room she was trying to ignore.

Morgan couldn't help but notice the difference in Aka's eyes—not the usual laissez faire. His eyes were filled with emotion. Morgan worried that Aka was on the verge of tears, something Morgan felt would take this precarious situation to an even more uncomfortable level, particularly with her mother.

"Grandpa," she said, "I know that you wanted to visit Steve. Would you like to walk over with me and see if he's home?"

Leilani looked at the both of them, surprised. Surprised that Aka even knew who Steve was much less had any kind of relationship with him.

Aka didn't answer.

"Let's go see if he's home," Morgan suggested, rising from her seat. "I'll finish my coffee when we get back, Mom."

Aka got up himself, looking down, no longer at Leilani. Without a word he headed for the stairs, grabbed the railing and descended the steps as though he was going to his doom.

"We'll be back in awhile, Mom," Morgan shouted as she hurried down the stairs behind Aka. She now thought that maybe it wasn't such a good idea to try to facilitate a reunion with her mother and grandfather, however, the deed was done and for now it was best to just put a break in the mounting emotion and tension between them.

Steve was home. He sensed a sadness in Aka and wanted to take him to the beach. Morgan thought it was a great idea. She would go back to the house, have coffee with her mother and see what she could possibly do to reconcile the obvious strain of this forced reunion.

"What's the problem with you and Grandpa, Mom?"

They sat on the back deck looking out over the golf course, her mother sitting in Aka's preferred chair.

She gave a gaze in Morgan's direction, as if pondering her answer, or to answer.

- 234 -

"Well?" Morgan asked again.

"Why do you need to know?" she responded in a refrained and calm voice. "Has Grandpa said something to you?"

"No; he only asks about you...how you are. I guess I don't 'need' to know, but you can cut the tension with a knife while we're visiting. He is your father, so, of course I'm curious." Morgan looked directly at her mother. "What if it was that way with you and me...it's so uncomfortable. And he's so old, Mom. I think it's pretty obvious he cares about you. I don't know whether you care about him but he cares about you and he's so old, Mom. He's here." She exhaled her angst. "He's trying."

"Why don't we leave the past alone, Morgan," she said without emotion.

"Okay, but can you try to make it more comfortable while he's here... talk to him?"

She turned to Morgan and gave a hint of a smile. Though her half-smile bewildered Morgan, Morgan smiled back.

"Yes. For you, I will," Leilani assured.

And she did. Aka returned with Steve and Piggy cookies. The Piggy cookies made Leilani laugh which delighted Aka. They sat on the deck with the cookies and coffee and Steve was surprisingly animated. Morgan was dumb-found by the change in Steve's demeanor: he kept the conversation going and, when he not only waved to Claire who had peeked out from her deck door but encouraged her to come join them for coffee, Morgan was shocked into silence.

Morgan thought it best to not spend the night on this visit. Her attempt at a reunion was a good try—not a success as she had wished but not a failure either. She felt comfortable to return with Aka in the future.

Leilani made dinner; Claire contributed and Steve ran home to get cottage cheese for Aka. It was a pleasant dinner with Aka contributing a bit to the conversation. He constantly watched Leilani but she only looked directly back at him a few times. After dinner Morgan and Aka headed back to Sunny Acres with OP preoccupied, chewing on a rib bone from Claire the entire ride home. It made a mess on the backseat but "It smells good," according to Aka.

Chapter 15
A Bible And a Fly Swatter

George stood in the doorway of the Samuel Pacific Imports office that led to Buffalo Books. Though Morgan detected the changed expression on his face, she didn't acknowledge it. And, George didn't say anything; he just stood there, looking at Morgan with an almost pained facial cast and a stance more like a toy soldier than his usual casual slump.

"So George, did you bring me an anniversary present?"

George said nothing. Morgan continued. "I've been working here a year now; can you believe it? So much has happened in this last year, don't you think?" She looked directly at George. Her heart began to beat a bit faster. "So much has happened; think about it: I've made it a year in one job; a year without the landlord finding out about OP; we got the entertainment for the men at the hospital." She kept on talking with her eyes fixed on the stiff figure of George. "Hey, Janet had Johan's baby...he actually stayed in one place long enough to make a baby." She smiled.

George moved from his station at the door. He pulled a chair over to Morgan's desk and sat down. Morgan looked panicked. OP got up from her bed to find affection from George. He stroked her head then told her to sit.

"What?" Morgan asked, her stomach tight.

"Are you busy here today?" George asked in a soft tone, not like George.

"Not really. What's going on, George?"

George reached over and locked the front door to the office, sat back down and placed his hand on Morgan's.

"What?" Morgan's voice displayed both annoyance and concern. "What, George. What's going on? What are you doing?" She pulled from George's hand. "Are you joking around?"

"Morgan, take a deep breath, okay," George said in a serious voice that scared Morgan. She didn't take a deep breath but gave George her full and undivided tension-filled attention. "I got a call from your grandfather, Aka."

"Did something happen to Aka?" her voice climbed.

"No, Aka is okay."

ZaneDoe

"What then? Come on, George," Morgan said filled with panic and feeling as though she were about to cry without being given a reason to do so.

"He called because he wanted me to be with you...when I told you—"

Morgan cut him off, "Told me what?"

"I guess Janie went by herself to feed the ducks at the park—"

Again she cut him off, "So?"

"Morgan, she didn't come back."

"Well—-"

"Let me finish, Morgan," George said calmly but firmly. "They found her on the bench, at the park...and she was gone, Morgan." George again reached for Morgan's hand.

"What do you mean 'gone'?" she shot back. Morgan felt immediately angry. "Just spit it out, George. Fuck."

George gently placed his hand on Morgan's chin and turned her to face him. He knew she knew what he meant. Like David, Janie was gone.

The phone rang.

"Let the machine get it." George waited for a response but Morgan just stared out in front of her.

"Would you like me to take you to Sunny Acres?"

"She's not there, George," Morgan's response was almost inaudible.

"I know, but Aka is."

"When did this happen? When, George?" She turned to look at him.

"I'm not sure. My guess is in the past few days. When did you speak to Janie last?" he asked to help determine an approximate time.

Tears overwhelmed Morgan and she couldn't answer.

George stood up, squeezed her shoulders and told her that he would be back shortly.

George talked to Ruth about leaving then called Rusty about watching OP for a while. He sat for a bit before entering the Samuel Pacific Imports office again.

"Would you like to go?" he asked Morgan who had her faced buried in OP's massive neck. She shook her head yes, stood up, grabbed her purse and handed the car keys to George.

They entered Sunny Acres together, George in the lead. There were several people behind the desk; they recognized Morgan so they just went about

A Bible And A Fly Swatter 1977

their business. It was like any other day: people shuffling along the hallways, visitors in the common area, several people on the patio.

Janie had just died yet there was nothing visibly or in the air to indicate the loss. Inside Morgan hoped that it was actually a different scenario and secrecy was essential. Maybe Janie ran away and this was a ruse so only her close friends would know the truth. Several preferable scenarios raced through Morgan's head as she followed George to Aka's room, whether they made sense or not. Once in Aka's room she knew by Aka's face that there was no trick or practical joke involved. Before Aka could say a word, Morgan turned and walked out of his room. She rushed down the hall to Janie's room—the feeling of panic, sadness and anger meshed together.

Morgan passed Xavier whose face also confirmed Janie's passing and she continued on to Janie's room. She could hear Mrs. Schwab talking in the bathroom. The room didn't look much different other than Janie's bed was made with a different bedspread. Janie never had personal affects adorning her side of the room so it was hard to tell that Janie was no longer there.

Mrs. Schwab came out of the bathroom, alone.

"Mrs. Schwab," Morgan said to get her attention then asked, "Where is Janie?" not truly sure why she asked.

"Hello Morgan," she smiled. "Miss Janie has gone to Jesus." Mrs. Schwab looked delighted, something Morgan couldn't take at that moment. She walked over to Janie's bed, opened the drawer on the night stand. There was nothing in it. She began taking huge breaths to hold back the fight between grief and indignation and her urge to scream or cry. She could feel adrenaline building and at the same time she felt physically weak. Morgan sat on the corner of Janie's bed and Mrs. Schwab began humming that progressed into a song. Nothing at that moment was feeling real to Morgan. Like with David, it all happened so quick and the reality was hard to grasp.

She climbed onto Janie's bed and leaned back against the pillow, staring out the window while Mrs. Schwab continued to sing, what seemed even louder, in the background. There were remnant fly-kill spots on the window. Morgan managed a slight smile at the sight, the remembrance. She reached for the fly swatter still sitting on the sill, twirled it in her hand then slowly tapped the end of the swatter on several stains on the window, slowly mimicking Janie's apt aim.

"Jesus has a gift for you, Morgan," Mrs. Schwab said with annoying glee.

ZaneDoe

Morgan swatted the fly swatter against the bed and ignored her. Mrs. Schwab continued to talk about Jesus and again broke out in song. Morgan tuned her out, didn't respond to anything she said but that didn't stop Mrs. Schwab. She became like a fly herself, buzzing and annoying Morgan to the point where she wished that she could give her a well-aimed swat.

Morgan watched through the window as Xavier watered the garden in the back. She stared at a visitor who seemed to strain making conversation with an old man that appeared to have left his body long ago. She kept thinking how Janie never belonged at Sunny Acres and found herself angry again as she sat in silence watching the "life" at Sunny Acres through the window as though watching a dull pointless movie. She watched an aide escort Albert fully dressed out to the patio—he looked miserable.

Much time had passed but Morgan didn't know how much. She just wanted to leave Sunny Acres at that point. She hurried off the bed and proceeded to the door still holding tight to the fly swatter. Mrs. Schwab was on her hands and knees by her bed, bent with her head parallel to the floor.

"Are you okay, Mrs. Schawb? Do you need help?" Morgan asked before leaving.

She answered but her voice was muffled as her head was half under her bed. Morgan walked over and bent down beside her.

"Can I help you?"

"I got it," she said in a whisper, pulling the Bible out from under the bed.

Morgan helped her to her feet. Mrs. Schwab sat down on the bed appearing exhausted.

"Here, sit Morgan."

"I need to go—"

"No, no," she interrupted. "We are alone."

Morgan looked around the room, yes they were alone and they had been alone. She assumed Mrs. Schwab was going to ramble on some nonsense related to her visions.

"Sit, Morgan," she demanded patting the bed.

It was obvious that this was important to Mrs. Schwab so Morgan acquiesced, sitting down beside her. Mrs. Schwab held the ribbon-wrapped Bible on her lap. She looked directly at Morgan, something Mrs. Schwab rarely did with anyone.

- 240 -

A Bible And A Fly Swatter 1977

"This is for you. This is a gift from Jesus," she explained with such passion that it was hard for Morgan to tell her that she didn't want it. "Jesus gave this Bible to Janie and I am suppose to give it to you." She placed the Bible on Morgan's lap. "You take it with you, Morgan. You read His words. He wants you to read this Bible. He told Janie that you must be given this Bible. It is such a wonderful gift from Jesus," she said, dreamy and heading off into her own world again.

"Thank you, Mrs. Schwab," is all Morgan could conjure to say and she said it so low that she wasn't sure that Mrs. Schwab had even heard her, but it didn't matter—Mrs. Schwab was back in her own world. She had done her brief connection to the world around her and she was due her time back into her own world again. Morgan looked down at the Bible tied up in a ribbon, as if it were a gift, lifted it with her one hand while her other hand gripped the fly swatter. She rose from the bed, unnoticed. She would never set foot in that room again.

Morgan convinced her mother that the curvature of her spine was causing her pain again. Her back was fine but her heart was once again in pain. With George aware of her state of mind, or heart, he kept an eye on both Morgan and OP, popping through the closet door to check on life in his neighbor's world of mourning. Morgan made use of her pain pills, snuggling up on the couch with her Bible and fly swatter and her wish for a foggy, numb, paralyzed state of existence for the time being.

"Maybe I shouldn't make friends with old people, George," she said have dazed.

"Death is a part of life, Morgan," George politely responded, keeping whatever sarcasm came natural to him to himself. "You made two good friends; you don't regret that. You'll be fine. Pop over, anytime, okay?"

Morgan nodded then closed her eyes.

She dreamed, and they were vivid dreams as though a separate reality but she could only remember the dreams momentarily when she awoke. She fed OP, made a piece of toast or made a cup of coffee, for the taste—she had no desire to be awake and ready to take on life—just yet. Then, Morgan savored a few pain pills and went back to sleep next to her Bible and fly swatter, never once opening the Bible.

ZaneDoe

The heart on her answering machine beat steadily. Morgan didn't care; she let it beat without response.

George had a conversation with Johan who compassionately understood: two deaths in such a short time were something Johan knew Morgan needed to handle in her own way. Though Mr. Smith was definitely the employer, the boss and she couldn't resolutely refer to Johan as her friend, he displayed a trust and sensitivity toward Morgan that went beyond one's average boss. There seemed to be an understanding between them from the get-go that neither could explain but both appreciated.

Janet couldn't have been happier to fill-in for Morgan at the office. She confused things regularly, and Johan had to respond to her calls and voluminous questions where he only had to touch base with Morgan on occasion. She liked to chat when Lacey called, which would have been ideal with Benny but Benny was gone and Lacey was all business. All things considered, Janet was enthusiastic and devoted behind that desk, working a full day with her baby close by. Morgan brought big OP to the office and Janet brought little Althena. Benny's desk was pushed to the corner and used as a storage table replaced by Ally's bassinet. Janet hung brightly colored ornaments from the *ficus* tree for the baby's entertainment—one shake of the tree and the suspended toys bounced and amused Althena like a good toy amused OP.

"Hello, Samuel Pacific Imports office, this is Janet. How can I help you?" she said with confidence and purpose. OP snored and sometimes barked—Ally giggled and sometimes cried. George checked in on Janet, as he had with Morgan although, unlike with OP, the baby made him nervous.

"You're not going to believe who stopped by," Morgan said to George while on her knees between closet doors.

"Come in," George demanded. And she did. "So," George continued. "Who came by? No, let me guess." He smiled. "Wackadoodle?"

"No, in fact I haven't seen her, thank God, for days…over a week, I think."

"Well…I didn't want to put anymore on your plate so I didn't say anything." George looked away from his magazine and directly at Morgan. "She's been helping Anna at the hospital. They're sort of redecorating, doing all kinds of clean up stuff—plants, pictures. You know, just brighten-the-place-up stuff."

A Bible And A Fly Swatter 1977

"You're right, I have enough on my plate and I'll pretend I don't know that. Guess again."

"Dan, our too-cool landlord?"

"Guess again?"

"The guys downstairs?"

"Wow, that would be a surprise, but no. I'll just tell you," Morgan said, "Steve and Aka."

"Steve from the beach, the surfer?"

"Yep," she said. "Evidently Steve visits Aka at Sunny Acres, takes him out places. I guess he wanted to come here." Morgan waited for a reaction from George but he didn't seem astonished as Morgan. "You don't think that is a big surprise? I was shocked."

"I think it's good," George answered. "So, what are you up to over at your place?"

"I'm baking."

"I could smell it."

"Then come over and visit and have some cookies. I'm making some to bring to Janet at the office."

"When are you going back to work?"

"Why, you miss me?"

"I miss OP," George stated sternly.

"Janet doesn't let you walk Althena?" Morgan smiled and George shot her a look. He wasn't a baby person. Janet was always insisting that he hold Althena while George feigned to be delighted but was in too much of a hurry at the moment. Without even asking, Morgan knew George wasn't the daddy type—except with a canine.

Morgan ducked down and exited back into her apartment. Minutes later George knocked on the screen door. Since Lorraine had been out of sight for several days Morgan took to leaving the front door open but the screen door locked.

"Have a seat," she said as George was already heading to the couch. He plopped down and put his feet up on the trunk coffee table.

"These muffins are flat as pancakes but the cookies are coming out perfect," Morgan remarked from the kitchen.

"Exact your recipe then open up your own cookie shop like that Amos guy in." George stared out through the front window at the trees and rooftops.

- 243 -

ZaneDoe

He was as much at home at Morgan's apartment as he was at his. They were roommates separated by the rarely closed closet doors.

"I wonder if I could...." Morgan chatted on adding the possibility of doggie cookies to the imagined inventory.

George's attention went to the Bible still wrapped in the ribbon. He picked it up, flipped it in his hands and asked, "Have you unwrapped your Bible yet?"

"You mean my gift from Jesus?" Morgan responded with a touch of mockery.

George quietly laughed then asked, "Really, have you opened it?"

"No. Why? Did you want to read it?"

"I don't know. It's wrapped in a bow, doesn't someone do that when they specifically want you to unwrap it...open it?"

"No," Morgan shouted back after closing the oven door. "But if you want to unwrap it, you can. Go ahead." Morgan had escaped into her baking. She was enjoying herself and wasn't interested in thinking about the gift from Jesus, Sunny Acres or the loss of Janie.

"You don't mind?" George was ready to untie the ribbon.

"No, I don't mind." The tiny kitchen was heating up so Morgan opened the kitchen window to let in some cool air. Curtains, windows and doors could be left open without fear of an invasion, and there was a sense of normalcy and relief, when Lorraine was absent from the complex—which Morgan was fully appreciating.

George carefully untied the ribbon and placed it on the trunk. The Bible was old and the first page was a yellowed translucent paper. He turned the page to find an envelope.

"There's an envelope, closed envelope, in the book," George shouted out to Morgan. She didn't respond. Morgan wanted to stay in the baking moment and wasn't interested in engaging in George's curiosity about the Bible. "Did you hear me?"

"Yes. Open it if you want. I don't really want to know. I'm busy perfecting my new business," Morgan quipped. She truly didn't want to know, at least not at the moment.

"Your name is on the envelope, Morgan." Which, halted her for a moment. She said nothing in response and continued on, removing the cookie sheet from the oven.

- 244 -

A Bible And A Fly Swatter 1977

George gingerly tore open the envelope, trying his best to leave it as intact as possible. He pulled a several page handwritten letter from the light-blue envelope.

"There's a letter...to you, Morgan," he informed.

"From Jesus?" she wisecracked.

George went to the last page of the letter.

"It's from Janie," he said a bit self-conscious, realizing that he had unveiled a letter to Morgan from Janie at a time which he was certain Morgan was not ready to read.

Morgan stepped out from the kitchen, not with enthusiasm but with apprehension. She stared at the letter in George's hand.

"Do you want to read it?" George shifted over to make room on the couch. "Sit down and read it."

"You read it," she said with a bit of anxiety .

"No, Morgan. It's to you. Sit down. Come on," he insisted.

"No. You read it. In fact, you read it to yourself," and she turned to go back into the kitchen. She felt her stomach tighten. She didn't want the sadness. She couldn't listen to it at that moment. She had cried enough for the time being and there was no way she would be able to read the words meant for her from Janie without falling back into grief.

"Do you really want me to read it, Morgan?" he asked.

She didn't answer.

George started from *Dear Morgan*. Several times Morgan peeked into the living room to witness George reading the letter. She was curious to see his expression as he read. She didn't want to read it, she knew that she wasn't ready, however, in her heart she did want to know what Janie had to say.

After *Love Your Friend, Janie*, George set the letter down on his lap. Attempting to take in the significance of what he had just read and knowing that Morgan made it perfectly clear that she was not ready to read the letter from Janie, he said nothing but pondered how Morgan would handle the contents of this letter.

"Coooookies," Morgan shouted from the kitchen.

It was too important for George to stay quiet.

"Morgan," he said in a raised voice, "you need to come in here. I'm serious. Forget the cookies. You need to come in here."

Morgan stepped over OP and stood by the couch.

- 245 -

"You need to know what is in this letter, and now, Morgan. This can't wait. It shouldn't have waited this long——"

Morgan cut him off, "I don't want to read it, George." She turned to go back into the kitchen. George hopped up and grabbed onto the back of her tee shirt.

Shocked at first but then thinking that George was playing around, Morgan pulled free from his grip and joked, "Okay, okay. You can have a cookie... for free."

George grabbed the letter and as Morgan shoveled a large cookie from the sheet with a metal spatula he began to read:

Dear Morgan

If it is you, Morgan, who is reading this letter then Mrs. Schwab did her job. Please thank her for me and Jesus. On this premise, I have several things that I would like to say to you, my friend. I want mostly to thank you for taking the time for me, for becoming my true friend. I have enjoyed your company and our conversations and so enjoyed our time outside of Sunny Acres.

"Stop, George," Morgan demanded, her eyes beginning to tear.

"No, you have to hear this, Morgan," George insisted like never before.

You brought life to my dreary existence and allowed me to escape from a world, well, a world I truly hated. I thanked God when we met. I had no idea that through you God would allow me to be with David once again in this lifetime.

"Enough," Morgan ordered. "I mean it, George. I'll read it some other time. Okay?"

George pulled the letter from his view. He knew that it couldn't wait.

"Okay, Morgan, seriously. I know this is upsetting you. I'm not trying to upset you," he said in such a sober and profound way that Morgan did not respond but continued to listen. "I'll skip this personal part, that can be for you to read in private at another time; that's up to you, but I need to read a part of this letter to you now." George persisted:

...I know that such matters can be overwhelming so, my dear, all you need to do is call my attorney. He is waiting for your call. OP will have her big yard and I will rest in peace knowing that my last best girlfriend is safe in what is now your home. I would like you to...

- 246 -

A Bible And A Fly Swatter 1977

Morgan grabbed the letter. She began to read the page George was reading from.

"I don't get it. George?" Morgan's emotions were overriding everything at the moment.

"Morgan, calm down. This is a good thing here. Morgan...Janie had a house. According to this, a duplex, and she left it to you. A yard for OP, Morgan!" George's smile filled the room. "You have a home, Morgan. It's all set up. It's been there, this whole time. You just never opened the 'gift from Jesus.' Clever lady. She set everything up for you."

Morgan stared at George in disbelief.

"Come on." George reached for Morgan's hand. He pulled her to the couch where she sat looking like a bewildered jackpot winner on a game show. "Just relax, and I'm going to read part of the letter to you and here," he said, "you look at this page. It has the address...the lawyer's name and phone number" and George read the details aloud while Morgan sat in stunned silence.

George stopped to laugh at the part where Janie warned that her sisters would not be happy but she *"took care of that too."* "She's something else," he commented with a big grin on his face.

Janie had arranged everything. She was savvy enough to know that Morgan was not savvy enough to handle the legal aspects of all that needed to be taken care of. She knew that Morgan, particularly if grieving, could not manage the details and that having to deal with her two expecting and greedy sisters could overwhelm Morgan. She only needed to call Janie's attorney and he would walk her through the process, and under Janie's instructions, with as little confusion or stress as possible.

The expression on Dan's face was priceless when he saw the "teacup" Newfoundland following Morgan as she carried boxes down to the VW Thing. George discretely got a photograph for posterity. Morgan had no need to hide OP anymore; she was moving out to her new home. George would soon be following, renting the adjoining abode beside her. Dan was doing a walkthrough, checking on the condition of the apartment before her last day though spending most of his time chatting about his rock n' roll pursuits. Morgan was busy along with George emptying out the apartment. They basically ignored Dan. He left the bedroom and walked over to the closet door that hid their secret passageway. George snapped his head around to look at Morgan.

ZaneDoe

"I still have to pack my clothes," she yelled to Dan then smiled at George. She had strategically crowded the closet with her clothing, hanging low enough as to hide the big hole in the wall

George jokingly lifted his thumb in the air. They would patch it up later, find some way to hide their friendship door. Morgan whispered to George on her way back down the stairs with another box, "No passageway in the new place or I'll have to keep your deposit."

Janie gave Morgan a home with a yard for OP. She was a homeowner, a proud homeowner and not just a homeowner but a landlord to tenants she couldn't love more. George lived next door and it wasn't long before Anna was also living next door. OP had a large yard with a lawn and the mobile home that once housed Janie's sister now was Aka's new home. Morgan never imagined such a perfect arrangement. The only conflict that was heard about the homes was what kind of dog George and Anna were going to get. George wanted a large dog, OP-like and Anna wanted a poodle—a dog George could not fathom walking. He continually warned Anna that OP would eat a small dog or use it for a chew bone or toy. "No she wouldn't!" Anna contested and the battle raged on. For the time being, OP would have to be shared.

Morgan made the long drive to pick Aka up from Steve's house at the beach. Like with Janie and Morgan, in spite of the huge age difference, Steve and Aka had become good friends.

"He's not here," Steve said in his predictable slow and apathetic manner. Morgan's disapproving expression inspired Steve to make the effort to explain. "He's still at the beach. Ya want me to go get him?"

"No, I'll go pick him up," she answered. She didn't want to wait for Steve to explain why Aka was alone at the beach, she just wanted to get there and make sure that he was okay.

"I can go get him," Steve offered again.

"No, that's fine. I want to take OP to the beach anyways," she said. "Thanks, Steve." She headed down the walkway then turned back to extend an invitation to dinner the next time he came to visit with Aka. He accepted with a nod and closed the door.

Morgan pulled up by the rocks, parked and with OP eager to run on the beach and play in the water, and Morgan eager to find Aka, they quickly

- 248 -

A Bible And A Fly Swatter 1977

hopped out of the car. She walked to the ridge and surveyed the long span of beach. She didn't see Aka and Morgan was immediately worried. There was only one person that she could see on the beach—a man by himself, playing the guitar. OP headed straight for the water with Morgan following at a fast pace while still searching for signs of Aka.

"OP," Morgan yelled.

Op stopped and Morgan raced the few yards to grab on to her collar. She wanted to keep her by her side as she searched for Aka. It was then that she saw in the distance two people sitting by the base of the cliff not far from the shore. It was Aka, and he was sitting with her mother. Morgan made her way to the rocks with a resistant Op in tow. She wanted to get closer, to get a closer look, without being seen.

Leilani was laughing, rocking back and forth like she always did when laughing uncontrollably. The sounds of the ocean prevented Morgan from hearing them but she could see Aka waving his hands and whatever he was doing or saying was thoroughly entertaining Leilani.

Morgan had no intention of interrupting.

Eventually, her mother got to her feet. She helped Aka to his feet. Together, with their pants rolled to their calves, they strolled hand in hand along the water's edge, letting the waves soak their bare feet and splash against their legs.

That was all Aka ever wanted—to be hand in hand with his daughter, his precious Leilani. Morgan felt blessed to witness her grandfather's dream come true.

1977: Never a year like it—before, or after.

Made in the USA
Charleston, SC
20 January 2012